EMERGENCE

Books by Douglas F. Sainsbury

Intrusion (2014)

Phantasm (2017)

EMERGENCE

a novel

DOUGLAS F. SAINSBURY

Emergence:
A Novel

Copyright © 2018 by Douglas F. Sainsbury

Published by: DFS 22 Vector Publishing
2391 Via Mariposa West.
Laguna Woods, California 92637
(708) 204-0098

This is a work of fiction. All the characters, names, incidents, organizations, and dialogue in the novel are either the products of the author's imagination or are used fictitiously.

ISBN: 978-1-54563-534-6

Printed in the United States of America

In memory of my beautiful daughter, Heather, and to my amazing son, Bryce; a father could not ask for better children

1

A sound from the kitchen? He rolled over onto his back and lifted a drowsy head to ensure his hearing was clear. Anatoly Terasenko had become accustomed to subtle noises in the middle of the night in his native Russia where citizens sometimes were taken and never heard from again. Now he lives in America, but lifelong reflexes are embedded deep in the human psyche. The clock on the nightstand flickered one fifteen. *Who the hell is in my house at this hour? I didn't hear the alarm in our security system.*

He glanced at Ludmila, his lovely wife, her measured breathing indicating REM sleep stage. *I don't want to scare her. Maybe it's nothing.*

More stirring downstairs. Anatoly's nervous system snapped to attention, a shiver down the spine. He retrieved his Smith and Wesson 29 .44 Magnum revolver from the drawer in the nightstand, brushed the thick mane of dark brown hair from his forehead, and slid out of bed.

Perspiration began to seep through trembling skin, his vision now almost completely adjusted to the darkness.

He tiptoed in the hall to the stairway and gripped the railing to steady a trembling body. Someone had opened the refrigerator creating a small halo of light to pierce the darkness in the kitchen. *Who or what could be in my house? An animal, a burglar?*

The bank cyber analyst descended the remaining few carpeted stairs and gripped his gun with both hands. He advanced to within ten feet of the kitchen, which was open to the dining and great rooms.

A figure in a white robe bent over at the waist was sorting through the contents of the fridge. Bottles clinked, and drawers opened and closed.

Anatoly flipped on the lights in the great room and shouted. "Turn around with hands up. Slow. Who are you and why are you in my house?"

The figure rose, closed the fridge door, and did what he had been told turning until he faced the man who issued the instructions. Now, however, darkness shrouded the kitchen and the figure's face. "Don't shoot, I'm Jer-"

Too late. The homeowner pumped three rounds into the torso of the figure hoping to hit the heart or other vital organs. The invader lurched backwards slamming into the refrigerator.

The terrified shooter knelt to one knee. *I hope he doesn't have a weapon. I think I hit him with every shot.*

Slowly the figure's head leaned forward behind the island as he straightened to an erect position.

Anatoly fired two of the remaining bullets in the clip into the figure but this time the intruder stood his ground.

"Get of my house, you bastard."

"Anatoly, I am not a burglar. I am Jeremy Chambers. This used to be *my* house. I was going to wait for you to get up in the morning, but I'm very hungry so I checked the fridge."

"I don't believe you. How did you get into my house? I call the police. Stay away from me. Why aren't you dead? I shot you."

The shots and resulting disturbance woke Ludmila who discovered her husband had vacated the bed and seemed to be talking to someone on the first floor. She swirled her robe around her shoulders and in stealth mode crept down the stairwell.

Her husband continued to kneel as he conversed with the apparition of a man in the kitchen. She screamed in Russian. "Anatoly, what has happened? What is that thing?"

Anatoly answered in Russian. "I don't know who he is. He says he used to live here, but I don't believe him. Go get a phone and call the police. I will hold him here." Ludmila raced up the stairs to their bedroom to retrieve one of their cell phones.

"Anatoly, relax. I'm not here to rob you or hurt you. I just came back from space. I'm really hungry. I was going to make a sandwich."

Ludmila flew down the stairs and shouted to her husband. "Both of our phones don't work. I can't call the police."

"That's right. I can't let you bring the police in. I want you to call Bob Pollard at the Chicago FBI office. You know him. He knows me and all the things I've been through. Use either phone. You'll see his number. Please call him and tell him I'm here."

Ludmila activated her phone and saw the cell number for Bob Pollard. She tried to clear the screen to call the police but couldn't. She looked at her husband who nodded. She tapped the number, and after four rings a man answered.

The FBI agent's eyes barely opened as he glanced at the digital clock on the night table. *Who the hell is calling me at this hour?* "Pollard."

"Mr. Pollard, it's Ludmila; there is a man here in a white robe. Says he is Jeremy Chambers. Anatoly shot him, but he did not die."

The FBI special agent in charge of the Chicago office ripped off the covers and sat coiled on the side of the bed. "Do not move from the house or talk to anyone else, and do not shoot or try to harm him. I will be there in forty minutes." Anatoly lowered his gun.

"Anatoly, thank you for tracing the guys who kidnapped my wife, Megan. They tell me she is better now." Jeremy wobbled while floating around the island, his feet six inches above the floor, to approach the nervous couple. "As you know I was taken in 2011 by an unknown force to a parallel universe to help work on some critical projects. Now eight years later they have returned me to earth." The Terasenkos's mouths opened in amazement. "I was given some special powers before I was taken, and I still have them. That's why I didn't die when you shot me. I don't know how long my powers will last, so I need to talk to Pollard to see what he wants me to do." He turned and walked back to the fridge and peered in. "Is it okay if I make a sandwich with this roast beef?"

"Yes, yes take whatever you want in the fridge. So you are really Jeremy? You scared the shit out of us." Anatoly and Ludmila sat on a couch in the living room.

Jeremy poured a glass of milk and carried it with his sandwich plate balanced on top of the glass as he gripped each passing piece of furniture to ground his floating body. He sat in a chair opposite the couple, smiled, and devoured his meal saving the chips and cookies for the end. When finished, he reclined and breathed deep. "I know this is a shock, and I'm sorry I scared you, but this house is where I wanted to come back." He slowly scanned the room. "So many memories of Megan and me raising our family in this house for ten years. Plus, my reentry here will be well disguised."

"How long will you stay here?"

"Don't know. It depends on what Bob thinks. Have you been happy in this home?"

"Yes, yes we have. This is hard for us. You don't seem real. You are like a ghost." The homeowners settled back and breathed easier since their guest did not appear to be aggressive or hostile.

"Yes, I guess I'm like a phantasm or ghost as long as I still have my powers." He leaned forward clasping the robe on his knees. "Speaking of powers, I will have to program your minds to keep my presence here a secret. You will not be able to share this situation with anyone. It's for your benefit as well as mine." The homeowners looked at each other, fear dissolving into amazement.

Anatoly's phone vibrated with a call from Pollard. "Anatoly, open your garage and move one of your cars to the driveway so I can pull in. I'm about ten minutes from your house. See you soon."

"Will do."

■ ■ ■

Anatoly slipped into a pair of topsiders and a jacket and moved his car to the driveway behind Ludmila's. He left the garage door open and retreated to the warmth of the house. Chicago in March can be a box of chocolates, and tonight the wind knifed between the trees and bushes creating intermittent whistling tones and a penetrating chill with the forty-degree temperature. The Terasenkos' house, located in Crystal Valley, a far northwest suburb of Chicago, and Jeremy's home before a celestial force seized and whisked him through a wormhole in space to a parallel universe where he participated in designated projects under the supervision of sophisticated aliens, felt familiar to the returning space traveler in spite of differences in the decorating taste of the new occupants.

Ludmila focused on the visitor still attempting to shake the remnants of sleep from tired eyes. *Can this really be the Jeremy Chambers we heard so much about from the FBI? I was expecting a taller, bigger man. So far he seems okay, and the fact he didn't seem to be hurt from getting shot verifies his reputation of having special powers.* To her, this figure was more of an oddity, a legend who existed only in the abstract.

Jeremy finished his meal and returned the dishes to the kitchen sink. He gripped the underside of the island counter and pulled up to force his feet to the floor. Defying gravity and bouncing above earth's surfaces made him feel like a freak.

Anatoly had camped out at the window to look for Bob's car. A Ford Escape rounded the corner, killed its lights, and entered the cul-de-sac. The weary homeowner met Pollard at the door in the kitchen that opened to the garage and hit the button to close the overhead door. They shook hands, and Bob ducked his six-foot five-inch frame in the doorway and hurried to embrace the figure in the white robe. He held Jeremy for a long moment then pushed him back to look at his friend whom he had not seen for almost eight years.

"You owe me a damn beer, bud," Jeremy said.

"I will definitely pay off that promise. Great to see you again. I had almost given up hope."

"I know, me too. The leaders never gave us timetables for our return to earth. Some guys came back in one year and others much later."

"I like your outfit; you look like the Pope."

"I can't wait to get into some jeans and a T-shirt."

"Hey, I just remembered something I've wanted to ask you. Did you visit your four friends up in Copper Harbor last fall?"

"Yes, I did. My appearance really shocked them, although they had an idea I might visit because of the way I asked them to make the trip up there. I'll fill you in on all that happened some other time."

"Good. Can't wait to hear it. I'll tell you a little secret; we spent some time following and observing the guys up there, but we didn't see you."

"Not surprised you were there, but I used my power so that only my friends could see me."

Pollard shook his head and turned to the host. "Anatoly, could you lend our friend some of your casual clothes? You and Jeremy are about the same size."

"Yes, yes. I'll be right back." He hurried upstairs and returned in five minutes with several varieties of shirts, jeans, and khaki slacks.

"Oh, thanks, Anatoli. I'll be right back." The new guest headed for the powder room to change.

"Can I get you something to eat, Mr. Pollard?" Ludmila asked.

"I would love a piece of toast and some strong hot coffee. Thanks," Bob replied.

Ludmila hurried to the kitchen to prepare the meal for the lawman. "I'm going upstairs and get dressed," Anatoli said as he took two stairs with each step Pollard munched on his toast and jam as Jeremy emerged from the powder room dressed in his new, comfortable threads while carrying the spare clothes and his robe over his arms. He joined the group in the great room and laid the clothes in a chair.

Bob placed the plate on the conversation table and settled back into his chair with the steaming coffee. He waited until Anatoli reappeared in a sweat suit and furry slippers.

"Bob, how are Megan and my kids, and when can I see them?"

"They're safe. I'll brief you on their situation after we finalize a plan for your new life. I've thought about this moment many times since you left." Pollard nodded toward Jeremy. "I concocted several different scenarios of how we should handle things going forward. Many variables are involved here, which will force us to be creative. I wasn't sure if you would have the powers you had when you left, but now we have that answer, which complicates matters. I also wasn't certain where you would emerge when you came back." Bob reclined, drew a deep breath, and sipped his brew while eyeballing his audience. "Appearing in this house is a real plus because it's not what most of our adversaries might expect. They'll probably look for you on the West Coast." He turned to face the Terasenkos. "Can we count on you to allow Jeremy to stay in your house indefinitely—and before you answer, you need to understand the possible danger. If some of the same people who tried to kill Jeremy and who kidnapped Megan discover he's living here in your house, you could become victims, too. I think you know what I mean about how vicious these guys are before you moved here from Russia. So take some time and let me know if you'll be willing to harbor Jeremy." The homeowners turned toward each other and spoke for several minutes in Russian and then faced the FBI agent and nodded, although Ludmila appeared reluctant. "Good. The tricky part will be protecting Jeremy, his family, and both of you while our government leverages his powers to protect our citizens and enhance our technology."

"Wait a minute, Bob. I have no idea how long my powers will last. I don't want to be in the middle of some government project and end up in a serious situation with these bad guys and find out my powers are gone."

"See what I mean about complications? You're absolutely right. We don't want to put you in high-risk situations, so we have to be very careful and resourceful in all we do."

"Excuse me, but I have to be at work at the hospital at seven thirty, so I would like to go back to bed for a couple hours," Ludmila said.

"Of course, of course." Pollard stood and shook her hand. "Thank you for your cooperation and for the breakfast and especially the great coffee."

"Why are there no bullet holes in the fridge?" Ludmila asked as she opened and closed the door in amazement.

"Oh that. I repaired them when I made the sandwich," Jeremy replied.

The stunned housewife shook her head. "Help yourself to more coffee; I made a full pot. Good night. You can use the guest bedroom at the end of the hall." Ludmila backed out of the great room and went upstairs.

Bob poured another cup of the dark brew and returned to the great room. "Anatoly, you probably need some sleep, too, so by all means go to bed. You need to go to work as usual and maintain your routine. Get some sleep; we'll update you tomorrow.

"Yes, I'm tired, and I do have to go to work in the morning." He turned at the stairway and waved to Jeremy. "Sorry I shot you. I'm glad you didn't die."

'Me, too! Don't worry about it. I would've done the same thing."

"Okay my friend, let's get busy and make a plan," Pollard said.

2

Bob Pollard and Jeremy Chambers moved the coffee table between them and prepared to brainstorm ideas for moving forward.

"Man, I'm so glad to see you here back home," Bob said. "Not as happy as I am to finally come back."

"It'll be great to have you on our team; there are so many things we can accomplish to protect the country with your unique powers."

"Slow down, Bud. I'm not sure how long I'll have these powers or even if they will let me stay here permanently. I'll help in any way I can, but I want some things in return—like the chance to see my family from time to time and live some version of a normal life."

"Understood. By the way, I forgot to mention Henry Barnes passed away last year."

"Yes, I learned of that when I received a telepathic message. I'm sorry he's gone. He was tough on me, but I liked his dedication to the job and all he did to try to protect my family."

"In addition to being my boss, he was also a close friend. The director assigned me as acting special agent in charge and in January promoted me to the job."

"Congrats! You deserve it."

"Thanks." Bob opened his iPad to a software page the bureau uses for project planning. "Now, first you'll be living here in your former house until we decide if moving you to another location is safe and makes sense. Down the line we may want to move you to other locations from time to time, similar to the witness protection program."

"Like I said before, I want to have your assurance I can see my family."

"I give you that promise, I just can't commit to a timetable. Oh, I forgot to mention—the director will ask the president to exercise his authority by signing a new executive order to give you Secret Service protection like years ago. They'll be coordinating with us."

"Fair enough." Jeremy visited the fridge again to make another sandwich. "The food where I was in space is a little shall we say . . . different. Took me a while to adapt to it."

Pollard nodded and returned to his project plan. He worked for twenty minutes typing ideas he had stored in a remote compartment at the edge of his brain while Jeremy enjoyed his second helping of earth food. He then asked his new colleague for his ideas, and the list grew to five pages. The two men explored the pros and cons of each possible course of action and then sorted it into groups based upon their projected percentage of success.

■ ■ ■

Bob and Jeremy interrupted their planning at the sound of the Terasenkos descending the stairs. The husband and wife appeared physically drained, not to mention emotionally spent.

Ludmila looked sharp in her uniform of crisply starched green scrubs as she held the fridge door open and asked the guests if she could serve breakfast, but both declined and said just coffee would be fine. Anatoly ground some beans and had the fresh brew ready in a few minutes.

Ludmila stood at the island facing the great room while sipping orange juice and munching cereal. Her dark hair was neatly rolled into a bun at the back of her head.

Jeremy noted she stood about five feet seven inches and maintained an attractive figure. Her dark eyes, however, betrayed a combination of fear and irritation at the sudden disruption in her otherwise mundane life. "How long will you be living with us? "

"It's up to Bob," Jeremy said.

"We'll make every effort to move him when we think it'll be safe, but I can't give you a specific date at this time," Bob said.

Ludmila involuntarily allowed a slight frown to frame her mouth. She nodded, put her dishes in the sink, and cast a derisive look at Anatoly who responded with a guilty expression while shrugging his shoulders, apparently reflecting a previous private discussion. She collected her purse and jacket then disappeared into the garage.

Anatoly realized he had parked behind his wife's car in the driveway and bolted out the front door to move it so she could back out. He closed the garage door just as his wife's car cleared the doorway and left his car in the driveway behind Pollard's Escape. He returned to the kitchen and served coffee to the two men in the great room and poured some into a large thermos he always took with him on the train.

"Anatoly, thanks again for putting up with us, but this is a serious situation, and your house is the perfect place for Jeremy for now. Seems like Ludmila is upset with us being here?" Bob asked.

"Jeremy's sudden appearance with the gun shots and him staying with us is overwhelming for her. We live a quiet life, and all the action of last night—she's just not used to so much going on, but she'll be okay. I will find a way to settle her nerves."

"Please tell her we truly regret turning her house upside down and will vacate at the earliest possible time."

"Personally, I think us being able to help you guys is exciting, and I will do whatever you ask."

"Thanks, you've been a big help in identifying the jerks who kidnapped Megan last year." Bob stirred sugar in his coffee. "I don't want to be seen leaving your home in daylight, so I'll stay until dark. Jeremy will close the garage door after I leave if you're not home by then. We still have plenty of work to do today. Thanks again."

"No problem." He took the thermos and his jacket from the mudroom on his way to the garage and left for the train station.

Jeremy and Bob discussed disguises, clothing, and other methods to mask the former spaceman's identity. By noon the caffeine had dissipated, and the men began to lose their ability to focus and to support increasingly heavy eyelids.

"I'm going to go up and take a nap. I'm tired after travelling a gazillion miles," Jeremy said.

"Right. I'm going to check some messages and make a few calls and then catch some winks. I'll use the couch down here."

■ ■ ■

At the top of the stairs Jeremy turned right, but stopped and turned around. The temptation to take a quick look at his old master suite overcame his respect for his hosts' privacy. A few steps to open the door and then enter the spacious bedroom. The Terasenkos' decorating taste differed from Megan's touch, but the space felt comfortable. Photos and portrait holograms of family members created the new owners' unique ambience. He approached the king bed and stroked the smooth white duvet conjuring images of his ten years with Megan and the kids in this house. The bathroom sparkled, indicating Ludmila's attention to cleanliness.

He lingered for several minutes before walking down the hall, stopping at Kelly's old bedroom, which Ludmila had converted into her crafts space.

Kyle's bedroom now served as Anatoly's home office with all the necessary equipment and a large desk and cabinet ensemble. Jeremy fought back tears before they could form and spill over his cheeks. *The bastards who orchestrated the plan to kidnap Megan and destroy our family are going to pay. The ones in jail are not the head of this beast. I'm going to kill the ones at the top.* He inhaled deep, coughed, and walked to the guest room. The sheets cooled and soothed his tired body, and sleep pulled him into a welcome state of rest.

■ ■ ■

Ludmila's car drove into the garage at four thirty, and she immediately used her cell phone to close the door. She noticed Bob Pollard sleeping on the couch and tiptoed to the stairway and then up with catlike steps.

Fifteen minutes later she returned to the first floor dressed in lounge pants and a sweatshirt.

The fridge door opening and closing combined with food bowls clanging on the island counter pierced Bob's nap bubble as he struggled to open eyelids seemingly cemented together from deep sleep. Finally his vision achieved 50 percent, presenting a wavy picture of a figure thirty feet away in the kitchen preparing food for dinner. He waited another couple of minutes for his eyes to fully adjust and then sat up.

"Hey there. How was your day at the hospital?"

"It was okay."

"Any unusual cases?"

"Nope."

Bob rubbed his eyes, stood and stretched. *Seems like she's really pissed. Glad I'm leaving tonight. I guess Anatoly will have to deal with her. Good luck with that!*

The weary agent moved to the chair he had used when he worked with Jeremy and decided no further conversation with the laconic nurse would be the best policy.

Ludmila continued assembling ingredients for a salad in a pot on the stove, then chopped chicken into its component pieces and slid them into a bowl before placing it in the fridge covered in Saran Wrap. Next she cut vegetables, dumped them into a bowl, covered it with Saran Wrap, and added it to the rest of the food for dinner in the fridge. She washed her hands, looked around the kitchen, and headed upstairs.

At 5:50 Jeremy glided down the stairs, yawning and stretching his arms. He plopped into the chair opposite Bob in the great room.

"Anything exciting happen this afternoon?"

"No, other than I think our hostess has a colossal case of the ass," Bob replied.

"I noticed that, too. I guess I can't blame her with me showing up in their kitchen in the middle of the night and Anatoly shooting me several times. Now she's stuck with me for who knows how long. I'll make sure I'm a good house guest . . . in my own house!" Jeremy laughed.

"I wouldn't worry about it, bud. She'll get used to you being part of her family. We really need to get you out of here ASAP, though, because the longer you're here, the more vulnerable you become."

"Maybe I should stay at your house."

"Don't know about that idea. The bad guys watch those of us in government law enforcement as much as we watch them. I won't rule it out, though, because it would be a lot fun having you live with me and Maggie, but you'd probably get bored real quick since we both work."

"Oh, I don't know. It's almost April, and the baseball season will be in full swing, so when the Cubs are in town, I can jump on the Red Line train and ride down to Wrigley to catch a game."

"No way, man! That's all we need. You could be attacked or kidnapped if the Russians spot you on the train, on the streets, or in the ballpark."

"Okay, I'll just watch the games on your TV and drink all your beer."

"Speaking of beer, I wonder if Anatoly has some on hand. Why don't you check the fridge?"

"Done." Jeremy opened the fridge and searched for some bottles or cans, but found none. "Sorry, no beer, but there is some Grey Goose. Care for a vodka tini?"

"Sure, on the rocks please."

Jeremy mixed two martinis and carried them to the great room. The friends clicked the TV on and searched the sports channels, agreeing on a Bulls game.

At 6:25 Anatoly's car pulled into the driveway, and he entered through the front door.

"Hi, guys. What's new?"

"We disarmed all nuclear weapons in all countries in the world, so they're going to award us the Nobel Peace Prize," Bob joked.

"Very good to hear. I see you have drinks to toast the achievement."

"Yes. We thought you wouldn't mind," Jeremy said.

"I'm going to change clothes. Is Ludmila upstairs?"

"Yes, but she's not in a very good mood."

"Thanks for the warning." Anatoly scampered upstairs.

The Terasenkos came downstairs fifteen minutes later. Ludmila sported a pouty face and Anatoly a wry smile.

The homeowners and their houseguests comprised an uncomfortable group at the dining room table, the only sounds for extended periods of time made by the tinkling of silverware on the bowls of food and tapping plates, the tension palpable.

Ludmila focused on her plate and the center of the table as she chewed her food in slow, rhythmic bites. She avoided Anatoly's repeated quick glances. The three men floated attempts at casual safe zone conversation, but questions directed at Ludmila died in soft-spoken one-word answers.

Anatoly took orders for coffee and spun some beans through the grinder as his sulking wife carried dirty dishes to the sink for rinsing and placement in the dishwasher. She washed her hands, turned, and said good night before gliding upstairs. Her dinner partners looked at each other and shrugged.

Bob and Jeremy finished a preliminary plan of action, realizing it consisted of only the bones and would need frequent adjustments due to the expected fluidity of the impact of the spaceman's return.

At 8:40 Bob stood, stretched, and shook his head to fling encroaching fatigue away from his mind. "Well, fellas, I'm going to shove off. Anatoly, don't forget to close the garage door after I leave." He hugged Jeremy and shook hands with Anatoly. "We have a great opportunity now, but also a ton of challenges." He stored his iPad in his bag and grabbed his jacket on the way to the garage. "Oh, I forgot to give you this." He tossed an iPhone and charger to Jeremy. "It's one of our special phones and has my number in the address book on speed dial. Make sure you take good care of it.

We'll talk every day." Jeremy nodded as he examined his new link with the boss.

3

Megan Chambers was still in a rehab facility in Newport Beach recovering from the trauma of the abduction last year. Her mother visited daily, and her father, Ryan, stopped by on his lunch hour and most evenings after work. The children, Kelly and Kyle, continued to see psychologists each week to deal with the ordeal of their mother's kidnapping last fall and now with her mental struggles. The kids visited Megan once not long after her rescue, but their mother's catatonic state and failure to recognize them proved devastating to the youngsters' psyches, so they had not returned to the rehab center since.

Today Ryan Murphy stopped at the facility on his lunch hour and joined his wife, Peg, in their daughter's room. Megan sat up in a chair staring out the window. Dr. Kahn entered and offered a cordial greeting to his patient and her parents, hoping to lift the pall permeating every square inch in the room; however, many months of Megan's static condition destroyed his effort. He motioned for the Murphys to follow him into the hallway out of Megan's earshot.

"I'm afraid your daughter has not made any progress since the kidnapping. She continues to be in a trancelike state. Although the distress of her ordeal inflicted deep mental damage, she has repressed most of the memories." The doctor allowed the gravity of this assessment to penetrate the parents' optimism for Megan's possible recovery. "We have observed her hallucinations of people beating her, animals attacking her, and an acute fear of being confined in small spaces."

Peg's countenance slid from dismay to frustration. "Isn't there something you can do? Different drugs?"

"I'm afraid not at this time. We have to exercise great care in prescribing the mix of medications because of possible adverse side effects, which could impact her general health. We have experimented with a couple of drugs that have performed well in combination in some limited tests, but unfortunately did not yield the results we wanted in her case. "

"So are you saying there is no hope?" Ryan asked.

"What I'm saying is she might remain in her present condition indefinitely, but she could snap out of it at any time. I don't want to color the prognosis by giving you false hope. You deserve the truth."

Peg covered her mouth with a shaky hand. Ryan curved an arm around her shoulder. He noticed an FBI agent at the nurse's station observing the conference with Dr. Kahn. The bureau has continued to provide twenty-four hour protection for the tormented patient in room 212.

Dr. Kahn motioned for the parents to follow him into the room once more. Megan had not moved, except for occasional slow motion blinking of heavy eyelids. Ryan continued to hold his wife and supported her as she walked unsteadily to the chair near the window.

The doctor asked Megan open-ended questions hoping to elicit a response, but none was forthcoming.

Peg stroked her daughter's hair and whispered positive thoughts and told her how much she loved her. But still Megan stared out the window, unresponsive. The distraught mother engulfed her daughter in an affectionate hug while wiping new tears from her cheeks. Ryan waited several minutes to allow the maternal embrace to perhaps spark a reaction, a sign of recognition. Megan did not move or speak. Her father then gently tugged at Peg's arm until his wife loosened her hold on their daughter and slid into her husband's arms, weeping in short convulsive breaths. Dr. Kahn held the door open as the beleaguered parents left the room.

Peg gazed into Ryan's red eyes looking for a sign of hope, a reason for optimism. "She's going to get better, right?" Her husband hugged her.

4

The new special agent in charge (SAIC) of the FBI's Chicago office reclined on his chair at his desk and massaged throbbing temples. He was used to the late hours, and now the clock read 7:47 on a Friday night. Henry Barnes, the previous SAIC, had shared details of a bizarre case involving a Chicago neurosurgeon, Dr. Dominic Cavallini, with Bob Pollard before Henry suffered a massive heart attack and died last fall.

Dr. Cavallini had participated in a secret project in Germany in 1998, or so he claimed. Barnes had met with the brain doctor on two occasions to reconcile certain facts in the file that didn't add up. Cavallini said he spent all of 1998 in Germany on the project and then returned to Chicago. Barnes suggested the doctor sit for a lie detector test to validate his story, but the neurosurgeon had balked and contacted his lawyer, who stonewalled Barnes. The persistent SAIC, however, contacted a retired scientist who had also participated in the secret project, but she had never heard of Dr. Cavallini, and his name did not appear on the roster of participants. Further, the project leader, Dr. Hoffmann, had allegedly been murdered about the time Cavallini returned home. Hoffmann's body was never found, and German authorities categorized the file as a cold case.

Henry Barnes thought this one-year, unexplained absence might have some connection to Jeremy Chambers's alleged disappearance into thin air seven years prior, so he continued to contact the doctor. However, Cavallini's attorney refused to allow the bureau to take any action against his client unless the FBI could obtain a subpoena and charge the doctor with a crime. In addition, the attorney raised the issue of a possible statute of limitations violation.

I wonder if Jeremy knows Cavallini?. After all, both of them are from the Chicago area. Bob retrieved the physical and electronic files and reviewed the facts from start to the present. *It still doesn't make sense. Are these guys acting in concert? Jeremy denied knowing Cavallini when I asked him. I need to talk to the doctor.*

The phone still had Cavallini's number available on speed dial. Bob called, and the doctor answered almost immediately, but his voice seemed overwhelmed by background noise. "Dr. Cavallini this is Bob Pollard calling. I replaced Henry Barnes as special agent in charge of the Chicago FBI office. Did you know Henry passed away last fall?"

"Hang on; I'm in a restaurant. Let me move to a place where I can get some privacy."

"Of course."

He excused himself from conversation with his wife and friends and moved down the hall near the restrooms. "I did see the news about Mr. Barnes. He was a sharp man, very persistent. I'm sorry he's gone. Now, you say you are the new boss in Chicago?"

"Yes. I was wondering if we could meet. I have some questions."

"No, no more questions. My attorney spoke to Mr. Barnes, and the matter was settled last year."

"There have been recent new developments I think you will be interested in learning."

"What kind of new developments?"

"We can't discuss this on the phone. Can we have lunch or dinner in the next couple days?"

"I told you, the case is closed."

"Dr. Cavallini, I'm not accusing you of anything; I'm asking for your assistance. This is highly confidential, top secret."

"How could I possibly help the FBI?"

"Please check your schedule and let me know what day works best for you; I will adjust mine to accommodate."

"Okay, how about Sunday night at Aureus. Do you know the place?"

"Yes, of course, it's one of our favorites. Let's say seven."

"Done. I put it in my phone. Good day, Mr. Pollard."

"Thank you, Dr. Cavallini."

The neurosurgeon stood in the hall, his dark brown eyes staring at the phone thinking it would reveal Pollard's news as patrons passed him heading to and from the restrooms. *What in the hell is this all about? I thought we put it to bed long ago. I wonder if this guy is as relentless as Barnes.*

■ ■ ■

The weary FBI SAIC arrived at Aureus, an upscale restaurant on Michigan Avenue, at 6:50 and returned the owner's greeting with a hearty handshake. A corner table was quickly cleared and cleaned for this frequent guest. Pollard ordered a glass of Chardonnay. The early crowd had finished dinner and filed out in mostly small groups.

Dr. Cavallini entered at seven sharp and exchanged laughs and greetings with the owner and members of the staff. He located Bob in the corner and weaved his way to the table. Pollard rose and shook hands with the neurosurgeon, who strained his neck to look up to this man who stood several inches taller than his five-foot-nine. The doctor ordered a glass of Cabernet and settled into his chair, casting a wary eye toward his host. They exchanged mundane small talk strangers use to get acquainted and take the measure of each other.

A waiter materialized, recorded their orders, and twisted the cork on a bottle of the Chardonnay Bob was drinking and poured a refill for the FBI boss.

"Well, Mr. Pollard, tell me why I'm here."

"I reviewed your file regarding the special project in Germany in 1998, and as far as I'm concerned the case is closed." Bob leaned against the back of his cushioned chair. "You are familiar with a case from eight years ago involving a man whose name is Jeremy Chambers, right?"

"Yes, why do you ask?" Cavallini shifted in his chair and cocked his head to one side.

"Do you think it's possible a person can be abducted by a force in space and taken to another planet, or even another universe—if such a thing exists—and then returned to earth?"

"I don't feel qualified to speculate on that. You need to talk to the quantum physics scientists and astronomer guys about such a possibility." His expression quizzical. "So, again, why am I here?"

"Let's suppose one or more humans were taken in the manner I described and in this faraway place in space they worked on projects to share their expertise in certain disciplines and also to receive advanced training and knowledge to share with people back here on earth to improve life." The waiter delivered the doctor's glass of Cabernet.

"Wow, that sounds like a stretch, but it would be wonderful."

"To pursue this further, let's suppose these people who come back were given special powers to enable them to assist countries and governments in working through the politics and the selfishness of mankind to keep us from blowing up the world. Does this scenario sound crazy to you?"

"Not crazy, highly desirable, but also improbable." The doctor leaned forward and lowered his voice. "Are you saying you know someone or more than one person who has experienced a round trip to space and is now back here and has special powers of some kind?"

Several waiters arrived and served the dinner with silent efficiency.

The men enjoyed several bites and reloaded wine glasses.

"What I'm saying, Dr. Cavallini, is my beliefs changed when Jeremy Chambers disappeared. We interviewed his friends at length, and their stories never wavered. Also, I was in the hospital due to gunshot wounds when Jeremy visited me. We had both been wounded in a gun battle at the wake for my partner who was killed in California. Jeremy transferred energy or power to my body somehow and cured all my injuries. Then he cured Paul Torchetti's terminal brain tumor. Paul was in the same hospital on a different floor and actually witnessed Jeremy's body evaporate." Pollard paused and studied the doctor's face, but did not detect unusual emotions. "In fact, Jeremy had been shot several times in the fire fight when I was hit, but his wounds miraculously healed almost immediately."

"Some of what you describe was on the news back then, but I didn't know you had been shot and cured. What does all this have to do with me?"

"With your expertise with the brain, do you think advances in artificial intelligence could give a human the kind of powers Jeremy possessed?"

"I have done research on AI, but am not aware of any human having those abilities."

"After reviewing your file, I thought perhaps the secret project in Germany might have some connection to Jeremy's powers."

"As I'm sure you're aware, I can't discuss that with you. It seems your imagination is working overtime."

"Maybe so, but I feel like I have to pursue Jeremy's story because this fragile globe of ours needs every possible chance to survive, and if there are people here on earth who have visited places and beings with superior intelligence, mankind needs to leverage that knowledge; don't you agree?"

"Of course. Our world grows more dangerous each year, so if there are any ways we can mitigate an unthinkable Armageddon, we should fully use such resources." The doctor shifted in his chair and forked the last piece of his sea bass and delivered it to his mouth. "But I still don't see how I can help you with your project."

"Can you share the research you conducted on AI?"

"I have published a few articles in medical periodicals over the last ten or twelve years, and some of my work is not yet complete. Our hospital includes a research unit, and docs with various specialties contribute the results of their studies to the unit's management who then decide which articles qualify for publication and to which journals they will be submitted."

"I see. Can you tell me about the projects you're working on now?"

"You will have to talk to management."

"Can you give me the contact information for the top person?"

"Sure. Here it is." Cavallini typed the information into his phone and sent it Pollard.

"Great. I'll give doctor Rosenzweig a call. Thanks."

"She may not be in a position to disclose the nature of our work at this point, but I'm sure she will be as accommodative as she can."

The men finished their meals and ordered a dessert to share. Dr. Cavallini ordered after-dinner liquors, and general conversation completed the meeting.

Stiff muscles and joints poked them as they stood and stretched before heading for the door. Once outside, Pollard tipped the valet and screwed his long frame into his self-driving car and departed.

The doctor stood on the sidewalk and watched the FBI boss's car disappear around the first corner. *I thought I was done with this cat-and-mouse game. Looks like Pollard is a damn pit bull like Barnes. I better call Rosenzweig and give her a heads up that she will be contacted by the Feds. She'll really love that!*

5

Jeremy spent most of his time in the guest room watching TV and reading. He only ventured down to the first floor for meals and to participate in small talk with Anatoly. Ludmila's attitude toward him had not changed; if anything, she appeared even more frustrated and terse. Jeremy's attempts at initiating conversation with the lady of the house were met with one word answers and rolling eyes.

The uninvited houseguest used his bedroom as a retreat from Ludmila's unhappy and possible expressions of disgust. However, after several weeks sequestered in this twenty-by-seventeen-foot room, Jeremy started hallucinating just after falling asleep. The dreams followed a pattern involving masked men chasing him through city streets and farm fields. The pursuers always gained ground until they could almost grasp his shirt. Jeremy would awaken with a start, sweat bathing his face and neck, his breathing punctuated by capricious gasps.

Boredom crept into his routine. Looking out the windows, which offered a view of the patio as well as the backyards of the neighbors on both sides provided temporary relief from his new gloomy existence. He looked forward to calls from Pollard several times each day, but Bob cut the conversations short due to an overflowing plate of FBI challenges.

On a Tuesday afternoon in April Jeremy tired of the novel he started a few days prior. He slammed the book on the night table and paced the room in the same pattern he had used hundreds of times. After a few laps he stopped at the windows and noticed Joe Serratella hauling out patio furniture, cleaning the various pieces, and raking the wet clumps of leaves embedded in many crevices formed between the concrete and the lawn. Next he swept the concrete and used the hose to push the winter's dirt into the lawn.

Jeremy watched his former neighbor and close friend for the hour it took for Joe to complete his cleaning, or was it his back telling him it was time to take a rest? The heavyset foreign exchange trader lumbered to the house and quickly returned to his patio with a beer in one hand and a cigar in the other.

He carefully lowered himself into a lounge chair and sighed as he allowed relaxation to wash over his tired muscles.

Jeremy shook his head remembering many afternoons and evenings he and Joe had shared on each other's patio enjoying beer, cooking steaks, watching baseball games on TV, and discussing the politics of the day. An urge to communicate with his former neighbor floated through his mind as he cast a longing glance at his friend who blew smoke rings, which collapsed into the light breeze. Jeremy's countenance changed abruptly as he recalled Pollard's instructions telling him not to contact anyone and that leaving the house was strictly forbidden. The urge to let his friend know he was back repressed the FBI rules. He focused on sending a telepathic message to Joe to let him know he returned and was nearby. Joe, however, exhibited no signs of recognition or of receiving his friend's thought. *Holy shit, maybe this is the end of having my powers . . . or could it be my bosses in the sky controlling me?* Jeremy turned in frustration and fell onto the bed as sleep encased his weary mind.

■ ■ ■

The remainder of the week consisted of one day cloned from the one before: Jeremy's nightmares woke him at four or five o'clock, and he lay in bed until six when he rose and took long showers. He meticulously shaved and dressed in loungewear before descending the stairs for breakfast and the next installment of Ludmila's cold shoulder. Then it was back up to the compact dimensions of his accommodations that seemed to shrink each day.

Saturday provided a transitory respite from Lumila's inimical behavior because she usually worked the morning shift at the hospital, and Anatoly typically ran errands early and was home by ten when he and Jeremy cooked breakfast together. Both men enjoyed the conversation on many topics. Jeremy especially enjoyed Anatoly's stories relating to cybercrime and the evolving tools he used to identify hackers and to help build electronic barriers to prevent penetration of his bank's firewalls. The men shared a common interest in sports: Anatoly followed Russian hockey players but also enjoyed baseball, basketball, and football, so they locked the TV into networks showing the games.

After a late lunch, Anatoly retired to his office to work, and Jeremy climbed the stairs to his room where a quick nap killed some time. The brevity of his sleep in the afternoon precluded the nightmares from assuming control of his brain. He rolled over on his back and stared at the ceiling for several minutes. A quick visit to the bathroom ending with cold water on his dry face drew him up to full wakefulness.

Birds' spring songs filtered through the partially open windows in addition to other sounds.

Joe scraped the iron stiles on his grill with a long-handle wire brush. *Looks like he's cooking steaks for dinner. Wish I could join him and Connie and the kids.* Joe sat on a recliner chair with a beer and dove into his iPad.

The urge to communicate with Joe overwhelmed Jeremy's sense of risk of incurring Pollard's wrath. *Besides, I'm not leaving the house, and I'm not actually going to talk to Joe, so what's the big deal? I just want to let him know I'm back. I know my powers are restored because I tested them on the TV.*

Jeremy ramped up his concentration and transmitted a telepathic message to Joe's brain. The effort encountered blockages at first, but this time he intensified his focus.

Joe shook his head and put the iPad on his lap. He looked around in a full 360-degree sweep but saw nothing unusual. The intrusion of strong impulses of something invading his mind deepened. He jumped out of the chair and surveyed the yard frantically. "Jeremy, is it really you? Are you back? Why can't I see you? I'm getting what you're saying. When can I see you? Not yet? When? You say you'll let me know when the time is right? Okay buddy, let's make it soon over here. Wait, don't leave . . ."

"Joe, what the hell are doing? Who are you talking to?" Connie Serratella shouted from the half open back screen door.

"What? Oh, no one. I, I saw something interesting on my iPad."

"Well, it sounded like you were talking to someone, but I don't see anyone. I think you're getting loony."

"Right, loony, that's me."

"It's almost time to put the steaks on. Is the grill ready yet, or were you going to talk to it to get it clean?"

"Ha, ha, very funny. The grill is clean. Don't worry; I'll take care of the steaks, and they will be the best you've ever eaten."

"You better get busy, or we'll all starve to death waiting for your gourmet touch."

"Okay, I'll call you when they're ready." *Maybe I should put one on the grill for Jeremy.*

6

J eremy reluctantly turned and lay down on the bed. He would have loved to go outside and join Joe at the grill and have a beer and a few laughs. But that isn't life for the time traveler these days. Now he lives in this dangerous invisible cocoon his family and old friends cannot visit. Too many flawed humans in faraway places are motivated to snuff out his powers and even his life. *I didn't sign up for this existence. All I wanted was to take care of my family, watch my kids grow up, and have a little fun along the way.* Sleep crowded out the melancholy thoughts inhabiting a weary mind.

The next afternoon the window pulled on his mind. *Maybe Joe's outside again.* Jeremy checked Joe's back yard, but no sign of his best friend, so he plopped onto the bed and stared at the ceiling.

Furniture scraping across cement outside woke him from a twenty-minute catnap. He leaped from the bed and checked the window. He saw Joe moving the patio chairs and table to one side so he could use the hose to rinse debris into the grass.

Holy shit, there he is again. I have to talk to him, even if it's only for a couple minutes.

The spaceman raced down stairs and out the rear door and then to the fence between the two yards. He crouched and looked around, all clear. Carefully he raised the latch and opened the gate leading to the side of the Terasenko's house, then quickly let himself through the Serratella's gate and into the yard. Joe did not see his visitor.

"Hey Bud, the patio's clean enough," Jeremy said in a muffled voice.

"What?" Joe spun around and saw Jeremy. "I can't believe it! Is it really you?"

"Shh, I'm not supposed to talk to you. Keep your voice down. Let's go next door." He led his friend into the Terasenko home.

The men embraced and laughed. "I'm so glad to see you, man. I thought I heard you talking to me yesterday when I was in the yard."

"Yes, you did, but I was here in this house upstairs at the window. I tried to send some thoughts to your mind, but I had trouble at first. I have no idea how long my powers will last. My bosses out there could cut me off at any time. I couldn't resist today, though. After I saw all four of you guys up at the UP, I got a severe case of homesickness. It's great to see you again."

"Yeah, me too. Why're you here, in this house?"

"This is where I told them I wanted to be for reentry, and they sent me. It's really an ideal location."

"Great. How long will you be here?"

"Don't know. Ludmila is a little nervous having me here. Anatoly fired a few shots at me the night I arrived because he thought I was a burglar. I healed myself quickly, and he seems fine now with having me here, but she's really uncomfortable, so I may have to move fairly soon."

"Where will you go?"

"I have to work that out with Bob Pollard. He wants to keep me out of sight so the Russians don't try to take me out again."

"Hey, you can stay at my house over here."

"No, I thought about that, too, but the bad guys are probably watching you, Carl, and Larry. I'll end up somewhere in the Chicago area, but I don't know where at this point."

"Man, I hope you get away from all this cops and robbers shit. We need to have some beers and play golf like the old days."

"You have no idea how good that sounds to me, but now is not the right time. Maybe someday if I lose my powers and we can let the Russians know I can't hurt them, we can get back to normal."

"That'll be great. Have you seen Carl, Paul, or Larry?"

"No. I've been here kind of' like a prisoner. You better go home because Ludmila will be here soon."

"Bummer. Wish we had more time over here to watch the Cubs now that they're good, and also to play some golf . . ."

"I know, bud, but you need to go. I'll let you know if things work out so I'm just the old Jeremy and we can get together. I'm going to have to program your brain so you can't tell anyone I was with you. Sorry about that." The friends hugged and Joe slipped out the side door.

Ludmila's self-driving car pulled into the driveway as Joe hurried from her house through the gate to his back yard as Jeremy followed part way and then retreated to the Terasenko's home. She took control of the car and braked to a stop as she watched her neighbor and houseguest.

■ ■ ■

"Hello, Jeremy. "

"Oh, hi Ludmila. How was your shift?"

"Okay, nothing special. I'll make dinner in about an hour so it's ready when Anatoly gets home."

"Sounds good. Thanks." She began pulling items from the fridge but watched him turn off the TV and go upstairs to his room for a nap.

■ ■ ■

Voices rattled in his brain, waking the voluntary hostage. As he ascended to lucidity, the voices identified as those of his hosts. He could visualize Ludmila and Anatoly in the kitchen speaking softly in Russian. Jeremy had acquired the power to translate most languages seamlessly in his mind. He lay still and closed his eyes to concentrate on the conversation downstairs. "He has been here for almost four weeks. We can't live our lives while he's here. I want him to go now," Ludmila demanded.

"He's been a perfect guest, no trouble. We need to help by hiding him until the FBI has a plan. We're doing our duty for our adopted country," Anatoly responded.

"We've already helped; four weeks is enough. I know he seems nice, but he gives me the creeps—you never know what he's thinking. And don't forget he programmed our minds so we can't tell anyone about him." She moved from the fridge to the island counter preparing lettuce and vegetables for a salad. "What if he can read our minds and influence our thinking and make us behave the way he wants? Our lives here are almost as bad as when we lived back home and the government controlled everything we did."

"We don't know the extent of his powers. Besides, we think in Russian first and we speak in Russian when we're not around Americans who only speak English."

"What if he understands Russian? You don't know how far his powers go." She slammed a steel-mixing bowl on the counter. "I want him out now."

"Not so loud. I don't think he speaks or understands Russian, but okay, okay I'll talk to Bob Pollard."

"Maybe working for the FBI has been a mistake. They control us, we have no friends, we're just spies—nothing more. They can dump us whenever they want. Maybe we should never have moved here. We live in his old house, for God's sake." Ludmila wiped tears from her eyes. "I miss my friends from the old country."

"I know; I miss them, too. I wish you could make some friends at the hospital, do social things with them."

"Some of the other nurses give me strange looks, and I hear whispers making fun of my accent. Besides, don't forget Henry Barnes told us when he recruited us to spy for the US government we shouldn't get too close to anyone."

"Yes he did, but that doesn't mean we can't have casual relationships with people here. I have some friends at the bank who accept everyone. We just have to be careful and not reveal what we're doing for the FBI."

"I'm not an extrovert like you. Even back in Russia it wasn't easy for me to make friends. I guess I'm really getting homesick."

"Well, after Jeremy leaves we can have our normal lives back. Things will get better, I promise." Anatoly coiled his arms around his troubled wife.

"We'll see."

Jeremy shook his head in despair. *Here we go again. I'm causing problems for these nice people. Everywhere I go people get hurt. Maybe the best thing would be if I can lose my powers, get back to being a normal human again. But I have no idea when my bosses out there will release me from this stifling life.*

■ ■ ■

This new development weighed on Jeremy. If he had to move out of the house, where could he find a safe place to hide? *Maybe Dr. Cavallini can offer a suggestion.*

Jeremy concentrated and sent a telepathic message to the doctor. Cavallini responded it would be too risky for Jeremy to move into his home. His wife, Sharon, would have too many questions regarding the secrecy involving Jeremy, which might lead to having to disclose facts about where both men had been for long periods of time. The less Sharon knew the safer she would be.

Cavallini suggested Jeremy move to one of his close friend's home temporarily, but Jeremy responded that the risk was the same as if he were to move into the doctor's home.

The neurosurgeon then suggested he check with Pollard. Jeremy reluctantly agreed.

■ ■ ■

"Pollard here."

"Hi Bob, it's AT. LT can't live with our guest here anymore. She wants him out now."

"Why, is he causing trouble?"

"No, it's just the fact he's here and has those powers or whatever they are. I like having him here, but she's all worked up."

"I know it's inconvenient, but your house is the perfect option right now. No one would surmise he's there. Can't he stay longer?"

"I'm afraid not, my friend."

"Well, how about another week?"

"I wish I could say okay, but if I want a reasonable home life and marriage, he has to go tomorrow."

"This is not good. I'm extremely disappointed. I'll stop by tomorrow in the late afternoon. I don't want to move him until it's dark."

"Okay. Sorry."

■ ■ ■

Having completed a day including cases involving police abuse, drug smuggling from Mexico, espionage in Europe, and various white-collar crimes in the Midwest, Bob Pollard pushed his chair back and closed weary eyes. *Man, I've only been in this job for less than a year, and I can feel the stress beating me up physically and mentally. Now I know how Henry Barnes got so wired and sick, then having that massive heart attack. I need to see my doc and ask him for something to help me deal with the pressure.*

He lurched forward opening eyes framed by red lines. His daily schedule on the iPhone flashed a note from Anatoly yesterday informing him Ludmila wants Jeremy out of their house ASAP. He had promised Anatoly he would drive out to the house tonight and take their visitor to a different location. *But where would he be safe and concealed from public scrutiny?*

He checked his phone—6:50. It would be dark by the time he drove from the city to Crystal Valley so removing Jeremy from the garage surreptitiously would not be a problem. Bob had not recently thought about possible hiding places with the weight of his current caseload consuming all his energy and mental capacity. *Guess I'll have to get creative on the drive out to the house and review my original ideas.*

Traffic moved above the speed limit on the Tri-State Tollway after the completion of the two- to three-year construction project to replace all bridges, add lanes, and repave the surface from O'Hare all the way to Rockford. The newly minted SAIC of the FBI's Chicago office pondered possible locations where he could hide Jeremy. *He can't stay at my house or any other agent's house, or his parents' home and not Megan's parents' home. The other possible sites he previously considered bubbled to the top of his mind. Maybe we could rent a modest apartment downtown or stash him in one of the museums, or the United Center.*

His exit on Randall Road appeared sooner than expected and interrupted the montage of ideas swirling through his mind. *I think one of the museums will work best. Which one? The Field Museum might provide the lowest profile. He'll need appliances for food preparation, a bed, and enough personal space so he doesn't feel claustrophobic. Maybe the boiler room.*

7

Stephanie Murphy reclined in her chair and stretched her arms above her head to full length while looking through the large glass windows of the office. The usual rhythmic hum of office activity and muffled conversation had dissipated as colleagues had left for the day, casting an eerie silence over the expanse of the suite. With a sigh, she secured a hair tie that instinctively fastened around her long auburn hair subtlety streaked with ribbons of blond. Her light brown eyes wilted under fatigue, but she was determined to finish her report before heading for home.

She had worked hard and made the required personal sacrifices necessary to graduate near the top of her class in both college and law school, resulting in an associate attorney position with Shields & Fitch, a large consulting firm specializing in corporate risk management. Her outstanding performance advising small and mid-level clients led to promotion to full partner after seven years. But if she were to be truly honest with herself, the sedentary and tedious nature of the work didn't fulfill her aspirations as she had once hoped.

She pushed her chair back and decided to get a cup of fresh coffee from the break room. On the way back to her office she lingered near the windows in the aisle, which provided a view of the shops and parking lot of the Fashion Island shopping mall here in Newport Beach. *I can't believe this place is still so crowded with the huge increase in online shopping over the last ten years. I guess these people still like the vibe and the game of seeing who's here and the thrill of being seen.* Reluctantly she returned to her office and her current project.

A recent assignment at the request of her firm's chief executive officer to investigate whether hackers had been siphoning funds from FiberLink Corp, a small, communications client based in Vista Nueva near John Wayne Airport that included few residential subdivisions, but several large commercial and industrial sections had created challenges in understanding the corporate structure and processes. Stephanie reviewed notes on the screen she had recorded during the past several days regarding the results of the most recent audit giving the company a satisfactory rating. The financials revealed large payments received from the city of Vista Nueva for consulting services provided by FiberLink regarding the quality and effectiveness of the city's communication equipment. But when she had visited the company last month, the Chief Financial Officer, Earle Claypoole, was unable to produce sufficient source documents to support the payments, a fact that, together with inadequate fire walls and systems security safeguards, led her to believe the firm may be subject to hacking. Mr. Claypoole told her he was working with the information technology team to review, evaluate, and tighten internal systems to protect the company from cybercrime, but the effort was still in its early stage as he could not devote much time to it because of other challenges like investing the firm's funds, paying bills, and developing plans for expansion of the business.

The young attorney also recalled the CFO had mentioned to her he and the mayor of Vista Nueva were brothers. Both lived in the lone upscale, gated community in town, belonged to the same country club in Irvine, and took family vacations together to exotic locations in the South Pacific and Caribbean. She noticed numerous pictures of the two men in Earle's office lining the credenza behind his polished wood desk.

The telephone ring jolted her concentration, and she exhaled before picking up the corporate phone. "Hello, this is Stephanie."

"Hi babe, how're you doing without me all this time?" Brad Wolfe asked.

The familiar voice surprised her. She took a deep breath and briefly shook her head, wishing she had checked the number on the console before she answered the call.

"I'm sorry, who am I speaking with?" she asked pretending not to recognize the voice.

"Hey, Steph, it's me, Brad!"

"Oh hi, Brad," she responded with almost no enthusiasm. "How can I help you?"

"Hey, that's no way to talk to the guy you wanted to marry a couple years ago."

Just hearing the words already started to irritate her. "So what's up? I'm really busy right now."

"I figured you'd be busy, as always, but I was thinking we could meet for lunch to catch up."

"No thanks," she replied in an emotionless tone. "I've really got a lot on my plate right now, and to be honest, I don't think there's any reason for us to get together."

"Aww, come on, Steph ," Brad said. "We're still fiends, aren't we? I know I didn't leave on a good note, and I apologize for that. It was totally immature the way I handled everything. But I'd really like to see you again. And believe it or not," he added softly, "I have changed."

Stephanie listened to the words but did not answer. Finally, after a long pause, she responded. "Listen, Brad, I really can't right now, but maybe some other time."

"Okay," he said with renewed hope in his voice. "I'll give you a call back in a few days, you know, after you've had some time to mull it over and you're not so busy. We'll plan something." Before she could answer, he added "Great! Talk soon." He hung up.

"Ugh!" She exclaimed as she placed the phone in the cradle. Saying "maybe some other time" was definitely the wrong response to give him. She unwound the conversation in her mind and concluded his eager reaction indicated he heard her say "yes." *He's already planning on a date and knows where they will meet.*

■ ■ ■

Brad called the next day, but this time Stephanie checked the number and let it go to voicemail. The following day he sent a text message, and then three more. Several days later he realized she wasn't going to respond, so he called again, several times in succession, letting the phone ring until it transferred to voice mail. After the third call, she picked up and answered. "What?" her irritation obvious. "I told you my job is crazy right now. Did you hear me?"

"I know," he whispered. "You're always busy; that's the story of your life. But even when you're swamped you need to take a break for lunch. I promise we'll make it a quick one. Okay?"

Stephanie sighed before answering, knowing he would not give up until she agreed to meet him. "Fine. I'll meet you at Logan's tomorrow. Be there at noon, and don't be late," still annoyed. She started to end the call, but heard him ask a question.

"Wait, I wanted to ask you something . . . Steph, Steph, Hello, hello?"

Pretending she didn't hear him, she clicked off the call. *No need to indulge him in additional chatter now since we'll have time to talk at lunch.*

Later that evening, the young attorney reclined in her chair and wondered about the reason for the sudden calls from her former boyfriend. The thought of meeting him for lunch surfaced many memories, most of which were bad, especially in the last two years of their relationship. However, they also reminded her of how attractive a man he always was, and at one time, she had wanted to marry him. *I wonder if he looks the same, or maybe heavier after two years? He was always a fitness nut, though, so he's probably still in good shape at thirty-six.* After picturing his short brown hair brushed forward and then up at the front and the perfect smile framing movie star teeth, she shook her head and blinked. "Don't even think about going down that path again Stephanie," she blurted out loud. "Because you already know it only leads to trouble." Her instincts told her he was up to something, an ulterior motive, but too early to know what that motive was.

■ ■ ■

Stephanie wore her muted dark blue business suit, beige blouse, and flat blue pumps she purchased earlier in the day. As she valeted her car, she saw Brad standing just inside the door of Logan's restaurant.

She walked in, and he smiled as he reached out to embrace her, but she reduced the gesture to a brief hug while keeping him at a distance.

"You look fantastic!" he said with a grin. "Thanks," she answered in a monotone.

As they walked through the atrium toward a table, she couldn't help notice thick biceps under the sleeves of his golf shirt. *Yep, still works out for sure, and he still has the same dark surfer tan he always had.*

He carried a blue blazer over his arm and wore designer jeans and a blue, unbuttoned golf shirt. "So, what have you been up to these last two years?"

"Lots of work. How about you?"

The waiter took their ice tea drink orders and left.

"Oh, I've been keeping busy, too. Changed jobs a couple times since I last saw you. Are you still with Shields & Fitch?"

"Yes," she said looking back at him and feeling there was more behind his question. "I made partner a couple years ago."

"Wow, congrats! Can't say I'm really surprised, though," he said with a wide grin. "I always knew you had it in you to be great at whatever you chose to do, but do you ever regret not hooking up with an actual law firm instead?"

"Sometimes, but I couldn't find anything in patent or intellectual property after I passed the bar. Unfortunately, IP in LA and Hollywood only operates on nepotism, and I don't have relatives in the business."

The waiter returned with the tea and took their food orders.

"So, do you like your job with the consulting company? I mean it's so different from practicing law."

"Yes and no. It's like anything else, you have good clients and bad clients." She didn't want to appear curious about his life since the breakup.

"I can understand that. Who are some of your clients?"

"Mostly small- to medium-size firms."

"Any names I'd recognize?"

"No, I don't think so."

"You still advising clients on their risk management programs?"

She paused wondering why the sudden detailed interest in her career. "Right, that's what we do." She cocked her head to one side. "Is there a reason you're asking?"

Before he could answer the waiter returned with fresh seafood salads and bread, making it easy for the conversation to transition to another subject.

"How is Megan doing, and the kids?"

"They've all had a tough time, but they're doing okay. Megan's still in therapy after the kidnapping, but the kids have held up pretty well, all things considered."

"I still can't believe how her husband—James, was it?—disappeared into thin air. Wonder if he faked the whole thing and is living on an island somewhere drinking mojitos."

"It's Jeremy. There was one witness who saw him evaporate and some other guys witnessed some events he experienced, so I'm a believer."

"I guess I'm old school—need to see it to believe it for myself."

The estranged couple continued to exchange neutral turf conversation as they finished their meal.

"Wow, look at the time, one forty-five. I need to get back to work." She stood and waited for him to walk her to the door.

"Yes, I need to get back, too. You know sales—you make your own schedule, but you need to bring home the bread at the end of the month."

"Right. Good to see you, Brad," she said without a smile.

"Let's do this more often. Who knows, maybe we can see a movie or go to Catalina sometime."

"Brad, having lunch was nice, but I'm not ready to jump back into a relationship with you. Let's just say goodbye for now."

"You know I'll be calling and texting you." Brad's grin broadcast his optimism.

"Yeah, and you know I'll be getting a restraining order," she answered with a wry smile before she slid into the driver's seat as her car drove itself back to her office.

Brad's smile twisted into a scowl as he watched her car pull away. *Damn, I thought I could reel her back in. Looks like I'll have to work a little harder to see what she's up to at FiberLink Corp. Earle told me she's been asking some alarming questions.*

■ ■ ■

"Hey Ace, it's Brad."

"What's up? I'm on my way to a meeting in a couple minutes," Earle Claypoole replied.

"I just had lunch with Steph; she was completely evasive about the names of her clients. How much do you think she knows?"

"I'm not sure how tenacious she is, but she sniffed around the audit and asked me for source docs, which you know I didn't have time to create, but I typed up a phony report yesterday, so hopefully it'll satisfy her next time she stops in or if she wants me to email it to her."

We need to be careful because she's like a pit bull when she investigates things. We can't let her stumble across our little golden goose."

"Agreed. We'll just have to play it by ear and see where she goes with it. I gotta run, bud."

"Okay, later." *This is getting too hot. We need to bring Phil up to speed.*

"Mr. Claypoole, please." Brad asked the receptionist at city hall in Vista Nueva.

"Who may I say is calling?"

"This is Brad Wolfe."

"Thank you, one moment, please." She came back on in twenty seconds. "I'll put you through, Mr. Wolfe."

"Hey Brad, long time no talk," Phil Claymore intoned.

"Hey Phil. I won't keep you because I know you're busy. I just had lunch with Stephanie Murphy, my ex-girlfriend from a few years ago. She works for Shields & Fitch, and they have a contract with FiberLink to review the company's enterprise risk management program. Earle told me she's been snooping around and pinned him down on some documentation to support the city's large payment for the consulting services we provided for you. Earle drafted a fake report he will show her next time she asks for it. I'm worried she may find some things we don't want her to find."

"Uh oh. Can't you throw her off the trail? After all you dated her back in the day."

"We didn't break up on good terms. In fact, I dumped her. I'll try to work my way back into her life, but she isn't real happy with me right now."

"Well, my boy, this one is your baby. If you can't get her to leave us alone, we'll all possibly go to prison."

"We can't let that happen. We may have to resort to other means to get her to back off."

"Like what?"

"I don't know. Maybe a car accident."

"That's too extreme. Think hard, my friend. I don't intend to go to prison. I think you, Earle, and I need to get together and develop a plan. How about Friday night at our country club in Irvine?"

"What time?"

"Say seven."

"Done. See you then."

8

Bob Pollard certainly didn't need this curve ball from the Terasenkos; his plate was overflowing with projects and cases. *I can understand Ludmila feeling nervous about having someone like Jeremy with all his powers and people who might be looking for him living in her house. Add to that the fact she and her husband are spies for the FBI and I'm sure she's scared. But damn, I was hoping we could get a few months for Jeremy to hide in their home while we see if the Russians have a clue he's back. It would buy us more time to decide on a secure, semi-permanent location for him.*

He called Anatoly and asked him to open the garage and make room for his car. The garage door immediately opened and then commenced its downward move before the car had cleared the driveway and come to a stop.

Bob entered through the kitchen and joined the Terasenkos and Jeremy in the great room.

"Ludmila, I understand your desire to get your lives back to normal, so I will take Jeremy when I leave tonight, and we will not bother you anymore."

"Thank you, Mr. Pollard. Please excuse me as I am working the early shift tomorrow and need some rest." She nodded to the group and headed for her bedroom upstairs but stopped half way. "Oh, I almost forgot. Jeremy, why were you and Joe sneaking between our houses this afternoon?"

"What? Are you crazy?" Bob shouted toward Jeremy.

"Sorry. I couldn't help it. I saw him working in his yard, and I thought I could meet with him for a few minutes without anyone knowing," Jeremy whispered.

"You idiot, you could have caused chaos if the wrong people had seen you. Ludmila saw you, so there might have been others. Good thing we're leaving tonight."

"Hey, man, back off. I said I was sorry."

"Okay, but promise you won't pull any more damn stunts like this."

"Sure, I promise."

Pollard shook his head and sat in a chair in the living room. He felt his face flush as his blood pressure pulsed through his fatigued body.

Anatoly decided to give the SAIC some time to decompress before speaking. "Bob, I apologize. I think my wife is overreacting because he hasn't been a distraction at all; in fact, he's been a model guest," Anatoly whispered.

"No need to apologize; I'd feel the same way if I were her," Jeremy said.

"Where will you take him, Bob?"

"Not certain yet, but I have some ideas. I'm going to use the bathroom and then we'll be leaving. You ready, Mr. Jeremy?"

"Yep. Not much to take with me."

Five minutes later the two men rolled down the driveway and out of the cul-de-sac en route to Pollard's condo, ostensibly only for tonight.

"You said you have some places in mind. I thought you might have one selected by now," Jeremy said.

"I do, but I didn't want to say it in front of Anatoly. Like all our innocent people who have some level of information of what's happening with you, the less they know, the better off they are."

"So where's my new home?"

"I reviewed a lot of possibilities in my mind, and I decided the Field Museum is our best bet, at least for now. You'll stay at my house tonight, and once I can get your new quarters ready, we'll move you to the museum."

"What? How can I live in a place like that? There are always people around."

"Yes there are, but they never visit the boiler room."

"You gotta be shittin' me."

"Take it easy. I've already arranged with the director of the museum to have things you need available down there, and you can come upstairs at night. Just use your special talents to program the security system and the guards to ignore you until you return to your den."

"Oh man, this will be a real palace. What about a bed, food, lights?"

"I said all will be handled for you."

"How long do I have to live in this rat hole?"

"Until I can come up with something better."

"I can think of something better. How 'bout a rental house in Corona Del Mar, or Newport Coast, or Emerald Bay?"

"Those are not in the budget, and you know it."

"Hey, I didn't ask for this fiasco."

"Seriously bud, I know that, but this is the hand we've been dealt, and we need to go with it as best we can."

"I wish I knew when, or if, my powers will be taken away. I need to see my kids and Megan."

"I wish I could give you a timetable for getting together with your family, but I can't at this point. Let's see how things at the museum go for a while, and if the coast is clear, I'll try to set up a time and place for you to meet your family."

"Okay, but it better be soon." Jeremy grimaced then looked out the tinted window into the darkness as the car cruised east on the Interstate 90 toll road toward Chicago. "Bob, what exactly will you have me working on for the bureau?"

"We need your skills to assist us with worldwide intelligence gathering. Our hands are full with all the amateur hackers out there. It's difficult for us to sort out what's real and what isn't. We need to continuously monitor the Russians, Chinese, North Koreans, and several countries in the Middle East and Africa."

"That's an awful lot for one person, even if I do have some special powers."

"Hey, I don't expect you to be a one-man band. You'll be our teammate with your ability to cut through a lot of the bullshit chatter we see every day, which will make us much more efficient."

"Okay, but just remember we have no idea how long my powers might last. I feel like I'm on a string that stretches many light years away to where I was for almost eight years. Those guys must be calling the shots on my life. I'm like a fucking puppet."

"I know what you mean. If you ever feel like you're losing it, call me ASAP. We'll put you into a new life, like the witness protection program."

"Another thing that bothers me is the fact that my powers can come and go. It's happened already when I tried to enter Joe's mind and couldn't, but then on another day I was able to. My space bosses seem to be playing with me, and I don't like it."

"I think all we can do is stay positive, and if they strip your powers, we'll move you until, or if, they're restored."

"Yeah, but I gotta tell you, this is a shitty way to live."

"Amen to that, but hang in there. Hopefully things will get better."

They swung by a fast-food restaurant and bought burgers and fries before Bob wheeled the car into his building's underground parking garage and the two men took the elevator to his condo.

"Maggie's working the night shift this month, so she won't be home until about eight AM. I'll get you out of here temporarily before she's back. Make yourself at home. I'll get us that beer I've owed you for eight years." Bob produced two beers from the fridge and handed one to his guest.

"Thanks. I really missed earth food and beer when I was away."

"Well, you'll have plenty of both from now on."

"Fine with me."

"Tell me your pants and shirt sizes and I'll have someone buy some clothes for you." Bob recorded the data in his phone as Jeremy indicated the types of items he preferred.

Bob clicked on a news station on the TV, and the men settled into their chairs and savored the addictive aroma and taste of their food.

The world had gradually slipped into a second Cold War as more countries acquired nuclear weapons. Ironically, this proliferation served as a deterrent to all-out war as no country wanted to lose its threat to use such force by firing the first salvo and facing total destruction of its people and land as well as providing the trigger for world nuclear conflict. The political landscape remained static as the stalemate simmered. In back channels, however, countries continued to form new alliances and amped up efforts to develop or steal the latest in artificial intelligence code that would provide leverage against enemies. Food and water shortages for a still burgeoning world population exacerbated strained relations between countries able to harness genetic engineering to augment their food supply versus smaller nations lacking resources to stay current with the latest technology.

"This world of ours is so fragile. All it'll take is for some rogue country or despot to feel squeezed enough to panic and push the damn red button, and we'll all be crispy critters in a matter of minutes," Bob opined.

"Right. I didn't realize so many more countries would get nukes while I was gone."

"You said you and others were working on things that could benefit us here on earth. When do your bosses intend to bring these improvements down here and give them to us?"

"No clue. We just worked on our projects and did what they instructed us to do."

"Come on, man, tell me specifically what you guys were working on."

"You know I can't go there. Even if I tried to tell you, they would not allow me to say the words. All I can share is they have a very orderly society; there is no disease, no conflict or crime—everything works perfectly. Transportation is precisely synchronized so no accidents occur. They are advanced beyond us by a ton. Hopefully someday they will teach us how to save our planet and get along with each other."

"Well, you knew I had to ask. All you said is really encouraging, and I hope they visit us earthlings soon because Lord knows we need guidance. If they have a method of improving human nature to delete all of our flaws, that would be a great start. Want another beer?"

"Sure. I had forgotten how relaxing a beer can be. Just one more and then I need to head to bed."

"No problem, bud. Let me know when you're ready, and I'll show you to your room."

9

Ludmila Terasenko's shifts at Good Counsel Hospital in Lake Barrington, Illinois provided a desirable variety of interesting medical challenges as well as unpredictable activity flow. Some days or nights the admissions tapered off, and many rooms remained vacant. However, during other shifts her floor bustled with new patients and increased medical staff. Ludmila's registered nurse certificate authorized her to perform several procedures and assist on many others. She enjoyed the nightshift most because it afforded time for her to engage in some personal online activities during dead time at the nurses' pod.

She could not recall exactly when her new life in America with her husband, Anatoly, morphed from the exhilaration of a fresh start away from the oppression in Russia to boredom and fear after her husband agreed to spy for the FBI. She missed the sameness of her routine in Russia in spite of omnipresent government eyes poking into every facet of their lives. Lifelong friends lived close, and she had been able to laugh and share events with people who spoke her primary language. Making friends in America did not come naturally for her. Hospital employees were cordial but distant, and she overheard some mimic her mild accent.

Three weeks after Jeremy Chambers floated into her home from wherever he had been in space, she fantasized frequently about her former life in Russia. Anatoly seemed happy and enjoyed his secret role as a covert FBI spy so her attempts to explain her malaise to him met with shock and disappointment. Jeremy the Spaceman living in her home for an indefinite period of time encroached on her privacy and added an unwanted level of danger to their lives. This visitor had special powers other countries coveted, and Russian assassins had made two attempts on his life several years ago. She decided to tell her husband Jeremy had to go. Four weeks of hosting this freak represented the outer limit of her patience, and she told Anatoly Jeremy must leave, which created a chasm between a couple previously cultivating matrimonial love. The issue wedged into their relationship, and the sharp edges began leaving open wounds that continued to fester each day Ludmila saw Jeremy in her home.

■ ■ ■

Two weeks after their guest departed with Bob Pollard, Ludmila received a call from a Russian-speaking man who wanted to meet with her. She refused unless he could identify himself and the reason for his request. He responded with a detailed profile of her life in Russia and her current situation since her arrival in America over eight years ago. *Oh no! The Russians have discovered Anatoly is working for the FBI as a spy. This is big trouble.*

The man identified himself as Ivan Markov and said he had a proposition for her.

She shook with vibrating nerves. *Here we go, an offer I can't refuse, and if I do it will mean Siberia . . . or worse.* Assuming she had no choice, a meeting was arranged during her lunch hour at a pizza restaurant near the hospital. She reeked of trepidation as her car drove itself to the restaurant and parked.

Markov, in his early to mid-sixties with a sagging belly and balding grey hair met her at the door and requested a booth at the back of a long aisle. "So thank you for meeting me today. You look lovely. You look like the nurses on TV in those medical shows," he said in Russian.

"Thank you. What is it we need to discuss?" she responded in Russian.

"Let's order first and then we can talk." He summoned a server and after asking his guest's selection of toppings ordered a pizza and two ice teas. "I am with our government intelligence unit, and we have a sort of permanent assignment to watch certain US citizens who may be involved with our ongoing diplomatic conflict with America. I am in charge of the Midwest region, and in particular, we have been observing FBI and other US activity the past several years." He sat back to allow this information to marinate with his fellow countrywoman.

"What does that have to do with me?"

"One of my drones saw the boss of the Chicago FBI pull into your driveway a few weeks ago. Why would he be visiting your home?"

The pizza arrived, and Markov licked his lips as he used a spatula to lift pieces onto each of their plates. They ate in silence.

"Did you hear my question?"

"Yes. I'm sorry; this comes as a shock to me. I'm not sure what you are talking about."

"Do not play games with me. We have confirmed this information.

Now why was Mr. Pollard at your house?" Markov's bushy eyebrows extending across the bridge of his dark red nose partially obscured the blood-shot condition of his eyes.

"He came to see my husband. I was upstairs so I don't know what they talked about."

"I think you know much more. Pollard did not leave until morning after you left for work. Why was he there?"

"I'm sorry Mr. Markov, I do not know any more. I need to get back to the hospital." She slid to the edge of her seat in the booth.

"Stop! You will not leave until I say you can." Markov dabbed the marinara sauce from the corners of his mouth. "Since you are not cooperating, here is the deal. You can have two days to try to 'remember' why the FBI visited your house and tell me. If you still can't remember, there will be consequences for you and your husband. Do you understand?" Markov edged out of the booth and bowed as he shook her hand.

She noticed his bloodshot eyes blinking in rapid bursts, which together with his stern countenance posed a menacing image. "Yes. Thank you for lunch." Ludmila resisted the urge to run out the door, turned, and forced a measured pace to her gait.

Markov smiled as he noted she had not eaten much, which meant more for him. He continued to savor this American food with the Italian name. *She is a cute one. Maybe I will get more from her than just information.*

■ ■ ■

The anxious nurse returned to her workstation and collapsed her head into trembling hands. Her station mates noticed and inquired if she felt ill. Ludmila forced a quivering smile and replied she was just tired. *My life is over. If I tell him about Jeremy, there will be violence, and if I lie, he will know because he seems to know everything anyway. He will make life for Anatoly and me hell, maybe even kill us.* She finished her shift and reclined in the seat as her car drove home. The car continued to idle in the garage until she told it to turn off and close the overhead door. Her body seemed to weigh a thousand pounds as she swung her legs out to exit and walk the few steps to the kitchen.

She hauled herself up the stairs to her bedroom, kicked off shoes, and lay down on her back on the bed. *This can't be happening. How could the Russians know so much about us? There is no good decision.* She slid into light sleep.

Anatoly bounded up the stairs at 7:10 and woke his drowsy wife. "Why so tired?"

"It was a tough day at work. I'll change clothes and make dinner in a few minutes."

Her husband pushed her back on the bed and straddled the lifeless body. He leaned in and kissed a dry mouth. Her body, limp; she didn't react and closed her eyes again. "What's the matter? I just want to give you some love."

"Nothing. It's like I said, I'm tired." She had crushed his libido, so he moved off the bed and began to undress. She changed into a T-shirt and jeans before heading downstairs. Soon kitchen sounds and spicy aromas filtered up to Anatoly who sat on the bed and pondered his wife's behavior. *Something really bad must have happened at work for her to be this distraught. I've never seen her so exhausted. Maybe the dinner will perk her up.*

■ ■ ■

Two days later Ludmila's cell phone rang. "Hello."

"Yes, Mrs. Terasenko, it is Ivan Markov," he spoke in Russian. "Have you made a decision regarding our conversation the other day?"

"Yes, but I can't talk here at the hospital. Can we meet again at the pizza place?"

"Of course. Same time?"

"Yes, that will work. Goodbye." She clicked off before he could respond. *Wait a minute, I don't think I can tell him about Jeremy because he programmed us so we don't have the ability to talk about him. I will have to stick with what I told him before and try to protect Anatoly somehow, but I think we both may be on our own.*

He met her at the door and again requested a booth in the back of the room. They ordered pizza and tea and Markov inched closer to his guest. "What do you have to tell me now?"

"I told the truth last time we were here. Mr. Pollard came to our house to see my husband."

"About what?"

"I was upstairs and did not hear the conversation."

"Come now, Missy. I told you we know he stayed at your home until morning. You must have been in the same room with him for dinner or watching TV. What did he say?" He grasped her hand and squeezed gently.

Ludmila instinctively recoiled pulling her hand back with a jerk. "I am not lying; he talked to Anatoly, not me."

"Maybe I should talk to your husband since you are playing dumb." He eased back and smirked. "Or perhaps we can find some other thing you can give me."

"What other thing?"

"Some time with me at my apartment."

"What? No, never." *I did not think about this. What a pig he is. Anatoly will not be able to tell him anything either except he talked to Pollard. I will have to warn him this man may contact him. What a fucking nightmare. He will send us back to Russia-or kill us.*

"Tell you what, Missy. We are interested in stories in the news over the past few decades about certain people who have gone missing for different periods of time and then returned. No one knows exactly where they were, and they just give some half-ass story about special projects or going to special doctors for radical health treatments. We think it's all bullshit." He moved closer to her again, and she inched away until she felt the edge of the seat. "You can do some secret research for us to find out who these people are and where they have been."

"How will I do this? There are people around me all the time at work, and I can't use a hospital computer."

"You can do it at home on your own computer or phone."

"Why don't you do this 'research' yourself?"

"Because the American Feds have become very good at identifying people from other countries who troll online, even in the deep web, and hack their systems. You are now an American and will not arouse suspicion."

"What if I say no?"

"You either do research or come to my place whenever I want you. If you refuse both of these fair offers, you and your husband will be hurt."

"How will you hurt us?"

"Come now, my love, as you know, we have ways. So what will it be?"

No choice is good. I better take what looks like the safest one. "Okay, I'll do the research."

"Good girl. I will call you tomorrow and tell you where to start." Ludmila sipped her tea and indicated she had to return to work.

. . .

Markov called Ludmila on her cell phone and provided guidelines regarding the types of research he wanted her to perform: identifying as many people as possible who mysteriously had gone missing, returned, or did not return over the last thirty years comprised her assignment. She started the work in her living room before her husband came home from his job at Heartland Bank in downtown Chicago. He often worked late and tonight missed the last express train; the milk runs stopped at every station extending the ride to an hour and twenty minutes.

Ludmila used several different search techniques to locate information on individuals worldwide who had gone missing during the prescribed timeline. Hits yielded news articles detailing scenarios from possible homicides, avoiding financial issues, people running away from family problems, human trafficking, others hiding from the police, or the mafia and kidnappings.

"Hi hon, what are you doing on the computer?"

Ludmila stopped her searches. "Come here Anatoly, we need to talk about something important." She patted the cushion on the couch next to her.

"What's wrong?"

"Come here and I'll tell you."

"I'm going upstairs to change. Be down in a couple minutes."

"Okay." She resumed her detective work.

Anatoly hurried down the stairs and plopped on the couch. "Now, what's this all about?"

Ludmila related her two meetings with Markov and warned Anatoly he may receive a visit from this malevolent man. She told him about her assignment and reminded him Jeremy had programmed their minds to prevent them from disclosing anything regarding the spaceman.

Anatoly leaned back, closed his eyes, and placed his hands on top of his head. "Holy shit. Just when things are going well, this bastard shows up. I don't know what I can tell him about Pollard coming out here."

"Maybe you can say he wanted to talk to you about the fact we live in Jeremy's old house and he was following up on whether we have heard anything from or about him."

"That may be the best idea. Have you found anything interesting in your searches yet?"

"No, but I'm amazed at how many people have disappeared all around the world in the last thirty years. I'm going to keep working on it because I want to give him some results as soon as possible to get him off our backs."

Anatoly rubbed her neck then slipped a hand in front and massaged her breast. "Maybe we can take a little break and go upstairs to search for other things."

She pushed his hand away and bounced further from him on the couch. "Leave me alone; I'm in no mood for sex."

"You never seem in the mood lately. Don't you love me anymore?"

"Our lives haven't exactly been normal for the past couple of months, have they? We have more serious things on our plates now than playing nooky. The sooner I get some information to that creep, the better off we will be."

Anatoly sloughed to the kitchen and checked the fridge for a snack since it appeared dinner would be delayed. He settled on chips, guacamole dip, and a beer, which he brought to his favorite chair and gave a voice command to the TV to tune to a news channel.

■ ■ ■

The magnitude of the universe of missing persons in online files amazed Ludmila. She had immersed herself in this new project the previous evening and summarily rebuffed her husband's request for dinner as she identified the scope of the various profiles of people around the world who ostensibly vanished from their lives. Her enthusiasm for succeeding in isolating names of persons Markov might find valuable transcended the fear of possible repercussions should she fail. This video game morphed into an obsession.

Concentrating at the nurse's station and caring for patients today proved difficult, almost impossible as she checked the time at intervals only minutes apart. Four o'clock appeared as a faint candle burning in the distant darkness. At 3:55 she signed off, closed down the computer, and programmed her car to drive five miles an hour faster than speed limits to reduce her travel time home without arousing the scrutiny of the police.

Once in the garage she sailed through the kitchen and took the stairs two at a time to her bedroom to change out of her uniform and into lounge ware.

Ludmila scooped mixed fruit from a large bowl in the fridge into a small salad dish and sat at her favorite position tucking her legs under her on a couch in the great room. She forked pieces of watermelon, orange, and pineapple into her mouth chewing slowly savoring the natural sweetness between searches on her iPad. Having isolated the entire collection of people who vanished, she initiated a method of sorting the population by type. Potential murder victims fit together in one file, possible runaways in another, and those who appeared to have been abducted for some kind of human trafficking into yet a third file. Reading profiles of hikers who had gone missing constituted a fourth group. The remaining cases had distilled through the aggregate into a narrow miscellaneous slice of the whole. Each individual's disappearance in this group yielded no plausible explanations; she targeted this type for more extensive research.

Anatoly trudged into the kitchen and placed his backpack on a stool at the counter and then took a beer from the fridge. He focused on his wife and shook his head. *Same as last night. I'll bet it's no dinner and no nooky for sure.* His "hello" greeting did not generate a response or acknowledgement of his presence in the house from the figure hunched over on the couch. He stepped upstairs at a slow and noisy pace hoping to provoke a reaction from the zombie now living in his home, but to no avail.

The beleaguered husband returned to the first floor in jeans and a sweatshirt ten minutes later. He checked the fridge and freezer for dinner options and settled on a lasagna microwave meal. He sat in silence on a stool at the island in the kitchen and ate his meal. *What has happened to our lives? This sucks. I thought we were safe here: we used to be happy. I guess everything is changed now because of that bastard Markov. How will we ever get rid of him?*

■ ■ ■

Ludmila's cell phone rang while she attended to a patient in a private room at the hospital. She recognized the number as that of Markov and let it go to voice mail. After returning to her nurses' station, she texted him indicating she couldn't talk but would call him on her lunch hour. He returned the text suggesting another meeting, but she demurred.

The stressed nurse had her car drive her to a fast food restaurant near the hospital. She ordered from the drive-through and parked in the lot to eat her lunch and call her tormentor.

"Hello, Mr. Markov."

"Yes. What do you have for me?"

She related her approach in organizing the results of her searches and mentioned she had concentrated on the group of people who had disappeared for no apparent reason. Some had returned to their previous lives, other had not. Markov wanted a list of these people, and she provided the names and last known locations around the world. A total of fifty-seven names comprised this list. She slowly provided each name and a brief recap of each subject's story. The forty-ninth name was that of Dr. Dominic Cavallini, a neurosurgeon residing in Chicago.

"A doctor from Chicago, eh?"

"Yes."

"Tell me, is he one of the people who returned to his life?"

"Apparently he did."

"Good work, my love." Markov smiled as he outlined additional segmentation of the other types she had identified and told her he would contact her in a week for an update.

He had referred to her as his "love" again. She shuddered at the thought of ever having to meet this man at a hotel or his apartment. She snapped off the call and bagged the rest of her lunch to toss into the trash at the hospital as her stomach churned.

Markov could hardly contain his exuberance as he reviewed the promising list of people to check. *I think I'll start with the computer engineer in India, the microbiologist in France, the astrophysicist in Brazil, and this Dr. Cavallini in Chicago. The neurosurgeon will be first since he's local. He was gone for about one year in Germany and then returned home after twelve months. Very encouraging.*

The Russian spy relaxed in his thirty-first floor apartment in a building on Lake Shore Drive just south of Chicago's Loop. His technical expertise developed in formal government training in Russia augmented his online analysis of Dr. Dominic Cavallini's life. He wrote notes on a lined tablet and then tapped into a secure Russian intelligence site where he recorded the results of his research in the file detailing his interactions with Ludmila Terasenko. *This story is getting interesting. I need to set up surveillance on the good doctor to see what his routine looks like.*

10

The Field Museum of Natural History, currently known as the Field Museum, is located at 1400 S. Lake Shore Drive on Chicago's near south side. The original title was the Columbian Museum of Chicago, which changed in 1905 to honor Marshall Field who was its first major donor and supporter. Established in 1893 as part of the World's ColumbianExposition, it's original location was in the Palace of Fine Arts in Jackson Park several miles south of the current location in a building that now houses the Museum of Science and Industry. Incorporated in September of 1893, its purpose was the "accumulation and dissemination of knowledge and the preservation and exhibition of artifacts illustrating art, archaeology, science and history." The current home of the Field on Lake Shore Drive was constructed in 1921 by William Pierce Anderson and reflects classical revival style.

■ ■ ■

Bob Pollard had rushed to engage a construction company a week ago to create a studio residence in the boiler room of the building to house Jeremy. The boiler and its attendant equipment was walled off, leaving an L-shape living space. A bed, microwave oven, small refrigerator, table, two chairs, one a recliner, and a large flat-screen TV completed living quarters for this special resident.

Pollard had briefed the Field Museum Director, Dr. James Cuthbertson, PhD, regarding the need to sequester Jeremy for an indefinite period of time and obtained the director's signature on a nondisclosure document on the SAIC's iPad. Bob also provided Cuthbertson with a schedule for food service to the boiler room and alerted him to the fact Jeremy would come upstairs at night for a change of scenery, disable the security systems, and induce the guards into a temporary deep sleep. In addition, Cuthbertson learned his mind would be programmed to never reveal Jeremy's presence in the building to anyone. This sudden intrusion into the director's daily routine played havoc with his sense of order. He wore well-tailored three-piece suits and a rotating variety of bow ties. *This is like a bad dream. It can't be happening. Program my mind? We'll see if that works! I hate having to wait on this "celebrity" guest in the boiler room; I'm not a damn butler! It feels like one big joke—but it's the FBI for God's sake!*

■ ■ ■

Jeremy woke early but lingered in the soft sheets of the queen bed in Bob's guest bedroom. *How can I live in a boiler room? It'll be torture. I guess he's right about no one ever thinking I would be hiding in a place like the museum, in the boiler room. Hopefully he can come up with a better idea soon.*

■ ■ ■

Five days later Director Cuthbertson knocked on the boiler room door at 6:25 in the morning and entered when Jeremy opened it and stood to one side to allow his guest to enter. Jeremy noted the receding hair line combed straight back allowing a shiny reflection of light on the director's ample forehead. Small drops of sweat dotted the surface. James flicked a condescending glance toward the "resident" and placed a canvas bag designed to keep food warm on the only table in the room. He asked the new tenant if he needed anything else, but Jeremy shook his head and quickly programmed his visitor's mind to prevent him from disclosing information to anyone.

The director turned to leave, but watched as his "guest" unloaded the food from the bag. *Funny, my mind is clear as a bell. Maybe his supernatural powers failed.*

Although Jeremy had already grown weary of his chicken coop accommodations, he had to admit the food was surprisingly good. Lunch included grilled salmon with mixed veggies and warm rolls and butter.

The lemonade proved tangy and refreshing. Now for dinner the comingled aromas of roast lamb, russet potatoes, green beans, and mint jelly teased his nose; his salivary glands began to generate moisture in anticipation of a tasty meal. Chocolate cake would provide a welcome finish.

Having sated his appetite, the reluctant tenant slid into his recliner and voiced the TV to a sports channel. His space was cramped because boiler rooms were not designed for residential living. Pollard had engineers wall off the heating equipment and created the *L*-shaped mini studio. A temporary door framed into a corner at the rear of the sleeping area allowed access to the boiler. The bed and nightstand were located in one alcove and general living quarters in the other, including a temporary toilet and shower facilities. Jeremy programmed his digestive system so that he could wait and use the men's room during his nocturnal visits upstairs in the museum after it closed, thus minimizing the need to use the toilet in his "suite."

Watching TV brought on drowsiness, and after an hour Jeremy's head drooped onto his chest. He woke in slow progression, finally achieving full lucidity after ten minutes. The small table clock Pollard had provided flashed 11:17. *Good, the museum has been closed since five o'clock. I'm getting claustrophobic in this cracker box. Think I'll go upstairs for my own private tour.* He strained for several minutes to summon his powers and quickly disarmed the security systems and put the guards to sleep.

Once on the first floor, Jeremy made his way in the dark to the main hall and headed for the information desk where he found a display with a map of the museum. A few night-lights provided minimal visibility, and the flashlight app on his IPhone helped, but reading the print required extra focus. The immensity of the space, profound quiet, and silhouettes of skeletons of very large animals created an eerie atmosphere. Static shadows streaked across the floor and walls.

The museum maintains several permanent exhibitions throughout the building. Although he had lived in the Chicago area for many years, he and Megan had never visited this cultural edifice. *I remember Kelly mentioned her fourth grade class came here on a field trip, and she raved about the place.* Through the darkness the enormous figure of Sue, the *Tyrannosaurus Rex* skeletal fossil, towered at the far end of the Main Hall. *I'll come see you later, Sue. Think I'll visit the Evolving Planet display first.*

He used the map to locate the exhibit, which follows the history and evolution of life on Earth over four billion years. He peered through the glass checking how organisms evolved. He smiled thinking about how this information fit with all he had learned during his time in space. *Wonder if religion could be compatible with the evolution process.* Jeremy noticed an adjacent dinosaur hall housing specimens from every era. He eagerly engaged the interactive displays. After completing his tour of this exhibition his aching legs begged for relief, so he decided to go back to his suite. *I will have plenty of time to visit the other displays; no need to rush.*

11

Brad Wolfe met the Claypoole brothers at their country club in Irvine as arranged. The three had a drink at the bar and traded friendly insults with other members before retiring to a private room.

"Brad, I'm concerned about your girlfriend's curiosity with the documentation supporting our consulting report on the status of the city's communication equipment and supplies," Earle said.

"Former girlfriend, and I know, we all understand what's at stake here. We need to find a way to throw her off track. We need to do something to get her off this assignment," Brad replied.

"You said maybe a car accident when we talked on the phone. Seems too radical for me. If she's hurt bad, or God forbid killed, we'll be up shit creek," Phil added.

"I know; I was just thinking out loud. Her sister, Megan, was kidnapped by some Russian guys last year and she's in a nut house, still hasn't gotten over the trauma. Maybe we can arrange for Steph to be taken and hidden somewhere for a while," Brad offered.

"Hey man, you keep coming up with possible serious criminal solutions. I don't really want to test the long arm of the law," Earle said.

"Me neither. Can't we just come up with a way to scare her so she backs off from her assignment?" Phil suggested.

A waiter knocked at the door and entered to refresh drinks and take the dinner order from the trio. He backed out of the room and closed the door.

"You may be on to something bro. Maybe we can get a guy to call and threaten her if she doesn't drop the job," Earle added.

"Are we assuming the phony report Earle created will not satisfy her?" Brad asked.

"I think she'll see right through it based on how she's been digging through our records. Too risky to count on her giving up," Earle said.

"How about we find a guy who speaks with a Russian accent to call her and threaten her with the same thing Megan went though, or worse," Brad proposed.

"Still criminal, but doesn't seem as sinister. But what if she refuses?" Earle said.

"I can't imagine she'll refuse. If she resists, he can give her some gory examples of what can happen," Brad replied.

The waiter returned to serve the meal and then left. The men tabled their discussion while they enjoyed their food.

"Okay, let's say we decide to use this plan. How do we find someone who can make the call?" Phil asked.

"I know some guys in my local hockey league whose families are from Russia; they're good guys, born in the states, good colleges and jobs. I might be able to convince one of them to make the call for the right price. I can tell him it's a prank," Brad offered.

"Sounds like our best bet," Phil said. Earle nodded in agreement.

"Good. I have a game in a few days. I'll mention it to one guy I think will be most amenable to the idea. By the way, I'm strapped for cash, so you guys will have to come up with the money," Brad said.

The brothers exchanged a dubious glance but agreed to finance the scheme, and the three friends clinked wine glasses to toast their collective genius.

■ ■ ■

Four days after Brad and the Claypoole brothers conducted their summit meeting, Brad's summer league hockey team played a game at a rink in Irvine. In the locker room after the game, he cornered Grigor Kuznetsov and invited him for a beer and burger at a restaurant nearby to discuss something important. The Russian accepted, and they drove separately.

"What is this thing you wish to propose?" Grigor had studied English in college and now maintained only a faded remnant of an accent.

"I recently have started dating my ex-girlfriend, and she's pushing me away, you know, playing hard to get. Anyway, I want to play a prank on her to scare her a little so she'll want to have me protect her." Brad focused on his friend's countenance to searching for a spark of interest and was pleased to see Grigor's attentiveness. "That's where you come in. You call her and say she needs to tell her boss she can't work on her current project because Russia has hacked the client's systems and any interference by her firm will result in trouble for her, her firm, and the client company."

"This sounds—how do you say it—bizarre. How do you fit into this picture?"

"I will take her out to dinner after you talk to her, and she will tell me all about what you said. I will then offer to talk to some of my Russian friends to help get the bad guys to back off."

"I don't know. I don't want any trouble. Besides, what do I get out of this?"

"Well, getting her back is worth a lot to me. I'll give you five hundred dollars."

Grigor pondered the offer between bites of his burger. He took a swig of beer and leaned back in his chair. "I think my part is worth at least one thousand."

Brad feigned shock. "A thousand? You have to be shittin' me." He sat back in his chair and contemplated the ceiling for a couple minutes. "You know, my sales have been slow the past few months so I can't afford that. How about seven fifty?"

"No, I think a thousand is fair."

"Well, I'll have to get a loan from my parents. I'll need some time—say a week."

"Take all the time you want. You see me every week at our games."

"Okay, deal." Brad continued his impression of a victim of extortion.

■ ■ ■

"Earle, Brad. I talked to my Russian friend last night and he said he'll do it."

"How much is going to cost me and Phil?"

"I went really low to start to see if I could get us a bargain. I told him five hundred and he came back with a grand. I really thought it was going to cost us ten grand."

"You mean Phil and me."

"Okay, okay. You know what I mean. I saved us—you—nine grand."

"When is he going to make the call?"

"We have a hockey game in a few days; I'll meet with him after the game and give him the details for the call."

"Alright, bud. This better work, or we'll all be in deep shit."

"No, I don't think so. I gave him the idea it's only a prank to help me get my girlfriend back."

"Call me or Phil after it's done."

"Will do. I'll stop by your office to pick up the cash."

The following week at his team's hockey game, Brad again asked Grigor to meet at the same restaurant. Money was transferred and instructions provided for the call.

■ ■ ■

Two days later the two men called Stephanie from Brad's car. He reminded Grigor to lay on a thick Russian accent.

"Hello, Ms. Murphy?"

"This is Stephanie."

"My name is Alexei. I call in reference to FiberLink."

"What about the company?"

"Me and my country hack into their system. We have valuable information we will use unless they pay us."

"What country are you from?"

"Never mind. You stay away from FiberLink."

"And what if I don't?"

"You and everyone get hurt bad."

"How do I know you are real?"

"Mr. Claypoole is CFO of FiberLink. We know everything."

"What is your last name?"

"Not important. You stay away from company. We are in their system, and we watch everybody. Good bye Ms. Murphy." Grigor turned to Brad and the two executed a perfect fist bump.

"Well done, my friend. I'm sure she's in a panic."

"Good. I think I convinced her."

"Yes, I believe you did." Brad took the burn phone from his accomplice for later disposal in the trash. *Can't leave any clues.*

■ ■ ■

Stephanie returned the phone to its slot in the large console in slow motion, but then picked it up immediately and dialed the number on the screen from the person who just called. A recording intercepted the call and indicated the number was unpublished. She could feel the blood rush to her head and flush every inch of her face. The hair on her arms stiffened and cringed; a quiver raced down a taught spine. She checked the phone number of origin, but the area code and prefix did not register in her realm of personal friends, family or business associates. *Holy crap. I can't believe this guy just threatened me. Who is he? How can I handle this?*

Should I call Mr. Schwedland, our CEO, let him know? It may be some sort of joke, but if it isn't and something bad happens it'll be my fault.

"Hello Lucille? This is Stephanie Murphy. I need to talk to Mr.

Schwedland. Would you please add me to his calendar as soon as possible? It's very important."

"Can I give him some idea of the nature of what you want to see him about?"

"I'm afraid not, confidential. It's extremely important, though."

"Are you resigning?"

"No, Lucille. Please check his calendar."

"I'm not trying to pry, just prioritizing the demands on his time; you understand. Let's see, does tomorrow at nine thirty work for you?"

"Yes, it does."

"Fine, I've entered it on his calendar and will send you a confirmation."

"Thanks, Lucille. Bye." Stephanie clicked off and reclined in her chair while twisting a thin strand of hair. The confirmation flashed up on her screen, and she immediately accepted. She lurched forward, speed-dialed her father, and left an urgent voice mail.

Another strong cup of coffee would help clear her mind and allow her to analyze this strange situation. She returned from the break room with the coffee and pulled up the FiberLink file. Checking her notes failed to reveal any new loose ends that had not already been identified. She traced her steps from the beginning of the assignment; she had followed her firm's protocol in examining the client company's physical and electronic security systems and the deficiencies she had identified in each area. FiberLink was a startup in 2012 and obtained financing from a venture capital firm. Earle Claypoole and two other men, all with extensive experience in the communications field, founded the company and owned all remaining stock. Claypoole held the most stock and highest position in the corporate structure as CFO. Another cofounder had been named president, but his role consisted of little authority, he was essentially a figurehead.

Attorney Murphy googled all three men and found their personal histories to be rather vanilla. She next examined their profiles on LinkedIn. Earle Claypoole's two partners had held high level jobs at several other firms in the communications industry and now hold key positions with FiberLink, but lower on the organization chart than Claypoole except for the figurehead president. She purposely saved Earle's page for last since he is the primary officer with whom she has dealt. His resume, although similar to his partners, also included a couple of gaps between jobs. She googled the companies and noted two of them had filed Chapter 11 bankruptcy shortly after Mr. Claypoole indicated he had left the firms.

Her cell phone rang; Ryan Murphy called. "Hi Angel. What's up?"

"Oh, Dad, I'm so glad to talk to you. I had a weird call from a guy who had a strong accent, maybe from a Slavic country or Russia. He threatened me and my firm if I don't back off the assignment I have on FiberLink. He said he has hacked into their system and knows everything the company is doing and who the key officers are. I asked him some questions to see if I could tell if it was some sort joke or prank, but he seemed knowledgeable and very serious."

"Damn. When will these assholes leave our family alone? Did you tell your boss?"

"Not yet. I have an appointment with him tomorrow morning."

"Good. You need to keep him informed even it turns out to be a joke.

In the world today there are too many jerks out there who can do damage to companies and people. Did your review of the company reveal any issues?"

"Yes, their internal and physical security systems are lax, and I have identified several level-five areas where they are susceptible to breaches. I was just researching the three principles online to see if there are any reasons to be suspicious."

"And?"

"Two of the guys seem clean, but the third one is the CFO and has a couple of gaps in his resume, and the companies he left went Chapter 11 shortly thereafter. I was about to see what I can find out about those companies when you called."

"Good work, hon. Let me know if this guy has had any issues with banks. If he has, maybe I can help."

"Thanks, Dad, I will."

"Oh, and call me after you talk to your CEO. Love you."

"Bye, and say hi to Mom for me and tell her I'll stop by soon. Love you, too."

"Will do."

Feeling a sense of comfort after hearing her father's advice, she turned back to Claypoole's profile. She minimized the names of the two companies on the screen and googled the first one. Information was sketchy, but news articles from 2008 indicated the company had lost substantial money due to internal fraud. Several employees were indicted after extensive Securities and Exchange Commission and State Attorney General investigations. Six employees pled guilty to embezzlement, money laundering, and securities violations; however, Earle Claypoole was charged, but acquitted. Review of the other failed company indicated a similar story in 2010, and again, Earle Claypoole avoided prosecution.

■ ■ ■

Stephanie left her office at nine fifteen the next morning and arrived at Albert Schwedland's Administrative Assistant's spacious wood cubicle complex at 9:20 outside his office.

"Hi, Lucille. I'm a little early for my nine thirty with the boss."

"Yes, you are. I'll buzz him to let him know you're here." She punched the familiar button on the console and notified the CEO his scheduled guest was here. Lucille Kalmin, tall, five eight, and slim for a middle-aged, unmarried woman presented a professional image to her boss's visitors. Short, light brown hair sculpted into perfectly formed curls appeared thin and brittle. She wore a light blue pinstriped business suit and dark blue flat shoes polished to a glossy shine. Her career started at Shields & Fitch twenty years prior after she landed a bachelor degree in business from the University of California at Irvine and ascended through various consultant positions until her mother who lives with her became ill four years ago. She applied for a job precluding travel allowing her to serve as a part-time caregiver at home. The CEO accommodated her by installing her as his administrative assistant when the predecessor in the position retired. "So how have you been, Stephanie?"

"Oh, about the same as the last time I saw you a few weeks ago. Just working and going to the beach when I can."

"Is there a new man in your life lately?" Lucille's social life had become severely restricted since her mother's condition had worsened, so working in this corporate environment provided some opportunities for her to live vicariously through a few of the women at the firm. She didn't really gossip, just served as a sounding board for the younger women, many of whom seemed to experience never-ending man problems.

"No, I can't find the time or the energy to date these days." *Sorry, I'm not sharing my personal life with Lucille or anyone at the company.*

Lucille's phone buzzed. "He will see you now; go right in."

"Thanks, Lucille. Nice to see you again."

Schwedland's rectangular office suite occupied a corner of the floor and offered views of Newport Harbor and Fashion Island shopping mall.

He met his visitor at the door and provided a warm handshake and welcoming smile. Having recently passed sixty, his compact body reflected dedication to a fitness regimen, and a deeply tanned face and forehead pushed back by a relentless receding hairline projected a natural aura of confidence. His reputation as a caring manager and leader endeared him to most employees in the firm. A grey suit, crisp white button-down dress shirt, and dark blue tie completed his usual professional image. He motioned Stephanie to a guest chair in front of his large, neatly organized desk while he took another guest chair facing her. "How's life treating you? How are your mom and dad? It's been a while since I've seen you."

"Oh their fine except they're heartbroken about what happened to Megan; she's still in the rehab center. I know it's been a long time since I've seen you, too long. Like everyone else around here I've been busy."

"That's the tradeoff we all have to pay for our careers. Now, what do we need to talk about?"

"I wish I didn't have to bother you with my problem, but I'm very concerned about my current client, FiberLink. I've been onsite at the company several times and have reviewed all their security programs and systems and have found some holes. I met with the CFO, Earle Claypoole, a couple of times, and after reviewing the financials also asked him about a report and supporting documentation for consulting services they provided to the city of Vista Nueva, and he couldn't come up with them. Said he would look further and would have them next time I visited their office or send them to me."

"Sounds like you're doing your job the way it's supposed to be done."

"I thought so, too until I received a phone call from a man with a strong accent, maybe Russian or Slavic. He threatened me and our firm if I don't back off digging into things at FiberLink. I tried to get his name, but he wouldn't share it. The phone number didn't ring a bell, and when I called back, his number on my phone was unpublished."

"Wow, do you think there's any chance it's a joke?"

"It's a possibility, but I don't think so. He told me they have hacked the company and know everything about it and the staff. I didn't want to take any chances, so I thought you should know."

"Thank you, good work. Did you call the police?"

"No, I wanted to tell you first."

"Okay, we need to get our public relations department up to speed on this and see how they think we should proceed." He called Beverly DeLucia and asked her to come to his office at once. "You did the right thing, Stephanie. After all the cybercrime in the past ten years, we have to give credence to any and all possible threats. This guy who called you didn't just mention hacking; he threatened to hurt you and our firm. That part is even more serious." there was a knock on the door, and Lucille opened it to allow Beverly DeLucia to enter cradling a folio in one hand and a large coffee cup in the other.

"Hi boss, Stephanie. What can I do for you on this beautiful day here in Paradise?" Beverly exuded buoyancy and an unwavering positive attitude. Standing five-foot, six-inches in heels, slightly overweight with light black hair, brown eyes, and Mediterranean, olive skin, she maintained a perpetual flexible smile, which slid from broad to narrow depending on the situation, but never sagged into a frown.

Schwedland motioned for all three to move to his small conference table. "Bev, we may have a dilemma with one of our clients." He nodded to Stephanie to recount the facts.

Beverly took notes as the story unfolded, but her countenance did not change. She sat back in her chair. "Well, I haven't run across one like this in my twenty-seven years, but you're right, Al; we need to treat any threat like this as legitimate; we can't risk that it may be a hoax and not address it. The physical threats here require we contact the police. However, since FiberLink does business both domestically and internationally, we need to pull Homeland Security in. They will probably throw it to the FBI. Anyway, we'll wait to see how the Feds want to handle it."

"Sounds like a plan. Now how do we execute our contract with this client? I don't want Stephanie or any of our people to go onsite and put themselves in danger."

"Absolutely right, boss. We'll just tell the company we're conducting offsite analysis to buy us time to get some direction from the cops and Feds."

"Okay, Bev you're driving the bus. Keep us informed."

"Always. I'll let myself out."

The troubled CEO's furrowed brow indicated frustration with yet another crisis to add to the overflowing pot of client engagements rife with issues. "You know, Steph, sometimes I just feel like bailing out in the middle of the day and going to the club to play golf. Out on the course I can forget everything about our business and just have a nice friendly battle with the little white ball and the hazards that challenge us on each hole. Do you play golf?"

This confession surprised her. "No, I never took it up, but my dad likes to play."

"The best part is when the game is over, we go to the clubhouse and have a burger and beer and laugh at all our dumb shots. It's a game of civility, although the wagering sometimes causes heartburn. The collegiality and being outdoors fosters an atmosphere devoid of all the proprietary garbage, so business people can be straight with each other and do deals on the golf course when they can't seem to get to agreement in the office. Does that make sense to you?"

"I think so. Dad always says the game takes your mind off your problems, at least for a little while, and he's told me about the business deals you mentioned."

"That's right, but the thing I like the most is when I'm on the first tee and I know it's impossible to score a perfect eighteen no matter how well I play. The thrill is the mental battle I will have with the course, identifying all the variables and developing a plan: The pros call it 'course management.' In every round I make a few good decisions and actually execute the shots properly to get a birdie or par, and sometimes an effective scramble out of trouble to save a bogey, which is one over par. I get a nice sense of accomplishment; the game recharges my engine and challenges the next day at the office don't seem so daunting. Golf is a great game."

"If it helps you meet the issues here at the firm, I guess I can see why so many men enjoy it."

"Sorry to unload my frustrations on you. Is there anything else we need to discuss?"

"No, I think the FiberLink saga is enough for today. I'll continue to review what I have on the company until you tell me what our next step is."

"Right. I'm sure we'll hear from Bev soon; she smiles a lot, but she's very efficient and attacks every problem head on. Thanks for coming up here today, and say hello to your folks for me."

"Will do." She rose and left the office. *Man, I feel much better now that the ball isn't just in my court alone anymore, but I'm not sure I fully understand what he said about golf. Must be a male thing. I wonder where we go from here?*

12

Sharon Cavallini heard the front door in the Michigan Avenue condo open followed by familiar footsteps on the polished hardwood floor. She looked up from her magazine. "Hi, hon, how was the battle today?"

Her husband leaned over and kissed his wife as he had done a million times before. "Same old. I really need to retire soon; the damn bureaucracy is driving me crazy. Thank God my patients are angels who help me keep my sanity."

"You know, I always thought office politics was confined to business and government, not hospitals and the medical profession."

"In the old days the docs had more control, but the focus on the bottom line brought in a lot of these hot shot MBAs who have one-track minds— profits. They're always coming up with what they think are more efficient ways to run the industry, but all they really accomplish is creating a lot of unnecessary pressure for medical staff and patients." He loosened his tie and laid his sport coat across the arm of the couch.

"It seems you complain about it more every year. You're going to be seventy-four next month; maybe you should retire."

"I really love my research work; I think I'm making a difference guiding the younger docs and residents. My experience is a valuable asset." He smiled and poured a glass of wine for himself and refreshed Sharon's. "Maybe I'll call David Waller at the bank's trust department and set up a meeting for us to talk about where we are financially and if we can bail out of the rat race in the next year or two. In the meantime, why don't we plan to go to our home in St. John in a couple weeks?"

"Meeting with David's a good idea. We were planning on going to St. John three months from now; do you really want to go so soon?"

"Like I said, the politics are getting to me, and I need to get away, read some books, swim in the clear blue water, and eat some of that great food you can only find in the Caribbean. We can call the kids and see if they can join us if they can sneak away from their jobs."

"Well, you know how much I love it down there, so I'll pack my bags tonight."

"I know you're always ready for the beach and those delicious tropical drinks. I'll go online and check flights tomorrow." He shuffled off to the bedroom to change.

Ten minutes later he emerged ready to prepare dinner. He had looked forward all day to preparing a pork roast with veggies and a salad. Cooking provided a welcome relief from the frustrations at the hospital, and Sharon deferred to his love of the culinary craft. He laced on his apron and set about the process.

The doctor's phone jingled when he opened the oven door and slid the meat in on the bottom rack. "Damn, it never fails. The calls always come when I have my hands in a salad, the oven, or making pasta." He shook the hot pads from his hands and toweled off before clicking on the phone. "Hello."

"Dr. Cavallini? Did I catch you at a bad time?" Bob Pollard asked. "Of course you did; I'm making dinner. Who is this?"

"Pollard here. Should I call back later?"

"No, not if it's something quick. Hang on while I set the timer on the oven."

"We need to talk in person ASAP. I have something important to share with you."

"This is getting old, Mr. Pollard. I had a tough day, and I feel like the Grinch right now. Can't you tell me over the phone?"

"Absolutely not. I wouldn't bother you if it wasn't urgent."

"Urgent? Is this life or death?"

"Indirectly it could be. Can I see you tomorrow?'

"Okay, but you'll have to come to my office at the hospital. I have patient appointments in the morning until eleven and after lunch until five."

"Great, I'll see you at your office at eleven. Thank you."

"Good bye Mr. Pollard."

"What was that all about?" Sharon asked.

"The FBI. He wants to talk to me again. This nightmare never goes away."

"Did he say what it's about?"

"No, but for once he said he has something important to tell me. Thank God it's not more questions." *When will this soap opera end?*

■ ■ ■

68

Pollard arrived at the hospital off north Michigan Avenue at 10:50 and after checking in at the desk settled into a chair with narrow wood arms and a well-worn cushion. He moved to another chair between an elderly man slumped forward in sleep and a young mother and her thirteen-year-old, presumably her daughter. Bob took an outdated *Sports Illustrated* from the table and turned the pages in rapid succession.

At eleven o'clock the receptionist called his name, and a nurse escorted him down a hall with doors on both sides to Dr. Cavallini's office. The men shook hands and the doctor motioned Pollard into a guest chair.

"First, thank you for giving me some of your time today. I'll be as brief as possible." Bob glanced at the ceiling searching for an appropriate way to open the conversation. "You recall our last meeting when I asked you about the possibility of people from earth going to places in space and then returning home?"

"Of course. A radical scenario like that is hard to forget."

"Well, what I'm about to share with you is confidential. Can I have your word you will never repeat it?"

"As long as the information won't get me in trouble, or worse."

"No, you won't be in harm's way."

"Okay, fire away."

"Not long ago Jeremy Chambers returned to earth from wherever he was in the heavens. He still has his powers, but he said he's not sure if he will be able to retain them or if the forces that took him will strip him of his 'magic' and make him a mere mortal again. Said he's experienced a couple instances when he was temporarily unable to invoke them, but recovered quickly. I'm hiding him in a temporary location until I can figure out a permanent home for him." He leaned forward, placing his hands on his thighs. The doctor held his chin in his right hand freezing his expression to avoid leaking his internal cauldron of emotion at this incredible revelation. He shifted to lean on the right arm of his chair. "Since he has his powers for the time being, he is a marked man for other countries that fear we, the US, will use him, and any other time travelers like him, as ultimate weapons to disrupt the balance of geopolitics in our favor." He paused to allow Dr. Cavallini to process the story.

"I'm flattered you have shared this incredible situation with me, but why do I need to know?" The doctor leaned forward so that their faces closed the gap creating a sense of professional understanding.

"I'm asking you to help me by examining his brain to see how it's wired, to determine whether we can duplicate his brain structure in other people, recruit an army—if you will—of these super individuals who can enable us, America, to truly be the only country that can head off the destruction of mankind."

"Wow!" Cavallini recognized the dangerous direction to which the conversation had pivoted and breathed deep to ensure his words would mask his unique perspective on the topic. "First, I'm not certain I can map his circuitry at a level where I can understand what specifically gives him these powers you talk about. Second, as you mentioned, his powers were given to him by some alien force, which must have intelligence far beyond ours. So how can we possibly expect to discover the origin and magnitude of such powers?"

"Good point. I'm an eternal optimist, so I guess all we can do is try."

"Where could I do this analysis? I'll need MRIs and other tests, equipment, and some very powerful computers."

"Right, issues for sure. I'm still in the beginning stage of spinning the concept around in my mind. Obviously I have to provide you with the tools you need to do the project." Pollard looked at the ceiling as if requesting divine assistance. "Is there any way we can use the equipment here in your hospital, say, in the middle of the night when the staff is gone?"

"Number one, that would be risky since we have cleaning folks and security guards in the building, not to mention a comprehensive system of cameras on every floor and outside around the building. Second, we have technicians who are trained to operate the equipment; and third some floors have patients and staff twenty-four/seven. So, I'm afraid I don't know how to do it."

"Are there instruction manuals?"

"Of course there are, but as I'm sure you know these machines are very sophisticated and sensitive." Cavallini regarded his guest warily and concentrated on selecting his words carefully hoping not to give any indication of his own supernatural powers. "If I attempt to operate them and make a mistake causing damage, we'll both be up shit's creek."

"Agreed, but as long we're brainstorming here, you recall Jeremy has powers, one of which is to program other people's minds not to pay attention to what he's doing, and he can also make them fall asleep for temporary periods of time. He might even be able to help you operate the machines."

Glad he doesn't know I have some of those same powers, but I can't let him in on that secret. This man thinks large, and the concept is an intriguing idea. It would be fun to give it try. Not sure how our leaders in the sky might feel about us freelancing down here on earth, though.

"Mr. Pollard, I have to admit your hypothetical scenario here has captured my interest, but one more important issue might be whatever force took Jeremy away and gave him these paranormal powers may not take kindly to him using these skills in the way you envision. They might pull them back at any time, placing us in a vulnerable position, don't you think?"

"I hadn't really thought about that possibility; like I said, I'm an optimist. However, maybe it's worth taking the gamble he will maintain his powers through all the testing, giving you the data you need to analyze."

Cavallini leaned back in his chair and folded his arms across his thick chest. He allowed several minutes to pass and projected a facial countenance of intense contemplation. "If his special abilities are revoked, it will put me in a very precarious situation. Not sure I can bite off that much risk. I have a wife, kids, and grandkids to consider you know."

"Understood. All I ask for now is for you to consider the idea. I will continue to anticipate any further obstacles. I haven't even discussed it with Jeremy, or the director in DC. I wanted to get your reaction and advice first."

"I appreciate your understanding and candor. I'll think about it and let you know in a couple days."

"Great. Thank you for your time. I'm looking forward to your call. Oh, I almost forgot, do you think there are any other people in our country who have been where Jeremy was and have similar powers?" The FBI chief aborted his exit from the chair to cast a penetrating look at the doctor's face searching for a sign of nervousness.

"No, I'm not aware of any other person or persons with his abilities." Cavallini felt the silent probing embedded in his guest's question and concentrated on controlling his facial features. "I'll show you out." The neurosurgeon led Pollard to the reception area where the men shook hands. *This thing is taking on a life of its own. At least he doesn't seem to be pressing me on my fictitious story about my year in Germany in 1998.*

Pollard sat in his government issued sedan, but hesitated before tapping the button to start the car. He selected the programmed instructions in its command center for the car to drive itself back to his office on the Chicago's near west side. *The doc seemed a little pensive when I first presented the idea, but I still can't tell if he's a spaceman, too, since he had an unexplained absence for a year back in the late 1990s.*

13

I t had been almost three weeks since Joe Serratella's brief encounter with his close friend and former next-door neighbor, Jeremy Chambers, and he couldn't shake his memory of seeing his buddy again. Last fall Joe and three other close friends had received anonymous instructions to travel to the Upper Peninsula of Michigan in September. The four men speculated the letter might have come from Jeremy, but no one could say for certain.

The trip turned into an adventure and Jeremy as well as Dr. Cavallini appeared on different nights at the lake and spoke to them.

Cavallini blasted in from nowhere appearing in an intense white light and thunderous crash onto the beach as the men enjoyed drinks and dinner from the grill. He shared general information regarding projects in space and told them Jeremy would visit soon.

Jeremy appeared in a similar fashion a few days later and said his bosses allowed him to see his friends for a short visit. He shared vague information about his experiences over the past seven years but would not elaborate or reveal specifics. He said his work was not yet completed in the parallel universe to which he been taken and that he had to return to his projects. He said he thought the force might allow him to resume his life on earth permanently, but did not know when. He told his friends, as Cavallini had, he would enter their minds and program them so they would not have the ability to share anything about this visit with anyone. Dr. Rindon attempted to test the prohibition by telling his wife, Myra, but the phone line would not connect.

Joe couldn't sleep at night after Jeremy's recent appearance—hoping he could reunite with his golf buddy had become an obsession—but there wasn't a timetable for when Jeremy would be allowed to live a normal life. The unique abilities he had acquired from the alien force transformed this ordinary human into a weapon many countries wanted to kidnap, or failing such an effort, eliminate him and the potential threat he posed to the balance of power among adversarial nations.

Joe wondered if his other three friends had received visits from Jeremy as well. *Maybe we could discuss it because we all had seen Jeremy in the UP and were, therefore, all privy to the same secret. The four of us haven't been together since the holidays; it's time for a reunion. Time to get our group back together.*

Joe sent a group text to Carl, Paul and Larry suggesting dinner as soon as schedules would permit. A plethora of responses, queries, and suggested dates back and forth ultimately identified a Saturday in two weeks as a viable date. All four men updated their electronic calendars. Carl and Larry offered to host at their country club in Bull Ridge. Joe reminded his three friends to turn off their cell phones so no one could pinpoint their location when they met.

■ ■ ■

The crisp spring air cleared the sky in the Chicago area and provided a clear view of a myriad stars and constellations. Joe did not notice the abnormally heavy volume of drone traffic circling in a ballet above his self-driving BMW. He reclined and pondered when he and the other three would see their time traveler friend again. He pulled through the gate after the guard cleared him and valeted the car at the entrance to the club.

Carl, Paul, and Larry leaned against the bar in conversation and greeted Joe with hugs and backslaps. Joe ordered rum and coke, and the four men retired to a private room Carl had reserved.

The group caught up on the status of family and the health of each man. Paul expressed thanks he still had no effects from the brain tumor and felt better than ever, and Carl proudly displayed his left hand, which had been badly burned on the grill at the cottage in the UP; Jeremy had healed both Paul and Carl through a transference of cosmic energy.

A waiter knocked and entered to refresh drinks and take dinner orders.

General conversation eventually exhausted topics, and the men reminisced about their trip to the UP last fall. They shared hearty laughs when Larry recalled the incident involving the flat tire on the van in Minocqua, Wisconsin, on the drive up north. He described Carl's escalating rant in the rain before a tow truck was called and hauled the vehicle to a service station.

"Do you believe how much that asshole at the repair shop charged us for two tires? Highway robbery, only because we were out-of-town city slickers; he knew he had all the leverage and could rip us off on the cost."

"Wait a minute, bud. I was with you at the shop, and the guy showed us the catalogue with the prices, so I don't think he screwed us at all over here. In fact, he didn't even charge us for the towing. And don't forget the rental company paid for the tires and the installation so the whole thing didn't cost us a dime."

"Yeah, I guess that's right, but it's the idea of how companies jack up the price of everything these days," Carl lamented.

"What the hell do you care, CT? You're worth multimillions and can buy an entire tire company if you want. Settle down or your blood pressure will be off the damn charts again," Paul said. The men laughed and worked on their drinks.

"The part I liked best was the fishing and how they seemed to just jump into the boat," Larry said.

"Doc, we were lucky you didn't put a hook in one of our eyes the way you cast your line," Carl added.

"What about the night we had dinner in that old log cabin restaurant/bar when the big guy with the shaggy hair and beard came in already drunk and pounded down a few beers, and then came over to our table to give us some shit about how it was his bar and told us to leave. Carl stands up and pulls out his gun and tells the Bear Man to back away or he will blow his fucking head off," Larry recounted as the others convulsed in laughter as he recalled the scene. "Bear Man says he ain't afraid of us city slickers and keeps on coming toward us. Then Carl blasts a warning shot through the ceiling. I thought my ear drums were shattered."

"Mine, too," Paul added.

"I always appreciate a reason to shoot my guns, especially in public," Carl said.

"I think the owner pissed his pants from the shot," Joe added. "He comes racing around the bar to our table and apologizes for Bear Man who had been dragged back to the bar by some other guys who knew him. Then he says our meal is on the house and offers to pay for the drinks spilled on Paul's clothes and the cleaning bill. So we get a free meal and the owner ends up with lost revenue and a large repair bill for his roof over here." The friends roared with laughter even though they had told these stories several times since they returned from the trip.

The waiter knocked and entered followed by two other servers each carrying entrees. They placed the food in front of the diners and let themselves out.

"You know, it's like I said when we were there in the clean air and the quiet. I could really see myself living in a place like that," Paul said.

"I don't think you'd like it so much in the summer when all the families with screaming kids, traffic, and packed restaurants create chaos up there," Larry said. "And I wouldn't be able to fly my drones without someone bitchin' about it."

"I really enjoyed the other restaurants where we had lunch and dinner. The people were nice, and some of the patrons at the one place joined in singing Sinatra songs with us when Joe played them on the juke box," Carl said. The others agreed as they finished hearty dinners and reclined in their chairs. Carl ordered a bottle of port for the post-meal toasts.

"I still can't get over how Cavallini and Jeremy appeared in those explosions over the lake," Larry recalled. "I think the animals are still running as fast as they can away from the state of Michigan."

"Yeah, and how about when Jeremy came down on the lake and walked on the water up to the beach," Paul marveled. "What I don't get is how he hadn't aged at all in the seven years he was gone. Has anyone seen Jeremy since our trip?" Carl and Larry shook their heads, but Joe selected the moment to sip his wine and did not react.

"This paranormal or supernatural stuff or whatever it is still baffles me. If I hadn't seen it . . ." Larry's thought dissipated.

"And the glow around him made him look like an angel or something," Joe added. He decided the conversation provided a perfect segue to share his recent visit with their friend from space. He opened his mouth to ask if any of the others had seen Jeremy recently, but his jaw temporarily froze, his speech a staccato, unintelligible stuttering as he tried to relate his experience with Jeremy, but his ability to speak failed.

"Hey pal, you all right?" Carl asked.

"Yeah, sure, just a nervous tic," Joe replied. *Looks like Jeremy wasn't kidding. I won't be able to tell them verbally, so I'll have to figure out some other method. Maybe I can do it with my eyes.*

"You been chewing on rocks?" Paul asked.

"No, no I'm fine. Had some dental work done a few weeks ago and now I have this tic and sore gums over here." The other three men seemed to buy the explanation. Joe could see the opportunity to share his secret slipping away. He riveted his eyes and squinted to draw his friends' attention and then raised and lowered his eyebrows in quick succession, but the others did not notice the signal.

"You sure you're feeling okay? You don't look so good." Carl asked again. "Anyone else feel sick, maybe food poisoning? If we've been given bad fucking food, someone at this club will pay big time."

Joe realized his effort to share his revelation was hopeless and felt a painful churning in his stomach. Sweat formed on his face, and he sat back in his chair as lightheadedness encompassed him. "You know, I think I am feeling a bit sick. I'm going to go home and sleep it off." He rose steadying by holding the back of the chair. Paul and Carl stood quickly and held his arms.

Larry checked his pulse and felt his forehead. "Hey man, you're white as a ghost. I'll drive you home and pick you up tomorrow to come back here for your car," the physician offered.

"No, no doc, I'll be okay if I sit here for a few minutes," Joe replied. "Well, if you don't look better soon, we'll take you home or to the hospital depending on how serious I think your condition appears to be," Larry insisted.

Joe sat and rested for fifteen minutes and gradually felt better. He stood, hugged his friends, walked to his car and programmed it to take him home.

About half way to Crystal Valley he began to retch and took control of the car to guide it to the side of the road. He exited carefully to avoid traffic coming from the rear and walked around to the other side of the car and vomited into the weeds. He wiped his mouth with a handkerchief and resumed his trip home. *Wow! I guess my old neighbor is punishing me for trying to tell our other buds about his visit to my house. I sure won't try it again.*

14

The vibration on Anatoly Trasenko's cell phone startled the banker as he hunched in his cube with low walls working on methods of strengthening his bank's firewalls to prevent cyber intrusions by bad actors in other countries, or possibly even the United States. "Hello," he whispered.

"Greetings, comrade Terasenko. I am Ivan Markov; perhaps your lovely wife has told you about me." He spoke in Russian.

"Yes, she mentioned you have her doing some research for you."

"Correct."

"Why are you calling me?"

"I have a project for you as well, and from my research on your current job, you will be most helpful to me and our mother country."

"I am an American now, not a Russian citizen."

"Yes, yes how they say here 'blah, blah, blah.' I want you to create a file of all of your bank's system security procedures and tools and save it to a thumb drive to give to me."

"You know I can't do that."

"Oh, but you can and you will because if you don't, things will go very bad for you and your wife."

"You can't do this to us. Leave us alone."

"We are from the same country; you know how we operate and get what we want."

"Our bank auditors will find out what I did, and they'll fire me."

"Not my problem, comrade. You will gather this information, create a file on the thumb drive, and then deliver it to me at a location I pick."

"And if I refuse?"

"Come now Anatoly, don't be stupid. If you refuse, I will have you brought to a hotel where you will watch me make love to your beautiful wife."

"No!" the frustrated banker looked around to see if his outburst had aroused interest of his fellow workers, but found no indication it had. "I will kill you if you touch her."

"Really comrade? It will be hard for you to hurt me since you will have a front row seat, but you will be wrapped in a strait jacket or tied up. I'm sure you'll enjoy the show. I have many men and some women working for me in this region, so controlling you and Ludmila will not be a problem."

"Stop, stop. I'll see what I can do about the file, but it will take me a while to figure out how without my bosses or the auditors finding out."

"I'm glad you see it my way. Today is Tuesday; you will go to a location I pick on Friday with the drive. I will call you on Friday morning and tell you the time and place and what to do."

Anatoly stared at the floor and did not respond. "Understood, comrade?"

"Yes," he mumbled.

"Excellent. I'm so happy you and I will be doing business together. Oh, one more thing, do not be so foolish as to contact the police. Your wife will suffer if you do." Markov smiled. "Do you understand?"

"I do."

"Wonderful. Have a great rest of your day, comrade Terasenko."

A beleaguered Anatoly clicked off the call and reclined in his chair rubbing his temples. *This is a fucking nightmare. What am I going to do? I have to give him the file; no way will I let that slimy bastard touch Ludmila.*

■ ■ ■

Anatoly decided to visit the café for some strong coffee. He bought a tall cup and found a table against the windows away from other employees. He pondered possible options, but they all led back to the scene in a hotel room with Markov raping Ludmila while he would be forced to watch. The coffee had cooled enough for him to take small sips. *Should I contact Pollard? It may be my—I mean our—only chance.*

"Pollard."

"Bob, it's Anatoly. I need to talk to you about something really important."

"Slow down. What happened?"

"Not on the phone. Let's meet after work today."

"Okay, how about Aureus for a drink at six thirty?"

"Fine. Is that the restaurant on Michigan Avenue?"

"Yes, just a couple doors south of Madison."

"Okay, see you there. Bye."

"Take care, my friend. Bye." Bob entered the appointment into his phone. *Now what can be happening with him? Maybe he has some good information on what the bad guys are up to at his bank.* An incoming call interrupted his thoughts.

■ ■ ■

Chicago's lakefront effervesced in the cool late May air creating in a unique vibrancy. The setting sun's late afternoon rays shimmered between the buildings, which had formed urban canyons and an appealing skyline.

Local residents and tourists alike strolled the paths of Millennium Park and the broad sidewalks on both sides of Michigan Avenue. Streams of people entered and exited the Art Institute and still others relaxed or clicked photos on the stairs between the famous iron lion statues.

Bob Pollard and Anatoly Terasenko arrived at Aureus within a few minutes of each other. Pollard followed the owner to his favorite corner table, ordered a glass of Pinot Grigio, and checked messages on his iPhone.

Bob looked up as Terasenko approached and noted the spy's stern countenance. "Anatoly, you look distressed. What's up?" Pollard stood and the two shook hands.

"We have problem, big problem, Bob. Both Ludmila and I have received calls from a Russian whose name is Ivan Markov. Do you know him?"

"I am familiar with the name; we know he's been in Chicago for about two or three years, and we have a file on his background and profile. What did he have to say to you and your wife?"

"He is bad man. I think he's a high level operative of the Russian government; he told us he is in charge of the Midwest region in the US for Russian intelligence." Pollard nodded, but did not offer any additional information from his extensive dossier on Markov, thinking *it's better if he doesn't know.*

Anatoly ordered a glass of Cabernet and leaned forward to mask his voice. "He threatened Ludmila if she refused to do research on people around the world who have gone missing in the last thirty years whether they came back or not."

"Holy crap, sounds like he's on the trail of Jeremy and maybe others."

"Wait, there's more. He called me and is forcing me to gather information about my bank's security systems and give it to him on a flash drive."

Pollard scanned the restaurant and whispered. "Do you think anyone followed you here?"

"Not sure, I wasn't really paying attention."

"Okay, we'll leave separately and don't be obvious, but check around you all the way home. If you see someone who might be one of Markov's flunkies, don't call me; send a text instead. Now, what do you mean he forced you?"

"He said if I don't give him what he wants, he will take Ludmila to a hotel and . . ." Anatoly's head drooped and tears formed in tired eyes.

"Easy, man. Take some deep breaths. What about Ludmila and a hotel?"

"He would have his goons tie me up and watch while he rapes her."

"Bastards. These guys are playing hardball now. Why didn't he do the research himself?"

"He said you Feds can identify and track foreigners who make such searches, but we are American citizens and would not be subject to as much scrutiny."

"Did she give him some names?"

"Yes, she did a thorough job and gave him a list of fifty- or sixty-some names."

"Do you recognize any of them?"

"No, but one is from Chicago. A doctor, I think."

"Do you remember his name?"

"No, but she can give it to you."

"When do you have to give him the information regarding your bank?"

"He wants me to deliver the drive on Friday of this week."

"Doesn't give us much time." Pollard held his chin in his right hand as a server asked if the men wanted refills on the wine. Anatoly indicated he would have another glass, but Bob switched to iced tea.

"I didn't know what to do. He told me not to go to the police, so I figured you are my only hope. Ludmila and I do not want to help the regime we fled from."

"You did the right thing, my friend. I need to think about what we can do to satisfy Markov without putting you and Ludmila in danger."

"I don't see how we have any choice but to give him what he wants."

"Never say never; every puzzle has an answer, sometimes more than one." They finished their drinks and Anatoly rose to leave. Pollard stood and they held their handshake several extra seconds. Bob noted fear melded with sadness in his friend's eyes and expression. "I'll call you tomorrow on your cell."

"I don't think I'll get much sleep tonight. Good bye."

"Take a melatonin pill. So long."

Pollard returned to his chair and nipped at his tea. He recalled Maggie was working the three to eleven shift at the hospital, and the thought of a microwave meal didn't excite his taste buds. He ordered dinner and another iced tea. *One more crisis to add to my collection; it never ends. I'll call Ludmila tomorrow to get more information on the research she's doing for Markov. I wonder who the Chicago doctor is.*

15

"Hey babe, how go the consulting wars?"

"Hello, Brad. Same old and don't call me babe," Stephanie frowned as she continued typing into her computer.

"Right. I was just thinking we could go to the movies on Friday night to get our minds off our jobs. The latest *Star Wars* film is out; is it the eighth or ninth in the series?"

"Not sure, but I'm going to my folks' house for the weekend. My mom needs some company."

"Oh, too bad. Maybe a rain check on the movies. How about lunch on Friday?"

"Brad, I told you I'm not ready to resume our former relationship."

"I know, but this is just two old friends having lunch. What's wrong with that?"

"I don't know . . . ," She stopped typing and looked at the ceiling. "Come on, I promise not to bite."

"Well, I would like to get out of the office once in a while. Okay, where do you want to go?"

"Let's see, somewhere close to your office so you won't get in trouble."

"Brad, I'm a big girl now, so I can handle my schedule. I do want to stay close to the office, though."

"Let's go to Gulfstream; I haven't been there in forever."

"Sounds good. What time?"

"How about eleven forty-five, you know, to beat the crowd?"

"That works. See you there on Friday. Bye"

"Bye babe."

"Don't call me babe, okay?"

"Sorry, old habit." Brad tapped off the call. *I was hoping she would be uptight after the call from my Russian friend, but she sure didn't seem like it.*

■ ■ ■

Stephanie walked to the windows in her office, wondering if having another lunch date with Brad is a good idea. *He hasn't acted like a jerk, so I guess as long as I keep him at arms' length I should be all right.* Her phone rang, smashing thoughts of Brad into thousands of virtual pieces. It was an internal call, but she did not recognize the extension. "This is Stephanie."

"Hi, Steph, it's Bev. I heard back from Homeland Security and since it's a physical threat and hacking, they're referring it the FBI. I spoke briefly with an agent, and she said we should conduct business as usual with the client to determine what the bad guys might do. I also called the police, and they will want to come out and take a statement from you, Al, and me. I told them the FBI is involved, which didn't make them too happy, and that we need to keep this thing confidential because at this point there is still a chance it's a hoax. I talked to Al, and we would like you to call your contact at FiberLink and ask some questions about your analysis, etcetera to see how he reacts. Sound like a plan?"

"Sure. I can follow up with him next week regarding some invoices we discussed last time I spoke with him."

"Perfecto! Let Al and me know how it goes."

"Will do. Bye." *Not looking forward to talking to Earle Claypoole again, but it's part of the job.*

■ ■ ■

"Hey, bud, it's Brad." Earle Claypoole told him he couldn't talk on the company landline but would call him back on his cell phone. They hung up, and Earle called back.

"How did it go with your girlfriend?"

"You and your brother are really funny about the 'girlfriend' thing. You know we broke up a couple years ago so she's not my girlfriend again . . . yet."

"Fine, what's going on since your Russian buddy made the call to her?"

"I called Stephanie and asked how things are going yada, yada, yada, and she acted like everything is copasetic, and so I'm not sure what's going on."

"This is your big plan, bud, so you best make it work, especially since Phil and I fronted the grand."

"Yeah, I know. I made a date with her for lunch on Friday. I'll see if I can get something out of her then."

"Do you think she went to the police after your guy called her with the threats?"

"Doesn't seem like it from the way she acted on the phone. I'll give you a call after lunch on Friday. Tell Phil what we discussed today, okay?"

"You bet; he's going to want to know if we're going to get a return on our investment."

"Right. Later." *I think these guys have more money than Warren Buffett, but they act like the measly grand is their only asset. Good guys, but they're colossal pains in the ass sometimes.*

■ ■ ■

Brad arrived at Gulfstream at eleven thirty and took a seat at the bar with a view of the front door. He ordered a vodka martini and looked around this popular restaurant famous for its fish and seafood. The wait staff all wore designer jeans, white shirts and ties, and seemingly, perpetual smiles. Sleek, horizontal dark wood and the high ceiling fashioned a comfortable and welcoming ambience.

Stephanie arrived at 11:50, and Brad aimed a kiss for her lips, but she deflected it and it landed on her cheek. A hostess led them to a booth. Stephanie ordered an ice tea and Brad asked for a second martini. "Sorry I'm late; the construction traffic around here is horrendous."

"No problem. So, you say things are same old since the last time we saw each other?"

"Right. Just working." She hoped her response appeared casual. "Anything interesting with your clients?"

"Not really." *Why is asking about my clients?*

A waitress brought the drinks and took their food orders. They clinked a toast. "Aren't you worried about driving after having some alcoholic drinks?"

"No, two is my limit, and I drink a lot of water to dilute the alcohol. Besides, I always let my car drive itself after I've had a few." He shifted to face her and read her eyes for indications of fear from the threatening phone call she had received, but so far, nothing. "I would think in your line of business you'd see some weird scenarios, like corruption and hacking."

"We do run across some of that, but mostly we just look at a company's risk assessments and internal controls." *What's with so many questions about my work and clients?* "Enough about me; what about your job?"

"Oh, I like the variety of clients I work with. Finding the right communications solutions for their needs, things like that."

"Do you provide tools for your clients to combat cybercrime?"

"Of course, I give them software ideas for all their commo requirements. Many of my clients are small companies that don't have in-house expertise in utilizing the cloud and other products out there to increase efficiency and security. 'WhatsApp' and 'Signal' are two tools I recommend because they allow the sender to set messages to disappear in a few seconds. Of course 'Blockchain' has been used for years to secure transactions, but it's just a matter of time before some hacker figures out how to compromise it. Some vendors have developed software like 'Touchpoint Manager' and 'CryptoStopper' to protect a company's files.

How about your clients? What do you tell them if you find deficiencies in your reviews?"

"Our contracts are to assess their various types of risk and how they impact overall enterprise risk. We sometimes offer recommendations based on what we know from what our other clients are doing, kinda' like best practices, but we don't name names."

"Hey, that gives me an idea. If you have clients having trouble controlling risk and some of the problems are commo related, refer them to me, and I'll fix them up with what they need."

Their salmon dishes arrived, and the former lovers savored their meals while engaging in small talk regarding the quality and taste of the lunch.

"Like I said, send those clients to me; I'm the commo doctor," Brad laughed.

Stephanie couldn't suppress a quick giggle, but immediately stifled it. Brad's sense of humor and perpetual optimism were a couple of traits that had initially attracted her to him. "Sorry, we aren't allowed to recommend specific vendors."

"Oh come on, Steph, who would know? I could really help your clients. Even better, I could give you a referral fee."

"No, I'm not going to put my credibility and career on the line. I also have to protect my firm."

"It would be a slam dunk. You tell the client there are people like me who have all the contacts in the communications industry, and then I take over."

"No, Brad; I have personal principles and will never compromise them." She stirred her ice tea with the straw.

"How about this: I give you a list of several guys, including me, who do what I do, of course not as well as me, and you put a star next to my name and maybe one other guy's name and tell your client to check us out. They will find me as the best, and I'll get the deals. It's a win-win, Steph."

"I said no. This conversation is making me uncomfortable. Let's change the topic. I have to get back to work in a few minutes." *I don't like where this is headed. He really wants me to participate in something unethical, and there's no way I'll do that.*

"Well, I admire your integrity, but just consider what I said. I don't think you would be violating your scruples." He still could not detect any fear in her voice or eyes about the Russian phone call. "How about the movie we discussed next weekend?"

"I'll think about it, but I need to spend time with my mom. Thanks for lunch; this place is amazing, and the food is out of this world."

"You're welcome, and, yes, this is a great restaurant. I'll walk you to your car." They stood in unison and headed for the door.

Stephanie purposely didn't turn around to face Brad as he opened the driver side door, but he spun her around and planted a kiss on her mouth before she could react. He continued to hold her as she squirmed to free herself. "Don't kiss me like that; we aren't a couple anymore, remember?"

"You mean yet." He tossed his head back and laughed, but continued to maintain a strong grip on her waist as she pushed against his chest.

"Let me go, Brad, or this will be the last time we see each other." He released his embrace and opened the door for her. "Hey, babe, chill. I'll call you next week about the movie. Say hello to your folks for me."

Stephanie didn't reply as she voiced a command for the car to drive to her office looking straight ahead while the car backed out of the parking space and drove itself away. Brad's aggressive move didn't sit well with her. *He was always touching me when we dated, and I liked it. Now, though, it feels dirty, and he seems different somehow. My parents still like him, even after he dumped me. He especially knew how to schmooze Mom. I don't think I will be going to a movie or anywhere else with Brad. It's just not the same anymore.*

■ ■ ■

Brad stood in the parking lot for several minutes after watching her car turn onto a main street. *She doesn't seem to be bothered by the phone call. Maybe she thinks it's a prank. I wonder if she reported the call to her boss or someone else in her firm. They can't trace the call because we used a burn phone card, and I dumped it. If nothing happens and they lay off FiberLink we should be home free.*

Brad called Earle Claypoole's cell phone. "Hey, bud, can you talk?"

"Yeah, I'm between meetings, but I only have about ten minutes."

"I'll make it fast. The lunch went okay. I tried to get her to talk about her clients, but she wouldn't name any of them. Also, she didn't act like she was scared by the phone call we made. I even suggested she refer some of her clients that have commo issues to me and I would give her a referral fee. She absolutely refused, said her 'principles' would not allow it and she will never go against them."

"What is she, some sort of ethics queen?"

"She's serious about her job and wouldn't budge on any of my ideas."

"You know, man, in my experience everyone has a price and can be compromised."

"That's probably true, but for now it looks like the coast is clear for us unless she resumes her audit of your company."

"If she does come snooping around again, what should we do?"

"Depends on how she approaches you. If it looks like business as usual with her audit, then the phone call failed, and we will have to do something to scare her."

"Like what? Don't give me those asinine ideas you had about hurting her."

"No, I was just thinking out loud when I mentioned those. We need to do something more sinister, like working on her mind. Let me ponder some possibilities, and I'll give you a call in a couple days."

"Okay. I'll update Phil; we're playing golf tomorrow at the club."

"Have a good game, and if she calls you or visits your office next week, let me and Phil know."

"Will do. See ya."

16

Morning in the boiler room does not fade in with light from the outside since there are no windows in Jeremy's new habitat. He wakes from his routine in total darkness. His iPhone displays 6:47. He sets his phone alarm for seven fifteen, rolls over, and closes tired eyes to grab a short catnap before starting the new day.

The alarm rings until he reluctantly shuts it off. A few minutes on his back, and he throws the covers off, turns on the table lamp, and then sits on the side of the bed to let his eyes adjust. The lights in his cozy bathroom shock him to full wakefulness. Trimming the new beard has become a welcome ritual, having never grown one before. After a quick shower, the spaceman towels off and brushes his newly dyed blond hair. *I really have changed appearance, a new me. Not sure if I like him—I mean me—yet.*

Breakfast of oatmeal, toast, two hard-boiled eggs, and coffee sate his appetite. *I sure do appreciate earth food after so many years of the pills and mush they fed us at the citadel. I can't get enough of the food I was used to before they took me.*

He relaxed with a fresh cup of coffee in the expensive recliner Bob had provided and propped his iPad on his lap. Pollard had given him a "job" of monitoring activity by US adversaries on the web, a mission he relished spending several hours each day performing. A review of his email inbox revealed only a couple of short status messages from Pollard; *no big deal.*

Next, he signed into a confidential FBI database that tracks selective chatter in various channels by potential enemies worldwide for indications of impending physical and cyber-attacks. His job had become increasingly difficult because the bad actors had embraced new technology similar to WhatsApp to eliminate messages within several seconds of publication. He also surfed the deep web or dark web, which is where hackers and other bad actors swim to communicate with one another and plot crime strategy on web pages that cannot be accessed in the surface web because they are not indexed by traditional search engines. Jeremy's special powers enabled him to view large segments of the dark web and the surface web simultaneously and connect seemingly disparate information and communication to gain a complete picture of what the lone-wolf hackers and the state-sponsored criminals were planning. He reported his findings in a secure manner to Pollard who then disseminated the intelligence throughout the FBI organization and Homeland Security, but only to those who had a need to know.

The iPhone rings at 11:35. "How goes the never-ending battle?" Pollard asks.

"Hi boss, same, same. I found a few interesting tidbits, which are included in my report to you, but I'm having some trouble with the disappearing narrative the bad guys are using the last couple years. When will our geeks find a way for us to capture the chatter and archive it so we can reference it on demand? The dark web makes our job more difficult."

"They're making progress, but it's hard playing catch up. The technology is progressing so fast it's a moving target. It's also hard to determine which flags we identify are real and which ones are red herrings. They try to lead us on wild-goose chases all the time, and we end up in dead ends; it's like a maze, and they are the ones who control and change the structure. Really stretches our resources. That's why you are so important to us; with your powers you seem to smell these false positives out quickly."

"I know what you mean. These bastards are shrewd, but they usually leave some markers from their bad habits I can spot right away."

"How are your accommodations working out?"

"Not exactly the Ritz Carleton, but I'm fine. By the way, when will I get to visit my family?"

"I'm working on it, bud. I have to find a way to mitigate the danger; we don't want to put anyone in a high-risk situation."

"Well, I'm getting antsy, so think fast."

"Will do. Talk to you tomorrow."

"Right, out."

Jeremy resumes his surfing in the database until noon. "Time for lunch. 'Smiley' Cuthbertson should be here soon," he chortled with a smile.

At 12:15 the museum director arrived with a cheeseburger, fries, a small salad, and a fruit plate for dessert.

"Thanks, man. I'm starved."

Cuthbertson rolled his eyes as he turned and left.

■ ■ ■

Jeremy watched TV for half an hour after his meal and then opened his iPad to continue his work for Pollard. He spent four hours searching for suspicious activity and followed three possible plots, but they all resulted in dead ends. Having completed his sojourn through the electronic, existential cyber world, he rose, stretched, and took a bottle of Pepsi from the miniature fridge. He paced his little living den as claustrophobia constricted his sense of space and stifled his personal freedom.

"I gotta get outta this damn dungeon for a while before I go crazy. It's Thursday in early June and many schools have finished the academic year so there should still be a crowd of families upstairs and I can easily blend in. I'm going up for some air." His isolation invited talking—mumbling, really—to himself. With a new sense of vigor he checked himself in the bathroom mirror and placed the thick-framed black glasses Pollard had delivered with uncorrected lenses on his nose and then regarded the quality of the camouflage and concluded it was perfect. He made faces emulating several different stereotypical male expressions and laughed at each fake persona.

Jeremy cautiously entered the main floor through a service door and wandered among the crowd viewing the attractions throughout the first-floor exhibits. A wave of exhilaration enveloped his body now that the perceptual bonds of the boiler room no longer restricted his pursuit of physical movement. He focused on patrons individually, but noticed he made some of them uncomfortable as they assumed he was staring. His reverie had temporarily masked the responsibility to ensure none of the visitors might be covert operatives of a sinister group. A ripple of guilt crept up his spine as he recalled Pollard did not want him in the museum except at night after visiting hours. *He can't really expect me to stay in that prison downstairs forever. I'm doing just fine up here with real people all around enjoying these wonderful exhibits.* He relaxed, found a bench against a wall, and sat watching patrons stroll and consult maps to locate their high-priority destinations in the building.

An elderly gentleman in a herringbone sport coat, grey dress slacks, and wearing a black beret cocked to the left stood with his hands clasped behind his back about thirty feet from Jeremy, the barrel of a pipe peeping out of his breast pocket. He casually moved toward Jeremy's bench and cast intermittent glances through rimless glasses with barely visible, deep-set small brown eyes at the seated young man. The old man removed his beret and used a handkerchief to mop his bald pate before placing the beret back on his head and adjusting its position carefully. As the man continued to approach the bench,

Jeremy noted his large, bent nose presenting an image of a scientist or college professor. The man's gaze intruded into Jeremy's aura alerting him to the old man's presence.

Jeremy concentrated on locking on to the intruder's eyes to determine if he had been recognized and if the man might be gathering visual information about his appearance. A quiver of trepidation fired a bolt of heat through the spaceman's body; could this "Einstein" penetrate his disguise and recognize his true identity? *The old man looks familiar to me, too. I can't place him, though.* Jeremy forced his mind to race back in time through his business career, but he could not connect this man's face with anyone he knew or with whom he had occasion to interact.

"Einstein" walked slowly past Jeremy glancing at him every few seconds. Once several feet past the bench, he pivoted in miniature steps one hundred-eighty degrees and walked past the bench again in the opposite direction.

Jeremy's discomfort continued to increase. He decided the only way to defuse the situation would be to go on the offense. He stood and moved to within three feet of his observer. "Excuse me sir, but why are you staring at me?"

The old man backed up a step and clasped his hands in front of his coat. "I'm so sorry, I thought I might know you, but I guess I must be mistaken."

"Who do you think I am?"

"When I was teaching at the university one of my students looked very similar to you. Same size, maybe a little thinner, but brown hair not blond, and he had the same eyes as yours, but he did not wear glasses. I didn't mean to infringe on your personal space."

Jeremy continued flashing through his mental recollection prior to his first job. He strained to recall his college friends, fraternity brothers and professors . . . *wait, this man looks like one of my profs.* "Where did you teach?"

"Vanderbilt University, why?"

"You look familiar to me, too. What courses did you teach? Did you ever lecture at other schools?

"Undergraduate and graduate philosophy and yes, I did participate on the lecture circuit until my health took a turn for the worse in 2006." He squinted and cocked his head to the right; *perhaps one eye is stronger than the other?* "I have a fairly good memory, especially of my former students. Did you attend college?"

This is getting too close to home. I can't let him know I went to Vanderbilt, I can't take a chance on him blowing my cover. "I was a business major at the University of Illinois in Champaign-Urbana. Did you ever lecture at U of I?"

"Yes, but I don't recall the year. Good school. Striking resemblance between you and one of my students."

"Really? What's his name?"

"It's on the tip of my tongue as they say, but I can't quite place him. Seeing you helps me visualize him, though. He was a good student and expressed interest in testing observations of the ancients regarding the possible existence of their concept of what we call heaven. I think I've got it! His name was Chambers, James, John: no Jeremy! I wonder what he's doing now. What is your name?"

Here we go. I need to steer him way off course. "George Chrystos."

"How about yours?"

"Professor Marvin Operman, now retired."

Jeremy extended his hand to meet the professor's bony appendage. "Pleased to meet you, sir."

The old man's grip, although thin, clenched into a vice-like wrap and seemed to project pulsing warmth. He maintained the handshake, pumping up and down for what seemed like a couple minutes as he continued to scrutinize Jeremy's features. "The pleasure is all mine. Hope to see you again."

"It's a small world; you never know."

"You are definitely correct about that. Take care of yourself . . . George." He released his grip and backed in short steps before finally turning and walking away.

Jeremy returned to the bench and felt his face flush. *Of course, Professor Operman, 401 Senior Philosophy, Tuesday and Thursday ten to noon. Holy shit, I wonder how can he remember me after all these years. Didn't seem like he bought the bullshit I gave him about my school and my name for that matter. I guess it's no big deal. I doubt I'll ever see him again.*

17

ob Pollard sat in his office contemplating the increasing number of high priority cases crowding his inbox. He had come to fully understand the level of stress pounding on his predecessor, Henry Barnes, exacerbating his health issues and ultimately contributing to his heart attack and subsequent death. Bob executed several deep breaths forcing exhales in slow rhythm as his primary physician had recommended to reduce stress.

He checked his growing to-do list on his phone and noted he had not heard from Dr. Cavallini in four days, two days beyond the doc's promise date; time for a call to check on his answer. He speed dialed Cavallini and frowned as the call defaulted to voice mail. "Hi, Dr. Cavallini, Bob Pollard here. I just wanted to follow up with you on our recent conversation to see what you think about my proposal. Please give me a call back soon." *I'm surprised he missed his own date to get back to me.* The besieged SAIC reclined in his chair and rubbed sore eyes before accessing a different case on one of his desk top computers.

Twenty minutes later his secretary buzzed and said Dr. Cavallini was on line three. "Hello, doctor, how are you?"

"Busy. Sorry I didn't call back on Friday; the office has been crazy, and Sharon and I are planning to go to our house in St. John in a few days."

"How long will you be gone?"

"Not sure, but probably two weeks, although she sometimes likes to stay longer, but I have to get back to my practice."

"Sounds like a nice vacation spot especially now in June; the hurricane season hasn't really started yet."

"Right, we love it down there. I've given your proposal some thought, and I think we need to add some flesh on the bones, lay out a plan, and assess the risk before I can commit to something as daring as you have suggested."

"Well, I'm glad to hear you're still willing to consider it. How about while you're gone, I'll work on an outline with as many details and risks as I can identify and then we can meet when you return."

"Sounds good. If you need to reach me, you have my cell number; I'll be on the beach sipping a margarita, or six."

"You sure know how to hurt a guy. Have a great trip. Talk to you in a few weeks, and thanks again for your help."

"Your thanks may be premature since we don't have a plan yet. Take care, bye."

"Bye." *Shit, I just gave myself more homework! He wouldn't go for it without the details, though, so I guess it will be time well spent. He has a good sense of humor, and I think we're starting to build some rapport. His year in Germany on the so-called special project still has a foul odor to it, though. I might have to find a reason to go over there across the pond and poke around to validate his story. Fat chance; I'm up to my ears with cases and crises here, so a trip like that is on the bottom of the pile.*

18

Days and nights piled into each other creating a seamless strand of boredom for Jeremy. After a close call with the professor he restricted his visits to the museum floors to after hours. He viewed one of the permanent exhibitions each night until he had seen them all. He especially liked the Inside Ancient Egypt display with its twenty-three human mummies and some 5,000-year-old hieroglyphs and the Ancient Americas exhibit, which displays 13,000 years of human ingenuity and achievement in the Western Hemisphere. He paid a second visit on a different night to the Egypt exhibition and engaged in manipulating the interactive displays.

Jeremy could feel a restlessness stir in his soul, and he longed to see his family and friends. *Who knows how long it will be before Pollard can figure out a safe way for me to see Megan and the kids? Damn, it better be soon, though.* He wondered how his close friends Paul, Carl, and Larry were getting along. His brief visit with Joe was a breath of fresh air, reconnecting the spaceman with society on earth, if only for a short time. *But, holy shit, was Pollard mad! I thought he was going to bust a blood vessel yelling at me. I can't take this life I have in a cocoon; I need to be around people. How can I figure out a way to see the other guys without Bob finding out and without putting the guys in danger.* He lay in bed trolling for ideas from the depths of his imagination, evaluating them, and then discarding each for one reason or another. Nothing seemed to work.

At 3:25 on a rainy June night a full bladder forced him to roll out of bed to use the toilet. The storm clouds bristled with explosions of thunder and beat on the large fortress-like building. Although the sounds were faint, he could hear the cacophony of the storm's irregular pounding. When he returned to the sheets and covers, a thought bubbled up and beckoned for consideration. His bosses at the space citadel had allowed him to visit his friends, albeit briefly in the UP of Michigan last fall. The aliens had provided instructions for navigating through space and a wormhole to arrive at the lake and, more recently, back to earth when he materialized in the kitchen of his old home. *I memorized the instructions, so maybe I can use them to transport myself to see the guys. Not sure I can pull it off without guidance from the bosses, but I'd like to try.* He also needed to inventory his powers to determine whether he could view his friends from his boiler room accommodations. He had not attempted such a feat since last year when he was able to enter his daughter's mind to provide her with direction in finding her kidnapped mother. The bosses had not allowed him to appear visible to Kelly during that ephemeral encounter.

■ ■ ■

The clock on his iPhone read 7:34, and Jeremy was already awake. He sat on the side of the bed after turning on the table lamp. The dimensions of this dungeon closed in on its tenant's psyche, squeezing his focus when he worked on searching for cyber plots and even when he watched TV. The walls seemed to inch nearer each day, and the ceiling appeared to drop at the same rate. Jeremy shook his head attempting to expel these depressing thoughts.

After a shower and trim of his beard, his mood swung to a more positive place. A knock on the door announced the arrival of Cuthbertson with breakfast. Jeremy let him in and cleared the table for the tray.

"How are you today, director?"

Cuthbertson produced a slight frown with the corners of his mouth. "I'm doing well, sir. Anything else?"

"Some storm last night, eh?"

"Yes."

"Would you like to join me for coffee?"

"No thank you, I have to get back to my *real* job."

"Maybe some other time?"

"We'll see. Good day, sir."

"See you at lunch time." The director did not acknowledge him as he closed the door and left.

This guy is about as stuffy as anyone I've ever known. What an asshole.

Jeremy finished his meal and voiced the TV on to the local ABC channel for the news. After a half hour of car crashes and results of violence on the south and west sides of the city, he opened his iPad and dove into his day job.

At noon, the director delivered lunch and quickly departed. Jeremy finished the food and relaxed in his recliner. *I need to see if I can make contact with my buds.* He summoned the instructions from his bosses in his memory and accessed auxiliary energy to invoke his special powers and then experimented by sending a telepathic message to Paul Torchetti. He failed to connect with his friend's mind. Several additional attempts did not work either. *I wonder if this is the end of the line for me; maybe I'm just a normal human now.* He tried to message Carl and Larry but could not establish a link with them either. *Damn, I must be too far away to make it work. I guess the only thing left is to try to transport myself to where the guys are and see them physically. Maybe I can do that, but then if my powers disappear again like they have a few times since I've been back, I'll be in deep shit. I can just hear Pollard shouting at me if that happened. It's a big risk, but I need to see the guys and my family; I can't live like this much longer.*

■ ■ ■

The restless spaceman waited until after dinner to try to visit Paul. First, he programmed Cuthbertson's mind to temporarily stop food service until he returned. Next, he geared up mentally to beckon his skills. He reviewed the instructions for transporting through the air one step at a time. His concentration paid off as he experienced invisible flight through the dark night to . . . the roof of a Walgreens store in Barrington, Illinois. *Well, this is the right town, but I don't think Paul lives on this roof.* He smiled at his errant aim. *At least I'm still able to make transport happen.* He had visited Paul's home in Barrington many times when they worked together so finding the correct location would not be a problem. The cool air and seemingly never-ending Chicagoland wind nipped at him. *Guess I should have worn the jacket Pollard gave me.* Gentle whipping of drone propellers reminded him of the need to get out of sight. He shuddered, squatted behind a commercial air conditioning unit to minimize his silhouette, closed his eyes, and refocused energy to penetrate layers of atmosphere winging him to the front porch of his friend.

Paul slept in his chair in the great room. Jeremy started to ring the bell, but caught himself in time and dropped his hand to his side. *I made it this far using my skills so getting into the house should be easy.* His first attempt, however, landed him in the vestibule between the outside door and the large dark wood front door decorated with etched glass patterns in the side panels. *Shit. I need more practice.* One last mental push, and he was inside the home. *Now I need to figure out how to wake him without scaring him to death. Where is Marie? She must be upstairs reading or watching TV in bed.* Jeremy stood to the side of Paul's chair and regarded his friend with affection. *Now that I'm face to face with him, maybe I can enter his mind and wake him slowly so he doesn't freak out.*

Paul winced and cocked his head in Jeremy's direction. He opened his eyes and bolted upright in the chair. "JC, is it really you?"

"In the flesh, bud."

Paul glided out of the chair and embraced his younger friend. "You look a little different, though, with the blond hair, beard, and those glasses. I can't believe it; I was just dreaming about you."

"Well, not exactly a dream; I entered your mind so I could wake you without giving you cardiac arrest. You look great. How do you feel?"

"Still completely healthy since you cured me of my cancer last fall up in the UP. Let's have a beer to celebrate." He guided his surprised guest to the kitchen and pulled two Coors Lights from the fridge. They returned to the great room and sat in chairs facing each other.

"Is Marie upstairs?"

"Yeah, I'll go get her."

"I would love to see her, but no, I don't want to put her in a bad position by seeing me and asking all kinds of questions. The less she knows the safer she'll be."

"Okay. Man, I can't get over how you haven't aged in the last eight years. When did you get back?"

"A few weeks ago. Pollard is hiding me in a secret location. He doesn't know I'm here; he would be super pissed if he did. I saw Joe not long after I arrived and programmed his mind so he couldn't divulge my presence to anyone. But I wanted to see you, Carl, and Larry too."

"You know, Joe invited us to dinner a couple weeks ago, and he acted strange after we finished the meal. He got sick suddenly and left early. It seemed like he wanted to tell us something but couldn't. Maybe it was about you."

"Glad my fix on his mind worked. How are the other guys?"

"We're all doing fine, but we really have missed you these last years since you disappeared. Are you back for good now?"

"I hope so. I completed my projects up there, so they don't need me anymore. I'm doing some work for Bob and the bureau during the day. My powers have been inconsistent, so I'm not sure how long they will last. It feels like my bosses from space are still pulling the strings on my life. I want to see Megan and the kids as soon as possible."

"You know they're still in California, right?"

"Yeah, I received telepathic messages while I was gone, and the bosses even allowed me to visit Kelly's mind last year when those assholes had Megan. How is she, do you know?"

"Can't help you there, JC, but the word is she's still in rehab. Being kidnapped and held for ransom must be pretty scary."

"I can't even imagine how she got through that nightmare. Pollard said he would work on a way for me to see them, but so far he doesn't have one."

"Want another beer?"

"No, I can't stay long, bud. It's great to see you."

"This is a real treat for me, man. I hope you can visit Carl and Larry too."

"I know, same here. I better take off. Great to see you, Paul." The men embraced as they headed for the front door.

"Wait, I should be able to transport myself from in here. I don't want to be seen on the porch." Jeremy closed his eyes and summoned his powers and disappeared only to reappear . . . in the kitchen. "Shit, I must not be following the instructions properly. I'll try it again." This time he remained in the kitchen. "Uh, oh. I wonder if my skills are gone." He executed several additional attempts, but could not exit the home. "Well, bud, looks like I'm not so special anymore. Pollard is going to go bat shit if I can't get back to my secret location before breakfast tomorrow morning."

"You're more than welcome to stay here as long as you want. I'll go up and get one of the guest rooms ready for you."

"Paul, thank you for the offer; I really wish I could accept, but I don't want to put you and Marie in danger, especially since I don't seem to have my powers. I can't protect you two."

"So, where will you go?"

"Not sure. I need to give it some thought. I think I'll have to call Bob and tell him what happened and where I am. He'll be furious, but I don't have much choice."

"I think you take too much blame on yourself. Look at all you've done for people. You cured Pollard and me a few years ago in the hospital, and then you cured me again after I had the relapse with the cancer last year. You also cured Carl's burned hand up at the UP."

"I know, but look at the grief I've put the people closest to me through. Megan and the kids had to move to California to escape the danger from the Russians chasing me and trying to end my life. Bob was shot at the funeral home, and poor Lorraine lost her life because I selfishly forced the FBI into letting me go see the kids in California. Then Henry Barnes dies of a heart attack from the stress I caused him and . . ."

"That's enough, man. You're not responsible for everything bad that's happened to us. You'd better call Pollard."

"Right. I'm not looking forward to this conversation."

19

Stephanie Murphy checked her email on her iPhone as the car weaved through the lunchtime traffic to her office building. Once in the garage, she put her phone in her purse and reclined her head on the rest at the top of the seat. Tears formed then slid down her cheeks. *What a fucking mess I've made of my life. I thought Brad was the coolest guy ever, and then he dumps me. I haven't found a good man since. I invested seven of my prime childbearing years in that relationship—for what? It's getting late for me to start having babies, and I need to have a loving, caring husband to help me give our kids good lives. I love my job, but I don't want to work sixty hours a week forever. I wish Brad and I could have the relationship we had before, but he isn't the same guy now.*

She checked her face in the car mirror. A small brown mole a half-inch from her mouth on her left cheek served to augment her beauty. *I hated that mole when I was growing up, but now it's kind of like an old friend.* The law partner wiped the smeared mascara from her face and prepared to walk to her office.

She broke into a modified jog to get to the ladies room to freshen up before anyone could see her. She hid in a stall until two ladies finished washing up and left. She emerged stealthily and checked herself in the large mirror above the washbasins and straightened her back to her full height. At five foot ten inches, she maintained her slender figure through a dedicated regimen at LA Fitness. Gymnastics and cheerleading experience in high school and college established an active, outdoor lifestyle, but spending so much time in the office suppressed her natural desire for meeting people and handling disparate types of cases. She reapplied makeup and then returned to her office.

The stressed attorney reviewed the FiberLink file again and wrote the key questions on a yellow legal pad she would ask Earle Claypoole regarding some missing invoices and other deficiencies she had identified. *Guess I can't put this off any longer.*

She speed-dialed Claypoole's number, and the secretary transferred the call after identifying Stephanie. "Hello, Mr. Claypoole, how are you?"

"Well, Stephanie, haven't talked to you in a while. I thought you forgot about us or maybe you decided everything here at our little company is in good order."

"I wish I could say you don't have any risk issues, but you remember from our meetings and discussions we have some concerns. Have you had a chance to look for the invoices?"

"Yes, I found them."

"Great. Can you email them to me?"

"Is that really safe? Maybe I should have copies made and courier them to you."

"No, I don't think that's necessary; email is fine."

"Okay. By the way, when will we receive your final report? We have a board meeting in two weeks, and I'd like to present the results of your review at that meeting."

"I still have more areas to review in addition to the invoices. If I can get some resources, we may be able to finish before your board meets, but I'm not making any promises."

"Understood. What other sort of issues have you found so far?"

"Since I have not had a chance to finish checking your firewalls and internal security procedures to draw conclusions, I'm not in a position to share what I have right now."

"With all the crackpots out there in cyberspace I hope we haven't been hacked. Have you found any evidence of that?"

"Like I said, everything is preliminary at this point, so you'll have to wait a while longer. I'm moving as fast as I can."

"Yes, I appreciate your hard work. I'm just really worried; if we are being hacked, we need to jump on analyzing the situation and finding a way to crush it before it does too much damage."

"I know what you mean, but again, I can't provide you with any details right now. However, if I identify some serious intrusions, I'll let you know right away."

"Okay, but if you find some evidence of hacking, we need to get on it ASAP."

"Right, will do. But for the less serious deficiencies I'll have to present my findings to our management first and then let you know."

"I'll send the invoices to you after we hang up."

"Great, thanks. Goodbye."

"Bye." *Doesn't seem like she knows anything we don't want her to know. I hope these invoices satisfy her.* Earle made photos of the invoices and sent the email with the invoices as attachments.

■ ■ ■

Stephanie visited the break room for a cup of coffee and to stretch her legs. *I don't like the way he kept pushing me for the results of my review; he knows we always share significant issues with our clients as we identify them, but he seems worried about hacking. Their firewalls and controls are not stellar, but I can't determine now if they will be showstoppers.* She checked her email inbox and noted the one from Claypoole. *This should be interesting.*

A careful review of the invoices for the purchase of communication equipment and supplies seemed to indicate some irregularities. However, she had also noticed a large credit on the company's income statement for a consulting fee. The contract was for a review of the communication structure and age and quality of the equipment used by the city of Vista Nueva. She had requested a copy of the final report from Earle Claypoole, but it appeared superficial and supporting documentation was sparse. The funds transfer representing the payment from the city of Vista Nueva was deposited into an account of a subsidiary of FiberLink. Stephanie consulted her notes and discovered the subsidiary appeared to be a shell corporation. Some funds were then disbursed the next day to BW, LLC as a commission for facilitating the consulting contract.

What the hell is BW, LLC? She googled the entity. *Holy crap! It's Brad Wolfe, LLC. He didn't mention he had FiberLink as a client. This is a hell of a lot of money for a routine commission, $750,000. I need to contact the city and check on its acceptance of the report and whether the few recommendations in the report were acted upon by the city. This is starting to stink.*

Stephanie typed an email to Al and Bev recounting what she suspected and suggested they meet. They both responded within minutes and Al invited them to his office in half an hour.

The three met, and Stephanie updated the others with all the details she could elicit. "Have you checked with the city?" Al asked.

"Yes, I have call into the controller's office, but they haven't gotten back to me yet."

She turning to Bev. "Any change from the Feds as to how we should proceed?"

"No, not yet. Mark Pawley, FBI special agent, has been assigned to our case due to his work in previous situations involving the Murphy and Chambers families. He told me once Steph gets some information from the city, we should update him."

"One thing you both should know: Brad Wolfe and I used to date until about two years ago when he broke up with me."

"Ancient history as far as our contract with FiberLink is concerned," Bev said.

"Well, maybe not. He called me a couple weeks ago and wanted to get together, acted like our relationship had not missed a beat. I ended up having lunch with him. He contacted me again recently, and long story short, I had lunch with him today at Gulfstream."

"Did he say anything about his relationship with FiberLink?" Bev asked.

"No, but he pressed me about my clients and wanted me to refer our clients to him if they needed communications help since that's the business he's in." She noticed the other two ready to ask the next obvious question, so she continued. "I told him no, I would not be part of anything unethical."

"Good response. Does he suspect you're on his trail?" Al asked. "No because I didn't find out about his connection with FiberLink until I received the email and invoices from Earle Claypoole after lunch. I also noticed receipt of a large payment on the income statement from Vista Nueva to FiberLink for some consulting work they did for the city. Then I found FiberLink paid a large commission to BW, LLC, which it turns out is Brad Wolfe's company. I'm really sorry I got us involved in this mess."

"No apology needed. You were doing your job and handled the situation the right way," Al said.

"Besides checking with the city, is there anything else you want me to do?"

"Not at this time. Let's see what the city has to say," Bev said. "Alright, we're through here. We'll wait to hear from you, Steph," Al said. Bev and Stephanie rose and headed toward the door. "Steph, one more thing." Bev closed the door as she went out. "I have to ask an awkward question. Do you have feelings again for this Brad guy?"

Stephanie hesitated, sorting thoughts at warp speed in her mind regarding how to respond. "No. When he first called I wondered if he was the same man I used to know, but when we had lunch two weeks ago, he was nice and funny like always, but something seemed different about him, so I decided to keep my distance. I knew then I'm not ready to rush back into a relationship with him. And today at lunch he confirmed my instincts."

"Dealing with someone's mind is one thing, but taking the blinders off so the heart can see the real picture is not so easy. You did well." Al looked down for half a minute. "If at any time you feel compromised by your situation with him, let me know, and I can have you switch assignments with another partner."

She stifled the moisture forming in her eyes. "Thank you for the offer, but I don't want to be a couple with him ever again, and I do want to work this contract to the end. You have my word I will never allow him to interfere with me doing my job."

Al smiled and patted her shoulder. "Okay, FiberLink is still your project." Stephanie smiled a thank you, turned, and left the office.

■ ■ ■

The fatigued attorney returned to her office, plopped into her chair, and held her face in her hands. Tears would not be denied as she rotated her chair around so she faced the window. She dabbed her eyes with Kleenex for the second time in a couple of hours. *This is turning into a bad dream. I'm so embarrassed I had to tell them about Brad and that I had lunch with him recently. They're probably thinking if I didn't want him back in my life, why would I have lunch with him . . . twice? I hope this doesn't blow up.* She spun her chair back facing the desk and her computer and searched for the City of Vista Nueva's website since she had not received a return call from the Controller's office. She navigated to the accounting department and found the page with the current financials. She explored the income statement looking for expense line items reflecting consulting fees. She clicked on the headings to get to the detail. None of the expenses matched the timeframe of the payment received by FiberLink except for an entry for $750,000 the same day FiberLink booked that amount in the shell corporation. *How could the city disburse that amount of money without corresponding documentation or at least an invoice for work performed?* She checked the line item for contractors hoping to find expenses that might be for commissions, but she could find none. *The only explanations are sloppy accounting practices, or . . . internal corruption. There's no way I can get hold of the city's books, but maybe I can check the city's annual audit.* She found the link and examined every line. No indication of any issues and the audit firm awarded a satisfactory rating. *I guess this will have to be turned over to the state's attorney's office or the Feds.*

She browsed the city website to get familiar with its government and the services it provides and learned the city includes several large commercial and industrial sections from which it receives huge tax revenues. Since the residential sections represent such a small share of the total tax base, the public services segment of the revenues easily covers the expenses and yields a large surplus. She checked the list of officers and one name jumped off the page: Phil Claypoole! *I forgot, he's Earle's brother. I wonder what type of relationship the city has with FiberLink?*

20

D ominic Cavallini sat in the front passenger seat of his C 63 S Cabriolet Mercedes coupe convertible with the top covering the cabin at seven thirty on this chilly Thursday morning. He scanned the latest news on his cell phone as the car headed for the hospital a few miles away. He punched the phone off and reclined while taking small drinks of his steaming coffee. *St. John will be so nice; I wish we were leaving on vacation today.* Life's complexities had been ramping up with yet another call from the FBI and Pollard's wacky project to test Jeremy's mind and analyze the results to use in programming other humans' brains to create an army of super people who would have only "good intentions" to resolve all of man's sins. *A noble, but impractical objective. I'm going to play along with his idea until he concludes the mission is impossible, as they say in the movies.*

The doctor did not notice a dark blue Tesla S trailing his car. The driver of the mystery car controlled the vehicle since he did not know Cavallini's destination. The Mercedes turned right off of Michigan Avenue into the employee entrance of the large hospital parking garage. The Tesla stopped at the entrance gate, backed up, and reversed course, slowly moved to the opposite side of the street and sat idling next to the curb. The vehicle's windows, darkened with tinting, obscured external view of the driver. He watched Cavallini walk through the elevated passageway between the garage and one of the hospital buildings in the enormous campus.

■ ■ ■

The screen on Ivan Markov's iPad revealed the results of his search for a Dr. Dominic Cavallini, neurosurgeon at Chicago's esteemed Northwestern Hospital. He shifted in his plush chair in his luxury apartment offering a view of Lake Michigan. The biographical information traced the doctor's history from a small town in Pennsylvania through college and medical school and a semester in Germany studying under the tutelage of Dr. Victor Schmidt, a world-renowned neurosurgeon. Dr. Cavallini returned to the United States to complete his internship and residency requirements. Since Dr. Schmidt had not expressed objections to Dominic's sharing the laser techniques he had taught the young student, Cavallini decided to introduce the practical use of lasers in brain surgery in America. This radical new technology application in the 1970s won Dr. Cavallini instant recognition and esteem in the medical community, including accumulation of substantial wealth. Wikipedia only briefly mentioned Dr. Cavallini's participation in a project in Germany under the leadership of Dr. Franz Hoffmann in 1998, and Dr. Hoffmann's mysterious death was officially classified as murder soon after Cavallini returned to his home in Chicago.

"This is most interesting. I think I will continue to have the good doctor followed to learn of his habits," Markov blurted out loud in Russian. "I need to know more about the project in Germany. Maybe I will call him and set up a meeting."

Markov then initiated searches on the other subjects he had identified from Ludmila's good work. He recalled he should be receiving information from Anatoly tomorrow, Friday; he expected the data would include much of what Russia already knew of Heartland Bank's internal security processes, but sometimes in his experience a nugget of previously unknown intelligence from a US bank or company shows up. He speed dialed Anatoly's cell. "Mr. Terasenko? It's me. Listen close," he spoke in Russian.

"Yes, I am here."

"I want to know how your assignment is progressing."

"I'm working on it, but it's hard to gather the information without my bosses finding out."

"You will do just fine, because if you fail, Ludmila is mine."

"No, no I will have the information. Where shall I meet you?"

"Not now. I will call tomorrow morning and tell you where to meet me. Oh, and don't bring the police or government guys with you. You understand?"

"Yes."

"Good. I will call at eight thirty tomorrow morning. Goodbye."

Anatoly dropped his face into his hands and rubbed his eyes. He still had several hours of work ahead to complete the task his Russian tormentor had given him in between his work for the bank. He alternated performing his real job searching for evidence of cyber-attacks against his bank with copying pieces of the bank's defensive security mechanisms to a flash drive as Markov directed. This approach meant extra hours of work in addition to his real job. He decided to update Pollard and moved to a small conference room for privacy. "Hello, Bob?"

"Hello, my friend. How goes your project?"

"I have a lot more to do, but now that most of my colleagues are gone for the day, it should go much faster. He called me a while ago and said he will tell me tomorrow at eight thirty in the morning where to take the drive. He also said no police, and you guys should not be there. What should I do? I hate hurting my bank like this."

"Are you in a place where you can talk freely?"

"Yes, I am in a conference room."

"Good. Is there some way you can delete or change a piece of code in a few strategic places in the information you are giving him that will disguise the real procedures?"

"I could do that, but then it may put Ludmila in danger if Markov finds out the information is phony. I can't take that chance."

"You told her about Markov's threat, right?"

"Of course; she's scared shitless."

"Understandable. Here's my plan. Have her drive to Palwaukee Airport in Wheeling, and I will send a helicopter to pick her up and bring her downtown to a secure location. Then we'll wait and see if he discovers the data is tainted. If not, she can return home. If he does find out we tricked him, she will be safe."

"Bob, that's fine, but what about me? If he can't find her, he'll come after me. You know how these old KGB guys are; they're ruthless."

"Right. Let's see; . . . after you give him the flash drive, take an Uber to my office, and we'll drive you to be with your wife where he can't find you. It's my guess the Russians already have uncovered many of the techniques the banks and major companies in the US have been using, so they may not spend much time looking for something new; it's like trying to find the needle in haystack, right?"

"Maybe that'll work, but Ludmila and I can't hide out and not show up for work for very long."

"You can call in sick for a few days. My guess is Markov will have his geeks work on what you give him right away, so we should know in a day or two."

"Okay, Bob, but I hope this doesn't blow up."

"I think we'll be fine; we've dealt with Markov before, and he's not the sharpest tool in the tool chest."

"I'm not so sure about that. He's an old KGB guy, and he may not seem smart, but he's politically savvy. I recall meeting some of their technical guys in Russia, and most are intelligent, so they may see through my changes and omissions. Will your men be near the meeting location?"

"We need to let it play out; I'm confident we can make it work. And yes, I will have agents in the area where you meet him, but we have ways of disguising our presence. We won't make a move unless we determine your life is in danger. Don't try to look for my guys; just know they are there."

"What about police?"

"No, we won't involve them at this point. Call me as soon as you know the meeting location."

"Will do, but this is scary, Bob."

"Hang in there; we take measures to mitigate all risks. Talk to you tomorrow."

"Right, goodbye."

21

Jeremy found a chair in the great room and executed several deep breaths, slowing exhales to calm his anxious body. He cradled his phone in one hand and tapped Pollard's number with the index finger of the other. "Bob, it's me. We have a problem."

"Oh? What happened?"

"Well, I felt cooped up in the boiler room and decided to see if I could use my powers to visit my friend, Paul Torchetti. I'm at his house right now, and I can't seem to find my powers, so I'm stuck here."

"Damn it! What the fuck is wrong with you? I told you the boiler room wouldn't be the greatest of accommodations, but it was only going to be temporary." The stressed SAIC rose from a chair in his condo and began to pace. "This is the second time you've fucked things up. Do you realize you're putting peoples' lives at risk?"

Jeremy held the phone several inches away from his ear. "I know, boss, it was stupid of me, sorry. What should I do?"

"I'll have to think about it and call you back. Do I have to tell you not to leave Paul's house until I can figure things out?"

"No. I'll be here waiting for your call." He punched off the connection and turned to his friend. "Holy shit, did he read me the riot act. He's going to think about what he wants me to do and call me back."

"Like I said, you can stay here as long as you want. What do we do about Marie?"

"I know, the last thing I want to do is place her in a tough position. If I remember correctly, you have some couches downstairs in your man cave, right?"

"Yes, and one of them is a foldout bed."

"That's good, but when Marie comes downstairs to do laundry, she'll see me."

"Right. There goes that idea."

"Wait a minute. Do you have a cot?"

"Yes, we have four; we use them for the grand kids when they visit."

"How about if I sleep on one behind the bar?"

"That should work. Also, I can volunteer to do the laundry for a few days or as long as you're here. It'll keep her upstairs as much as possible, and I can smuggle food down to you a couple times a day."

"Not perfect, but at least it'll give Pollard an option for a few days."

The friends continued to brainstorm possible issues and corresponding solutions. Jeremy's phone rang, interrupting their plotting. "Shit, I forgot to put it on vibrate; hope it didn't wake Marie."

"Paul, who are you talking to?" Marie shouted from the top of the stairs.

Jeremy dove behind a couch out of sight of the stairwell. "No one, hon; just babbling to myself and the TV. Sorry to disturb you."

"Okay. I'm going to bed. Don't stay up too long."

"No problem, be up there in a little while, hon."

Jeremy cupped his hands around the phone and whispered "Bob, we're trying not to let Marie know I'm here."

"Well, finally thinking with the right head. Have you tried using your powers again?"

"Of course, about two hours ago; no go. But Paul and I have come up with a plan that should buy us some time. If I have to stay here, I can sleep in his rec room downstairs without Marie seeing me."

"Good. Keep trying to recapture your magic every hour or so; maybe it'll return. Your plan to stay there will give me more time to find a place for you to hide. I left a message for Cuthbertson to stop delivering meals since you're temporarily out of the boiler room. He seemed relieved."

"I already programmed his mind not to deliver meals until further notice. Sorry, man, but that guy is a real dork. I'll keep trying to get my space skills back. I'll call you right away if I succeed."

"You better. Bye."

"Bye." He tuned to Paul. "Well, that was fun. At least he seemed to cool off somewhat toward the end. He told me to try to get my skills back every hour. I'm beginning to think my space bosses have pulled the plug on me."

"Never say never, JC. I don't think your so-called bosses would abandon you after using you for seven years."

"I wish I had your confidence. The thing that bothers me is it seems to come and go. Makes me think the bosses are monitoring my behavior and deciding what they think is proper, or what they like, which is even scarier.

"How so?'

"Look at it this way: maybe they're using me for amusement or diversion. They treat me like a puppet pulling the strings to force me to do one thing or another. If they get bored they could put me in some dangerous situations, but other people might be affected, too."

"Seems to me they've treated you pretty well. From what you told us they're working on things to make life here on earth better for mankind, right?"

"Yeah, basically, but their intelligence is so far beyond ours it's impossible to know their true intention. I'm going to give it another try right now. " He closed tired eyes and concentrated his focus and energy, but he did not transport. He tried again and again, without success.

"Well, bud, I guess we have our answer."

22

Stephanie's phone console buzzed. She picked up, and her administrative assistant said she had a call from a Mr. Hastings at the city of Vista Nueva. "Hello, this is Stephanie."

"Hello, Ms. Murphy, it's Andrew Hastings from the accounting department at the city of Vista Nueva. I'm returning your call from a couple days ago. *His voice indicates a level of maturity; probably older, maybe close to retirement age, but you can't really tell without seeing the person.*

"Thank you for the quick response, I know you must be very busy."

"Name of the game for just about everyone these days. How can I help you?"

"I'm with Shields & Fitch, and we currently have a contract with one of your consultants, FiberLink. I have reviewed your financials on your website and the annual audit report as well, and I have a few questions I'd like to ask if you don't mind."

"Sure, I'll answer any questions I'm allowed to."

He must be a long-time employee. "Perfect. I noticed the city recently purchased a consulting contract from FiberLink. Your income statement reflects a commission of $750,000.00 paid to a third party manufacturers' rep, but I can't locate an expense for the consulting contract itself."

"Let me check on that." He drifted off the call and his keystrokes in his desktop sounded like a machine gun "Yes, here it is. We contracted with FiberLink on April 16th 2019: We booked it under administrative expense."

"Why would you book it in that account if it was for consulting services?"

"This has been the practice over the sixteen years I've worked here. I questioned it when I first started and was told this is the way they have always done it."

"Seems to be buried in that account. How much was it for?"

"It was for $3,750,000.00."

"Okay, so the commission was for twenty percent. Does that seem like an abnormally high figure to you?"

"Honestly yes, but as I said before, that's the way they have done things around here forever, so I just book the entries the way they tell me to. The outside auditors have not cited it as a problem since I've been here."

"Seems like a strange accounting system to me. Do you have a report of what FiberLink found in their review of the city's communication systems and equipment?"

"Yes."

"Could you email it to me?"

"Sure."

"Great and thank you so much for your help. I really appreciate it."

"Glad to help. Is there a problem with this transaction?"

"I'm not sure; I just have to understand the way your city does business. Thanks again, Mr. Hastings. Goodbye." She dropped the receiver into the console and reclined in her chair while checking the notes she scribbled during the conversation. *Wow, I can't believe the irregularities in their accounting system. How could a reputable audit firm allow entries that are clearly outside the scope of generally accepted accounting rules? Looks like I need to make a couple more calls.*

■ ■ ■

Stephanie broke for lunch at one o'clock to avoid the traffic and lunch crowds and programmed her car to drive to a sandwich shop a couple miles from the office. She often eschewed eating in the building cafeteria to get away from the chatter and the pressure of the job to clear her mind and occasionally read a novel while having a light meal.

She ordered a salad and Diet Coke and sat at a table by the window. Today the novel would remain in her purse, and it would be a working lunch. Her plan involved gathering all relevant facts, organizing them, and preparing a report she could present to Al and Bev and whoever else needed to see it. *The relationship between FiberLink and the city of Vista Nueva appears to reek of something sinister and the fact Brad Wolfe is a player is surprising and disappointing.*

Stephanie lingered in the sandwich shop and refilled her drink. She tore the note pages from her legal pad and laid them on the table in chronological order. She checked her laptop and found the email from Hastings with the report attached, which reflected that FiberLink performed a review and recommended a few action items, a couple of which involved the city engaging

FiberLink to obtain and sell communication equipment and state-of-the-art software systems to Vista Nueva . . . *another opportunity to fleece the city.*

The timeline started with the city's contract for the consulting services from FiberLink on April 16th and then the booking of the transaction in the Administrative Expense account and subsequent payment to FiberLink. The date of the city receiving the report of review was April 28th. The city also paid Brad Wolfe a commission fee of $750,000 on April 30th. The young attorney added notes on some pages, crossed out other entries, and changed still more. Having clarified what she knew so far, she collected her notes and returned to the office.

■ ■ ■

Back in the office, Stephanie phoned Bender, Cohen and Burke, LLC, the city's external audit firm, and after a ten-minute wait spoke to Ira Cohen. "Hello Mr. Cohen, I'm working on an engagement my firm, Shields & Fitch, has with a small company called FiberLink, which has done business with the city of Vista Nueva. Could I ask you a question pertaining to your most recent annual audit of the city's financial position?"

"Depends on what the question involves."

'Of course. I would not bother you if it were something proprietary or confidential. The city purchased consulting services from FiberLink and paid a fee of $750,000 to BW, LTD for arranging the deal. When I checked with the city, I asked the man in the accounting department where he booked the expense for the consulting services, and he said it was in the administrative account. They booked the commission in the third party vendor account, which is fine. My question is, why did they book the purchase in the administrative account instead of the appropriate expense account? Your audit did not reflect an irregularity with this transaction. Doesn't it seem unusual for the city to use this type of entry?"

Ira Cohen paused before answering and sighed. "Yes, you are correct. We have been the city's auditor for twenty-one years, and in year one we asked about this practice. The answer was vague, and we were referred to their attorney who told us there was no intent to deceive, but they didn't want to broadcast how much money they spent on goods and services. The attorney said the entries were readily available to anyone who reviewed the city's financials, but you would have to look at the details."

"So you gave them a satisfactory rating in spite of this practice?"

"Yes. Our position has been from the first year that the fact the information is available is all that's technically required, even though it's not in the account where you would normally expect to find it." Cohen quickly added, "The city's management explained to us that its tax base composition is heavily weighted toward commercial and industrial, and those entities pay some huge taxes. The city takes in far more than they spend on services and materials, resulting in eye-popping surpluses. So management decided long ago they would pay top dollar for the best quality of everything they needed, and they didn't want to make those expenses front-page news, if you know what I mean. The way they account for those expenses accomplishes two objectives. One, the data is ostensibly available, but not featured, and two, by buying top quality for top prices they are able to shrink their surplus somewhat."

"Not sure that makes a whole lot of sense to me, and I would think the optics are not great either."

"Agreed, but as long as what they do is legal, we don't have a problem with it.

"I see. Well, thank you for the explanation and the help." She clicked off the call. *Holy crap, this is getting weirder by the minute.*

Next she phoned Lee Enterprises, LTD, manufacturer of communications equipment and software products, she but experienced difficulty with the international telephone systems.

After some back and forth with Vista Nueva's purchasing department, Stephanie connected with the department manager, Ms. Sylvia Kirkwood, and explained who she was and questioned whether the city had acted on the recommendations in the report from FiberLink. Ms. Kirkwood placed her on hold while she checked her records and rejoined the call in minutes. "No, not yet."

"Why?"

"The report was vague, and the recommendations were for the purchase of some equipment and software we have had in place here at the city for over a year. I wanted to clarify our action plan with the mayor before I implemented FiberLink's ideas."

"What did the mayor say?"

"He told me to just order the things they recommended that we don't currently have."

"Did you order them, and if so, from whom?"

"Not yet, but I need this job, so I will order some equipment and software off their report."

"Whom will you order from?"

"Well, the mayor insisted I order through FiberLink."

"Are their prices reasonable?"

"Honestly, I use three vendors that would beat FiberLink's prices by twenty-five percent."

"Did you mention this to the mayor?"

"No, I've been down that road before, and he told me to do what I'm told, so I will order from FiberLink."

"Thank you Ms. Kirkwood. Goodbye."

Wait until Al, Bev and the FBI hear about this! She added the new information gleaned from the audit firm and Ms. Kirkwood to the rest of the facts and typed an outline for her report.

23

The vibration of his phone on the desk at the bank startled Anatoly. *Eight thirty. Damn, it's Markov. I'm not looking forward to talking to this asshole.* His palms moist, he hunched over his desk to shield the upcoming conversation. "Hello, Markov."

"Hello, my good friend. Are you ready to hand over the drive today?"

"Yes."

"Very good. Listen close. You will go to Buckingham Fountain at exactly noon. You will go to the south side of the fountain, then face fountain. Look to right and see benches. Go to benches and sit down. At twelve thirty put drive far under seat of bench. Wait five minutes then walk away. You understand, comrade?"

"I'm not your damn comrade, and yes, I understand."

"Ah, why so mad, comrade? You are saving lots of trouble for you and lovely Ludmila. No tricks, no police, no Feds. Understand?"

"Yes."

"Goodbye, comrade."

Anatoly exhaled. *Glad that's over; I can't stand talking to that bastard.* He waited a few minutes to recapture his composure moved to a conference room, and called Bob Pollard.

"Hello, my friend," Bob said.

"Hi, boss. He just called and told me to go to Buckingham Fountain at noon and sit on a bench on the south side of the fountain. He said at twelve thirty to put the drive under the bench, wait five minutes, and then leave."

"Okay. That gives us some time."

"Boss, he said no police, no Feds."

"Right, like I told you we have ways of making ourselves blend into our surroundings, so don't worry."

"Easy for you to say. Is Ludmila okay?"

"Yes, I had her picked up by chopper, and we have her here in an apartment where you will join her. Did you jazz up the code in your data on the drive?"

"Yes, but I'm nervous about it. If he finds out I screwed the drive, he'll look for me forever."

Understanding his spy's fear, Pollard provided some solace. "Try to relax, man. First, he'll have to take possession of the drive and transport it to what he deems a safe location. Then he'll have one of his techie goons check it out. This is all going to take some time, and you'll be long gone from the scene and in the apartment with your wife."

"Okay, but I'll be scared until I'm in the apartment with Ludmila. She must be a wreck."

"She's fine. The fridge is stocked with food . . . and beer and vodka. We're having new clothes brought in for both of you."

"How long will we be cooped up in there?

"Not sure. Like I told you we need to wait a couple days to see if he's pissed that the data is corrupted because then he'll try to call you. And that's another thing; when you leave the fountain, go to Michigan Avenue and grab an Uber to my office; wait, better yet, have him take you to the AT&T building on Adams and get out. Then walk through the building to the Monroe Street entrance. We'll pick you up there and bring you to my office. Also, turn your cell off so he can't track your location."

"Okay. I hope this plan of yours works. Hey boss, don't hang up yet. What kind of car will I be looking for?"

"It'll be grey Honda Accord with a license plate number ending in 338. Agent Eldrick will pick you up. He is my deputy SAIC."

"Okay."

Anatoly's nerves tightened to the extent they seemed so taut they might snap like a violin or guitar strung to the breaking point. Several cups of regular coffee only exacerbated his tension. Working on bank matters proved almost impossible as his mind shifted to the upcoming trip to Buckingham Fountain. He checked the time on his desktop computer seemingly every ten seconds. His boss had stopped by his cube at ten fifteen to say "hi" and see how his ace cyber analyst was doing and noticed immediately an unusually agitated Anatoly who continually shifted in his chair and couldn't seem to maintain eye contact for more than a few seconds. "Hey Terasenko, why so antsy today? You feel okay? You don't look so good." Roland Hartung asked. He headed up the IT Security Unit as senior vice president.

"No, I'm fine, too much coffee."

"Found any hackers today?"

"What? Oh, I thought I had a good lead, but it turned out to be nothing."

"Oh yeah? What country did it look like was going to hit us this time?"

"It was China, but I verified it is legitimate."

"Well, maybe the next one will be a score for us."

"Yes, we just need to keep surfing."

"Right. Say, I'm a member of the Union League Club, and a few of us are going there for lunch. Want to join us? I have a reservation for noon. It'll take us a few minutes to walk over there, so we're leaving here at about eleven forty-five."

"Oh, sorry boss, I'm meeting a friend for lunch today, but thanks for the invitation."

"Well, maybe next time."

"Right, next time."

"Don't forget we have a staff meeting tomorrow at seven thirty."

"I have it on my calendar." Anatoly rubbed his temples as Hartung walked away. *He will not be happy when I don't show up tomorrow.*

The frazzled analyst noted the time at 10:55 and began checking his desk drawers for things he might want to take with him. He packed a few personal items in his backpack and made a feeble attempt to return to his work, but could not concentrate. Time slowed to a crawl until eleven fifteen. The cafeteria opened at eleven for lunch, so he went downstairs and bought a sandwich and bottle of Pepsi. He visited the men's room at 11:40 and lingered near the elevator long enough to see Hartung's group file into one of the cars on their way to the Union League Club.

He returned to his cube and shut down his computer, perhaps for the last time, exhaled as he glanced around the cube, and then left the office suite.

Puffy white and grey cumulus clouds dotted the sky, and a cool June breeze combined with a mild seventy-four degree temperature provided strong incentive for employees in Chicago's Loop and surrounding area to enjoy alfresco dining at the city's many fine restaurants or a leisurely stroll. Anatoly donned sunglasses and exited his building at 11:50 for the short walk from La Salle Street to Buckingham Fountain, dodging pedestrian traffic on the crowded sidewalks. The harsh winters in Chicago made people pay the price for beautiful days like this. His stomach churned as negative thoughts raced through his mind.

He arrived at the fountain with a minute to spare and blended in with small groups of visitors. A large group of tourists stood on the west side of the fountain against the short fence ringing the monument. A tour guide gesticulated while explaining the history and features of this iconic Chicago landmark.

Anatoly strolled nervously around the fence line from west to north to east and finally arrived at the south side. He noted the benches to his right but stood observing the water spewing from several of the bronze figures and the occasional plume jetting high in the air from the central part of the fountain. The west wind carried a thin mist of water toward the east, encouraging some young visitors to retreat to avoid getting wet while others laughed and allowed the mist to provide a light shower on happy faces. *I wish I could join these people in enjoying this beautiful monument.*

Look at them; they haven't a care in the world. If they only knew what danger exists everywhere, even in downtown Chicago, they wouldn't be laughing and getting their faces wet.

He turned and found a seat at the end of one of the benches. *I sure would like to be able to sit here for hours and take in this magnificent day.* He cast furtive glances in every direction hoping to identify a person who might be the one who would retrieve the thumb drive after he placed it under the bench, but none seemed likely. He also tried to identify which people might be FBI agents, but couldn't find any with certainty.

His phone flashed 12:17, and he pulled his lunch from the backpack and consumed the meal in slow motion to pass the time. At 12:28 he unzipped a small pocket in the backpack and palmed the black thumb drive into his right hand. He pretended to check his pants pockets and then feigned looking for something under the bench using his right hand as if reaching for a piece of paper and deposited the drive on the ground as far under the bench as he could. He then zipped the backpack, shut off his phone, stood, and walked slowly around the monument to the west side and headed then for Adams Street.

He felt a burning on his neck like someone following and breathing on him. Turning around to check would draw attention, so he forced his vision forward. The sidewalks teemed with workers hurrying to and back from lunch as he ordered an Uber ride, and a car appeared in two minutes.

Once on Adams the car stopped in front of the AT&T building on the corner of Adams and Franklin, and he quickly exited and pushed through the revolving door into a lobby opening to an atrium several stories high. The building was built by the firm of Skidmore, Owings & Merrill, completed in 1989 and soared slightly over one thousand feet. Its postmodern architectural style and Gothic detailing accentuated the strong vertical lines. The lobby featured rose-beige and gold colors in the tile floor and on the walls to create a warm, yet imposing great hall effect.

Anatoly had used this welcoming shortcut many times over the years, especially in winter to get a break from the wind; the long vertical and horizontal lines were reminiscent of Frank Lloyd Wright's Prairie Style. This stately edifice remained one of his favorite buildings in the city. He walked at a measured natural pace and arrived at the north end of the lobby opening to Monroe Street. He navigated the tall, heavy revolving door and once out of the building, moved to the side in front of the red granite blocks forming the base of the structure to await his ride.

■ ■ ■

Time slowed against a surging sense of danger for the FBI spy as he stood against the building, checking every grey car and license plate number. *It's almost one o'clock; where the hell is he? I need to get out of downtown and I want to see my wife.* He studied the face of each passerby for . . . what? Bad guys look like ordinary citizens, so he resigned himself to the conclusion that searching the sea of humanity for a Russian killer is futile. *Where is Eldrick?*

At 1:17 a grey Honda Accord, license plate ending in 338, with tinted windows pulled to the curb as the front passenger window rolled down. A large African American man motioned for Anatoly to get in. The driver extended his massive hand, which engulfed Anatoly's. "I'm agent John Eldrick; pleased to meet you, Mr. Terasenko. Sorry I'm a little late—traffic."

"Pleased to meet you, too. Boy, am I glad you're here. How long will it take to get to the office?"

"We're going to take a circuitous route to lose anyone who might be tailing us. Not likely they will, but we'll use an abundance of caution."

"Okay. I won't be able to relax until I'm in the apartment with my wife."

"I can understand that. Now is not a time for this car to drive itself because I'm going to go north for a few blocks and then turn west for a few more before we head south and then toward the office. Let's both keep an eye out in the traffic to see if anything looks suspicious. I'll check the rear-view mirror, which is how we're most likely to spot a tail, but sometimes these bad guys like to come up one side of our car to get a look at who's inside. I don't know if you noticed, but our license plate doesn't have M on it, which would be a dead giveaway that we're government. Did you have lunch?"

"Yes, I had a sandwich and cola at the fountain."

"Did you see any suspicious guys in the area?"

"No, just a whole lot of people out for the lunch hour and one tourist group."

"Great day to be out and about."

Anatoly couldn't focus on the conversation, and frustration began to set in. "I'm really tired; this thing has me emotionally strung out." He hoped the FBI agent would take the hint and just drive.

"Gotcha. Just check the right side of the car every couple minutes if you don't mind, and I'll shut up."

"Thanks, Mr. Eldrick, I appreciate it."

■ ■ ■

Twenty minutes later they arrived at FBI headquarters on Chicago's west side as Eldrick drove quickly into the underground garage. The two men took the elevator to Pollard's office.

"Well, my friend, I see you made it in one piece," Pollard extended his hand and shook with Anatoly.

"Yes, I feel a little better, but I need to see Ludmila."

"Of course, and we'll leave here shortly. Did you have any trouble with the handoff?"

"No, it seemed to go okay. Did your agents see who picked up the drive?"

"It was interesting. You never know what might happen in a situation like this. After you left, an old man in a beret and sport coat using a cane for support wandered over and started looking under the bench. He used his cane to poke the drive out from under the seat and picked it up."

"Was he Markov's guy?"

"We thought so at first. Just like us, the Russians use many disguises to preserve their identity and send us on wild goose chases looking for people who don't exist. Anyway, this old man—he looked like a scientist or college professor—examined the drive for a couple minutes when out of the trees a guy walks fast up to the man, bumps him hard so he falls to the ground. The guy pries the drive out of the scientist's hand and starts to run away." Pollard pauses. "Then the scientist trips the guy with his cane. The Russian drops the drive but grabs it immediately and slugs the old man on the side of his face."

"Oh my God, is he okay?"

"A couple of our agents came to check on him, and later we had him taken to the hospital. Our other two agents followed the thief, but he disappeared into the crowd. We used our drones to track him from the air before he ducked into a building on Michigan Avenue. Our people checked the building but could not find him. My guess is he bolted out the service entrance in back and had a car waiting for him."

"Holy crap, this is like a movie."

"Right, sometimes it seems like one of those Jason Bourne flicks, but this is real life. We have had Markov under surveillance for as long as he's been in the Chicago area. We'll see if he attempts to call you."

"But you told me to turn my phone off so he can't locate me. How will we know if he tries to call?"

Pollard smiled. "John and I will take your phone with us to lunch tomorrow or Sunday at Aureus and turn it on. If Mr. M wants to talk, we'll offer to buy him lunch, but he won't know where you are."

"Wow, are you sure Hollywood isn't out here filming you guys?"

"You should know real life is brutal, Anatoly; just think back to when you lived in Russia. Your parents had to deal with the oppression of the KGB, and your lives were no picnic either under the watchful eye of the GRU, the Main Intelligence Directorate of the Military in Russia."

"Oh yes, I remember those days, and I never want to go back there."

"Right. Why don't you go down to the garage and get into the car.

John will show you which one we'll take to the apartment. I'll be down a few minutes; I'm going to check on the old man at the hospital."

Eldrick led Anatoly to the elevator. The car Pollard would use to transport the spy to the apartment was a four year-old 3 series BMW with tinted windows. The FBI had several foreign model cars to appear discreet and avoid detection since many US government and local agencies use American-made cars with the *M* on the license plate.

The weary SAIC clicked off the call with the nurse's station at the hospital and joined Anatoly in the garage. "The nurse said the old man had a severe wound on the right side of his head and was scheduled for some treatment. They were going to keep him in the hospital for a few days under observation and for testing. However, she said when she checked on him a half hour later, he was gone. She notified security, and they searched the entire floor and then other floors but couldn't find him. Hospital security called the police, and they are taking statements and preparing their report as we speak. Poor guy was apparently picking up something he thought was trash or something he thought you might have lost. Wrong place, wrong time. Now he may end up on the missing persons list."

"That's a shame. This is like the Cold War, but with higher stakes because of all the electronic tools and nuclear weapons countries have access to now. When are we ever going to learn?"

"I know what you mean, but I guess that's why we have jobs. We're going to wait a few minutes after John drives the Honda out; he'll take it home. Then we'll take off for the apartment. This way if anyone followed you here, they'll continue to follow John to his house and will see he's alone."

"But he might be in danger if the bad guys break into his house."

"Believe me, John can take care of himself, and his house is loaded with electronic cameras and other devices I can't mention."

"What if the assholes cut off the power to his house?"

"We installed a generator that kicks in immediately if he loses power, and our people will be notified if anyone attacks the house in any way. We all have these protection tools at our homes."

"Well, I hope he's okay."

"Right. Now, let's go see Ludmila."

■ ■ ■

Pollard smiled as the Terasenkos embraced and cried; the couple swayed as they sobbed and expressed love for each other in Russian. "I'm going home now. I'll check on you every day. Here're a few prepaid phone cards. I have the numbers so I can call you, and you can use them to call me on my government phone, if necessary. Have a great evening." He winked even though they would not see it.

Anatoly phoned Bob on Saturday to see if Markov had tried to contact him on his cell, but Pollard indicated not so far. Pollard told him he and Eldrick were having lunch at Aureus on Sunday figuring two days would be plenty of time for Markov to discover the flash drive contained only bad information.

■ ■ ■

The two FBI agents settled into chairs at their customary table in the corner at Aureus at twelve thirty on Sunday. They nursed glasses of ice tea and ordered an appetizer. At 1:20 Anatoly's phone vibrated. Pollard raised his eyebrows and smiled at Eldrick. "Hello?"

"Who is this?"

"Well, Mr. Markov I presume. How nice to hear your voice. What can I do for you?"

"Who are you?"

"Special Agent in Charge of the Chicago FBI office, Bob Pollard. What is your title these days, Ivan, KGB asshole in charge?" Eldrick held his mouth to stifle laughter.

"So, Mr. Pollard, the FBI pig in charge. Where is Terasenko?"

"Oh don't get so upset. He's in a safe place in Europe on the French Riviera. Where are you?"

"I don't think he's in Europe. I have business with him. Where is he?"

"My friend and I were having a nice lunch until you called and spoiled it. Tell you what, since I'm a nice guy I'll buy you lunch if you'd like to join us so we can talk." A long pause ensued.

The former KGB officer fired an angry face at the phone and mouthed an expletive in Russian. "Okay, I'll come to lunch with you."

"Great, we'll look forward to seeing you. How long before you can be here? We can order for you."

"No, no I'll order when I get there." Markov understood food doctoring is always a potential hazard in the espionage business.

"Okay, that works. I'll give you directions to the restaurant."

"Don't make me laugh; your phone, or I mean Terasenko's phone, tells me where you are. I'll be there in half an hour."

"Super, we can't wait. Goodbye." Markov ended the call without acknowledging. The agents burst into hearty laughter. They placed their food orders and requested refills on the iced tea.

■ ■ ■

Markov arrived at Aureus at one thirty and spotted Pollard immediately. He walked to the table and refused to shake hands with either of his hosts; although Markov maintained an austere countenance, the imposing figure of John Eldrick seemed to intimidate the short, portly Russian.

"Ivan, thank you for joining us; we weren't sure you would," Pollard began the conversation. "Let me introduce you to John Eldrick, deputy SAIC." The three then eased into their chairs. Markov met Eldrick's penetrating gaze with one of his own.

The FBI agents had already ordered, but Pollard told the waiter to hold the meals until Markov's selection would be ready to serve with the other two. "Why don't you order your food and then we can discuss your concerns," Pollard suggested.

"I only want iced tea and spaghetti with meat balls."

Pollard signaled a server who arrived in seconds and took Markov's order.

"Now, my friend, you said you are looking for Anatoly Terasenko?"

"Yes, and I'm sure you know where he is."

"Why do you make that assumption?"

"Cut the shit, Pollard, you're hiding him. Now where is he?"

"Slow down, friend; you're not in a position to be making demands of us. I told you he's in a safe place, and you do not have a need to know where," Pollard leaned forward while placing his forearms on the table.

Markov reclined in his chair and his ample belly bunched up on itself forming a bumpy slope. "He gave me a 'gift,' and it isn't something I like, so I want to return it to him and ask him to give me what he knows I want."

"A gift, you say? What kind of gift?" Pollard enjoyed playing with his arch adversary.

"None of your business."

"Really. Well I guess we're through here. John, let's go." The agents rose to leave.

"Okay, okay wait. He said he had found an interesting article about our homeland he wanted to share with me, but it turned out to be one I have already read."

The food arrived temporarily halting the conversation.

"Ah, I see. So this article is of no use to you, is that what you mean?"

"No time for your little games. Where is Terasenko?"

"Round and round we go, where we stop nobody knows . . ."

"You push me to the limit with your riddles. You know what is on the thumb drive, so let's get serious."

"Serious it is." Pollard squinted, his eyes unblinking. "Like I said before, you have no need to know where he is, and you have no right to any information on the drive. Therefore, you will probably have to spend time and resources yourself to try to hack into the bank's systems. No freebies today."

"We have ways of getting what we want, as you well know."

Pollard flashed a grim look at his lunch guest. "Markov, we have been watching you and your comrades since you came to Chicago, and we know you watch us. So here's something for you to think about. If any harm were to come to Anatoly or his wife, or if we find you have been snooping around the bank's system, we will come after you full force."

Markov leaned forward and formed a sarcastic smile; he was used to the gamesmanship between the various intelligence agencies of both countries. "My country always plays by the rules just like your country. If the bank is hacked, it could be China or your little friend in North Korea, or many other nations that hate the United States."

"If we see it's your country, I will personally visit you, but it won't be social. Remember, we're not in Russia now; we're in the US, and we won't tolerate threats against our citizens and institutions." Pollard leaned back to signal the substance of the meeting was now off the table.

"Too bad for you." Markov rose prompting the agents to rise as well. Eldrick watched Markov's hands and prepared to draw his weapon if the Russian made a threatening move. Markov noticed Eldrick's edginess and laughed. "What, you think I shoot you guys here in this nice restaurant?

You know us better than that." He made no move to shake hands with his adversaries and stepped away from the table, turned, and walked out.

The agents sat down and finished the remainder of their meal and lingered over their iced teas. "I'd almost love to have that bastard try something so I could go after him. He and his goons killed Lorraine, shot Jeremy twice, and me once, and he thinks he can waltz in here and demand we give him the bank's security systems? What a shithead."

"Easy, boss. You know this is the game we've been playing with them for decades, and it's not going to change any time soon, so try to relax."

"You're right, but these assholes made it personal for me. I'd love the opportunity to return the favor—just wishful thinking on my part. Thanks for spending part of your Sunday in this mess, partner."

"Bob, you know the word 'weekend' doesn't exist in our world; Saturday and Sunday are just days, like any of the others, that's all."

"Say hello to Cynthia for me."

"Will do. Call me if you need anything else."

He flashed a grin. "I think maybe I just might have your number, but hopefully I'll not have to use it." The colleagues/best friends shook hands and John then left the restaurant.

Pollard stopped a few feet from the table as Anatoly's phone vibrated. He smiled. "Did you forget something, Markov?"

"Yes. Is that huge black man still with you?"

"Why, what difference does it make?"

"I want to discuss something between only you and me."

"Okay, go ahead."

"Is your friend there?"

"No, he left a few minutes ago."

"Good. I have been working on a research project, and maybe we can help each other."

"How so?"

"I am interested in people who have disappeared and then come back to their lives, or sometimes not. You recall Mr. Jeremy Chambers before he went somewhere—some say maybe into space—but has not returned."

"So?"

"I have found an interesting group of people who have mysteriously vanished, and some have returned."

"Go on."

"One such person appears to be a doctor who lives here in Chicago, a neurosurgeon named Cavallini."

Shit, what now?

"What about him?"

"He was gone for about a year in Germany and then came back here."

"Okay." *Wish I knew where this is going.*

"Do you know him?"

"Maybe."

"If you do, why don't we get together again and share our information?"

"Why would we do that?"

"Come now, Pollard, we are both after the same goal. People who have super powers are very valuable to a country in many ways."

"Do you know if the doctor has these 'special powers'?"

"We have been watching him, and we think he does have them."

"Why?"

"I think we should meet and share what we know about this man."

"And if we meet and share whatever information we have, what then?"

"Maybe you and I could use his skills for our mutual benefit."

"What benefit?"

"Monetary benefit."

"Man, this is really bizarre, Markov. How long do you think our leaders would allow you and me to use the doctor for our exclusive benefit?"

"Of course we would keep our activities confidential. Your president and Putin would never know."

"Are you nuts? Why would the doctor agree to work with the two of us?'

"He is family man, no?"

"So let me get this straight. You want us to hold this innocent American citizen hostage to do our bidding for our mutual financial gain, and if he doesn't cooperate, you want to harm his family?"

"What is your FBI salary?"

"You're a fucking scumbag. You asked the wrong guy to help you with this shitty scheme."

"We know where he lives."

"Don't even think about it, Markov."

"Oh, but I have, Pollard. Good day." Markov tapped off the call. "Wait, Markov . . . Markov." *Holy shit, I need to get to Cavallini quick!*

24

Jeremy woke with a stiff neck after sleeping on the cot behind the bar in Paul's basement rec room. Turning over during the night was an engineering feat, and he didn't think he could last too long if Pollard didn't move him soon. He had tried to use his powers each hour before retiring for the night, but the tank came up empty each time. *Damn, I go from a spaceman with special skills wanted by the Russians to an ordinary slug with no skills who the Russians want to kill because they'll think I could regain my powers. Shit! Doesn't look like I have much upside.*

Paul closed the door to the basement and stumbled down the stairs with a large clothesbasket, which he dropped in the laundry room. He had hidden two small bananas under a shirt in the basket and handed them to his secret guest. "Here, these aren't much, but maybe they'll tide you over 'til later. He whispered. "Any luck with the magic?"

"No, but my neck is stiff from the damn cot; guess I'm human after all."

"I'll go up and when Marie leaves for her book club meeting at nine thirty, I'll cook some breakfast for you and make a couple sandwiches you can put in the little fridge for lunch."

'Thanks. Hey, bud, I hope Pollard can move me soon; I don't want to be a burden to you and Marie."

"Don't even think about it. I'm really glad to see you again, JC, and I'll take care of you for as long need be."

"Yeah, well let's hope for something good to happen."

"Great to see you. We'll just have to think positive. I'm going to get the laundry going and then see if Marie's up and cooking breakfast. Make yourself at home."

"Thanks again, man. See you later."

Paul finished with the wash and bounced upstairs with newfound energy.

Jeremy sat on a stool behind the bar ready to duck if Marie happened to come downstairs. He tried to invoke his powers, but failed once more. He had plugged in his phone and put it on the floor last night. Now fully charged, he called Pollard's government number. "Good morning, boss. I'm still only human."

"Bummer. I haven't had a chance to work on a new place for you; several other emergencies have cropped up. I'll work on it today, though, I promise. How'd it go last night?"

"I slept, but on this cot I ended up with a pain in the neck."

"I can imagine. I need to go, but I'll call you in a couple hours."

"Roger that." Jeremy clicked off the connection.

25

Although she normally didn't drink coffee after lunch because the caffeine kept her awake at night, Stephanie headed to the cafeteria for a large cup of Seattle's Best regular blend and did not add sugar or cream. She developed her goal for the afternoon to craft a synopsis of the information she had assembled with her conclusions at the end. If it were going to be perfect, it would require sharp focus.

Her phone buzzed—Brad's number. She let it go to voice mail. *He's the last person I want to talk to now.* She tasted her coffee at frequent intervals until it had cooled to allow for larger swallows. Yellow legal pad pages covered her desk, forcing her to place a few on the floor. The excitement and importance of the project and the caffeine launched her heart rate into high gear. FiberLink, the city of Vista Nueva, the accounting irregularities, the Claypoole brothers, and Brad's involvement played out like a dystopian puzzle. *My mind is spinning; I need a break. Three forty-five already?*

A quick stop at the rest room and then to the cafeteria for another infusion of the strong coffee, but in a smaller cup this time, provided a chance for her to cleanse a brain overloaded with facts, speculation, anger, and fear. *How can Brad be mixed up in this mess?*

She reclined in her chair sampling the fresh brew and reviewing the first draft of the report. A second pass through the document resulted in some fine-tuning and careful thought about the conclusions.

The screen on the last page flashed accusations, which if true could lead to legal trouble for the individuals, and if untrue, maybe even her firm in this ugly play. Stephanie's heart raced. *I can't say these things. What did I learn in law school: gather the facts, define the issues, apply the law, and render a decision. But I'm not a judge; my role is to present the facts objectively leading to possible dispositions. Other people will ultimately decide where it goes from here; glad I don't have be the one with the final say.* She quickly revised the language in the conclusion section with qualifying terms like "may," "might," and "could." She felt her heart beat closer to a normal rate. After printing out a copy of her report and placing it on top of the yellow legal pages with her notes, she placed the bundle in a new file folder, which was added to her other work papers for the FiberLink job in a large expanding folder and then put the complete file in her credenza. Although her firm had been committed to automating the review process for several years, she routinely printed documents and included them with handwritten notes in her files as backup in the event of electrical or software issues.

She collapsed into the contour of her chair and rocked for several minutes. The clock read 5:22. *I'm sure Al and Bev haven't left yet; most everyone at the firm is inundated with work, so we all work into the evening almost every day. However, the late hours offer a residual benefit—a chance to make better time on the freeways for the trip home.* "Well, here goes," she muttered out loud. She sent the email to Al and Bev and asked when they would like to meet.

Replies snapped into her inbox in less than a minute. Al wanted the two of them to come to his office immediately. Stephanie finished her coffee, grabbed her folio, and headed for the CEO's office.

■ ■ ■

Stephanie and Bev arrived at Al's office almost simultaneously. Lucille buzzed her boss and told the two ladies to go in. Al greeted both with warm handshakes and motioned them to the conference table. "Well, this job has blown up, and it's still a few weeks until Fourth of July fireworks." Both ladies nodded. "Steph, walk us through the facts beginning with the first time you determined something that wasn't quite right."

"Sure. It was when I noticed the large commission paid to BW, LLC and the expense on the city's income statement for the consulting fee. Earle Claypoole told me his company had won the consulting contract. He couldn't produce the RFP (Request for Proposal) when I initially asked for it, but said his firm had done business with the city many times in the past, and the RFPs were only a formality because Vista Nueva had been happy with FiberLink's work. When he did send it to me, it looked like he had doctored some sections of the proposal, or maybe even forged them." Al and Bev shook their heads. "That led me to the city's accounting department and the weird booking for the fees in an account that didn't make sense to me. In the meantime, I get the call from the Russian guy or wherever he was from telling me to stay away from FiberLink." Al and Bev took notes. "Then Mr. Cohen of the city's external audit firm explained why the city did its accounting in such a strange way, and it sort of cleared it up. The real kicker came when I spoke to Ms. Kirkwood in Vista Nueva's purchasing department, and she told me the mayor instructed her to buy some equipment and software FiberLink recommended in their report.

She said many of the recommendations were for outdated items. She also told me she had to purchase some of the items the city doesn't already have from FiberLink at greatly inflated prices. I was shocked; the mayor, Phil Claypoole, is Earle Claypoole's brother, which adds another twist to the story. I started to connect the dots, and the picture doesn't look pretty."

"Boy, it sure doesn't. Bev, where do we go from here?" Al asked. "I'll let agent Pawley know, and I'll send him Steph's report."

"Good. If this proves out to be fraud, I'm certain the media will have a field day with it."

"Yes, and that's why we need to keep it confidential until the FBI completes its investigation and the Department of Justice decides how to handle any legal issues," Bev cautioned.

"I should mention Brad called when I was working on this report, but I let it go to voice mail. I'm sure he'll call again soon, and Earle Claypoole will also be following up with me on his consulting review and the status of our appraisal of their risk program. What do you want me to do?" Stephanie asked.

"As far as Brad is concerned, you can speak to him, but of course don't share anything about our review, and don't accept any invitations for dates. For Claypoole, just stall him and tell him we're short of resources because it's summer, so people are on vacation, etcetera. We need to buy time to allow the Feds to dig into this mess," Bev said.

Stephanie let the mild insult from Bev regarding not sharing information about the review pass, but a slight frown revealed irritation. *Damn! I'm a partner for God's sake; how can she think I would ever blab about what I know? I don't give a shit if she's under pressure and just spewing the company line. She owes me more respect than that.* "Sure, no problem; I'm well aware of the rules." The response surprised Bev, who shot a questioning glance at Stephanie, but then turned to face Al.

"Bev, let Steph and me know what Pawley says. I think we're done here," Al adjourned the meeting. "Steph, hang on for a minute." Bev gathered her folio and left the office.

"Sure."

"I saw the look on your face when she told you not to say anything about this fiasco, and I know you were upset, but she was just touching all the bases like she's trained to do, so just let it slide off your back, okay?"

"I guess you're right, but being treated like I'm some teenybopper pisses me off. It's been happening all my teenage and adult life, and I'm tired of it. I'm thirty-four and want people to treat me like I have a brain."

"And you're absolutely right. Just cut her some slack; she's one of our most dedicated employees."

"Okay." Ripples of frustration subsided but would take a while longer to dissipate. She let herself out.

■ ■ ■

Special Agent Mark Pawley of the Los Angeles FBI office, which is responsible for Orange County in addition to some other contiguous counties, read Stephanie Murphy's report of issues at FiberLink and the City of Vista Nueva on his iPad. *Holy shit, another case involving the Murphy family. Great people. I wish they could just enjoy their lives, but ever since Jeremy Chambers disappeared eight or nine years ago, members of the family have been plagued by danger from Russian thugs chasing Jeremy, and they even kidnapped his wife, Megan. Now the younger daughter, Stephanie, uncovers this fraud scheme. I hope we can button this one up without any harm coming to her.* He called his boss, Hector Gomez, Assistant Director in Charge (ADIC) of the LA office, to give him the thumbnail sketch of the report and then emailed it to him. They discussed maintaining confidentiality as their investigation commenced, and Pawley said he would update the boss daily, or more often if the situation dictated.

"Hello, Bev, it's Pawley. I just read Stephanie's report. Looks like we have boys helping themselves to some money that doesn't belong to them. I'll have a couple of agents who will see what details they can dig up on the Claypoole brothers on a covert basis and another agent who will research Brad Wolfe. We need a little time to develop profiles and look into their personal finances."

"I thought you would approach it that way. One thing to keep in mind— Brad Wolfe has been contacting Steph frequently and has taken her out on dates a couple times in the last two weeks. I think she said they dated for several years, and then about two years ago he dumped her. Now he's come around to maybe reestablish the relationship. I told her not to ignore him, but not to share what we know and not to see him, but he is apparently very persistent—calls her all the time and wants to take her out, so we need to find a delicate balance in how she interacts with him. If she were to refuse to see him, we don't want him to feel like she's on to the scheme, you know what I mean?"

"Yes, you're right. We'll move as fast as we can to wrap up our work and then hand it off to the DOJ. Do you think this Brad fella might try to harm Stephanie?"

"I don't know him at all, only what Steph has told us about him.

Sounds like he's a party boy and likes the good life. She said she never quite knew his financial situation, but she said his car was repo'd a while back. I suppose we can't rule out he might try to get physical with her."

"Tell her I'll assign an agent to trail her for protection. If this guy tries anything, we'll do whatever is necessary to keep her safe. I'm also going to have one of our agents who specializes in forensic accounting work with her on the documentation and financial issues."

"Good. I'll tell her. I assume you and I will maintain a line of communication."

"Oh absolutely, both ways. Hopefully we can get this case resolved with no one getting hurt."

"Yes, we all want that result."

"Talk soon. Bye."

He contacted several agents and briefed them on the facts and their assignments and then emailed the report to them. *This job doesn't get any easier.*

26

Bob Pollard drove to his condo, contemplating how to explain his conversation with Markov and the new threat he posed to the neurosurgeon.

The weary agent poured pretzels into a bowl and sat down in his chair as blood drained from his face. A couple of deep breaths to compose tense nerves, then he told his phone to dial Dominic Cavallini's cell. "Hello, Doc, it's Pollard. How are you?"

"I'm fine. Did you finish the plan for our project?"

"No, haven't even started on it. Something important has come up and it involves you. Can you talk?"

"As a matter of fact I'm at our place in St. John; the whole family is here, kids and grandkids. I'm on the beach and everyone's in the water, so I can talk. What happened?"

"Sorry to interrupt your vacation. I had a conversation with a Russian intelligence officer about a matter that doesn't concern you, but then he tells me he has been working on finding other people who may have special powers like Jeremy Chambers.'"

"Okay, but what does it have to do with me?"

"He said he has done research to locate other people like Jeremy and you are one he has identified." Pollard paused to allow the doctor to process this startling news. "He said if I don't meet with him to share what he and I know about you to get what he wants regarding the other matter, he'll use you and your family as bargaining chips."

"What?" Bargaining chips, like pieces of trash? Sir, I'm damn tired of all this cops and robbers shit."

"Understood, but we need to address the possibility you and your family may be in danger. Here's my idea for us . . ."

"Bullshit! I don't care about your ideas; get him off my back now."

"Dr. Cavallini, I'm truly sorry you're involved against your will, but I need to make sure you and your family are protected."

Cavallini shook his head and lowered his voice. "Mr. Pollard, your agency has dragged me through all kinds of hell the last few years, and it has to stop now. Give this Russian asshole whatever he wants, and my family's safety will be guaranteed."

"I wish it were that simple. Our country's security may be jeopardized if I give him what he wants because it will lead to more of these demands."

"I don't give a shit; you can't put my family at risk; it's totally unacceptable."

"I understand how you feel, but I'm going to assign agents to provide protection for you and your family."

"No, you need to put our lives first. Give him what he wants."

"Let me ask you a crucial question. Did you travel to the place where Jeremy Chambers was, and if so, do you have powers similar to his?"

The doctor squirmed in his beach chair. *I don't want Sharon or the rest of the family to know about my time in space and my special skills because they would be in even more danger.* "You'll have to make your own decision on that; my family's safety is all I care about."

"Why can't the answer be between just you and me?"

Cavallini pondered the possibility; everything in his life the past few years had been building to the point where he was forced to share his secrets with someone. *I guess if I am going to disclose, telling the FBI is the best option.* "Okay. Yes, I do have unique powers, but they are not exactly the same as Jeremy's. I won't get into how or why mine are different because it's too complex, and you don't need to know anyway. So, now that you know about me, how can you protect Sharon and the rest of my family without us telling them the truth?"

"Thank you for sharing. I know it can't be easy. I've suspected you might be like Jeremy for some time, but it's good to get your confirmation.

I have thought about what we can do to protect your family, and frankly, the options are limited. I can assign agent surveillance for all of you at all times without your family knowing. I'm sure the director in DC will lend me some resources from other offices based on the nature of this situation." He paused to allow time for the doctor to ponder this best solution. "Of course another option is to let your family members know there is a reason they need protection, and we could move them to safe houses, but their lives would be disrupted and I'm sure they'd be terrified."

"I don't want them living in fear for who knows how long. Can't you go after these bastards and either take them out or lock them up?"

"Nice idea, but the Russian intelligence organization is like a snake; you cut off the head and another one takes its place. Besides, the relationship between our two countries is so complicated at every level that moving on Markov and his team now could trigger a catastrophic international incident." Bob paced the floor in his den. "I have another question. Since you have special powers, can we leverage them to assist in protecting your family in a covert way?"

"Possibly, but it will be tough to use my skills without them noticing and asking questions I don't want to answer. I guess for now your idea of watching them is the best plan."

"Not ideal, but we'll have to make it work. I'll put the wheels in motion. When will you be returning to Chicago?"

"We're here for nine more days."

"Okay. If you notice anything unusual before I can get some agents down to St. John, call me. I should have a team on the way by tomorrow night, and I'll stall Markov. Again I'm sorry, Dr. Cavallini."

"Yes, me too. Goodbye."

"Bye." Bob pulled a beer from the fridge and settled into his recliner. *Damn, this is getting crazy complicated. The director will be thrilled when I lay this one on him. I wonder how many other people have been where Jeremy was taken and how many have returned to earth and how they are using their powers. I hope the doctor doesn't lose his like Jeremy has. So far, it appears the Russians don't have any of these space people, or Markov wouldn't be so hell bent on using Cavallini as a pawn.*

27

Another night of twisted rolling and turning in the restricted boundaries of the cot in Paul's basement rec room aggravated the stiffness in Jeremy's neck, and now his lower back started to bark. *How am I going to survive any more nights in this damn mummy casket?* He sat on the edge of the cot rubbing tired eyes and checked the time on his cell: 6:37. He used the bathroom and retreated behind the bar waiting for Paul to bring breakfast. A quick attempt to see if his skills returned failed once again. Despair filtered through his mind as he checked the news and sports results on his phone to kill some time, but he was reluctant to leave the cover of the bar area in the event Marie decided to come downstairs unexpectedly.

At 7:10 Paul appeared with some coffee, cereal and a banana. He didn't want to cook eggs or bacon because Marie would wonder why he was avoiding his normal routine of only making coffee and waiting for her to join him and cook the meal. "How'd you sleep, JC?"

"I'm grateful for your hospitality, but the cot is twisting my body in ways I never imagined it could survive. Other than that, I'm okay."

"Here is your first gourmet meal of the day. Once Marie leaves for her book club meeting, I'll cook a great meal for lunch."

"Thanks."

"Have you talked to Pollard yet?"

"No. If I don't hear from him by nine thirty I'll call him."

"I wish we could let Carl and Larry know you're back."

"I know. I can't wait to see them."

"I'm going back upstairs. Call or text me on my cell if you need anything."

"Will do, and thanks again."

Paul settled into a chair in the great room nursing a cup of steaming coffee while he browsed favorite sites on his cell. After finishing the coffee and completing a routine circuit of his favorite sites on the phone, a yawning spell preceded an overpowering weight of fatigue as a curtain of sleep pushed his eyelids down.

■ ■ ■

Since Paul's plan of sequestering Jeremy in the basement without Marie finding out has worked so well, the secret guest decided to catch the baseball highlights on ESPN with the sound turned off. He sat in a comfortable chair and put his stocking feet on the coffee table.

At 8:05 he thought he heard the shuffling of footsteps on the carpeted stairs. He looked for a place to hide, but he was in no man's land and only had time to dive between the coffee table and couch but banged his elbow on the table.

"What was that? Is someone down here?" Marie dropped the laundry basket at the bottom of the stairs and cautiously approached the TV area furniture cluster. "Who are you? I'll call the police. Paul, Paul, come here."

Jeremy rose rubbing his elbow. "Hi Marie, it's me, Jeremy. Sorry I scared you."

"Jeremy? You don't look like Jeremy, he has brown hair and no beard."

Paul stumbled as he tried to hustle down the stairwell. "Marie, it's okay, hon. It's Jeremy, and we need to hide him here for a while." He turned to his friend. "Sorry, bud, I fell asleep upstairs."

"Well, we'll just have to make the best of it. My fault anyway for not staying behind the bar." He walked to Marie whose expression flashed a combination of fear, joy, and then recognition. "I'm sorry about this, Marie, but when I came back to earth a few weeks ago, I just wanted to see Paul, and now I've screwed things up for both of you. I needed a disguise so the bad guys would have trouble finding me, and now I've lost the special powers I used to have."

Marie's face gradually faded into a smile and she embraced her long-lost friend. "Well, you scared the crap out of me, but I'm so glad to see you." She held Jeremy tight in a long hug. "You haven't aged since I last saw you; how can that be?"

"Great to see you, too, Marie. Not aging is one of the benefits for being gone so long. Anyway, I have to tell you, you can't say anything to anyone that you have seen me. Since I lost my powers I can't program your mind to prevent you from letting someone know I'm in your house, so I have to rely on your promise not to tell, okay?"

"I promise." She turned to her husband. "Should I cancel my book club meeting today?"

Jeremy answered before Paul could speak. "No, go ahead with your normal activities. If the jerks are watching, you need to go about the things you normally do."

"Well, okay then. Can I make you some eggs or pancakes?"

"Pancakes would great. Thanks."

The men watched Marie ascend the stairs, and soon the aroma of breakfast food from the stove wafted down the stairwell.

"Do you think she'll be able to keep my secret?"

"She's always been partial to you and Megan, so I'm sure we can count on her not to blab. Are you going to tell Pollard about Marie finding out?"

"Not sure. Like you said, we can trust her to keep quiet, so I don't want to burden him with any more of my fuckups. But I do want to see what he's up to and if he's thought of a new hiding place for me."

"We'll keep our fingers crossed, but I like having you here; it's been a long time since we had a chance to spend some time together."

"I know. It's fun for me, too. I just wish it were under better circumstances." He opened his phone and called the Chicago SAIC as Paul trudged upstairs.

"Pollard here, hi Jeremy. How'd it go last night? Did your powers come back?"

"Hi, boss. No, I'm still sterile. Been sleeping on a cot and have some aches and pains, but okay otherwise. Do you have a new home for me?"

"Not yet, but I'm working on it."

"What else is going on?"

"Are you alone?"

"Yes."

"We've had some trouble with our Russian friends; they are putting pressure on the Terasenkos for some information we don't want to give them."

"What information?"

"Not important. They're threatening some nasty consequences if we don't give them what they want, but we're working on some plans of our own."

"Can I help?"

"Not without your special skills. I need to ask you a question." He contemplated briefly the best way to ask and decided the direct approach would work best. "Do you know Dr. Dominic Cavallini?"

"Why do you ask?"

"Because he's like you; taken away for a year back in the late '90s, and when he returned, he told me he has skills like yours. The damn Russians are using him and his family as leverage to get the same information I mentioned before."

"What? Well, yes, I know him and we've become close friends. I can't believe those asshole Russians are using him and his family in this chess game. Are you going to help him?"

"Of course. I'm borrowing agents from offices around the country to protect him and his family. I'm also sequestering the Terasenkos, as well as you. We're stretched pretty thin."

"Sounds like it. I need to get my skills back so I can help. Maybe if my space bosses see Cavallini is in trouble they'll restore my powers."

"That would be nice. Had a call from agent Pawley in California, and he said Megan's sister, Stephanie, is involved with a white-collar crime situation, and the LA office is providing protection for her."

"Steph? What the hell is going on? Is she in trouble?"

"No, she has a client they suspect might be skimming money from the city of Vista Nueva. They're still gathering the facts, but it appears her old boyfriend may be part of the scam."

"Wow, Brad Wolfe? I guess I can believe it; he's always promoting the playboy image, likes to play the big shot, and although he apparently makes a lot of money, he's always in debt, in over his head."

"He may be in deep shit this time. Once they have the case together, they'll arrest those involved and refer the case to the DOJ."

"Steph's a great kid—smart, gorgeous, and a good athlete. I hope she doesn't get hurt in this mess."

"Right. I'm sure the LA office will keep her safe. I need to make some calls; talk to you later."

"Okay, bye."

Holy shit, he knows about Cavallini. And the Terasenkos have to hide, Steph's in trouble—what the hell else can go wrong? Those fucking Russians.

28

Brad Wolfe left his final sales call of the day in Irvine. He checked the time—5:47—and smiled as he would have time to do some reconnaissance on Stephanie Murphy before leaving for his dinner engagement at seven thirty with the Claypoole brothers at Martin's, a high-end restaurant on Pacific Coast Highway in north Laguna Beach.

Traffic started to build as he took the 405 north to the 73 into Newport Beach. He parked in the Fashion Island lot across the street from the office building where Shields & Fitch rented three floors of office suites. He knew Steph worked later than five or five thirty, like most of her colleagues, so arriving in the shopping mall lot at 6:25 should require only a short wait until her car emerged from the employee section of the parking garage. He tapped the button on his phone to call her, but as usual she let it go to voice mail. *I really need to talk to her; it's been a while, and Earle hasn't heard from her either. I don't like this silent treatment. I need to get her out on a date so I can find out what's happening.*

At 6:46 Steph's car exited the garage and turned left heading for PCH. She sat in the passenger seat as the car followed her program instruction while she checked email on her cell. She and Brad had mutual friends who told him she had purchased a condo in Huntington Beach on an upper floor with a partial ocean view. He followed at a reasonable distance to avoid detection but did not notice a silver Nissan Sentra three car lengths behind him as Special FBI agent Jesus Garcia recognized him from the pictures provided by agent Pawley and the license plate number on his car.

The condo building, inland four blocks, provided outside parking for its owners, and Steph's car obediently pulled into her assigned space. Still engaged with her phone, the presence of Brad's car in an empty space directly across from her did not arouse suspicion. Brad walked to the passenger side of her car and tapped on the window, startling her as she fumbled the cell.

"Hey babe, roll down the window." He gestured by rolling his hand from top to bottom. She lowered it half way.

"You scared the crap out of me. Why are you here?" She forced an unsympathetic expression to mask anxious fear.

He held his arms off to his sides, palms facing her. "What am I supposed to do? You never answer the phone or reply to my friendly emails."

"My job takes most of my time."

"Well, you need a break from the grind, babe. Remember, we said we were gonna go to the movies one of these weekends? It's been four or five weeks since then." He leaned against the roof with both hands.

"Don't call me babe, and I never said I would go. I told you when we had lunch I wasn't going to get back into a relationship with you."

"Aw, come on, we always had fun back when we were good. We got along fine at lunch a few weeks ago."

"You're making me regret I ever agreed to go out with you then. Pleave me alone."

"Steph, we can still be friends, go places, and have some fun. Why can't you see that?"

"Brad, why can't you see we're done, and I don't want to see you anymore?" She attempted to open the door, but he blocked it. "Let me out."

"Not until we plan a weekend together. Maybe Vegas or San Fran. We'll have a ball."

"Let me out, or I'll set off the alarm."

"No, you're not going to do that, Missy." He grasped her right arm immobilizing it. "I'm not leaving until you say yes."

"Oh, I think you'll be leaving in less than one minute," agent Garcia walked to the car and grasped the larger man's arm with a hand like a steel claw.

"Who the fuck are you, pal. This is none of your business, so get lost."

"Doesn't matter who I am; you're bothering this young lady, and it seems like she doesn't want to talk to you. Now let go, or you'll have more trouble than you ever dreamed of." Brad noticed the shoulder holster under the man's sport coat housing what looked like a Glock 22, .40 caliber.

"Are you a cop or something? Me and my girlfriend were just having a nice chat, nothing wrong with that, so you can leave."

Garcia squeezed Brad's arm and punched him in his ribs on the left side. Brad released his grip on Steph and reached for his ribs, his face reflecting severe pain. "I warned you, but you just kept running your big mouth. Now get away from this lady and don't ever try to touch her again." He shoved the hulking man from the car.

Brad staggered toward his car coughing to catch a breath. "I'll see you later, asshole." He slumped into his car and punched the button for home.

"Thanks, Mr. Garcia. I didn't think he was going to let me go.'"

"My pleasure, Ms. Murphy. You have my number, so don't hesitate to call. I'll be watching out for you every day so I don't think Mr. Brad will bother you again. I think he saw my gun, and I didn't tell him I'm FBI. We have a rotation of agents keeping an eye on you twenty-four/seven."

■ ■ ■

Brad drove to the entrance to the parking lot and then pulled to the curb with his right turn blinker on. His ribs screamed as he rubbed them, and he continued coughing while breathing spasmodically with great effort. *Son of a bitch, who is that guy? I think he's an undercover cop with the gun in a shoulder holster instead of in his pocket. I'm going to get some of my hockey buds and teach the bastard a lesson.*

He drove to Martin's, an upscale restaurant on PCH, and valeted the car. Breathing improved, he checked in at the desk at 7:30 and headed for the restroom. He splashed cold water on a grimacing face and returned to await the arrival of the Claypoole brothers who walked into the waiting area at 7:35 laughing at a shared joke. They shook hands with Brad. The hostess led them to a table next to a window with a view of the Pacific Ocean on the opposite side of PCH.

"Well, loverboy, how're you doing with the little consultant?" Earle asked.

"Not too good. I followed her to her condo and talked to her in the parking lot because she won't answer my calls. I tried to convince her to spend a weekend with me in Vegas or San Francisco, but she said she doesn't want to see me anymore. I had hold of her arm and said I wasn't going to leave until she agreed, but then this short Mexican guy shows up and punches me in the ribs. He had a gun, so I think he's a cop, the little bastard."

"Shit. Things seem to be going south in a hurry, pal. If he's a cop we need to lay off the girl; we can't afford a high profile with the fucking police," Phil said.

"I'm thinking the opposite, boys. It's time to play some damn hardball with her."

"Are you fucking crazy? We need to keep what we're doing under the radar," Earle added. The server took their dinner orders and poured a glass of Cabernet for each. They toasted and attacked the delicious pretzel bread.

"Wait, hear me out, guys. I'll round up some of my hockey friends, and we'll mark up her car with our keys when it's in the employee garage where she works. Then I'll have my Russian friend call her at work—she won't answer, but he'll leave a message that if she doesn't back away from her contract with FiberLink, she could get hurt."

"Damn, Brad we went over this before; we don't want any criminal stuff. Can't you get that through your head?" Earle said.

"Don't worry, it's just to scare her and get her thinking about her own safety."

"I don't like it. What about that cop?" Phil asked.

"He won't see us scratch her car, and my Russian friend will only make phone calls, so she won't be physically hurt. We'll only be screwing her up mentally. I know her; she doesn't do well under pressure, and she'll back off the audit."

The meals arrived, temporarily quelling conversation. The men savored the prime steaks and fresh side orders of mashed potatoes and creamed spinach as the server refilled their wine glasses.

Earle nodded toward Brad. "If this blows up, it's going to be your ass, bud, because we'll say we had nothing to do with it. We had a good thing going for almost ten years running this scam, and now this little bitch is exposing us. I don't want to do any time in the damn pen."

"Easy, none of us want that kind of trouble. Tell you what, if this plan doesn't motivate her to leave us alone, we'll stop trying to scare her and see where the audit goes." Brad messaged bruised ribs and slurped his wine.

"Okay, but what if she figures out how our scam works?" Phil asked.

"We'll just say it was oversight. She already knows my company doesn't have strong internal security processes," Earle said.

"Do you think they'll be smart enough to link the funds from the phony consulting contract back to us?" Phil posed.

"The shell company and moving the money through several accounts should cover our tracks," Earle said.

"I hope so, bro." Phil exhaled and loosened his tie. "I still don't like the idea of scratching her car. All the parking garages have a million cameras, and she'll know you had something to do with it."

"Okay, okay. We'll forget keying the car and just stay with the phone call," Brad agreed.

Earle ordered an after dinner liqueur, and they toasted the now-precarious status of a plan revealing cracks.

29

Bob Pollard arrived home at eight fifteen after a long day and night in the office orchestrating strategies for his various ongoing cases. He changed into shorts and a tee, found the last beer in the fridge, and thrust an exhausted body into his recliner. He checked email on his phone and replied to agents around the country working the usual mix of diverse investigations. The phone buzzed, interrupting his response to an agent in Arizona working a drug case. "Pollard."

"Mr. Pollard, it's Dom Cavallini. We have a problem here in St. John."

"Hello, Doc. What is it?"

"Since you called yesterday I have noticed a couple shifty men hanging around the resort, and they appear to be watching me and my family. When will your agents be here?"

"I checked with them earlier today, and they said they're booked on a flight at 2:20 arriving in Miami at 6:33. They were to change planes and fly to St. John at seven forty-five and be there at about eight thirty, so you should see them soon."

"How will I know who they are?"

"Don't worry, they know who you are and will find you in a discreet manner so your family won't know their identities. In the meantime, keep your eye on the guys you mentioned, and if they make a move on you or anyone in your family call me immediately, and I'll get the local police involved."

"I told you I don't want my family mixed up in this crap."

"Right, but if someone is threatening you, we need to head it off, even if it turns out to be a false alarm."

"Okay, but this is getting scary."

"Try to remain calm, and if the bad guys move on your family before my agents get there, use your powers in a subtle way so your folks aren't aware of what's happening."

"Easier said than done."

"I know, but if they question you, just pass it off as coincidence."

"I'll try to figure out a way to do it; no other choice. But if it doesn't work, I will have big problems with Sharon and the others."

"Hopefully it won't come to that. Talk to you later."

"Goodbye."

■ ■ ■

Dr. Cavallini gathered his wife, two daughters and two young grandchildren and propelled them to his condo in the resort. The kids wanted to know why they couldn't spend more time in the ocean, and Sharon fired a questioning look at him, having noticed the urgency in his voice and uncharacteristic, panicky manner. Dominic forced a smile she pierced like a knife though lemon meringue pie, so he knew he owed her an explanation when they were alone.

"What the hell's going on?" She cornered him in their bedroom, hands on hips.

"Did you see the sky? A big thunderstorm is heading this way."

"So what? It rains for a while almost every day here at this time of year. We could've moved into the lobby."

"Right, but the thunder will scare the kids."

"I don't know what's going on with you, but we can't be afraid of the ten million things that could happen every day. We came down here to relax and have fun, remember?"

"And we have been having fun and will have some more tomorrow, I promise."

Sharon shook her head, picked up some clothes, and headed for the bathroom to change.

Holy shit, I hate lying to her. Pollard's people better get here soon.

The frazzled doctor found some ice cream in the freezer and polled his troops for orders. The kids sat at the kitchen island while the adults enjoyed their bowls of the creamy treat in the great room.

Sharon emerged in casual clothes, launched a menacing frown at her husband, and then joined the kids.

Cavallini's phone buzzed; he juggled his ice cream, finally pushing it onto a table. Hands freed, he checked the number, which had a Chicago area code, but he didn't recognize the exchange. He rose, walked out on the patio and closed the sliding door. "Hello."

"Hi, Dr. Cavallini. My name is Howard Pruitt. I work for Bob Pollard, and I'm here with agents Striekar and Bressler. When can we meet?"

"I'm in a tough spot here. I don't want my family to know what's happening, so I need to be careful where I go. I think my wife already suspects something is going on because I'm very concerned for my family, and I guess she can see it in the way I'm acting even though I'm trying to appear low key."

"Understandable. If it's not possible to meet, can you describe the men you observed watching you and your family?"

Cavallini provided descriptions of the perceived Russian thugs and agent Pruitt reassured the distressed neurosurgeon. The agent said he would call in the morning and also gave him the phone numbers of the other agents as they would be rotating around the clock on this protection assignment. Cavallini plugged the information into his phone.

The doctor returned to his condo; Sharon joined him in the kitchen and whispered. "Who was on the phone?"

"Oh, it was the one of the docs from the hospital asking for a second opinion." Sharon's skepticism was palpable, but she did not press him.

After forty-five minutes of TV and board games, members of the family said their good nights and drifted off to bathrooms and bedrooms.

30

After Marie Torchetti cooked breakfast for her husband and special guest, she left for her weekly book club meeting at the home of one of her girlfriends. Paul and Jeremy sat in front of the TV in the basement rec room discussing old times and how both their lives had taken weird turns the last eight or nine years.

"I'm so thankful you were given the ability to cure my cancer . . . twice! I can't ever repay you for that."

"You already have by being my best friend and supporter when we worked at Castle Rook. You were the only person who accepted what was happening to me; you never questioned it."

"I guess I had an advantage of witnessing a couple of those strange occurrences later on, so it was easier for me to believe some powerful force influenced you."

"Right, but before you saw a couple of those events, I had already been affected by the force, and you listened to my crazy story and jumped in to help. Friends like you are hard to find." The men executed a fist bump.

"Do you need anything else from me?"

"No, bud. The food in your restaurant here is out of this world; pardon the pun."

"Okay then, I'm going upstairs to make some business calls. See you at lunchtime." Paul shuffled up the carpeted stairs.

Jeremy called Pollard and both quickly learned nothing new had transpired at either end, resulting in a brief conversation. The exhausted time traveler quickly tired of the recycling sports stories on ESPN and news on ABC. He clicked off the TV and checked his phone but found nothing of interest. With pains still pulsating in his neck and back in rhythm with his heartbeat, he stretched out on the couch for a nap.

■ ■ ■

Paul's descent on the steps to the basement alerted his light-sleeping guest. "Ah, I see you found a good place to rest your aches and pains."

"Yeah, this is much better. I feel like I actually got some sleep. What did you bring for lunch?"

"I cooked some tilapia on the grill out on the deck. We also have Caesar salad, asparagus, fresh croissants with real butter, fruit for dessert, and iced tea to drink." He placed the tray on the coffee table, and the men ate while watching *The Leadoff Man* on Comcast Sports Net before the Cubs afternoon game against the Mets. "How's your consulting business going?" Jeremy asked.

"I've been lucky; many of my former clients at Castle Rook have taken me on to continue assisting them. No complaints and I really like setting my own schedule. The money isn't bad, either."

"Good for you, but then I always knew a guy as smart as you would do well after the fiasco at Castle. If I ever get out of this ridiculous life I've been leading I'd love to join you. I could help you develop clients who are in the energy field to open up a new business line for you."

"Great idea. Let's plan on it; we'd make a great duo, so hurry up and make all the bullshit in your life disappear."

"I'm tryin', man. Can't wait to be just an ordinary human again.

Maybe since I lost my powers the bosses are sending me a message that it's okay for me to go back to my former life. I'll have to be careful, though because the Russians won't believe I'm normal and will want to kill me just to be safe."

"Well, we need to keep you hidden so they can't find you. In the meantime, I'm grateful you're helping the FBI fight these assholes."

"I'm not much help lately, but if I get my skills back, I can continue to do some good things for Bob."

"I'm gonna head upstairs; I have a conference call in twenty minutes. Let me know if you need anything."

"Will do, and thanks again for everything you've done for me."

Jeremy watched a couple innings of the game, but felt drowsy after the large meal. He settled in on the couch again and fell asleep immediately. He dreamed of his job in space and wondered if he would ever be called back. The intense tug of his exposure to a utopian life and the tranquility of a far-away place where things worked and people behaved like they should serve as addicting nectar in his mind. He longed for the life in the space city free of fear, hate, greed, and all the other foibles of mankind on earth.

The buzzing of his phone pulled him away from warm memories of an environment so perfect he wished it could be duplicated on earth even for one day so people could know what's possible. "Hello."

"Jeremy, it's Dom Cavallini. Can you talk?"

"Good to hear from you; sure, I can talk. Pollard told me about your situation down there in St. John. Are you okay?"

"So far, but I've seen some creepy guys eyeballing me and my family. Pollard sent some agents down here, but I'm in a bad position because I'm trying to keep my talents secret from my wife and the others. If I have to use the skills to protect us by taking one or more of these assholes out, my family will wonder how I did it."

"Wow, I see what you mean. Why did you call me?"

"I had an idea; if you can transport down here and use your powers to neutralize these guys, I won't have to use mine, and my year in space will remain a secret. Can you help me?"

"Man, I wish I could, Dom, but my powers deserted me a couple days ago. I'm hiding out at a friend's house until Bob can find a better location for me."

"Damn. How'd you lose your skills?"

"Don't know and not sure if it's permanent. I keep trying to refocus to get them back, but no luck. I'll keep at it, and if I'm lucky and become special again, I'll come down there."

"That's a bummer. Thanks for trying; I hope it works because I can really use your help. Talk to you later."

"Sorry. Bye."

Now I'm causing more problems with a close friend. Shit, when will it ever end?

He ramped up his concentration to maximum and relayed a mental request he hoped would be heard by his bosses, but could not invoke his abilities.

Damn.

31

Frequent reports from his comrades in Chicago and the Caribbean pleased Ivan Markov. Although he and his men had not located the Terasenkos, he knew Bob Pollard had to use assets to provide twenty-four hour protection for the Russian couple and for Dr. Cavallini and his family as well. FBI resources were already stretched thin, and if Pollard had to borrow manpower from other FBI offices, the bureau's domestic web would be even thinner and vulnerable thus facilitating Moscow's activities.

Markov sat in the living room of his Lakeshore Drive apartment, watching people frolicking at Oak Street Beach and the plethora of sailboats on the Lake Michigan, twirling a glass of vodka before swallowing a mouthful.

"Artemi, you see how my plan is working? FBI agents spread all over the place. They don't know what we do next," Markov spoke in Russian and laughed.

Artemi Radulov, a tall man who shaved his head daily sat across from his boss. He smiled exposing a chipped front tooth and answered. "Yes, captain."

"It's almost time to follow up with Pollard to get a new thumb drive with the bank's security procedures, or Dr. Cavallini and his family will have to suffer." He laughed again and quickly drank more vodka, allowing a narrow stream of the clear cocktail to ooze from the corner of his mouth. "The Americans are so fucking stupid." Artemi nodded.

"You see, I have Pollard in a box; if Cavallini is one of these freaks like Chambers and can work magic, his family and our men at the resort will see it. I suspect the good doctor doesn't want his wife and kids to know he's a spaceman because then they will be at risk like him, and Pollard will lose his leverage of having Cavallini as a secret weapon. But if he isn't a freak, our guys will scare the hell out of him and the family." He bellowed with hilarity at his genius and poured more vodka into Artemi's glass and then his own.

■ ■ ■

Markov munched a cracker with cheese, and when he had chewed sufficiently, he sipped his drink and punched Bob Pollard's number. "How are you this fine day?"

"Hello Markov. What dragged you out of your snake pit?"

"Still angry, I see. Do you have the good information we discussed the other day?"

"I told you to go scratch; you're not getting it."

"I'll bet the Terrasenkos would feel better if you had Anatoly get the real data and give it to me so he and his wife don't have to hide like unsociable outcasts, don't you think?"

"No dice, Markov. You will get nothing from us."

"So uncooperative. On another matter, how is Dr. Cavallini down in the Caribbean?"

"I spoke with him last night; he's doing well." Pollard winced. "Listen asshole, if your goons get physical with him or his family your boys will end up at the bottom of the ocean."

"But Mr. Pollard, if the neurosurgeon has super powers like that little shit Chambers, he will be able to ward off my men. But then of course his family will know he's a freak and will be scared for their lives for as long as they live."

Bob Pollard felt loathing for his job creep back into his mind, the vice ratcheting another notch, and he had no answer, no solution, but he had to finesse his adversary into thinking he has a plan. "Don't take me on, Markov."

"Good bye, my friend."

"Why would I be friends with a prick like you, Ivan?" The line went dead.

"You see, Artemi, if you plant the seed, the tree will grow. You still have to nurture it every once in a while." Markov slapped his ample thigh as he laughed into a coughing fit. Artemi flashed his toothy smile.

32

The sun angled downward toward the ocean as cirrostratus clouds floated in front of it spawning colors, transitioning from yellow to orange to pink and purple, an iconic Southern California Chamber of Commerce trademark. Brad Wolfe and the Claypoole brothers ignored nature's splendor as they continued to speculate what Stephanie Murphy might have deduced thus far from her analysis. The veil of mystery Shields & Fitch erected by the sudden lack of sharing of information about the status of the review distressed the trio. Now the steaks did not soothe the palate as they had in the past, and the after-dinner liquor lost some of its bouquet as they speculated whether the Murphy girl might be penetrating that veil and connecting the links in the chain in the correct order, thus exposing the fraud.

Brad remained at the bar nursing several vodka martinis after the brothers departed. The young bartender poured less vodka with each succeeding refill to slow his customer's slide into a dangerous state of intoxication. He tried to engage Brad in conversation, as it was apparent something bothered him, but Brad resisted the temptation to share the frustration of his quandary. He thought about his entire relationship with Steph. *I wonder when I stopped loving her; she would be a perfect wife.*

Attractive, smart, fun to be around, and with a rich old man to boot. I guess I like money and all it can buy too much. She didn't seem to care that much about an upscale lifestyle and just wanted a career, marriage, and kids. All that's fine, but I love fast cars, trendy bars, and exotic vacations. I also told her I want a mansion on top of a mountain in Newport Coast or Laguna Beach someday. Now she can't stand me and I'm going to have to fuck with her mind. Seems like a long way to fall.

■ ■ ■

The bartender suggested Brad head home and get some sleep. The weary patron struggled to his feet and stopped in the men's room before instructing his car to drive to his condo in Emerald Bay.

. . .

Morning filtered through the parted curtains in his bedroom, drawing him to wakefulness at a slow, leisurely pace. He glanced at the digital clock on the night table: 8:37. He had not scheduled sales calls today, but he had promised a client in Utah he would call at ten forty-five. *Damn, I think that cop broke a couple of my ribs; it hurts every time I breathe.* The injury prevented him from finding a comfortable position during the night, and he paid the price with lack of sleep. After rolling and turning throughout the evening hours, exhaustion finally intervened at four AM, pushing him into a deep sleep. *It would be nice to get a couple more hours of it.*

The ubiquitous marine layer, this month known as June Gloom, extended far inland and would not burn off until between eleven and twelve. Brad debated whether to go to urgent care to have a doc check the ribs, but decided to wait it out for a few days and if it didn't improve, he would then make the visit.

A piece of toast, a banana, and several cups of strong coffee provided increasing lucidity as he sat in front of the TV and checked the baseball scores. He pulled up his calendar on the phone and noted a hockey game scheduled for next Tuesday night. *My Russian buddy, Grigor, will be happy to make a quick grand for one more call to Steph.* He laughed, then coughed as pain rifled through his chest; *I guess I can't do anything to disturb the damn ribs.*

. . .

Earle Claypoole rose early on this Saturday morning to play a quick eighteen holes before the marine layer burned off and the intense sun with its high UV ray count in the middle of the day would make golf a chore instead of a pleasure.

He declined an invitation to a poker game in the clubhouse when he finished his round, but he lingered on the terrace with a beer chatting with other club members and then ordered a burger and fries for lunch. He show-ered and called his brother, Phil, from his car in the parking lot. "What are you up to today?"

'We're just going to cook out. Want to come over?"

"No, we're busy, too. I think we need to talk about our 'partner.' I'm getting nervous since all his plans have failed, and now the cops are involved. Can you meet me at the Yard Manor at the Spectrum for lunch?"

"What do you have in mind about Brad, bro?"

"Not on the phone. I have a couple thoughts, but let's discuss them at lunch, okay?"

"You're on. What time?"

"Let's say one thirty; most of the lunch crowd will be gone by then, and we can find a quiet table or booth."

"That'll be tight because I'll have to get home and help the wife get set up for the cookout, but it'll work. See you then."

"Good, bye, bud." Earle ended the call.

33

Jeremy tried to continue his investigative work for Pollard through the FBI system, but without his special ability to recognize various types of cyber-attacks, he couldn't identify potential enemies. After experimenting with several approaches for three hours, he gave up, closed the computer he borrowed from Paul, and lay on the couch. Sleep came quickly.

Marie and Paul's feet on the stairs awakened Jeremy. The Torchettis's solemn expressions foretold a problem. "Hi guys. Everything alright?"

"Marie needs to tell you something."

"Oh, Jeremy, I'm so sorry. One of the gals at the club meeting asked about you, and before I could catch myself, I said you are at my house and you look great. It just slipped out. Of course they all jumped on my stupid mistake and started firing questions at me." Her reddened eyes evidenced an extended crying session.

Jeremy stifled a rising sense of anger and framed a controlled smile. "Marie, everyone can slip up sometimes, so don't worry about it. How did you answer their questions?"

"After I composed myself as best I could, I told them it was a dream I had last night, but they saw right through that lie. I'm so sorry; please forgive me."

"Like I said, forget it; you didn't do it on purpose. Now, we need to figure out where to go from here." He nodded toward Marie. "Your friends might want to stop by and see me for themselves. Paul, can you prevent them from coming into the house?"

"Sure, I can tell them I'm sick and they need to leave. But I just had a scary thought; what if one of them calls the media? We'll have a damn circus at our front door."

"Is there a better place I can hide in the house—the attic, the garage?"

"Well, those would be better than behind the bar."

"Wait a minute. I have a thought. Remember when you dressed like a woman after you were shot at the funeral home? Maybe you can borrow some of Marie's clothes and impersonate her, just drive out of the garage like you're going to the grocery store."

"You're right; it did work back then, but if her friends or the media come up to the car and get a good look at me, they'll see through the disguise. Even if I shave my beard they'll see I'm not Marie." Jeremy paced the floor while looking at the ceiling. "We may have to keep that as a last ditch option, though. For right now, what do you think is better, the attic or the garage, Paul?"

"It's summer, you'll cook like a pig up in the attic. The garage is the best bet. I have some cabinets in there we can clean out to make room for you. This is such a shitty situation; I'm really sorry, JC."

"Forget it. Time to head for my new quarters." He gathered his few belongings and followed Paul and Marie upstairs.

■ ■ ■

Paul looked out his front window as drone traffic gradually increased forming a circular pattern with the Torcheti house as the focal point.

Jeremy had been sequestered in the garage cabinet for two hours with some food. Using bathroom facilities would be an issue they hadn't discussed. He would have to make a run for it in the darkened house when necessary. Paul had closed all curtains to provide as much privacy as possible.

"It'll be just a little while before the media assholes show up with their choppers and trucks," Paul said.

"What will you tell them, honey?"

"I guess all I can do is tell them I'm having stomach problems and I'll deny Jeremy's here."

"Three of my girlfriends have called already, but I didn't answer. Their voice mails are so gossipy it's sickening."

"I know. We'll just have to deal with it."

Thirty minutes later six television trucks with multiple satellite dishes on top stopped and parked in front of the Torchetti's home. Neighbors hurried to the front door and rang the bell to see what had created all the buzz. Paul patiently cracked the door and explained he was sick and had no idea why the media was at the curb. The neighbors congregated on the sidewalk and questioned the TV reporters about their presence in this quiet upscale community. Jeremy had given him the number for the special phone Pollard had provided.

Paul called, but Jeremy did not answer, and the call defaulted to voice mail. Paul left an urgent message for Jeremy to call him.

Soon the police arrived as people streamed in from all directions and congregated on the lawn and in the street. Officers blocked traffic at both ends of the street and a captain knocked on the Torchetti's door. Paul relayed the same story, but the cop asked if he and his men could have a look inside the house. Paul said no, asked them to leave, and mentioned they didn't have a warrant anyway. The captain reluctantly returned to his cruiser and radioed the station. Fifteen minutes later he returned to the door with his iPad in hand. He showed Paul the warrant and pushed it through the slightly open door to the reluctant homeowner.

"Harboring a fugitive? What kind of crap is this?" Paul asked.

"If this Mr. Chambers is truly in your home we need to talk to him. He's been missing for about eight years and a lot of people have questions for him."

"One minute, officer." Paul closed and locked the door and spoke with his wife who sobbed convulsively. They decided they had no choice since a judge had sanctioned the warrant.

"Okay, you can come in. How many men will be with you?"

"Thank you, sir. We have a team of seven."

The police entered the home and inspected the house as Paul and Marie sat on a couch holding hands. The search began on the second floor and attic, then filtered down to the first floor, and finally the basement rec room. They returned to the great room, and the captain stood before the harried homeowners. "So far we haven't found anything except a cot behind the bar downstairs. Seems like a strange place for it. Why is it there?"

"Just didn't have anywhere else to store it, so I put it there temporarily," Paul replied.

The captain looked askance at Paul. "The only place left for us to search is the garage. We can go through the kitchen, right?"

"Yes, the door is next to the fridge through the mudroom." Paul and Marie exchanged fearful glances. They heard the cops moving things, opening doors, checking inside the cars and trunks, and the cabinets. "Unless Jeremy took off out the back door before the police arrived, looks like it's over, hon," Paul arched his arm around his distraught spouse.

"Poor Jeremy; it's all my fault." She continued sniveling.

The police team returned to the great room, and the captain stood in front of Paul. "It appears no one else is here. We apologize for the intrusion. We have to take these situations seriously. I'll clear the media and gawkers away from your home." He motioned his team out the front door and began to clear the sidewalk and street of the crowd that had swelled to several hundred people.

Paul and Marie huddled on the couch for another thirty minutes relieved, but curious about how Jeremy had not been found. "He must have found a better place to hide in the garage, maybe up in the rafters. I have some old plywood sheets up there that would shield him. But that's crazy; the cops would have checked that, too," Paul offered.

"I hope he's safe. I'm so glad they didn't find him."

Paul rose and opened the curtains, revealing a quiet street. A few neighbors stood on the sidewalk chatting, but when they saw Paul, they drifted off toward their homes. "Marie, come here." Marie joined her husband at the window. "You stay here where any of our friends can see you while I check the garage and talk to JC."

Paul entered the garage warily and stood facing the cabinet his friend had used to hide. "Jeremy, where are you? How did you avoid the cops?" He turned in a slow three hundred sixty degree circle. "Well, here goes." He moved to the cabinet and slowly opened the double doors. A shuffle of some of the ski clothes did not reveal his guest. *Holy shit, where is he?*

He searched the space thoroughly and was satisfied Jeremy no longer remained.

In the house Marie's sobbing dissolved as she blew her nose into several pieces of tissue. "He's not in the cabinet, and I couldn't find him anywhere. I called and he didn't answer," Paul said.

"Where could he be hiding?"

"No clue." Paul sat next to his wife. "Hey, maybe he got his magical powers back and transported somewhere. I can't explain it any other way."

"I hope you're right, hon."

Paul sighed; he didn't need this kind of excitement. He knew he should contact Pollard and update him on the bizarre sequence of events at his house. *The FBI chief will not be happy.* He checked the Chicago office on his phone and dialed the general number. Again the call fell to voice mail, and Paul recounted the facts. A frightening thought crashed into Paul's mind: *what if his bosses took Jeremy back to space? Are they mad at him? How long will he be gone this time? Oh shit, we've really screwed things up.*

34

Dominic Cavallini lay awake most of the night evaluating various threats possibly facing him and his family. *I sure don't want to use my powers unless I absolutely must to save us from kidnapping or from being killed. I hope these Russian guys are just doing intelligence gathering to report back to their boss. I can't let them use their guns.* At 4:37 sleep overcame the somnolent doctor.

Noises in the kitchen and great room woke Sharon and Dominic at 6:50. "What the hell is going on?" Dominic speculated the bad guys might have broken into the condo.

"Take it easy, hon. Why are you so jumpy? It's just the kids up early to get started on the day. You know how they love to play at the beach," Sharon said.

"You're right. I didn't get much sleep, so I'm wound kind of tight."

"I've never seen you like this. Now tell me what's bugging you."

"I guess it's all this never ending drama with the FBI; it keeps resurfacing. Barnes was an okay guy and Pollard is too, but every time I think we're through with it, I get another call."

"Well, hopefully we won't hear from them anymore, so relax and enjoy our family. You know, they can't always join us down here with their jobs and the kids in school. Let's treasure it while we can."

He rubbed his eyes, yawned, and leaned over to kiss his wife. "You're right as usual, dear." He stood and stretched before heading for the bathroom to shower.

■ ■ ■

The doctor cooked breakfast for everyone and decided not to do the dishes as the kids raced through the front door carrying plastic inner tubes followed by parents holding thermoses of coffee and coolers with drinks for the kids. He didn't want to leave his tribe even for one minute.

Dominic had rented three cabanas to provide respite from the intense tropical sun on the beach, and the adults set up blankets and beach chairs under the colorful umbrellas. He used the safety of his large sunglasses to allow him to shift his vision from side to side without detection. Periodically he leaned to one side to catch a glimpse of the area to the rear.

The morning provided beachgoers cooler temperatures and lower ultraviolet ray counts than later in the day. The family enjoyed the clear water as the kids splashed and used the inner tubes as boogie boards to ride waves to shore as their parents stayed in the water to serve as lifeguards. After three hours the parents began the negotiation process to round up the kids to head to the condo for lunch and a nap. Avoiding the midday sun was a necessity for the sake of sensitive skin.

■ ■ ■

After lunch the kids lay in bed whispering and laughing until eyelids weighed down by exhaustion cast a dreamy shroud of sleep over each. The adults relaxed in the great room checking phones for emails, texts, and news.

Dr. Cavallini tried to mask the now-permanent pensiveness spawned by the threat posed by unknown foreigners who might harm his family.

Sharon continued to monitor his countenance for clues as to what bothered him. "You need a margarita to calm your nerves, hon. I'll make one for you."

"No thanks, it's too early in the day to start drinking. I'm fine."

"Define 'fine'."

"You know how it goes when I'm down here. I always think about the patients I've seen recently and how they're doing. That's why I check with the staff at the hospital each day. I doubt it'll change—old dog, new tricks."

"I can hardly wait to see what you'll be like when you retire. Maybe you should take up yoga to relieve the stress." She sat next to him and massaged his shoulders and back.

"Not a bad idea. I'll sign up when we get home."

"Something you can do while we're here is get a massage over by the pool house."

"I think I'll be fine just vegging out here and at the beach."

"Well, I'm out of ideas, dear." She headed for the kitchen to get a piece of fruit.

"Thanks for your help." The doctor fought the urge to let his guard down.

A hard knock at the door startled the family members, and Dominic raced to see who it was through the door's peephole. A man with a resort maintenance shirt and cap knocked again.

Cavallini normally would have opened the door to greet the visitor, but not this time. "Who is it and what do you want?"

"Sir, I am from maintenance; I need to check the kitchen sink. We've had some problems with drainage, and we're checking all units to find out where the problem is."

"Ours is working fine, so the problem must be somewhere else."

"That's good to hear, but the manager wants us to check each unit and have the tenants sign a form that we did the inspection."

The doctor assessed the intrusion as routine and legitimate and opened the door.

Four men burst into the unit with guns drawn and quickly herded the adults into the great room. The leader placed his index finger in front of his mouth as his friends applied duct tape to the mouths of the adults and applied plastic constraints to their wrists behind their backs. The leader instructed everyone not to make a sound or they would be shot.

After the adults answered his query regarding the location of the kids' bedrooms by nodding to the hall, he and one of the other intruders followed the parents into the kids' bedrooms to wake them and cover their mouths with tape. The adults led the shocked children into the great room followed by the two captors. The parents tried to reassure the kids with loving eyes, hoping they wouldn't scream, but the youngsters uttered guttural, muffled noises through the tape.

Sharon cast a terrified glance at her husband, who shook his head in dejection. *Damn, how could I be so stupid to let these assholes in? Now we have to find out what their plan for us might be. Where are the FBI agents? They probably figured from the uniforms these guys really do work for the resort. Shit. I wish I could call Pollard. I'm going to have to use my special skills; there's no other way to keep everyone safe. Sharon will be pissed.*

The intruders' leader returned his PYa pistol (replaced the Markarov PM pistol in 2003) .38 caliber to his pocket and straddled a kitchen chair facing its back. He looked at each adult maintaining a smirk and then pushed his cap back on his head, revealing closely cropped, dark brown hair. Cavallini estimated he could be in his late thirties or early forties with a solid build. His English wasn't tainted with an accent, but the doctor knew he worked for a Russian based on Pollard's call. The other men positioned themselves in the room to surround the captives. One had closed the curtains.

"You wonder why we're here. You don't need to know except that our boss wants something, and if he gets it, we'll leave, and you will not be hurt. If he doesn't get it, we will receive instructions from the boss about what to do with you. For right now we wait."

The Cavallini clan took turns looking at each other and focusing on the doctor for an explanation. They speculated in their minds perhaps he was involved in some situation gone bad, or maybe this is a case of ransom. Children whimpered as parents moved close touching the little ones with their bodies.

■ ■ ■

"Hello Mr. Pollard. How are you this fine day?"

"Screw you, Markov. What do you want this time?"

"Just like before, the thumb drive with the correct information. Has Terasenko created it?"

"I said no, you're not going to get it."

"What do you hear from the good doctor?"

"He's fine."

"Really? Why don't you call him right now; you may find he's got a case of laryngitis and can't talk."

"What do you mean?"

"Go ahead, call him."

Pollard placed Markov on hold and tapped Cavallini's number. No answer, voice mail. He called agent Pruitt. "Pollard here. What's up with the Cavallinis?"

"Nothing boss, they went to the beach this morning and came back to their condo at lunch time and have been inside ever since. Why?"

"I have Markov on the other line and he's implying something's wrong. I tried to call Dom, but he didn't answer, and it went to voice mail. Stay on the line while I get back to him."

"He said everything's fine, Markov."

"I'm surprised to hear that. My man says Dr. Cavallini is in his condo with his mouth taped and his hands tied behind his back, just like his family." Markov chortled until he coughed.

"Don't try to bullshit me, you asshole."

"Such language, so nasty." He paused to cough again. "I'm tired of this game. Now listen to me, you worthless government piece of shit. My men have taken the Cavallini family prisoner and they will be hurt if I don't get the new thumb drive. If you don't believe me ask your men down there in Paradise to go check on them. Then call me back. Good bye."

Pollard switched back to agent Pruitt. "Are you there?"

"Yes, boss still here."

"Markov claims his men are holding the family hostage in the condo. Have you noticed anything unusual?"

"No. Like I said, they came back from the beach and have not left the condo."

"You need to check and verify everything's okay. I'll stay on the line."

"Okay, will do." He circled the building and returned to the call. "I don't see anything wrong. The curtains are closed, but I figure some of them are taking a nap."

"It's beginning to look to me like we have a big fucking problem. Markov isn't bluffing this time. Did you see anyone go into the unit other than the family?"

"No, except for some maintenance guys. They must have some type of issue."

"How many maintenance guys?"

"Looked like four. The doctor let them in."

"Damn. It's them. Are they still in the unit?"

"Yes. They had uniforms . . ."

"Shit. You know how easy it is to knock some guys out and steal their clothes. Get the other agents with you and wait for my call."

"Sorry boss. Will do."

What a fucking nightmare. Now the doc will have to use his powers, which will put his family in danger. Damn.

■ ■ ■

The Russian leader's phone buzzed in the Cavallini condo. Markov delivered news he had spoken to Pollard, so the FBI agents would be watching the unit with renewed vigilance. He told the leader he would call back with word on whether he was successful obtaining the thumb drive.

The leader listened and nodded several times but did not speak.

The neurosurgeon struggled to break free of the white plastic strips used by the police to bind perpetrators' hands, but they are designed to tighten if the captive attempts to free himself or herself. He looked around the room at his wife, daughters, their spouses, and the horrified children.

How could I let this happen? The kids will be scarred for life. Wait; maybe I can reverse their memory of this terrible experience. I've never tried it, but I may have to. I need to decide when to use my skills to stop this tragedy. As long as these bastards don't hurt any of us, I'm going to wait it out and hope Pollard gives them what they want.

35

Earle Claypoole relaxed at the bar at the Yard Manor restaurant in the Irvine Spectrum shopping mall, a sprawling collection of upscale stores, a huge movie complex, a large Ferris wheel, other rides, and a wide variety of eating establishments. He nursed a beer and watched the Dodgers game on one of the numerous TVs behind the bar.

Phil Claypoole entered and joined his brother at the bar and ordered a beer. The twosome then asked the hostess for a booth in a corner, and she led them to one away from other occupied tables.

"Good choice coming here after most of the lunch crowd is gone," Phil said.

"Yeah, this works."

They ordered salads and settled back in the booth. "Okay, what about our friend Wolfe?"

"He's leading us into trouble with all his stupid ass schemes. I'm thinking you and I need to distance ourselves from him in case things blow up," Earle explained.

"He's making me nervous, too. Where do we go from here?"

"I think we play hard to get when he tries to contact us. Don't answer either our cell phones or business phones and if he shows up at our offices, have someone tell him we're in meetings. We're at a point now where we don't want to know what he's doing or saying to anyone. This way if the cops sniff around, we'll be clean, no knowledge of what the asshole is doing."

"What if he caves and spills his guts to the cops?'

"Like I said, hear no evil; see no evil, however that thing goes. We just disavow any knowledge of his scam."

"What if that auditor finds out the report we have for the consulting contract on the city's communication systems is phony?"

The server delivered their meals, and the men paused their conversation while they ate.

"It's like we said before, my company has sloppy accounting procedures, and we don't know who could have created phony papers," Earle said.

"Do you really think they'll buy it?"

"Don't forget, the reason we have Shields & Fitch doing this review is because we know FiberLink's security procedures have some flaws. This way Brad takes the fall, and we skate."

"I hope you're right. We've been riding this gravy train for a long time, and I don't want this idiot to ruin it for us," Phil shook his head.

"Right. We still have some risk, but I think we can work around it."

"What if he shows up at our houses?"

"Have our wives tell him we're sick or we're at meetings. We have to stay away from him and avoid knowing what he's doing, treat him like poison."

The brothers fist bumped and finished their salads.

■ ■ ■

Brad spent most of the weekend in his condo on the couch watching TV to allow his sore ribs to heal. He experienced pain when he breathed too deeply and also when he coughed or sneezed. He made several calls to the last personal cell number he had for Stephanie, and as expected, she didn't answer so he left voice mails apologizing for the incident in her building parking lot. *The little bitch will have a nice surprise when Grigor calls her next week.*

Monday he had two appointments scheduled, one in Irvine and the other in Mission Viejo, but he was still moving in slow motion, as the ribs didn't seem to want to heal. After having his car drive from his luxury condo with an ocean view in Emerald Bay to his meeting with a longtime client at the latter's office in Irvine near John Wayne airport, he took him to lunch at a restaurant in the nearby Marriott hotel. Brad ordered a continuous stream of vodka martinis to control the pain in his chest. The client inquired about his discomfort, and Brad told him he had fallen at home and caught his ribs on the corner of the kitchen counter. He took the client back to his office and continued to have trouble breathing, so he had his car drive him home. He called the client in Mission Viejo and cancelled the afternoon meeting.

Finding a comfortable position on the couch proved impossible, so the afflicted salesman took a couple more Aleve and crawled into bed but again turned and rolled, unable to find a position to lessen the pain. The pills finally provided enough relief from the throbbing ache for him to drift off to sleep.

At nine fifteen he woke with more pain as the Aleve lost its effectiveness. Hunger also rousted him from bed, and he checked the fridge, but the microwave meals didn't look appealing.

He had a taste for Mexican food and called his favorite nearby restaurant to place an order for delivery. The owner asked why he wouldn't be coming in; Brad was a celebrity of sorts in the restaurants he frequented as his loquacious personality entertained the regulars. He used the same explanation he had given the client at lunch.

He lumbered around his condo rubbing the sore ribs and took the food out on the balcony to eat. A beer washed the tasty enchiladas down, but the combination also gave rise to heartburn. *That fucking cop screwed up my weekend, and now I'm still in pain, the little bastard. Too late to call Grigor; I'll just have to meet him at the hockey rink tomorrow. I can't wait to see his face when I tell him about making a second call to Steph; he seemed to really enjoy the first one.*

■ ■ ■

Grigor asked Brad why he didn't dress for the game Tuesday night in the locker room, and he repeated the story about the kitchen counter yet again. Brad told his Russian friend to meet him after the game, and he would have a proposition to present.

Brad watched the game from the stands and waited for Grigor outside the locker room. The Russian emerged a half hour after the end of the game, and the two men drove in Brad's car to the same burger place they had visited a few weeks ago.

"Remember that phone call you made for me to the consultant?"

"Of course, I scared the shit out of her. It was fun."

"I know; you did a great job. Well, how would you like to make another call to her for the same money?"

"I can use the grand, so yeah, I'll do it."

"She may not answer so you'll have to leave her a badass voice mail. I'll write a little script for you to follow. Okay?"

"Just tell me when you want me to do it."

"Tomorrow morning. Let's meet at your office at about ten."

"Sounds good, See you then."

■ ■ ■

Wednesday at ten Brad waited in the reception area of Grigor's company, an established venture capital organization. Grigor led Brad to his office and shut the door.

"Okay, bud, ready to shock the little lady?' "Oh yeah, I hope she answers when I call."

"I doubt it, but we'll see." Brad handed some typed text on a piece of paper to the eager Russian. "Here's the script I wrote for you to read."

"Nice, this is much stronger than the last one; it should really scare the crap out of her."

"I think it will. Read through out loud a couple times to practice, get the right tone in your voice."

"Good idea." Grigor eagerly repeated in a heavy Russian accent the vitriol Brad had composed.

"Excellent. You may have a career in voice overs after this performance."

"I would like that. Do you have any contacts in Hollywood?"

"A few, but let's make this call and we can deal with your job opportunities later."

"Here we go." He dialed Stephanie's personal cell number on the prepaid phone card Brad provided. She didn't answer, and the call transferred to voice mail. Grigor injected emotion and animation into his presentation of the threats in the script, using his thick Russian accent.

"Good job, bud. Here's five hundred of the thousand I owe you. I'll give you the rest on Friday night at the next hockey game." He pushed an envelope across the desk.

"Thanks, man; pleasure doing business with you." Grigor opened the envelope and gave a cursory look at the bills. He smiled his approval. "See you Friday, friend."

36

The leader of the gang in the Cavallini condo walked to a corner of the great room near the windows. He called Ivan Markov to discuss the situation; his report pleased the boss. He nodded and whispered acceptance of instructions from Markov who mentioned FBI agents were in the area.

Dominic scanned the room, hoping to see something to trigger an idea, a way out of this mess. He could invoke his powers to loosen the restraints on his wrists and free his hands, but what then? *These assholes hold all the cards; I wonder how long they'll keep us here . . . more important, what will they do next?*

The leader told one of his comrades to check the fridge and get some food for his group. Plenty of ingredients for sandwiches and condiments appeared on the island as the subordinate found bread and slapped together enough for all four goons. He also found potato chips in a cupboard and beers in the fridge. The captors sat at the kitchen table and enjoyed their meal. Conversation in Russian produced sporadic laughter and grunts. As the group finished the meal, two men collected their guns and visited the bathrooms, and then entered separate bedrooms to sleep. The leader and remaining comrade worked on their beers and smoked cigarettes.

Dominic noted a burgeoning fear in the faces of his family members. *So the bastards are taking shifts to sleep, which means they intend to be here a while. I wonder if the FBI knows what's happening to us; wish I could talk to Pollard. If he doesn't give them what they want, we're screwed.* He glanced at his grandchildren. *Look at the poor kids; they're terrified.*

A knock at the door spooked the two Russians into alert mode. Guns in hand, the leader asked who was there and agent Pruitt gave his name impersonating resort management, careful to overcome the habit of prefacing his name with the title of agent.

"Dr. Cavallini, I need to talk to you about your reservation for parasailing tomorrow."

"Thanks, but a few of us are not feeling well; I think it's food poisoning," the leader responded in slow, perfect English.

"Sorry to hear that. Is there anything we can do for you?"

"No, we just need to rest and take some medication we have here."

"Okay then. I hope you all feel better; let us know if you need to go to the hospital; we'll give you a ride."

"Will do, and thanks again."

The visitor's fading footsteps clacked on the tile floor in the hallway.

Agent Pruitt retreated to his car where two more agents waited. He called Bob Pollard for further instructions.

"Thanks for the update. I guess we couldn't be too optimistic they would open the door. I want to stall Markov as long as possible, but we need to be careful for the family's safety. I'll get back to you in half an hour, but if anything changes as far as you can tell, call me," Pollard said.

"Roger that."

■■■

Pollard paced his office slurping coffee. Markov had a point about Cavallini using his powers in view of his family and the abductors; the family would be added to the growing list of people in danger of future kidnapping or worse. *We can't provide protection for so many people twenty-four/seven, but the doc might have no choice, and I don't want to give that asshole Markov the bank's security processes. Time to call the bastard.*

"Markov, it's Pollard."

"Good. Do you have the new thumb drive?"

"What if I say no?"

"Bad answer. Cavallini and his family pay for your stupidity."

"What if I say you'll never get the thumb drive?"

"Then the good doctor and his family will be punished."

"How?"

"As you know, we have many options."

"If you harm them your boys will die, too. How do you think you can save them?"

"Sometimes, Mr. Pollard, it's more about country. You understand that, right?"

"So, you'll sacrifice your guys after they kill a bunch of innocent people?"

The Russian boss paused. "Cost of doing business."

"You really are a despicable piece of shit."

"The clock is ticking. I give you one more hour. Goodbye." Markov snapped off he call.

Doc will have to demonstrate his powers to save his family even if it reveals his secret to them. No choice when lives are at stake. We'll deal with how to protect them later.

■■■

Thirty minutes had passed when Jeremy concluded an extended transport maneuver and floated through the window of a bedroom at the Cavallini's resort condo where one of the Russian captors lay snoring on top of the duvet of one of two queen beds in the room. Jeremy hovered unsteadily a foot above the floor, lost his balance and lurched to the side where the man slept. He knocked a clock off the night table to the floor, but quickly retrieved it and placed it back on the table. The Russian continued to slumber. *Damn, I need to practice transporting now that my powers are back—at least for now.*

He surveyed the dark room, the man in the fetal position on his left side; he noted a PYa pistol, the standard weapon for Soviet Special Forces and secret police on the bed under the perpetrator's right hand. He knew pulling it slowly away would most certainly wake him; after all these clowns are assassins. The spaceman used logic to wrest the weapon without all hell breaking loose. He focused his brain and induced the man's mind into a state of temporary suspension, incapacitating him. He decided to test the effectiveness of the exercise by tweaking the abductor's ear with his finger and raised his right hand in a fist to smash the goon's face if he woke. *Success! That should have wakened him if my power didn't work.* This knowledge bolstered his confidence, so he slid the gun from under the limp hand and stowed it in his belt. He patted down the man's body to identify other weapons and found an ankle holster with a PSS silent pistol caliber 7.62, a smaller gun, which he extracted and added to his belt. Next he took a pillow-case from the other bed and used it as a gag by twisting it into a taut rope and inserting the middle into the sleeping assassin's mouth and tying it behind his head. Jeremy then stripped the other bed of its sheets and twisted them into long, narrow lengths to use as makeshift restraints. He tied the slumbering Russian's feet together and wrapped the other rope sheet around the neck and tied it to the foot restraints. Since the abductor's legs were still in the fetal position, when he woke, he would increase the pressure on his neck if he extended his legs.

One down, more to go. Powers, don't fail me now.

178

37

Stephanie held the cell phone after the mysterious Russian man ended the call in her voicemail. *Another call from this monster. His threats are scarier. I can't live like this. I never dreamed someone would want to kill me; I'm just doing my freaking job.* She clicked the phone off and felt her face flush.

Time to call Al and Bev—again.

Lucille answered CEO Al Schwedland's line and put Steph on hold while she checked with her boss. She apologized for interrupting his meeting with team leaders of various company projects, but Steph's request to see him was urgent. Al adjourned the meeting, and the team leaders left his office sporting bewildered looks, murmuring and speculating what could be so important for Al to abruptly stop the meeting. He instructed Lucille to have Steph come to his office immediately and to summon Bev as well.

Steph collected her folio and coffee and headed for the boss' office, but stopped briefly in the ladies room to compose. She stared at the image in the mirror; a woman who appeared years older than thirty-four gazed back at her with dreary eyes. *I need to snap out of this trance.* She inhaled several deep breaths, exhaling slowly at a restrained pace as she had been taught by her father. Now somewhat relaxed, she practiced a few expressions of alertness and confidence.

Bev had already arrived at Al's office, and the two of them sat at the conference table. Steph joined them.

"Do we have more trouble?" Al asked.

"Yes. I just received a voice mail on my personal cell from that same guy, maybe a Russian, and the threats are much worse this time. He said if I don't back off the FiberLink review, I will be killed."

"This is getting out of hand. Bev, call the FBI and report this to agent Pawley and ask what we do next. I think we need to find out who this bum is and get him behind bars."

"Will do." Bev turned to Steph. "Is that FBI agent who helped you in the parking lot at your building still protecting you?"

"I believe so, but he told me to go about my normal routine and he or the other agents will be in the background, but not far from me at all times."

"Good. Your safety is paramount. Now, where do we stand on the risk review of FiberLink?" Al said.

"Earle Claypoole has called and left a few messages wondering where we are and I've been stalling, telling him we are stretched for resources and the review is taking longer than we expected."

"So, do you think he suspects anything?" Al asked.

"Not sure. I'm continuing to review their consulting report, and he still owes me a copy of the RFP, but I also have a few more things to verify."

"Have you had any contact from or with Brad?" Bev said. Resentment welled in Steph's face, and she felt a flush in her chest.

Here she goes again treating me like a teenager. "No, I said I wouldn't have anything to do with him. He tried to drag me out of my damn car, for God's sake." Her voice rose.

"Okay, okay, I'm just covering the details," Bev forced a sarcastic smile in response to Steph's venom.

"I thought we covered that base last time we met," Steph fired back. "Easy, ladies, we're all on the same team here and we need to focus on the challenge in front of us," Al said. "Anything else we need to discuss?"

Both women shook their heads, and Al stood to signal the meeting's end. Bev left immediately, but Steph intentionally fumbled with her folio and coffee. "Why does she keep treating me like a child?"

"Like I told you last time, she's all in on her job and doesn't realize when her style offends people sometimes. Don't worry about it; we just need to keep you safe." Al reached an arm around her shoulder in a brief hug.

"I'll try, but maybe she should take a class." She turned and left the office.

■ ■ ■

The young lawyer returned to her office and sat at her desk twirling a lock of hair while looking out the window at the Fashion Island shopping mall. *How great would it be to not have the stress of this job, to be able to go shopping whenever I want, have lunch with friends, and then go to the club to play tennis and swim and a concert at night? I had those things in the summers home from college and law school, but I guess we all have to grow up at some point. I didn't ever think I'd fear for my life, though.* She rotated the chair back to her desk and the City of Vista Nueva consulting report.

Although sparse, it covered the routine issues for such a contract. She examined each section and then attempted to match the items to the support documents, which consisted of recaps of alleged interviews with city employees and lists of various types of communication equipment in the city's inventory. The conclusion section was general and unlike any such reports she had seen at other companies recommending the city purchase a short list of common equipment and systems that would be obsolete in a few years. She also could not verify the city acted on the recommendations in the report; she only had Ms. Kirkwood's comment Phil Claypoole told her to order the things the city doesn't already have in place. *Anyone could have fudged everything in this document. I think Earle Claypoole threw it together in a couple hours to cover his ass. But it's all bullshit. If the auditors had looked at this $3.75 million expense like I'm looking at it, they would arrive at the same conclusion as mine. So here we have a consulting contract for an outrageous fee, almost no work product, and minimal action by the city on FiberLink's advice. A lot of money involved, two brothers dealing with each other through Brad, and he receives a huge fee for his expertise. Fraud. Holy shit, this is bad.*

She called Al's office and Lucille attempted to engage her in personal conversation, but Steph shot it down by telling her they could discuss those things some other time. "Al, I have some news on FiberLink." She explained the last piece of evidence establishing some sort of scheme to extract funds from the City of Vista Nueva involving the mayor of the city, his brother, the CFO at client FiberLink, and one Bradley Wolfe.

"Wow, well done, Steph. Update your report and come see me when it's ready and make twenty-five copies. Bev will get agent Pawley, and he can direct us from there."

"Will do, Al"

■ ■ ■

Agent Mark Pawley accompanied Bev to Al's office; Steph arrived ten minutes later. Al waited until the police chief of Vista Nueva and the commander of the Orange County Sherriff's office stepped into the room.

"Thanks to all for joining us again today. We have new information confirming some of our presumptions regarding the business practices of our client, FiberLink, and other players who we think have colluded to steal funds from the city of Vista Nueva," Al focused briefly on each attendee. "I'll turn it over to Stephanie Murphy, a partner in our firm, who will walk us through the sequence of events, the evidence she's uncovered, and the conclusions we've drawn. Then Mark Pawley, FBI, will address us regarding next steps. We need to ensure strict confidentiality in this matter at all times. Steph."

Stephanie distributed bound copies of her report and verbally presented the facts with supporting documentation implicating the Claypoole brothers, Brad Wolfe, and an unknown man with a thick Russian accent. Each person in the room raised eyebrows as they followed her presentation while glancing at the written report.

No one asked questions, so Pawley stood to address the group. "I've spoken with the local authorities here today and with the Department of Justice chief for the LA region. We're confident we have enough evidence for the DOJ to proceed with indictments. Our next task is to coordinate taking the individuals Ms. Murphy mentioned into custody, seize whatever other documents or materials might be pertinent to this case, and for the DOJ to refer the matter to the grand jury to determine the strength of the case." Several attendees added notes to their report booklets. "Does anyone have any questions or comments?" Bev asked about the timing of the apprehension of the people involved, and Pawley said it would be decided by the DOJ. "Thanks to all of you for adjusting your schedules on short notice and special thanks to Ms. Murphy for her excellent work identifying this scam and documenting it so thoroughly." He led the group in polite applause.

38

Wednesday morning Brad Wolfe's ribs finally started to feel better, and the pain had subsided incrementally. He woke early at six forty-five and enjoyed breakfast on his balcony, but the marine layer, June Gloom, partially veiled his view of the ocean. He checked the calendar on his phone, finding only one conference call with a client in Silicon Valley at ten, but no appointments. He scanned the domestic and international news on his phone and then checked baseball box scores followed by a review of his bank accounts. *Where does all the money go? I'm bringing in over a million bucks a year, but I'm always short, and now I owe Grigor five hundred by Friday, and my mortgage payment is due next week. I guess my lifestyle burns the cash faster than I can bring it in, even with the free money from the scams. No choice, I'll have to tap into my home equity line of credit to get me through until some commissions come in.* He transferred $5,000 from his home equity line to his checking account. *My balance on the equity loan is approaching the credit limit. Shit, I need to make some calls to get my clients to cut those commission checks; they always drag their feet on payments of this type to conserve cash. Guess I'll have to be my own collection agency—again.*

Since it was too early to call the Claypoole brothers, he took a leisurely shower and shaved and then flicked the TV on to ESPN. At eight thirty he muted the sound and called Earle Claypoole. No answer, so he left a voice mail with the news Grigor had called Stephanie and scared her once more. Same result when he called Phil. *Those guys never answer their damn calls anymore.*

He waited until nine o'clock and called Steph's cell; predictably she didn't answer, so he left another apologetic voice mail. This general lack of communication with Steph and the brothers exacerbated his already high level of frustration. It was like a dark curtain had been drawn across a stage concealing the people he wanted—needed—to talk to. *I hate not knowing what's going on. Makes me think something bad might be happening behind the scenes.*

. . .

Mark Pawley and his team mapped a campaign to raid the offices and homes of the Claypoole brothers and Brad Wolfe. The action would take place at six o'clock on Saturday morning. Two-dozen agents comprised the group that would execute the bust. Although each situation included its own challenges and complexities, the FBI had long ago developed templates for various types of intrusions and could merely plug names into the boxes, and with some tweaking use the element of surprise and careful planning to achieve their objectives. Agents undergo extensive training for such operations, and every detail is triple-checked. The templates include anticipation of unforeseen events and flow chart or decisions tree measures to react to them.

After briefing Pawley on Shields & Fitch's consulting contract with FiberLink in preparation for the FBI incursion, Stephanie decided to spend the weekend at her parents' home in the city of Orange. She did not want to be in her condo in the event Brad might stop by and cause another scene in spite of his apologies in the several voice mails and texts he sent since the episode in her building parking lot. Her parents welcomed the opportunity to have her in the safety of the family homestead where Megan's kids also lived.

Now that the FBI was close to bringing this sting to a close, anxiousness seeped into her mind: *What happens after these guys are arrested and end up in prison. I doubt they'll spend more than a few years locked up. When they get out, will they come after me? Will I have to run to stay ahead of them the rest of my life? What about my career? I'm beginning to wonder if I did the right thing by digging into their little caper too deep. I had to do it, though, because it's my job and the honest thing to do. Dad wouldn't hesitate if he were in my shoes. My stomach's doing flips.*

■ ■ ■

After his ten o'clock conference call, instead of calling the Claypoole brothers' personal cell numbers, Brad first calls the general number for FiberLink and then the City of Vista Nueva and in each call asks to speak to Earle and Phil, respectively. He knew the calls would be directed to the brothers' secretaries, and he would have a chance to ask them to interrupt the brothers because his call was urgent. After placing him on hold, however, the secretaries came back on the line and told him the brothers were unavailable. *What the fuck? It seems like the boys are avoiding me. What the hell's going on?*

I don't like where this thing is heading. Maybe the boys know something I don't. Maybe I should visit their houses.

Brad next texted Steph insisting she reply because he had something critical to share with her. He waited thirty minutes with no answer and knew from her recent behavior she would not be responding. *Damn, shut out again. This is getting depressing.*

His stomach rumbled indicating the lunch crowds would be herding into the restaurants soon. He directed his car to drive to one of his favorites, a nearby BK's restaurant.

At 11:50 he still beat most of the throng and found his usual seat at the bar. Several regulars had already found stools and worked on their drinks. Brad exchanged loud greetings and fist bumps with them, and a vodka martini materialized in front him. He cracked a few jokes and livened up the heretofore mundane conversation at the bar. Brad had been a star patron at this and many other restaurants and bars in Orange County over the years as his charismatic personality and gregarious style naturally attracted followers. A striking, virile appearance and enduring smile showcasing flawless teeth endeared him to almost any group. His presence was magnetic to people; his quick wit and focus on each individual who spoke fostered an instant mutual bond. Brad possessed an arsenal of jokes and stories he could summon at will, which created a festive environment in which people would relax allowing intimate details of character to bubble up from deep in their souls.

"How about you and me stepping out for dinner after you finish your shift, Julie?"

"Gee, Brad, what took you so long to ask me today; you usually hit me with that come- on before you're sitting on the stool." Julie, a lean blond who had known her handsome customer for several years engineered a coy smile as she drew a microbrew for another customer. "You're losing your touch."

"Maybe so, but I fell and hit my ribs a few days ago, possibly broke one or two, and I haven't been feeling the best since then. So what is your answer? I'll take you to an upscale place you'll love."

"You know I like the way you flatter me, but as I've told you a thousand times before, my husband, Josh, would not allow me to go out with you."

"Oh well, why don't you divorce him, and then we can date."

"Divorce is not in my future; we're very happy."

"Never say never," Brad said cocking his head to the left. Julie smirked and turned to ring up a sale.

As Brad's glass hit empty, Julie replaced it with a fresh martini, as she knew her regular customers' preferences. He ordered a sandwich and small salad and continued to banter with his friends at the bar. After he finished the meal, Julie placed his favorite beer in front of him. A half hour later he said his goodbyes, winked at Julie, who rolled her eyes, and directed his car to take him home.

Brad paced the great room in his condo, his nerves wound tight as guitar strings. He settled into a chair on the balcony and put on sunglasses as the marine layer had burned off in late morning. He placed several cold calls to old clients to see if they needed any communications equipment or software and to introduce them to new products, but no appointments emanated from his efforts. He called two former girlfriends to get a date for the weekend, but they both had plans and admonished him for not calling for so long. *Great, I can't even get a date with my old reliables. I'm losing my touch.*

■ ■ ■

Thursday offered more promise as Brad's ribs continued to heal and the pain subsided. He still popped Tylenol and Advil at night, however, to facilitate sleep. A check of his calendar on the phone reminded him of a visit he had scheduled for eleven thirty with a client in San Clemente followed by lunch. With time to kill before he had to shower and prepare to drive to the client's office, he thought a brief run would give him time to contemplate his current situation.

He stretched on the sidewalk in front of his building and started to jog at a comfortable pace, but after four hundred yards, sharp, stabbing pains pierced his chest as the ribs sent a reminder his injuries had not completely healed. He slowed to a walk holding his ribs with his right hand and bent over at the waist. A runner proceeding in the opposite direction stopped and asked if he was okay; Brad thanked him and said he was just winded. *I play hockey, basketball, and surf with no problems and now I'm like an old man with these busted up ribs.* Dejected, he walked back to his building and stripped off his clothes before heading to the bathroom. *I think I'll go see the brothers at their homes tonight. I need to know what the hell's happening around here.*

39

Earle Claypoole called Stephanie's office and, as usual, she did not pick up, so he left an urgent voice mail indicating he had some new information for her regarding the risk review. He thought this ploy would arouse her seemingly dormant curiosity and she would call back to learn the latest.

Two hours later Earle ended a call with a customer, exhaled, and shook his head. *I can't believe she wouldn't call me after the voice mail I left. Things are too damn quiet.*

He speed dialed his brother's cell. "It's me; can you talk?"

"Hold on." Phil Claypoole rose from his desk at City Hall and closed the office door. "Now I can. What's up?"

"Did you get calls from Brad on your personal cell and then through your office general number?"

"Yeah, you?"

"Yep. He's starting to panic. He may show up at our houses soon. Let's plan on going out to dinner the next couple nights."

"Okay with me. Should we go to the club?"

"No, that'll be the first place he'll check. I'll find a couple out-of-the-way restaurants where he'll never find us."

"Fine. What else is happening?"

"I left an urgent voice mail for the Murphy girl, told her I have some new info on the risk audit she's doing to see if that would motivate her to call me. That was over two hours ago, and she hasn't called me back. I'm getting a funny feeling about our little escapade."

"Me too. What do you think is going on?"

"I'm beginning to feel like she's maybe figured everything out and is reporting it up her chain of command to let them decide what to do next."

"And that would be what?"

"Probably the police, maybe even the State's Attorney or the Attorney General. We could be getting visits from some of those assholes soon."

"Shit, I was hoping Wolfe's scare tactics would get her to back off.

What do we do if the cops come to see us?"

"Like we said a few days ago, we know nothing of what Brad's been up to, and I'll tell them my company's security procedures are weak and that's why we brought Shields & Fitch in to help us improve, etcetera."

"We're covered on the recommendations you made in the report. I just hope they don't want to see how we acted on the advice in the report because the systems and equipment you and Brad suggested are not the best available," Phil said.

"Well, the phony bill of lading for the equipment you ordered should cover our asses, and I'll tell them the fake RFP I created is part of our crappy procedures."

"Looks like we're in good shape."

"Right. Don't forget to tell Judy to tell Brad you're out to dinner with business people."

"Earle, you know she's a great wife; she's used to my crazy schedule and always tells me who called or stopped by."

"Yeah, you're right about that, and I'm lucky Cathy is like Judy, too. Brad won't get anywhere with either of them. Let's go to Mason's in Orange tonight, and we won't tell the wives where we'll be, so there's no chance they can accidently spill the beans."

"Sounds like a plan. What time tonight?"

"Let's go straight from work."

"Got it, see you there."

"Good, see ya."

■ ■ ■

Brad donned his swimsuit and headed to his complex's pool and spa. He splashed in the refreshing water and scouted for attractive women but found none up to his standards. The bubble jets in the spa soothed his healing ribs.

After an hour with no dating prospects in view, he returned to his condo, showered, and shaved. He checked his mailbox but found nothing other than grocery flyers and requests for donations from several charities.

Typically heavy traffic on the I-5 freeway increased the length of his trip to Earle's home in Irvine. He arrived in the driveway at 6:47 and rang the doorbell. Cathy Claypoole opened the door in shorts and a tank top.

Tall and slim with colored brownish-blond hair that had almost grown out revealing light brown roots, she exuded casual confidence.

"Oh, hi Brad. What brings you down here?"

"Just looking for Earle. We need to discuss some business. Is he here?"

"No, he had to meet a client for dinner and went straight from the office. Can I give him a message for you?"

"I haven't been able to contact him lately, and we have some things to take care of. Just tell him I stopped by."

"I know what you mean; I haven't seen him much either with his busy schedule. I'll tell him you stopped by. Nice to see you, Brad."

"You, too Cathy. Thanks."

Can you believe this shit? I can't even catch him at home. I wonder if Cathy is covering for him. Sure didn't seem like it though. Damn. I hope I find Phil at home.

Phil's wife, Judy, told him her husband was at a business meeting too and had left from work. *I wonder if the brothers are at the same meeting. Probably not, we haven't done any phony deals since the one Steph's working on. Everywhere I go lately I'm hitting a brick wall.*

■ ■ ■

Mark Pawley sat at the small conference table in Al Schwedland's office sipping black coffee. He, three of his top agents and Al squeezed around the table. "Okay, Al, I wanted to have you in on our plan because we may need a few of your people to assist us in some of our searches since your firm conducted the audit, and they will know where we're most likely to find what we're looking for. It'll save a lot of time."

"No problem. I'll give you whatever you need in terms of manpower. Do you want Stephanie to be at the FiberLink office to assist you?"

"Not sure, but on second thought, it may be a good idea. Thanks. Now, the first thing is the warrants. The judge had no problem granting them after we presented our facts." Pawley distributed copies authorizing the FBI to search the homes of the Claypoole brothers and Brad Wolfe.

Separate warrants would open the door for the agents to search Earle's office at FiberLink and Phil's office at Vista Nueva City Hall. "We're all set to enter the premises on Saturday morning. Now I want input from you guys on how many folks you'll need for your assignments." The four team leaders presented their estimates by location with Brad's condo requiring the smallest team.

"Great. Now I want to review the timing of our visits because the element of surprise is one of our best weapons. I'll be with the team at FiberLink and at exactly six o'clock AM all four teams will approach their assigned sites and demand entrance. The warrants will be our tickets for entry." He glanced at each team leader for agreement, and all nodded. "We probably will be catching our subjects sleeping, which is fine because they won't have a chance to hide things. The sheriff will provide officers to cover the rear of the homes, and he will handle the arrests. We'll take the documents and computers out in boxes and bring them to my office for review. Any questions?" There were no questions, so Pawley continued covering the remaining items on his checklist.

40

Dominic Cavallini scanned the room populated by terrified members of his family and two professional assassins. The kids' expressions reflected prolonged horror, which saddened the neurosurgeon the most. *The poor kids don't deserve this bullshit. I'm going to have to use my powers to incapacitate these thugs.* He surveyed the room to anticipate the best options for putting these guys to sleep and getting the family out of the condo to safety. *First, I'll cause the jerks to fall asleep. Next, I need to free myself from the restraints; I've already loosened the ones on my hands. Then I'll untie the others, but I think I'll leave the tape on the kids' mouths so if they scream it'll be muffled, and hopefully won't wake these bastards or the other two goons in the bedrooms. After we leave the condo we'll go to the administrative office, and I'll call Pollard.* He looked around the room searching for any detail he had not identified. *Looks good. Here goes nothing.* He inhaled fully and was about to invoke his powers when he noticed a shadow in the hallway leading to the bedrooms. He aborted his efforts and watched the shadow. *Are those jerks awake and coming in here? If so, I'll have to devise a plan B . . . fast.*

The figure creating the image in the hall peeked around the corner and smiled at Cavallini. *Holy shit, it's Jeremy! I thought he had lost his skills, but he could only be here if he transported. If he has his powers, I won't have to use mine.*

Jeremy put the intruders into trances, crept into the room, and removed the tape from Dominic's mouth. "Why didn't you take these assholes down?"

"Not so loud," he whispered. "Long story, but I don't want my family to know I have our unique abilities; that way they shouldn't be targets for these bastards. Anyway, I'm glad you're here, partner." The two men hugged and began untying the others while motioning them to remain quiet by placing index fingers against their mouths. Jeremy programmed their minds erasing knowledge of Jeremy's visit. He and Dominic told the adults to leave the tape on the mouths of the kids and to get them out and go to the resort office as fast as possible. The parents untied their children's restraints and carried them out of the unit. "What about the two guys in the bedrooms?"

"I put them out; they're sleeping like babies. We need to get the guns from these two. Check the pants for foot holsters with a second gun; the two in the bedrooms both had them in addition to their other ones."

"Will do. I'll take Mr. Leader here." The doctor confiscated his weapons while Jeremy did the same to the other comrade. The two spacemen used the white plastic handcuffs to bind the two captors and duct taped their mouths.

"I'm going to call Pollard and let him know we're free of these pricks," Jeremy said. "Doc, why don't you check on the two in the bedrooms; I had to use bed sheets and pillow cases to tie them up and gag them. Not sure that'll hold them for long. You can use the rest of the little tools they used on your family to secure them better. Can I borrow your phone? I left in such a hurry I forgot to bring mine."

"Good idea. Here's my phone. Check the recent calls, and you'll find Pollard's number." The doctor flipped his phone to his partner and then gathered what he needed and headed for the bedrooms.

Jeremy tapped Bob Pollard's number in the recent call menu. "Hi, boss."

"Hi, Dom. What's the current status?"

"No, boss, it's Jeremy. I borrowed Dom's phone."

"Jeremy? Where the hell are you?"

"Easy, boss, I'm in St. John at Doc's condo. I was able to get my powers back and transported down here when I received a telepathic message that the Cavallini family was in danger. Not sure how long I'll be Superman this time either."

"Wow, that's great to hear. Did Doc use his powers?"

"No, not before his family raced out of here, but after they left, we agreed he would invoke his talents with mine to hold these assholes until you can have your guys and the cops arrest them."

"Good work. I need to call Markov to let him know his threat has failed. Oh, here he is now calling me. I'll call you back after I talk to him. Later."

"Bye boss."

■ ■ ■

"Hello Markov, how goes the war?"

"Shut up Pollard, I have no time for your bullshit. The deadline has now passed, and you did not call me. Do you have the good thumb drive, yes or no?"

"Wow, why so angry?"

"The drive, do you have it?"

"No, and you will never be getting it."

"Very big mistake. Now Doctor Cavallini and his family will suffer because of you. I will be instructing my team after we hang up."

"You may find they're sleeping on the job, Mr. Big Shot."

"Very funny. You will regret not working with me. Bye."

Pollard sat in his office with his phone in the center of his desk. He waited for Markov to call back; the phone rang two minutes later.

"What did you do to my men? They don't answer my calls."

"You should know better than to fuck with me, Ivan. You have no business trying to extort proprietary security information from Anatoly and threatening innocent people. So now your little team in St. John is under arrest and won't be available for your espionage tricks."

"Why should I believe you?"

"Go ahead, check with some of your other goons to verify what I'm telling you is the truth. Your boys are out of commission for a long time."

"You won't get away with this."

"Look at it this way; you lose four of your best men. No problem; 'it's just a cost of doing business.' I'll be coming for you next Markov; I taped all of our calls. Have a nice day." Pollard punched off the call.

Bob smiled and called Jeremy. "What's the status down there?"

"We talked to your men, and they're working with the local police to process the goons. What did Markov have to say?"

"He's not happy. Do you still have your powers? Can you transport back here?"

"So far, so good. Where do you want me to land?"

"For right now, I think you're better off back at the museum.

Everything's already set up until I can come up with a better arrangement for you. I'll have Cuthbertson resume your meal service."

"Glad you mentioned that. When can I see my family? You promised from day one when I came back."

"Yes, and I'll make good on it, but you move in dangerous circles, Jeremy and I have a lot of lives to consider. I'll try to have a plan for you in a week or two."

"I understand the danger, but if my powers don't crap out on me, I can transport to California and see my wife—former wife, that is—and kids."

"But that's what I meant about other people I have to protect. Your kids will want to be with you all the time and won't understand why you can't reconstruct your old life with them. See what I mean?"

"Yeah, I do, but I'll be able to program their minds to prevent them from talking to anyone about the fact they saw me. That reduces the risk, right?"

"Yes, to a degree. I'm just thinking about the emotional impact on your kids having a chance to see you again; who knows what it might do to their fragile states of mind?"

"I'm willing to take that risk; I have faith they're stronger than you realize. They're older now, too, and will be better able to handle the emotional side."

"Could be true, but don't forget Kelly has had to undergo some therapy to deal with your disappearance and last year when you visited her mind to help find her mom. Like I said, man, I owe you a lot after what you did for me when I was shot at the funeral home at Lorraine's wake. I'll keep my word."

"I know you will, but I've missed a huge part of my kids' growth and development, and I don't want to miss any more."

"Understood, bud; we'll get there. Thanks for bailing out the doc and his family."

"Glad I could help. Just know I'm going to bother the hell out of you until I see my family again. Bye."

"I don't blame you. Bye."

41

Jeremy and Dominic embraced and exchanged farewells, and Jeremy then disappeared to transport to his familiar basement accommodations in Chicago's Field Museum. Everything looked the same, and he felt warm comfort and a sense of security in his cocoon. He checked the time on his phone; it read 11:38 on this Thursday evening.

A quick shower and clean clothes brightened his spirits as he found a beer in the small fridge and some pretzels to munch while watching TV. *This is isn't the greatest living space, but it's clean and comfortable; could be worse.* He watched an old James Bond movie and marveled at the level of sophistication of the technological devices used in the spy world back then; many of them were considered science fiction at the time. *Now look how far we've come with all sorts of futuristic tools and weapons that make the ones from the old movies look like toys.* He plugged his phone into an outlet to charge.

Fatigue gradually enveloped him and elevating his eyelids became laborious. He clicked off the TV and crawled into bed; sleep came in minutes.

■ ■ ■

Friday ushered in more hot, humid temperatures in Chicago, and the lack of wind this morning allowed the confluence of pungent vehicular exhaust and fusion of different food aromas emanating from restaurants to form a stifling blanket over downtown and the lakefront. Cirrus clouds floated in slow procession from west to east across a sky partially obscured by a pervasive haze, and the sun's ultraviolet rays began to build in intensity.

Bob Pollard loosened his tie and reclined in his chair. He checked a box on his computer file of active cases in his region to indicate the siege in Dominic Cavallini's condo in the Caribbean was now no longer critical. He smiled and slurped some coffee and called Jeremy. "Good morning. Did you have a good trip back?"

"Hi, boss, yes all went well, and I'm still armed with my secret weapons."

"I checked with my guys in St. John, and they said the perps will be arraigned today in the local court. I'm going to talk to the DOJ about getting them extradited to the US to stand trial since their crimes were committed against American citizens."

"Good, I hope those assholes get five hundred years apiece in the pen."

"Me too; we'll see. Did Cuthbertson deliver your breakfast?"

"Yeah. I have to thank you for the good food in this hotel—makes life a little more bearable."

"Can you gear up to work on uncovering some cybercrime in our system today since you have your skills back?"

"Sure, I was just about to log in. If my skills crap out on me again, I'll call you right away."

"Right, but let's think positive and hope they never fail anymore."

"I have mixed feelings about that. I would really like to just be a normal human again—no more spy stuff. On the other hand, I know my powers are useful in helping keep our country safe. I hate how my experience has affected so many people, putting them in danger. But for now, I'll do my best."

"And I'll do my best to let you visit your family again."

"By the way, what's the latest on the shit with Stephanie Murphy's company?"

"I talked to Mark Pawley yesterday, and they'll be moving on the subjects soon. Stephanie apparently did a great job of digging into the scam, and Mark thinks their case is solid."

"Good for her. Steph was always a bright girl; it's too bad Brad turned out to be such a shithead. She dated him for several years."

"I know, but sometimes you don't know what a person is like until you uncouple and look at them objectively. It appears like she has a great career ahead of her."

"Yep, I think Megan was always a bit jealous of her little sister. Any word on how Megan's doing?"

"Last I heard her parents see her every day in the facility, and there doesn't seem to be much change in her condition. "

"Damn, a big example of how I've fucked things up. I wish the docs could do something for her—new drugs or treatment . . ."

"I know what you mean. Try to stay optimistic, bud. I gotta go, talk to you tomorrow. Bye." He tapped off the call.

■ ■ ■

Jeremy worked in the FBI system until noon and then opened the door for Cuthbertson, who wheeled in a lunch tray.

"How are you today Mr. C?"

The director said nothing and left without looking back. *I won't miss that stuffy bastard when I get out of here.*

He enjoyed the food and clicked on the TV to catch up on the news. Spending time on the small phone screen and having to navigate through various sites didn't appeal to him except to get the late sports results. Watching the TV provided huge HD images in super-sharp resolution and didn't require searching for websites or apps. Soon the images on the large screen began to slowly collide and fade. The voices from the audio blended into an incoherent stream of staccato hums. Sleep slid its soft curtain of darkness over the spaceman.

■ ■ ■

Jeremy woke at 4:20, his body heavy from a sedentary day. He put a small pot of coffee on and checked his phone. The only emails he received were from Bob, so he skittered across the web in search of interesting morsels of information. YouTube yielded several humorous videos and the Weather Channel offered spectacular pictures of a serious storm spawning tornadoes racing across Kansas. The Cubs game started at three this afternoon, and currently the Cardinals were batting in the top of the fifth inning leading by two runs. He tired of the small screen and punched the TV on and tuned to ABC for the early evening news.

At five o'clock a knock at the door meant Mr. C delivering the dinner meal. Jeremy called for him to come in. The director wheeled the tray to his guest's chair. Jeremy decided attempting to engage this condescending oaf had been fruitless, so he pulled the cart closer and uncovered the entrée plate. Mr. C hesitated for instructions, questions, or conversation, but none ensued after three minutes, so he pivoted on his heels and left.

Jeremy shook his head.

The meal of pot roast, green beans, salad, and cheesecake for dessert sated his appetite, and he redirected his attention to the news. Boredom crept in, producing its silent internal agitation, and Jeremy scanned his mind for things to defeat the mind-numbing vexation. Having the opportunity to see and talk to Joe a few weeks ago rejuvenated his sense of his old life. He invoked his celestial talent and acquired a mental frame of Joe in real time.

Joe's family had finished dinner, and he had gone to the family room to watch the end of the Cubs game but soon dozed off from the great lasagna, salad, and Italian bread meal Connie had prepared.

Next Jeremy checked in on Carl, who had finished dinner and worked in his basement on his new pastime, making pipes for smoking. He told his wife, Lani, it helped him relax, and she found the wafting aroma of the smoke drifting up the basement stairwell pleasing.

Dr. Larry Rindon had received a package with a new high-powered drone and assembled the various parts in accordance with the instructions on the kitchen table while Myra rinsed the dinner dishes before putting them in the dishwasher and then hurried to the family room to watch her favorite series on Netflix.

Jeremy mentally framed Paul Torchetti's home and found him and Marie sitting on the couch in front of the TV. Marie still appeared sad and guilty after she had exposed Jeremy's return to earth, and her home, to several of her friends, causing the incident with the police searching the house but finding no trace of Jeremy. *My terrestrial bosses gave my powers back just in time to transport out of their garage. That was a close one. I hate to see Marie so bummed out; I'll have to find a way to make it up to her.*

■ ■ ■

Longing for the companionship of his old friends tugged at Jeremy's heart. Living in virtual isolation seemed to push his mind into the top layer of depression. *I can't live this way, cooped up in this cracker box indefinitely. Working in the FBI system for a few hours each day is interesting and feels productive, but there are many more hours when the walls close in on me, and I need human interaction. Helping Doc Cavallini broke up the boredom temporarily, but now I'm back to the same old grind. I need to see the guys again. Pollard won't like it, but my life has some gaping holes in it until I can see my family. Having lunch or dinner with my friends would be the next best thing, so Bob will just have to accept it.*

■ ■ ■

Jeremy launched his plan by sending his buddies a group text suggesting they meet for dinner tonight at Carl and Larry's country club in Bull Ridge at seven. He told them he would be there and that they should not share the planned rendezvous with anyone, including their wives. He waited for acknowledgments from each man and received responses immediately.

Pollard will be pissed, but oh well.

42

Light Santa Ana winds from the north and east accompanied the sun to greet Friday morning and bathe So Cal in its warmth. At seven the temperature slowly had risen to a comfortable sixty-eight as Stephanie pulled into her company's parking garage. She looked forward to the last day of the week when most of her colleagues returned from field assignments for meetings and writing reports; and hopefully she could leave a couple hours early in the afternoon. Today, however, her nerves were wound tight with the knowledge tomorrow would be a landmark day in her career and life.

The CEO had scheduled her to assist Pawley's FBI team raiding the FiberLink office to secure computers and other documents pertinent to the scam she had uncovered. Although she did not believe Earle Claypoole would be in the office on a Saturday morning at six o'clock, the thought of pouring over company files and paper documents invoked memories of all her meetings with Earle and his phony RFP and consulting report for the city of Vista Nueva designed to disguise the fraudulent scheme the Claypoole brothers and Brad Wolfe had engineered. As she sipped her coffee and munched a blueberry muffin, a sudden realization raced across her mind. *What if this scam is not the first one these guys have pulled off? I wonder how long this has been going on. Was Brad involved in criminal activities when we dated?* A sickening acid ball of indigestion gripped her abdomen. Could her entire relationship with Brad have been a charade?

She threw the muffin in the garbage and hurried to the rest room.

She bent over the toilet until the convulsions of retching occurred, but nothing came up—dry heaves. She washed her hands and toweled cold water on her face, forcing her makeup to smear and run. Stephanie stared at the image in the mirror. *All those years of dating, even talk of marriage, were really just bullshit. How could I be so stupid? The amorous words, the vacations, concerts, and the sex. I feel violated; that bastard—I hope he goes to prison for a thousand years!* Anger trumped her inclination to cry as she wiped her face with paper towels. A few deep breaths brought her down from the cliff of rage she felt.

Now somewhat composed, she returned to her office and closed the door. She used her compact mirror to reapply makeup and finished the cup of now-cool coffee. *Tomorrow will be a memorable day.*

■ ■ ■

Stephanie bought a salad and Diet Pepsi in the building cafeteria, declining an offer to join her peers for a Friday meal at a favorite Mexican restaurant near the building. She ate in the solitude of her office while reviewing emails on her iPhone. Several phone calls on her business line had stacked up a batch of voice mails, and she played them back between bites. Two were from Earle Claypoole, wondering when results status of the risk review would be available and of course, one from Brad to add to the three he had left on her personal phone. The sound of his voice picked at the emotional scab she had developed in the morning, but now she fended it off with a newfound sense of revulsion at the deceit of the eight years of their previous relationship. She recalled how she had fallen into a bout of depression when Brad inexplicably seemed to drift away two years ago.

She laced her hands behind her head and studied the ceiling as memories of how she tried to elicit reasons for his sudden disinterest yielded no results. She laughed and shook her head, thinking about the dating services she had contacted and the few dates they arranged, but the men seemed creepy.

She rose, walked around her desk, and looked through the glass of her office to the rows of cubes housing colleagues. She swirled the Diet Pepsi before sipping on the straw and smiled at her initial temptation to date a couple men in the office as a reflexive weapon to punish Brad, but her personal principles and forceful warnings from her father had talked her off that dangerous emotional ledge.

Back in her chair, she pulled up the FiberLink file on the office desktop computer and transferred notes into her iPad to take in the morning. She spent the balance of the afternoon returning phone calls and decided to leave at four for her parents' home in Orange anticipating a conversation regarding the FiberLink situation with her father.

Special Agent Jesus Garcia sat in his car in the Fashion Island parking lot facing Steph's building. Since he did not see her leave at lunchtime, he took the opportunity to swing by an In-N-Out Burger location for a quick salad before resuming his observation post. Even with the windows rolled down, the eighty-seven degree heat spawned rivulets of sweat on his neck. He had moved his car several times to take advantage of finding partial shade from the trees on the parkway. He munched a Snickers bar when Stephanie's car emerged from the parking garage. Jesus fumbled the candy onto the floor and started his engine and followed his subject using a special FBI tracking device synched in with FBI drones and choppers in the area that locked on to her vehicle even when it was well out of sight.

The traffic on the I-55 freeway poked along with its usual rush hour traffic snake dance. Stephanie seemed oblivious as her car drove itself while she checked emails on her iPhone. Jesus drove his car himself attempting to zigzag between lanes to close the distance between his car and hers. He deduced from the route she had selected as the one to her parents' home in Orange as he had followed her there several times in the past few weeks.

Stephanie's car transitioned from the 55 to the 5, but the traffic bumped along at the usual Friday snail's pace. Ultimately she exited at Seventeenth Street and used other surface streets to proceed to her parents' home in a gated community in the north side of town.

Garcia had made up some time and caught sight of her car as it turned right several blocks ahead. He slowed as he noted her stopping at the guard-house and then proceeding through the upright gate. At this point he continued on to a favorite restaurant at the Circle in Old Town Orange for dinner and to meet with the agent who would take the next shift.

■ ■ ■

Friday for Brad had been a cruise day; there were no appointments, and he didn't feel like making any calls other than to check with some clients who owed him money. Active waves at the beach beckoned surfers. After a leisurely morning he changed into his wet suit, grabbed his board, and headed for Huntington Beach.

Several of his surfing tribe already were engaged in various phases of the sacred pastime paddling out, sitting on boards staring at the incoming swells, or riding the breaking surf to shore. Brad high-fived several friends as he waded into the water and paddled out to join many other surfers. He loved capturing the exhilaration of catching the right wave and scrambling to his feet and balancing for a long ride. Escape to this fantasy world lasted three hours before he carried his board back to the car and secured it to the roof. His ribs had healed, and he no longer had to avoid this favorite activity.

The exercise had stimulated his appetite, so he thought about what to do about lunch while soaping up in the shower. BK's sounded like the perfect solution, and his car navigated the short drive to his favorite haunt.

"Hi stranger, what'll it be today, the usual?" Julie asked from her position behind the bar. Brad nodded, so she created a vodka martini and slid it toward Brad.

"Julie, you and me should really get together. Do you surf?"

"No, I never had time to learn, and my husband doesn't want me getting hurt and not being able to work."

"Well, tell him you'll be receiving lessons from a pro: me."

"Tell you what; I'll ask him if he wants to come along, and if he says yes, you can give us both lessons."

"Naw, that won't work; you know what they say about three's a crowd."

"Too bad, I can't do it any other way. Sorry."

"One of these days you'll say yes when I ask you out, and you'll be sorry you waited so long."

"Oh well, my loss. You want a sandwich?"

"Yeah, make it a roast beef on sour dough." He admired her slim, but shapely figure. "You need to stop playing hard to get."

"One time I didn't, and the lucky guy is now my husband."

Brad shook his head and joined the conversation the regulars had started an hour before he arrived. Four more martinis and a beer chaser put the self-anointed super salesman in a semi-state of euphoria. After two hours he visited the men's room, then staggered into the bright afternoon sun and sat in his car. *Steph said she's staying at her folks' home on the weekends. I think I'll pay her a visit there.* He checked his iPhone to see how long it would be before she would be at the house in Orange. *It's now 5:17. By the time I get there with this Friday afternoon traffic it'll be six thirty, and she'll be sipping a glass of wine. I never thought she would be a problem interfering with my part-time income scam. She needs to be stopped.* He knew in his intoxicated state he couldn't drive so he directed the car to go to Ryan and Peg Murphy's house in Orange, a route the car had taken many times when he and Steph were dating.

He stopped at the guardhouse and Clyde, the guard on duty, knew Brad for several years when he used to pick Steph up for dates. "Hey Brad, haven't seen you here for a long time. Where you been?"

"Oh, you know Clyde, working sales is a tough job with all the travel." Clyde noted Brad slurred his speech and his eyes appeared glassy.

"You okay?"

"Yeah man, just had a couple pops at lunch. That's why I let the car drive over here. I'll be fine in an hour."

"Okay, but you take care of yourself." He pushed the button to open the gate.

"Will do, Clyde. Thanks." Brad took control of the car, drove around a curve and stopped at the curb. He opened the glove box and removed his Smith and Wesson Model 29 .44 magnum revolver. He checked the magazine verifying it was full and then put it in his pocket. The Murphy house was only three blocks away.

He approached at a slow pace and saw Steph's car in the driveway. "Perfect," he mumbled. He parked on the street in front of the home instead of the driveway in case Ryan pulled up and parked behind him blocking his escape route. *Time to give the little consultan' a scare.*

43

Ivan Markov could hardly contain his rage after the last call with Bob Pollard. He spoke in Russian. "Artemi, you know how bad our boys in St. John fucked up my plans?" Artemi shrugged his shoulders. "I can't ask boss comrade for more time or computer guys to hack the bank's systems to find out how their security works so we can infiltrate and steal customer information and money. Having Terasenko do it for us was best plan, but now I have to pull one of my guys off his assignment and have him do it. I lose the four guys in St. John, so now my team is short. How am I going to get my jobs done on time?" Artemi shrugged again.

Markov paced and swigged his vodka on the rocks, searching for a solution. *I need to get someone who can get into the bank, someone who has access to the systems and understands IT.* He scratched his bald head as an idea surfaced. *One of my guys who knows a bank guard told me the bank has some state and federal regulators who have desks in the bank permanently. I think I'll target one of them who might want to make a little money on the side.* "Artemi, I'll have one of our best agents pose as a reporter to get an appointment with the office of the comptroller of the currency examiner in charge. We need one of our women who can schmooze and also must speak perfect English. She can tell the examiner in charge (EIC) she's doing a story on bank risk management."

"Boss, I recommend Anastasia Alexandrova. She knows how to influence naïve Americans, she speaks fluent English, and she is very—how you say—voluptuous," Artemi offered.

"Good choice, comrade. Once she is in with the regulators, she can get friendly with them and find out who needs money. Then we can turn him into a mole for us, and he will provide an accurate thumb drive with all the information we need. I'm sure Anastasia will charm those Feds and find the weak link for us."

"Boss, do you want her to screw the guy?"

"If that's what it takes, my friend." Ivan smiled for the first time in a long while and drained the remainder of his vodka. "Set it up."

"Will do, boss."

■ ■ ■

Bob Pollard rose from his chair and poured another cup of hairy, dark coffee. *I need to switch to decaf; this shit is winding me too tight.* He paced to break the monotony of sitting for long periods even though emails and phone calls occupied his mind as time raced. After Jeremy saved the Cavallini clan and the four Russian thugs were arrested, he thought an opportunity presented itself to take down Markov and really dent the Midwest segment of the Russian espionage operation in the US. GPS tracking devices on certain phones narrowed Markov's probable location to be in the lakefront area. *Could be an office under a phony name or even an apartment in one of the high-rises. I think I'll have John Eldrick see what he can come up with.* He hit the single button to speed dial his longtime partner who was working a multiple murder case in the south suburbs. "John, Pollard here. How goes the war?"

"Been interviewing persons of interest. This job doesn't get any easier, boss. Talking to the families of the victims is the toughest part."

"I know, bud. Hang in there. I have a change of pace assignment for you; I'll have someone else replace you on the murder case."

"Okay. This mess is depressing."

"I'd like you to find out where our little rat Markov is hiding. We need to bust him and cripple his operation in the Midwest, at least for a while. You know they'll find some other goons to bother the shit out of us, but it'll take some time, slow them down, and give us some temporary relief."

"You want me to come in to the office?"

"Yeah, but it's getting late for today, so finish up there and come in tomorrow. We can brainstorm some ideas on how to smoke him out of his hole."

"See you in the a-m. Bye."

"Later, bye."

■ ■ ■

Anastasia Alexandrova knocked on Markov's apartment door. Artemi squinted at the peep hole to verify her identity, pulled the door open, and glanced both ways in the empty hallway out of an abundance of caution. Anastasia, her flowing dark brown hair swaying in back, exchanged furtive smiles with Artemi and followed him into the living room. Her smooth stride and tight-fitting business suit over an attractive figure portrayed an image of elegance and sophistication.

Markov took her hand and kissed it. He stepped back and observed, "You look lovely as always, my dear."

"Thank you, Mr. Markov. Why did you send for me?"

"I have a special job for you. Please sit down." He motioned her to a sofa. Ivan sat next to her. "Artemi, get Anastasia something to drink. What do you prefer?"

"Green tea, please." Artemi retreated to the kitchen.

"How have you been? I have not seen you for months, it seems."

"I have enjoyed my assignment reviewing the state of Illinois systems. Yesterday I was able to isolate their state employee health care files. I'm in the process of selecting the best ones for us to use for identity theft purposes."

"Excellent. I wish all the operatives on my team could match your success rate. Now, let me tell you about what I want you to do." He took her hand and stroked from the wrist down to the fingernails. Anastasia did not recoil from this advance; she had experienced many types of aggressive behavior by men in the course of her work and possessed confidence in her ability to manage such situations.

Artemi returned with tea for her and more vodka for Ivan.

"We have not been able to obtain a thumb drive with the Heartland Bank security systems and protocols from one of their IT guys who is a Russian defector. The FBI is involved, and they refuse to give us what we want, and now they have hidden the bank's IT man. I cannot afford to pull someone off my other jobs who has IT expertise to hack in and get all the information." He continued to stroke her hand and she crafted an artificial smile. "So, we know the bank is large enough to have state and federal examiners permanently onsite. I want you to pose as a reporter and get in to see the OCC EIC and tell him or her you are doing a general banking story on risk management. Once you're in, get to know the staff and find the weakest one, someone who needs money and will gather the data for us. We will make him an offer he can't refuse."

"What if the weakest link is a female?"

"No, a woman will be jealous of you and will be too hard to break down. Take the next weakest until you get a man."

"What if he wants more than money, like sex?'

"We need to give him what he wants. Do you have a problem with it?"

"I've done it before—more than once."

"Good, good my dear." Ivan leaned and kissed her on the mouth and stroked her breast. She did not recoil, but remained stoic and did not move. "What's wrong, you said you've done it before," he scowled.

"I have a personal policy not to make love with my colleagues, no matter what their level. Sorry."

"Too bad. Maybe we can talk about how your career can advance quicker after you finish the assignment."

"Anything else?" she frowned. "No, you may go."

"Thank you." She sipped her tea and rose, and Artemi let her out. "I'm going to get me some of that one day." Markov said. Artemi glanced at the ceiling.

■ ■ ■

John Eldrick remained in his seat after the FBI team leaders in the Chicago office left Pollard's office at the conclusion of a special meeting, which had begun at seven thirty on this Friday morning. Pollard had called the meeting to reallocate resources with Eldrick moving to a new assignment.

"More coffee?"

"I can use some. Thanks." Pollard filled their cups at a credenza and returned to his desk but sat opposite John in a guest chair.

"This Markov is a slimy little bastard; you saw him at Aureus, remember?"

"How could I forget a bum like him?"

"That's him alright. He uses kidnapping and extortion to get what he wants, and I'm sure he would have had his goons murder Cavallini's family if Chambers hadn't arrived to blow up the whole affair. So, we're dealing with a cold-blooded killer just like the old days with the KGB."

"I recall from our training the Russians have several foreign intelligence agencies working together and that murder and assassination are some of their favorite tools."

"Right. After all the incidents with their agents chasing Jeremy and attempting to assassinate him eight years ago, I've put in some extra time studying the structure of their foreign intelligence program. Our best information tabs Markov as a senior member of the SVR RF, which is their external intelligence agency. This outfit is responsible for intelligence and espionage activities outside the Russian Federation."

"Is this the group that succeeded the KGB?"

"Right again. This agency reports directly to the president of Russia.

There are many other subsystems in the intelligence web; most of them have authority for domestic activities. The GRU is the largest and is primarily responsible for nuclear security and is the military arm of the foreign intelligence architecture, but they have agents worldwide, and they work with the SVR." Pollard paused to nip at his coffee and allow Eldrick to follow the complexity of the Russian intelligence structure. "The SVR breaks down into several subunits; I won't describe them all except for a few. Directorate S deals in illegal intelligence and trains and plants illegal agents abroad who conduct terror operations and sabotage in foreign countries, biological espionage, and recruitment of foreign citizens on the Russian territory. Directorate X is the scientific and technical intelligence arm, and Directorate KR carries out infiltration of foreign intelligence and security services and also conducts surveillance over Russian citizens abroad."

"These guys are creepier than I thought."

"Yes they are. In fact, a rumor has it there's a secret special ops unit called Zaslon in the Directorate S, which operates covertly. This elite unit has about 500 agents who speak several languages and have extensive military experience. I believe Markov is running a wing of Zaslon, so we're up against their best."

"Wow, I guess I didn't realize how well-organized the Russians are."

"Now that you have the crash course on these bad actors, our dilemma is we have not been able to pinpoint Markov's headquarters. Although we have identified and tracked him for several years, members of his team are in deep cover and many are legal immigrants to the US; some are scientists and other professionals."

"So you want me to locate the bastard, but when I do, what's our next move?"

"We need to assemble all the evidence we've gathered and arrest him for a long laundry list of crimes."

"Maybe the goons we arrested in St. John will do some singing and give us some juicy intel."

"That's the plan." Bob leaned toward his partner. "John, I know you and I have seen some bad shit over the years and have been in uncomfortable situations, but I can't emphasize enough how dangerous Markov is. He's a throwback to the old KGB assholes who were ruthless killers. You need to be extra careful."

"Got it. I like the challenge of this assignment, and I really want to nail that little bastard; thanks for thinking of me, boss."

"I would not trust anyone else on this one. By the way, I think Markov is scared of you." Pollard reclined in his chair and laughed.

"What do you mean?"

"When we met him in the restaurant his eyes bugged out of his head when he saw how big you are and that you are a black man; you intimidated the little shit," Pollard couldn't stifle a giggle.

"Good, I'll take any advantage I can get."

"Roger that. After we finish here, see Dave Swayne; he has our dossier on Markov and his group so far. Dave thinks Markov and his boys have dedicated secure commo lines, but they also use burn phones to stay in the shadows where we can't find them."

"Can't wait to get started." Eldrick rose and left the office.

Pollard walked around his desk and eased into his chair. *This will be our best chance to nail Markov and his band of hoods. I need to rein John in; he's maybe too eager, and I don't want him getting hurt.*

44

Brad Wolfe breathed deeply to shake the alcohol-induced cobwebs from his mind. Walking slowly and deliberately, he approached the Murphy's front door. *Time for some payback, Stephie.* He rang the bell, and Peg Murphy opened the door. "Brad, how nice to see you. Come on in." She bear-hugged him. "You still look great. I'll tell Steph you're here. Do you want something to drink?"

"Thanks, great to see you too, Peg. Ice tea would be fine." He found a large chair in the family room.

Peg and Steph, dressed in shorts, a tee, and flip flops, walked in from a hall, which led to a wing housing most of the bedrooms. Peg veered off to the kitchen to prepare drinks.

Brad stood when he saw Steph. "Hi, babe. You never answer your phones, so I thought I'd stop by. Glad I caught you at home." His manufactured smile scarcely masked his contempt for the woman who once occupied a special place in his life. Peg brought tea for three. "Peg, could you give us some privacy?"

"Oh sure, honey." She retired to her bedroom.

"Brad, what are you doing here? I told you I don't want to see you ever again, especially after you hurt my arm in the parking lot. So please leave."

"Not so fast. We had a good time at lunch and then you act like we're enemies. Why can't we still date once in a while, you know like old times?"

"It's over; you're not the guy I thought you were, and I won't put up with you hurting me physically. So just turn around and leave . . . now."

"Sorry, no can do. You've been fucking up my finances with your shitty little audit at FiberLink. You need to back off or you might really get hurt."

Stephanie' eyelids expanded at this revelation. "I can't believe you're involved in the scam I uncovered with the Claypooles. I always knew money is at the top of your list, but I never dreamed you would get involved in stealing." She stood her ground.

"I like to live large, and it takes more money than I could make at sales, so my arrangement with the boys is an easy way to supplement my income."

"It's a crime; didn't that ever occur to you?"

"Come on, Steph, grow up. No one was hurt by our little game, and the payoffs have been generous."

"What about the taxpayers of Vista Nueva? And the shareholders of FiberLink?"

"They never knew what we were doing; out of sight out of mind, as they say."

"Bullshit. The fact they weren't aware they were being ripped off doesn't mean they weren't harmed. You guys need to pay all the money you stole back to those people." The young attorney shifted on her feet, sensing the situation could escalate from Brad's menacing stare.

"No chance, babe. That money is ours. I have expensive taste, and it takes lots of bread to finance the things I want. No way I'll give the money back."

"Do you realize what kind of trouble you're in?"

"What'd you mean, trouble?"

"I have to report what I find in my review, and I found the phony RFP and consulting report; I confirmed all the fraud, so my boss will have to take appropriate steps."

"What steps? You're not going to report anything but a clean audit to your boss, bitch." He removed his gun and waved it back and forth. "This is serious shit, Stephie, and I'm not going to let you or anyone fuck it up. Let's go; you're coming with me, and don't even think about screaming to for your mom. Or I'll drop you where you stand" He motioned for her to head to the front door. "Wait, get your purse and give me your phone. We're going to take a ride to your office and change your report." She shuddered as fear bubbled up her spine. She picked up her purse and retrieved the iPhone and handed it to him.

"No, I'm not going anywhere with you." She started to back away forcing confidence in her face, but barely hid intensifying panic in her chest. "You won't shoot me. You may be an asshole, but murder isn't something you'd do."

"You never did really know me, did you babe? I need to have your company give FiberLink a clean bill of health with maybe a couple suggestions how to improve their security. Let's go." He grabbed her arm and pointed the gun in her back while pulling her to the front door. She resisted only slightly; she never had a gun in her back before and now couldn't judge Brad's level of intoxication or willingness to use the weapon.

Once outside he scanned the neighborhood while holding the gun in his pocket and escorted his hostage to his car. He pulled her around and motioned to the driver's seat while he settled into the passenger side. He pushed the button to start the car and asked her for the street address of her office in Newport Beach. She recited it, and he punched the information into the navigation system and tapped "go."

As the car cleared the driveway and turned to head for the freeway, Ryan Murphy's car passed going the opposite direction as he drove Kyle home from baseball practice. He saw Stephanie's grim expression and honked his horn, but Brad's car did not respond and continued on. His daughter had shared all the depressing details of her FiberLink risk review and ugly encounters with her former boyfriend, and he sensed she might be in a precarious situation. He pulled into his driveway and called Peg to ascertain why Steph would be driving Brad's car. Peg told him she didn't know they had left, that Brad had shown up, and he and Steph were in the family room. Ryan updated her on what he had just seen and asked where Kelly was, and Peg said she was attending a sleepover at a friend's house since it was Friday night. Ryan told Peg to lock the door with Kyle inside and to call the FBI.

"What's wrong, Grandpa?" Kyle asked.

"Nothing, son, I just need to pick up Steph. See you soon." Kyle raced from the car and bolted into the house. Ryan called Steph's cell, but it rotated to voice mail. He left a message for her to call him ASAP and asked where she was. He then backed out of the driveway and headed for the freeway, uncertain where he would go. *Damn it! This shit never stops. I guess I'll have to take my family to Idaho to be safe.*

45

Jeremy waited until 6:50 Friday night before transporting to the country club. He landed awkwardly in the parking lot and a valet attendant turned and saw him just as he tripped. "Are you okay, sir?"

"Yeah, I just stubbed my toe on a crack in the blacktop." He entered the clubhouse and noticed his four friends at the bar. He joined them, and they all shouted greetings, slapped backs and exchanged fist bumps. Carl led them to a private room and ordered a bottle of white wine from the waiter.

The men relaxed and commented on Jeremy's different appearance; Larry whistled at the blond hair. After one glass of Chardonnay, the bottle had little left, so Carl ordered another while the men placed their dinner orders.

Jeremy recounted his adventures since returning to earth as Joe and Paul nodded at the parts they had observed when the spaceman visited Joe's back yard and when he hid in Paul's house.

The meal arrived, and the group temporarily suspended conversation to eat. After dessert Carl ordered an expensive bottle of Port, and they reclined in the high-back chairs. Carl produced a pipe and fired it up while explaining how he made this smoking device and others in his new collection. Cigarettes and cigars were banned from inside the club restaurant, but pipes were exempt from the rule.

■ ■ ■

At 8:40 Jeremy experienced a shooting pain from his left eye to the center of his brain. He screamed and stood holding his face and head. The others leapt to their feet and crowded around him, asking what happened. After several minutes the pain subsided, and they all sat down. Jeremy continued to rub his forehead and moan softly. His friends regarded him with genuine concern, not speaking.

Jeremy drifted into a trance-like countenance, and his eyebrows appeared to furrow and then release as if he were listening to conversation. He cocked his head. "Oh no, leave her alone," he shouted.

The others fired questions at him, but he held up his right hand to silence them. "Sorry guys, someone's in trouble. I gotta go. Glad I was able to see you all. Oh, I'm going to have to program your minds to erase the fact I was at our meeting here." He stood and hugged each man and then stood away from the table, closed his eyes, and strained. Seconds later he was gone.

46

Stephanie stared at the road as Brad's car bumped along in traffic on the 5 and then the 55 freeway; Friday nights in Southern California always extended the rush hour when some people ventured out for the evening and then, combined with workers driving home, clogged the freeways.

Brad saw Ryan's name appear on her phone's screen and smiled as he put the device back in his pocket.

"You aren't going to shoot me, Brad. It would complicate the trouble you're already in." Stephanie's voice quivered.

"You don't get it, do you, bitch? I can't let this income stream dry up; I need the money. All we have to do is doctor your report and have you tell your boss you made a mistake and everything will be cool. If you do anything to fuck this up, I will kill you."

Stephanie began to believe her captor was losing his grasp on reality and actually might shoot her. A chill zipped up her back. She couldn't tell him the raids were scheduled for tomorrow morning and if he saw her file, he'll know the latest version of the report was final and could not be changed. She faced the road and decided any further conversation with this monster would be fruitless and might even provoke him to do something stupid. Once again thoughts filtered into her mind about her relationship with Brad back in the beginning when they used to laugh and have fun. *How could I have missed the signs? Now he may kill me.*

They pulled into the garage assigned to her building, and she drove the car to her reserved space. Brad exited first, then told her to get out slow.

They entered the building and stopped at the reception desk. "Hi Ken, I need to do a little last-minute work on my project. This is Brad, and he's assisting me." Ken, the uniformed guard asked for the visitor's driver's license and had him sign in. He buzzed them through the electronic gate, and they took the elevator to Steph's floor.

"Well done, sweetie. Now let's get into your office and do some surgery on that report."

She led him to her office and he told her to sit in her desk chair while he looked over her left shoulder. She booted the computer and retrieved the FiberLink file.

Brad placed the gun on the desk, pushed her aside, and leaned over while he read the report. He shook his head and mumbled at the findings and conclusions, which could send him and the Claypoole brothers to prison. "This is bad shit, you little bitch." He slapped her face with the back of his right hand. She squealed and held her left cheek. "You start changing things right now, and then you're going to write an email to your boss and tell him you had to make some corrections to the report, which you will attach to the email." He backed away as Steph rolled her chair to the center of the desk and began to alter paragraphs in the report as she massaged her face while tears spilled on to her lap.

Brad stood waving the gun back and forth. "Did you tell the police about what you found?"

"No, no I swear I didn't."

"You're a fucking liar; I can see it in your eyes. What did you tell them?"

"I didn't tell them anything; my boss met with them."

"What are they planning to do about this?"

"I don't know, I'm just a peon here."

"Wrong, you told me you're a partner; that's not peon status." He slapped her again in the same place on her left cheek, which caused her to lurch to the right, moving the chair and almost dumping her to the floor. "You better stop lying to me, or I'll kill you right here and dump your body down the garbage shoot. Now, what are the police going to do?"

Steph realized she had arrived at the point of self-preservation and that Brad was delusional and would no doubt shoot her. "The FBI is going to raid FiberLink tomorrow morning."

"And what else; there has to be more." He grabbed a handful of her hair and yanked it back. Tears steamed in rivulets on her cheeks, and her convulsive sobs combined with the position of her head stretched backward hindered her speech. "They're going to raid your house and the brothers' houses, too."

"Damn. You're the one who started all this bullshit. I want you to call the FBI guy in charge and tell him to shut it down, or I'll kill you."

"I don't have his number. I didn't deal with him."

"Then call the LA FBI office and ask for him. What's his name?'

"I think it's Pawley. Brad, please drop this whole thing and run away. I swear I won't tell anyone."

"No can do; I'm in too far to turn back. Call the LA office and get Pawley's number, now!"

Steph sniffled and did as she was told with trembling hands. The receptionist at the LA office said she couldn't give agents' numbers to the public, but she would get a message to him and have him call her. Steph provided her cell number.

Brad used his phone to text Earle and Phil about the FBI raid scheduled for tomorrow morning and told them to leave tonight. Minutes later as Steph worked on revising the final report, Brad's cell buzzed. "Hey Earle, why haven't you answered my calls or texts until now?"

"Been busy, bud. What's this shit about some FBI raid; is it a fucking joke to get me to call you?"

"'Fraid not. I'm in Steph's office, and she's revising her report that accuses us of fraud and embezzlement, and I'm having her send an email to her boss telling him she was wrong and that FiberLink has weak security but is clean otherwise. I'm going to have her call him, too, but I wanted to get the revisions in writing."

"How did you manage to get her to do these things when you said she wouldn't talk to you anymore?"

"Never-mind, long story; let's just say she's convinced. You guys better get the hell outta Dodge tonight. I'm going to leave as soon as Stephie finishes the assignments I gave her."

"I can't believe all this is for real."

"Your choice, bro, you can roll the dice if you want, but a lot of shit's going to come down on us if we don't get the hell away from here."

"I'll talk to Phil and get back to you."

"Okay. Let's all stop at Walmart and buy some burn phones so the Feds can't track us."

"How will we get the prepaid numbers to each other?"

"I don't know; we'll have to meet up at some point and exchange them. We can't use our business or personal phones anymore."

"Right. See you later."

Steph finished the revisions and email and sat back in the chair rubbing her face and whimpering. Brad checked her computer and read the revised report and proposed email to the CEO. He had her make a couple minor changes and then hit send. He then thrust his face inches from hers. "Print out a copy of the revised report and the email to your boss. Now we're going to call Mr. Schwedland and fuck up his weekend. Call him." He folded the copies and put them in his pants pocket.

"I don't have his number." He slapped her again.

"Do you think I was born yesterday? Every business has a master list of every employee's contact information. Now pull it up on the screen."

Her eyes blurred from full-scale weeping as she accessed the firm's roster and clicked on Al's name. Employees were not allowed to maintain the master list contact information on their cells for security reasons.

"That's better. Call him and say you revised the report and he has it in his email; he can read it on his phone." Steph tried to recover from the beating she had taken and fumbled at keying Al's number into her phone. "Hurry up, bitch."

Before she could call, her cell buzzed with an incoming call from Mark Pawley. Brad looked at the name and grabbed Steph by the hair again. "You tell the FBI asshole what you're going to tell your boss and tell him to stop the raids tomorrow. Got it?" She nodded and took several deep breaths to moderate her composure and vocal rhythm. She relayed the message as Brad moved the phone slightly away from her ear so he could listen, too. Pawley sensed tension in her voice.

"Steph, I'm surprised you have changed your mind. What happened?"

"After I checked my file one last time, I noticed some things I missed during the review process. I didn't want us to accuse people of things they didn't do."

"Okay then, but it seems strange; I thought we had everything locked down. Does Al know?"

"Not yet, I sent him an email and was about to call him when you called."

"Well, I'm disappointed all of us put in so much work for nothing, but we have to do what's right. Thanks, Steph. Are you okay? Your voice seems different."

"No, I'm fine, just a summer cold. Bye and thanks."

"Right, I hope you feel better. Bye."

Steph called Al, but his line was busy (with a call from Pawley), so she left a voice mail.

"Good job, you little slut. Now it's time for me to take off for calmer waters." Brad collected Steph's phone and instructed her to lead him to a utility closet. She rose as her body shuddered.

"Are you going to shoot me? Please, please don't, Brad. I did everything you wanted. Please don't kill me."

"I'll decide in a couple minutes. Now get going."

47

Anastasia Alexandrova smiled at the security guard at Heartland Trust and Savings Bank and presented her phony driver's license and passport as two pieces of personal identification required for entry to bank premises. She signed in on Monday morning indicating she had an appointment with Ms. Irene Barbaro, lead examiner in charge of the relationship with the bank on behalf of the Office of the Comptroller of the Currency's Supervision and Regulation Department. She waited in the anteroom to the lobby for ten minutes until an administrative assistant arrived to escort her to regulators' quarters on the fifteenth floor.

Ms. Barbaro extended her hand, shook with Anastasia, and waved her into the office. "So, Ms. Alexandrova, you are here to do a general article on how American regulators evaluate banks' risk management systems?"

"Yes, ma'am and thank you for allowing me to be here. My magazine, *The Crucible,* back in Slovkia will be most happy to show how you Americans review your banks so our regulators can measure how well they are doing in supervising Slovakian banks."

"I'm afraid we can't share our proprietary protocols and tools, but we can talk in general terms. Your name sounds Russian."

"Yes, my father is from Russia and my mother is Slovakian and they live in Slovakia."

"Interesting. Well, I have arranged for you to interview several of our examiners who are working on different segments of the bank's risk program." She extended a sheet of paper reflecting the agenda for the day, including the names of the examiners she would be meeting and the times of day for each. The examiner for her eleven o'clock interview would be taking Anastasia to lunch in the bank cafeteria. "Would you like some coffee before you get started?"

"Green tea, thank you." Irene heated a cup of water and brought it to her guest on a tray with a tea bag, cream, and various sugar alternatives.

After several minutes of general conversation, she led the reporter out to the floor where the examiners each had small cubicles with low walls and introduced her to a woman who would be her first interviewee. Irene smiled and returned to her office.

Anastasia used the recording feature of her phone and also typed notes into her iPad in each interview. At lunchtime, Examiner Randall Mehler took Anastasia to lunch, affording the visitor an opportunity to use her expertise and skills in personality evaluation to probe Mehler for information about his personal life and finances. At the conclusion of the meal, her assessment pegged this man as having his financial life in order and would not make a good target for her to recruit.

Anastasia's arrangement with Ms. Barbaro was for a full week of scheduled interviews with two open time slots Tuesday through Friday, allowing her to speak to examiners she had previously interviewed to answer new or follow-up questions she might have. She requested that the eleven o'clock slot each of the four days be allocated as open, giving her leverage to return to people she identified as possible marks for her recruitment efforts. Tuesday and Wednesday did not yield any targets, but on Thursday morning she interviewed Herman French, a forty-three-year-old with four kids and a wife who worked part time at T. J. Maxx.

Anastasia scheduled French into the open slot at eleven to explore whether he would be a good candidate to recruit. She flirted and leaned forward displaying her ample cleavage, capturing Herman's attention.

"Wow, this is getting out of hand Ms. Alexandrova." He moved slightly away.

"Please, call me Stasi. I think we are becoming good friends."

She learned two of his kids were in college, one at Illinois State and the other at College of DuPage, which appeared to be placing stress on his family finances. She goaded him into discussions regarding education and health care costs as well as the onerous Illinois state income tax. He lamented the fact his wife couldn't go full time to provide more assistance with the bills.

On Thursday at lunch Anastasia offered to buy him a drink after work, which he pondered and then declined, but she put her arm around his shoulder and coaxed him by whispering in his ear. Because her perfume was intoxicating, he agreed to stop with her for one drink.

At five thirty they visited a nearby watering hole offering muted lighting, and she led him to a booth against the back wall. After one drink he attempted to leave, but she held his arm and stroked his thigh with her other hand. He agreed to stay for one more, which turned into three more. She had consumed several mouthfuls out of a small bottle of Pepto-Bismol in the ladies' room when they arrived to coat her stomach, which would allow her to drink heavily without getting drunk. Herman drifted into a mellow state of euphoria between the number of drinks he was not used to having and the amorous fondling by his companion.

Anastasia scrutinized him carefully, and when he seemed most vulnerable, she told him quietly she had a proposal for him. "If you will create a flash drive with the bank's security protocols, third party software, and firewalls—all of those things, I will give you fifty thousand dollars."

"I don't know; I shouldn't do something like that. If they catch me I'll be in big trouble. I can't think straight right now. How much did you say?"

"Fifty thousand. Think of what that money will do for your family. Will you give me the flash drive tomorrow night?"

Herman squirmed and closed his eyes to organize the many thoughts floating through an alcohol-clouded mind.

"Fifty grand, baby. That will make all your troubles disappear." She rubbed against him and traced his face with her index finger.

"Fifty grand. I could use that kind of money."

"Tax free," she added.

She continued to paw him but executed a pregnant pause to allow him to convince himself he should accept her offer.

"Okay, I'll do it."

"Wonderful, darling. I'll have the eleven o'clock time slot with you again tomorrow, and I'll take you to a nice place for lunch."

"We're not supposed to accept gifts like lunch from people outside our agency." She looked at him, cocked her head, and displayed a grin with a full mouth of perfect white teeth. "What the hell, if I'm going to take the fifty, what's the harm in a lunch?" She nodded and kissed his cheek.

Anastasia took out a credit card, but Herman gave her a twenty dollar bill to pay for part of the bill. She folded the bill in half, and as they left the bar she slid the cash into his pants pocket. They walked as far as Madison Street together, and then she kissed him on the mouth, turned, and headed east while he stood staring at her derriere before turning and heading west to the train station.

■ ■ ■

Friday morning Anastasia interviewed Herman at eleven o'clock but did not mention their arrangement. As promised, she took her target examiner to lunch at a steakhouse on Monroe Street a few blocks from the bank. They settled into a secluded booth and ordered a drink and expensive steak sandwiches.

"Well, my love, do you have something for me?"

"Yes. Here it is." He passed the drive under the table. She glanced around the restaurant discretely, swept the small device into her purse, and then kissed him with an open mouth. Anastasia anticipated his uncertainty regarding the sequence of events and said she would give him the cash after work at the bar. He relaxed; they laughed and enjoyed the meal.

"I can't stay long tonight; one of my younger kids has a Pony League game."

"No worries, dear. We'll just have a couple drinks to celebrate and you can catch your train to make it to the game." After an hour and a half, they returned to the bank.

Anastasia found a small conference room and plugged the flash drive into her iPad to verify the information. She reviewed the data Herman had gleaned and smiled at its organization and depth. *Well done, Mr. Herman; this is just what I wanted.*

At five o'clock she waited for him in the lobby, and they walked to the same bar they had visited last night. She again requested a booth in the back of the dimly lit room. She nudged her body against his and kissed his cheeks, then his mouth. They ordered drinks and some appetizers. When the server had delivered the food and drinks, Anastasia produced five manila envelopes and opened them on her lap. She fanned the bulging bundle of $100 bills in each packet so he could confirm she had brought the full amount. She passed the envelopes to him after he had opened his backpack, and he quickly slipped them inside.

Herman French reclined and exhaled; he was a happy man. "I feel like I just won the lottery."

"Yes, you did. Don't deposit more than ten thousand at any one time; you know the money laundering rules." They both laughed, and then she turned to face him as her countenance dissolved from merriment into an earnest expression. "Let me ask you an important question, my darling. Do you have access to the type of information on the flash drive you gave me at lunch for other banks you have examined?"

"Sure, I have access to our files, why?"

"I was thinking maybe we can do some more business together. You can make a ton of money with me, baby."

"You mean like we just did today?"

"Yes, of course. I have a lot of money to exchange for more flash drives. Are you interested?"

"Wow, that's a big risk. I can't afford to get caught."

"Neither can I. Tell you what: I'll even add some spice to the deal."

"Spice, what spice?"

"If we can establish an ongoing relationship, I'll take you to a hotel from time to time and give you more spice than you've ever had."

"Whoa, I don't know about that." She leaned against him and rubbed his thigh while kissing him tenderly. "Well, maybe I'll think about it."

"Good, I'm sure we can make some beautiful music together."

"Like I said, I'll consider it. I need to bolt or I'll miss my train. Thanks for everything, Stasi." He kissed her and stood to leave.

"Goodbye, my love, I'll be calling you next week." She blew a kiss off her outstretched hand. He returned the gesture and hustled out the door. *That pig Markov will be pleased I opened a new channel for us to gather information on Americans.* She swirled her drink, wiped her mouth vigorously with a napkin, and motioned for Artemi, who had occupied a table fifteen feet away and had witnessed her tryst with French, to join her. He slid into the booth, and they exchanged a passionate kiss.

"I thought you told Markov you don't get involved with coworkers," Artemi mumbled in Russian as he withdrew a couple inches from her lips.

"That rule is only for him; he disgusts me."

48

The slight tremor in Stephanie's voice combined with the inexplicable request to abort the operation tomorrow morning confirmed the concern in Mark Pawley's mind after Peg Murphy's frantic call an hour ago, but he concluded Brad must be pulling the strings, so he played along to protect her. After he clicked off the call, however, he speed dialed Al Schwedland who was attending a charity event in LA. Al didn't pick up on the call, so Mark sent him an urgent text.

Al called in two minutes. "Hey Mark, couldn't take your call, I'm at the Opening Ceremonies of the LA Special Olympics. I just stepped into the hall so I can talk. I'm scheduled to speak in ten minutes. What's up?"

"I just had a call from Stephanie Murphy telling me she made some mistakes in her review and the three guys we targeted are innocent, said she found some things in her review she missed the first time. Sounds to me like Wolfe put her up to the call; she seemed nervous and her voice was different. She said she sent you an email and tried to call you, but my call to her interrupted."

"I haven't had a chance to check my email since I'm up front with the other speakers. Hang on, let me see . . . yes, here it is. Holy shit, I can't believe this."

"Me either, so let's assume she's being coerced. The call from her came from her office. We need to act fast with a plan B. If any of the three guys are holding her against her will and forcing her to do things she doesn't want to do, we should move up the raid to tonight because the three perps will be taking off soon. I'll work on getting my teams together and coordinating our move tonight."

"Mark, make sure nothing happens to Steph."

"Right, her safety is paramount. I'll send a team to your firm's location and keep you posted."

"Thanks, and if you need me for anything, call and I'll leave here right away."

"Will do, but I think it's in our hands now." He ended the call and contacted his team leaders on a conference line.

■ ■ ■

Stephanie whimpered as she picked up her purse and started for the door to her office with Brad at her back. As the pair passed through the doorway, they heard a crash to the right a few cubicles down the aisle.

Jeremy Chambers had fallen onto a desk and then to the floor. He stood up rubbing his left arm. "Hold it right there, Brad. Let Steph go."

"What the hell? It can't be little Jeremy, can it? What's with the blond hair, glasses and beard? You stay where you are or the bitch gets one in the back."

"No, no you're not going to do that. Put the gun down and your hands up. Your little game is over." He took several deliberate steps toward the kidnapper and the hostage.

"I heard all about your supposed super powers, but I still don't believe it. You've been hiding in here for an hour; I didn't hear you come in."

"No, that's wrong, Brad. I transported from Chicago a few seconds ago, and I do have special skills."

"Oh yeah, show me an example, you little shit."

"Okay, I usually don't announce what I'm going to do in advance to assholes like you, but I'll make an exception this time. I'm going to put you into a state of suspension until the cops arrive."

"Really? I haven't been in 'suspension' for a long time, like the last time I was drunk. So go ahead Mr. Big Shot."

"Put the gun down and let Steph move away from you."

"Not a chance shithead. She's my ticket outta here."

Jeremy concentrated to cast the spell on the captor but didn't feel the usual rush of energy that accompanied such efforts. He opened his eyes as panic slid across his face. *Shit, I'm not getting my vibes; hope I'm not vulnerable.*

Brad didn't notice any different feeling; he stepped to Stephanie's left and raised the gun and fired two rounds at the intruder. Jeremy anticipated he was a target and started to dive behind the cubicle to his left, but one of the shots punctured the right side of his abdomen. He screamed in pain as he bounced off the chair and onto the floor.

"Nooooo! Jeremy, are you hurt?" Steph screamed.

"Okay, slut, we're leaving now." Brad pulled his hostage by the arm toward the doors to the hall. "Where's the utility closet?" Steph pointed to a door twenty feet on the left. He pushed her to the door and tried the handle, but it was locked. "Do you have a key?"

'No, only the housekeeping staff has them."

"Fuck. Okay then, we're going to the men's room." He asked her for directions, and she led him to the door. He pushed her inside but didn't have materials to gag her and tie her hands and feet. "I can't leave you here unless I shoot you, but then I lose my leverage. You're coming with me until I'm out of the country, and don't even think about screaming or running. If you do, I'll kill you and then the cops will kill me."

"Is that what you want? Death by cops?"

"Shut up. I either get out of here alive and go to someplace safe, or they get me. I'm not doing any time in prison as some guy's wife. Let's go to the elevator." He brought her out of the men's room and down the hall to the elevator bank. He pressed the down button and held it down with a shaky hand, thinking it would speed the car to their floor.

The doors opened, and a bald man with white hair and a deep tan in a flowered shirt and khaki shorts stood at the rear of the car. "Good evening, going down?"

Brad pointed the gun at the mystery man. "Who the fuck are you?"

"I'm here to see my friend, Jeremy Chambers. Do you know where he might be?"

Brad displayed his gun and moved toward the elevator. "Okay gramps, get out, and don't try to follow us or the bitch dies."

Cavallini stopped at the threshold of the car and held the door with one hand. "Why are you holding this poor girl at gunpoint?"

"None of your business. Now get out of the way."

"I'm afraid I can't do that, sir."

Brad pushed Stephanie until she was even with the doctor.

Dominic Cavallini held his right hand at face level with his palm facing Brad and Stephanie and froze Brad's mind and body in instant suspension. He stepped out of the car as Stephanie gushed tears when the doctor took her in his arms and whispered soothing words of comfort, then after her weeping faded, he asked. "Where's Jeremy?"

"He was shot, over there. Who are you?" she pointed to the area of the office where he had fallen.

"A friend. Stay here, dear. I'm going to check on him."

"What if Brad wakes up? I'm still scared."

"He'll wake up when I let him. The FBI and police are downstairs in the lobby and will be up here in a minute or two." He walked deliberately to where she had indicated his fellow spaceman had fallen.

Jeremy stayed on the floor and out of Brad's sight and had removed his shirt to use in applying pressure to his wound when Cavallini came around the corner of the cube. "Fancy meeting you here, my friend." The doctor helped the wounded man to his feet as Jeremy moaned in pain.

"Doc, how did you know I was here?"

"Did you forget our bosses know all? They sent me to help you. Now, let's do a little magic and heal your body." The doctor focused on the wound and removed the shirt as the bloody tissue quickly morphed into smooth healthy skin.

"Thanks, man. I owe you."

"Bullshit, you saved my family in St. John. Just returning the favor."

A commotion near the elevator broke the eerie silence in the empty office. The two friends ducked behind the cube wall. "I think we should get out of here before the law sees us." Cavallini woke Brad after he saw an FBI agent had taken his gun and patted him down and then erased the fact he had appeared and froze Brad from Steph's mind.

"I lost my powers, I can't transport," Jeremy whispered. "You can piggyback on me. Where do you want to go?"

"Pollard has me staying in the boiler room of the Field Museum."

"Wow, first class."

"Pollard had it fixed up so it's not too bad. Do you think it will work if I go with you?"

"Let's find out." Cavallini closed his eyes, and the two men disappeared.

■ ■ ■

Earle Claypoole sat in front of the large screen TV in his family room mulling the astonishing news Brad Wolfe had shared with him a few minutes ago. *I guess it wasn't a joke; he sounded tense. I need to throw some things together and get out of here.* He couldn't risk his story about passing off the phony consulting contract with the city of Vista Nueva as sloppy business practice; he knew it wouldn't fly with the Feds after Brad's warning.

He assembled personal documents and financial records in his home office, locked file cabinets, and placed them in his briefcase. A quick note to his sleeping wife, Cathy, that a business opportunity had been offered to him and he had to leave for a meeting tonight covered this base. He signed with love and left it on his desk. He also took the key for his safe deposit box at his bank. He looked around the office checking for any details he might have missed, and seeing none, he headed for the garage.

■ ■ ■

"Hey, it's me."

Phil Claypoole was about to crawl into bed but sat on the edge to answer the call from his brother. "He bro, what's up? I'm just getting ready to hit the hay."

"You better get dressed. I just had a call from Wolfe, and he said the cops and Feds are going to raid our houses tomorrow morning early. He's at Murphy's office, and he read her report on my company. It accuses us of fraud. He's going to flee the area and told me we should, too."

"Are you shittin' me? I thought we were home free. What about our plan to play dumb and chalk it up to sloppy record keeping by FiberLink?"

"Yeah, me too, but I don't want to take a chance since the Feds are involved. I'm on my way out the door, and I'm going to stop and buy some burn phones like Wolfe suggested. We can figure out a way to contact each other later. The point is the damn heat's on, and we need to get out—now."

"Holy shit, this is for real. I'm pulling my pants on now. "Later, bro,"

"Good luck to both of us." Phil clicked off, but the phone call and his stumbling in the bedroom woke Judy who groggily asked him what he was doing. He told her it was Earle who wanted a document and he had to go downstairs to the office to get it.

Phil duplicated his brother's movements in collecting the items he wanted to take with him, but didn't think to leave Judy a note.

49

John Eldrick hoisted his large frame from the guest chair in Dave Swayne's small office at FBI headquarters in Chicago. Swayne had schooled him on all the information he had developed on Ivan Markov and his band of thugs over the last several years. The group appeared to be highly organized and efficiently run, although the recent arrest of four members of the unit in St. John when they held Dr. Cavalini's family hostage definitely represented a setback, and the impact on the gang's ability to reconstitute itself could not be estimated. Swayne surmised Markov might move his headquarters after this incident, which would increase an already enormous challenge for Eldrick.

John returned to his office and reviewed Swayne's report in detail, including positive IDs of his operatives in the Chicago area. However, the FBI had successfully learned of the residences of only three low-level goons because they had been careless in failing to slip their FBI tails when returning home. All the other IDs were of operatives in the open in the metro area when they were engaged in their assignments. Markov and his top lieutenants had many years of training and experience enabling them to use stealth in maintaining effective obscurity in eluding any adversaries' tracking attempts. The only time John had seen Markov was at the Aureus Restaurant when the Russian came to meet with him and Pollard. Swayne had given Eldick several photos and short videos of Markov in disguises at various locations in the city, but the Feds had not been able to locate his residence or headquarters.

Eldrick stared at the yellow lined tablet on his desk next to the Swayne file. He asked an administrative assistant for a map of the six-county region and used a red pen to circle the places Markov had been photographed. He connected the red circles with straight lines, but no definitive pattern emerged. *This little bastard is slippery, but there must be a way I can find his nest, and when I do, I'll make him pay.* He tapped the red pen on the tablet and rotated his head to loosen the tightness in his neck. *They use burn phones and library computers to communicate, so we haven't been able to track them electronically. I'm beginning to think the only way we're going to flush out Markov is to pressure one of his peon goons who will lead us to his home.* He checked the three names of Markov's sycophants whom he had his agents follow home. Not much was known about any of them as each of their files was thin; *must be new guys.* Eldrick printed the file on Andrei Donskov.

Mr. Donskov had entered a new high rise south of the Loop on Prairie Street east of State Street and two blocks from the lakefront. Tracing this man's movements for a few days to establish his routine would require another resource or two to provide surveillance twenty-four/seven. He called Pollard to request two agents expecting pushback from his boss, but surprisingly it was granted. *Wow, Bob must want Markov as much as I do.*

John contacted the two men Pollard assigned and set up a meeting for tomorrow, which gave them the rest of today to debrief their respective team leaders on their cases.

The next day Eldrick shared the file information with his two agents, and they established a rotation for watching Donskov's building and following him whenever he left or returned home.

■ ■ ■

"Did you get good video and audio of our friend Herman at lunch and here in the bar?" Anastasia asked Artemi in Russian as he blew in her ear and kissed her cheek.

"But of course, my sweet Stasi."

"Good; it will be our private insurance policy to use if he decides to double-cross us. I'll go to Markov's place tomorrow and give him the flash drive and tell him I may be able to get security data on other banks in the city from my little pet, Herman."

"I'm sure Ivan will be happy."

The couple continued their clandestine tryst in the booth in the darkness of the bar.

■ ■ ■

Anastasia rang the bell at Markov's condo at eight the next morning, and Artemi let her in. They exchanged coy smiles as he led her into the living room.

Markov wore a grey athletic sweat suit striped in red down the arms and legs as he reclined on a couch, checking his messages on a burn phone. He stood at the sight of Anastasia and kissed her hand. "Well, my dear, how was your week?"

"Very productive. Here is the flash drive. I verified the data after he gave it to me." She handed him the small device.

"Excellent, excellent. I may have to give you a bonus." Artemi turned his head toward the window to shield a look of exasperation.

"I may have more good news, boss. I planted a seed in Herman's mind about providing security data on other large banks in Chicago and the area around the city, maybe even big banks in other states. He said he would consider my proposal."

"Do you really think he will go for that?"

"I think there is a good chance; he can take the pressure off his finances with the money I gave him, but now he's getting greedy; he's thinking of some nice toys he can buy for himself."

"He may not want to draw attention to himself if he starts spending money on cars and vacations."

"Could be, but you know how strong the pull of big money is; he may not be able to resist."

"More banks gives us more information we can exploit for ourselves."

"Wonderful."

"I thought you might enjoy the news."

Markov pulled her to him and kissed her mouth aggressively, but she pushed against his ample chest and belly. Artemi took a couple steps toward the struggling couple, but Anastasia successfully separated from her boss.

"You must learn to reward your superiors, comrade Alexandrova," Markov blubbered.

"I rewarded you with the drive and the possibility of more data. That's my job. I owe you nothing more."

"You must remember how we do things in my unit. I am boss, and I demand complete loyalty."

"Loyalty in our work, but not personally."

Markov pushed her back with such force she started to fall, but was caught by Artemi. "Is there anything else for me in this meeting, Mr. Markov?" She stared at him impassively.

"No, no, get out; go back to your old unit and think about what I said."

"Oh yes, I'll think about it. Goodbye." She turned and whispered "Bastard" to Artemi as he let her out.

50

Dominic Cavallini held Jeremy's hand as they floated to the floor in the latter's hideaway in the boiler room of the Field Museum. "Thanks for the piggyback ride Doc, that's the best landing I've had since I started transporting."

"My pleasure. You'll get better with more practice."

"You mean if I ever get my skills back. I can't believe our bosses let me get shot."

"I've been with them longer than you, and I've found they have a purpose for everything they do. They sent me to rescue and heal you, so you were never really in danger." Cavallini walked around the modest accommodations, nodding and smiling. "You were right; your FBI boss did a nice job making this space livable and comfortable."

"It's okay, but it closes in on me sometimes and I go stir crazy. The food has been great, though."

"Well, I better be going home; Sharon will wonder where I've been tonight. Take care, bud, and let me know if you need some help."

"I will, and thanks again for bailing me out."

"It may be your turn to save my ass next time, guy." The men hugged, and the doctor evaporated.

Jeremy brushed his teeth and rolled into bed when his phone buzzed. "Were you in California today?" Pollard was not happy.

"Yes I was; sorry, boss. Stephanie Murphy was in trouble, and I had to help."

"Mark Pawley called me and told me someone had temporarily immobilized Brad Wolfe, allowing Stephanie to escape and Pawley to arrest the bum. You have to stop leaving your little palace there, pal. When you do, it creates too much risk to a lot of people."

"Understood, boss, but I thought I did the right thing in helping Dr. Cavallini in St. John, and I couldn't let that asshole Wolfe hurt Steph. I know I'll have to be good now—no choice."

"What do you mean?"

"It happened again as I confronted Brad when he was holding Steph hostage. I lost my powers, and he shot at me twice and hit me in the midsection with one round."

"Are you shittin' me?"

"I wish I was. I thought I was going to bleed to death like a human, but Cavallini showed up and froze Wolfe and then healed me. He programmed Brad and Steph's minds to erase any knowledge of either of us being there. Then we transported back to my boiler room as the police and FBI showed up at Steph's office. They didn't see us."

"Holy shit. Why do you keep losing your powers?"

"Damned if I know. I still don't have them; I had to hitch a ride with the doc to get back here."

"Well stay there, no more fucking freelancing. I'll talk to you tomorrow. Bye."

"Got it. Wait, do you have a plan for me to see my family yet . . . ?" Too late; Pollard had tapped off.

■ ■ ■

John Eldrick assigned himself the afternoon shift from two o'clock until ten to observe Andrei Donskov. John met agent Richard Olsen outside Gibson's Steakhouse on Rush Street. Olsen, dressed in a Cubs hat and T-shirt, had texted his boss informing him the Russian spy was having lunch with several other men. Richard had staked out a seat on a bench at a bus stop across the street. His boss walked to the same bench and sat at the opposite end.

Eldrick wore a Bears hat and T-shirt with number 72 on the front and back. John settled into the mode of a man waiting for the next bus and focused on his phone. He texted with his teammate on a secure line to avoid having to speak. John asked how long the subject had been in the upscale restaurant, and Olsen replied since noon. Eldrick commented the Russian spy business must be good. Olsen smiled and replied the two of them were in the wrong business. Nothing unusual occurred during the morning shift, and Richard rose, stretched, and ambled off heading south.

John had participated in hundreds of surveillance and stakeout missions and marveled at how criminals had enough money to take three-hour lunches and dinners at the most expensive places in town. *As always, crime pays very well.*

At 2:40 Donskov exited Gibson's, made a quick one-hundred-eighty degree visual sweep of the crowded street, and seemingly satisfied he was not under observation, jumped into a self-driving UBER car in a northbound lane on Rush. Eldrick snapped a picture of the Uber car and entered the image into a secret FBI app that beams the image to a FBI drone, which in turn, locks on and tracks the car. John hailed an Uber car and drove it himself to follow Donskov's vehicle north a couple blocks where it turned left and left again heading south.

Donskov's car weaved in a random pattern heading east, then south, west, then south again for several blocks. He exited the car at the northeast corner of Randolph and Wabash and hurried into a building to a pedway entrance. He then used the underground tunnel system to walk east to Michigan Avenue and then south to a garage entrance just north of Monroe Street where he surfaced and hailed another Uber car to take him to his apartment on Prairie Street.

John saw his subject exit his car and head into the building, so he stopped his car and exited. He knew the subject had a head start putting him several minutes behind the Russian and once inside, found no trace of the man. He did notice the pedway entrance sign and thought it would be fruitless to dive into the underground without knowing which direction to go. He left the building and hailed another Uber car and set the destination for Donskov's apartment building to resume his watch.

The Russian operative had spent considerable time underground walking and did not arrive at his apartment until after Eldrick had set up at another bus stop bench kiddie-corner from the building.

Donskov stumbled out of the car and weaved his way to the entrance. John regarded his adversary with amusement as he filmed Donskov's drunken dance through the glass door. *I guess the vodka at lunch was potent.*

Donskov did not reappear before ten o'clock, probably sleeping off the vodka stupor. Bruce Randolph, the third member of John's team, arrived at 9:55 to relieve his boss. Eldrick updated him regarding what he and Olsen had observed so far and warned him Donskov was probably an expert in using the pedway system, which provided cover from FBI drones and other aircraft, and that the spy may be sleeping off a hangover from lunch. The men said goodbye, and John hailed an Uber car to go home.

■ ■ ■

Eldrick and his team maintained surveillance on their subject for a week, sometimes in restaurants where Donskov met with others in animated conversation in Russian, but he did not commit a crime or appear to participate in any organized espionage activity. They concluded he was a soldier and remained in the city in ready mode when an assignment might come his way.

The FBI team decided to take him down and interrogate him for information about Markov; they would use the threat of deportation as leverage to hopefully get him to flip. Things would not go well for Donskov back in the mother country if the intelligence leadership suspected he had been compromised in spite of his pleas to the contrary. The plan was to snatch him when he exited the building in the morning.

On Friday At seven thirty the spy exited his building and before he could hail an Uber vehicle, Eldrick's team descended on him and forced him into a black van, which skidded west toward FBI headquarters.

Donskov's eyes bulged at the surprise seizure as Olsen and Eldrick searched him, confiscated his two guns, and bound his hands behind him with plastic restraints. "Who do you work for?" John asked. The Russian did not answer and maintained a stoic expression. "Do you speak English?" Again, no reaction. Eldrick's nose almost brushed against his captive's. "Listen, boy, when we have you at headquarters you better learn English fast and tell us what you know, or I'll ship your sorry ass back to Moscow." Donskov's eyes betrayed his trepidation, but he did not speak. Apparently he understood some English.

The van pulled into the garage at headquarters, and Donskov was pulled out, pushed to an elevator, and taken to an interrogation room.

Eldrick summoned an employee fluent in Russian, and the three-man team launched a verbal assault on the spy, but he continued his laconic demeanor. Eldrick told the translator to share with the subject a series of threats, including the deportation possibility.

Donskov became agitated and whispered to the translator in Russian he didn't want to go back to Russia. Eldrick asked him questions about his role in the organization in Chicago and for the names of others in his unit and information flowed like a rushing river after a hard rain. Then John leaned over his prisoner, their faces an inch apart, and asked the coveted question: "Where does Markov live?"

Donskov squirmed and feigned no knowledge, but Eldrick shouted the query repeatedly. The spy shook his head as sweat beaded on his forehead.

Again, Eldrick's nose almost touched against his captive's. "You're going to MOSCOW!" Finally the subject caved and provided the address.

Eldrick instructed Olsen to have the Chicago police arrest Donskov on suspicion of espionage and take him to jail. Next he and his team met in his office and planned strategy for capturing the big prize, Markov.

51

Jeremy tested one more time to see if his special powers had returned, but they had not. He rolled over in bed and descended to the lower depths of sleep immediately.

A knock at the door startled him awake; he hustled to the door, shaking his head to gain lucidity. He inquired who was there and Cuthbertson responded in his usual monotone voice. Jeremy opened the door, and the director delivered breakfast, asked if his guest needed anything more, and receiving a negative reply, pivoted on his heels and departed rolling his eyes to express his disdain.

The food and especially the strong black coffee facilitated the spaceman's bourgeoning level of alertness. He watched ESPN for sports highlights and then CNBC for financial and political news before attempting to regain his unique skills but with no success. *No use signing on to the FBI system since I can't do the work they expect.*

He shuffled to the bathroom to shower and shave and then dressed in a blue Cubs shirt, beige cargo shorts, and a Cubs hat and headed upstairs to the museum.

At 11:08 he opened the service door to the first floor, which bustled with visitors and conversational sounds cascading in random directions throughout the huge room. Jeremy strolled around the floor stopping briefly at "Sue" to once again ponder the majesty of this enormous specimen. He completed the circuit ending at the same bench he had occupied several times in the past when he had ventured out of his subterranean refuge.

The crowd invigorated his sense of humanness. He watched and smiled at a group of children pointing at "Sue" and squealing with delight at the far end of the room.

Gradually a presence to his opposite side crept up his spine like an electronic charge. He turned to see an old man in a sport coat and black beret forty feet away staring at him. The old man began a slow, small-step march toward Jeremy. *Looks like the same guy I saw a few weeks ago.*

The intruder stopped three feet from the bench, and Jeremy spontaneously rose to greet him. "Ah, Professor Operman, right?" He extended his right hand to the visitor.

"Yes, George it's me. How have you been?' "Oh, same old. You come here often?"

"My life is rather mundane, but I enjoy making the rounds of all the wonderful museums we are so fortunate to have in Chicago. I see new things on every visit, even if nothing has changed."

I wonder what that means. "No doubt, we're definitely lucky to have so many great cultural opportunities, professor."

"What about you, my friend? This is the second time I've seen you here."

"Like you, I enjoy this museum and its exhibits. I also like the architecture of the building itself."

"Yes, I agree; it's a special place. Do you live nearby?"

"No, I'm from Crystal Valley, way out northwest of the city. How about you?"

"I live downtown in a modest condo." The professor scrutinized Jeremy as the hint of a smile edged up from the corners of his mouth. "What do you do for a living?"

Jeremy sensed the educator weaving circles, which he might use to unmask the spaceman, an unwelcome intrusion. "I work in the financial services industry doing research, primarily in the energy field."

"Really? What is the name of your company?"

"Well, actually I'm between jobs at the moment." *This is getting uncomfortable.*

"I see. Where did you last work?"

Jeremy wanted to lie about his job at Castle Rook Investments and the fact it was eight years ago, but something tugged at this strategy, pulling it out of the way like opening a curtain and exposing the truth. "It was a while ago at Castle Rook Investments, but I'm sure you never heard of the company."

The professor looked down for several seconds, then raised his head and fired a laser look at the young man's eyes. "I'm sorry, Jeremy, I've been playing with you. I know everything about your life. You're a good man, just a little headstrong sometimes." He tilted his head as if to look behind his young friend's eyes to view the thoughts racing through his brain. "We're on the same team, you and I."

"What do mean, same team?" Jeremy shifted from one foot to the other and he could feel the hair on his arms begin to stand on end.

The professor glanced over each shoulder and lowered his voice. "You recently visited the Caribbean to assist our mutual friend Dominic Cavallini, and then you went to California to help Stephanie."

Jeremy retreated two steps. "Holy shit! Are you a . . . I mean are you like me?"

"Quiet down. Not only am I like you, I'm one of three Earth supervisors."

"This is unreal; how many more of us are there?"

"You don't need to know, but now you are wondering if you will ever recapture your powers, right?"

"Yeah, I need them as soon as possible. I guess you know I was in your class at Vanderbilt."

"Of course I've known all along and wanted to see you after all this time. Now, what will you do if I give your special talents back to you?"

"Wait, did you take them away from me?"

"No, our bosses did, but they have authorized me to reinstate them for you under appropriate circumstances. What do you want to do now?"

"I want to see my kids and wife. It's been way too long, and I've put them through a lot of shit."

"Yes, they've had a tough time. I can make it happen for you, but unfortunately I will have to program their minds to forget your visit. It's still too dangerous for them."

"When will it stop being dangerous—when can I just be a damn human again?'

"This is a difficult war; we're fighting against many bad actors in our world, and it will continue to take time."

"Which means never for me. I didn't sign up for this, Professor Operman. Why was I selected?"

"You know the logical answer to that. Think about your projects in our other place."

"Okay, I know it was for my expertise in energy and rare earth metals. But it has turned my world upside down; it isn't fair."

"I didn't ask for my role either, but we both know life isn't fair, right?"

"Yeah, yeah, but that doesn't make it any easier. Why didn't you tell me you are like me when we first met here a few weeks ago?"

"I wanted to monitor your progress a while longer. I have to issue reports on all my people to the bosses quarterly."

"You mean they grade us?"

"They evaluate our performance to ensure we are still a good fit for our tasks."

The professor's former student shook his head, hoping the new pieces would fall into some kind of logical order. "When can I see my family?"

"Here is how I'm going to handle it. I will select a date and at the appointed hour, your children will be transported to your old home in Crystal Valley since the Terasenkos can't go back there until Mr. Markov is out of the picture. You will meet them there."

"How long will we have?'

"I'll bring them in shortly after it gets dark. The Terasenkos have several lights connected to their home security system, so you won't have to worry about turning on lights that might cause suspicion." Jeremy started to speak, but Operman held his palm up silencing him. "Then I'll bring you in. I'll fix Mr. and Mrs. Murphy's minds not to detect the kids are gone from their house, and after I take the kids back to California, I'll fix their minds, too. I will also hold off on giving you your powers back until after you have seen your family."

"What? Why can't I have them now?"

"I've noted you have exceeded Bob Pollard's instructions several times. Meeting your family will be emotional for you, so I'm withholding the skills until after the visit, and then I'll decide when to return them to you."

Jeremy shook his head. "But how long will we have?"

"That night."

Jeremy's head drooped in dejection.

"If feasible, I'll arrange for other visits until it's safe for you to return to some semblance of your former life."

"Dr. Operman, I no longer have a former life." Jeremy sat on the bench.

The professor placed a hand on the young man's shoulder. "I'm sorry I can't promise more than that at this point in time."

"Well, I'll take it; it's certainly better than nothing. When can I see Megan?"

"She's had a difficult time since you were selected, as we both know. She's not been able to cope with events very well and is currently in a trance-like state in a facility. After you meet with your kids, I'll find a way to get you out there to see her, but—fair warning—you may be disappointed if she can't shake loose from the trance." Jeremy squirmed for a minute then nodded.

"Thanks, professor. I owe you a lot."

"No, mankind owes you, Dominic, and others like us more than they can ever repay. Take care; I'll be in touch, mentally if not physically."

"So long and thanks again."

Armed with new intelligence secured from Donskov, John Eldrick established a surveillance schedule for the building in which Ivan Markov lived. John had received two additional agents from Bob Pollard for a temporary period of time to set up the plan to capture the elusive Russian boss.

With a total of five agents the new schedule included five shifts of five hours each, except one shift was reduced to four hours and would be rotated between team members to the extent possible. Each agent, three males and two females, had been fully briefed on Markov's disguises and the routines and habits developed from recent observation, but the depth of the information was sketchy at best. Now with his address at a high rise building on Lake Shore Drive on the Gold Coast, tracking and documenting his comings and goings would be much easier.

The team implemented observation the day after Donskov revealed the key piece of information. Eldrick coordinated FBI air surveillance with drone operators, helicopters and light aircraft to augment the ground efforts of his team.

Copious photos and narrative on Markov's movements created an expanding profile of the reticent leader over a two-week period. John convened a meeting on a Tuesday consisting of himself and three of the other four agents in his headquarters office; they incorporated Olsen in via Face Time from his post near Markov's building.

"From the intel we've gathered, I think we're ready to move. We've established he doesn't leave his apartment every day; more like three or four days a week when he has not received visits from his goons. However, it appears he regularly leaves the building at nine o'clock on Thursdays and goes to that trendy Mediterranean restaurant, Doria Mediterranean Cafe on north Halsted Street. Nice job, Bruce, to get in there and be our close-up, first-hand watch on the activities. Markov stays for several hours, meeting his operatives and extending into and well after the lunch hour." He glanced at each agent to measure level of engagement and, satisfied, continued.

"My first thought was to snatch the bastard as he exits the restaurant, but I rejected that idea because if his goons draw weapons and start shooting, bystanders could become innocent victims." John referred to his notes. "Grabbing him on Thursday morning would be better, but he's alert, and his driver comes out of the underground garage hot, so we might have a tough time stopping his car. That leaves the most logical choice; we'll wait for him at his building in the afternoon when he's tired and maybe a little careless. We'll post agents in the garage and have a car or two available if he somehow escapes back on to the street, but it's unlikely since his car will be facing the interior of the garage. We'll let him drive thirty or forty feet into the garage and then surround the vehicle from protected positions." He again surveyed the team. "Sound like plan? What did I miss?"

Team members pondered the options. Jolanda Messner leaned forward. "John, what if his driver takes off in the garage? Our people could be hit by the car or shot."

"Good observation. We'll have weapons drawn and shoot the tires of the car to hopefully disable it. If we get rounds coming at us from inside the car, we'll return fire as appropriate. This is a dangerous project, and these guys are elite SVR, but we're elite too, and our training is as good as theirs. Of course we'll have a large manpower advantage as we always do, and we'll be wearing full body protection. Any more questions, comments?" Hearing none he continued. "Okay, today is Tuesday; I'll meet with Pollard this afternoon and get his buy-in and feedback, and if he's good with the plan, we'll expand our team and prepare for Thursday."

52

Professor Marvin Operman transported Jeremy to his former home in Crystal Valley at 9:30 PM two days after their meeting at the Field Museum. The two men emerged in the family room and verified the drapes were still closed and two lights were illuminated by timers.

Jeremy fidgeted and paced the room as Operman disappeared to fetch Kelly and Kyle Chambers from their grandparents' home in Orange, California. *I wonder if the kids will still be angry with me for leaving them for eight years. I missed so much of their lives while they grew up. I wish I could turn the clock back and never have had to leave them.* Still, without powers, he could only wait and depend on the professor.

Fifteen minutes later he heard a whoosh as Operman appeared holding hands with Jeremy's children. The awestruck father's lower lip quivered uncontrollably as he extended his arms out in front of him.

"Dad, is it really you?" Kelly asked.

"Yes, guys, it's me, in the flesh this time. I've missed you two more than I can ever tell you."

"Dad, why is your hair blond, and why do you have a beard; you never used to have one?" Kyle asked. The kids moved toward their father slowly at first, then raced into his open arms. He hugged them and kissed the top of their heads. All three sobbed tears of jubilation. When Jeremy looked up, the professor signaled he was leaving and pointed to his watch he would return before dawn. Jeremy nodded and continued to embrace his children.

"It's a disguise, Kyle. I don't want some bad people to know who I am. I wear glasses, too, but not tonight."

"Who is the man who brought us here? How did he do it?" Kelly asked.

"He's a good friend, and he knows some magic; it doesn't matter how he got you here, the important thing is we're together for a while."

Operman dissolved and Jeremy disengaged from the two youngsters, holding them at arm's length. "Let me see you guys. You look great. Let's sit down; I want to hear all about what you've been doing." The trio moved to a sofa and sat with Jeremy in the middle.

"Dad, are you going to be with us for good now?" Kelly asked through convulsive sniffles.

"No, honey, I have to go back, but one of these days, I'll be home with you."

The answer precipitated tears on his daughter's face. Kyle also succumbed to intense crying.

Kelly looked through bleary eyes. "Not fair, why can't you be with us now?"

"It's very complicated, Kelly Bird. When I do come back for good, I'll try to explain it to you both." The kids continued to lean into their long-lost father with their arms around his waist.

The children gradually settled down from weeping and took turns telling their dad about their lives since they last saw him. Jeremy listened attentively. He savored every word and nodded occasionally.

"Dad, this looks like our old house. Is it?" Kyle asked. "Yes it is, bud. It's the best place for us to meet."

"Can we go see our old rooms?"

"Yes, but they'll look different since other people bought the house from Mom."

"Where are the people who own the house now?" Kelly asked.

"They're out of town. He didn't want to overload the kids with an explanation of where the Terasenkos were and that they were hiding from bad actors too. The three continued the conversation to catch up on their lives.

An hour later he asked if they were hungry and checked the freezer.

Finding some chicken and a bag of vegetables, he cooked a meal as the kids sat on stools at the kitchen island alternately continuing to update their father on what he had missed.

I can't believe they're so grown; I missed so damned much and I can never get it back.

■ ■ ■

John Eldrick arrived at FBI headquarters at 6:20 on Thursday morning to review his plan to capture Ivan Markov at his residence on the lakefront. He had scheduled a meeting of the team tasked with the take down of the sinister

Russian espionage boss for seven o'clock. *I'm going to get that slimy son of a bitch, and I hope his conviction gives him a nice long vacation in prison.*

Eldrick and the team verbally rehearsed each step in the capture operation; it seemed airtight. Agent Olsen would leave his post at Markov's building and go to the restaurant before nine o'clock to prepare to observe Markov and his band of comrades and report their activities to Eldrick and his team via texts. After Olsen left the building, surveillance would be handled from the air. Team members recited their assignments. "Okay, looks like we're ready. We'll leave here at one fifteen and take up positions outside the garage and in the garage. I will deal with the security boss for the building when we arrive; I don't want to alert them until the last minute because you never know if they may be on Markov's payroll." He solicited final questions, and since there were none, he adjourned the meeting.

■ ■ ■

At 9:37 Markov, Artemi, and two other SVR members took the elevator to the underground garage and piled into a large silver Mercedes sedan with tinted windows. They sped out of the garage entrance and drove to the restaurant.

Agent Olsen had already taken up a position at a table for two against a wall and with a clear view of the corner booth used each week by the Markov group. He was casually dressed and brought copies of several newspapers to peruse after a leisurely breakfast and lunch, thus allowing him a cover for remaining in the restaurant over a long period of time without attracting attention.

Markov and his entourage settled into his usual booth, and the wait staff immediately brought several bottles of expensive vodka to the table. The men toasted and feasted on a variety of appetizers. Occasionally an individual soldier entered from the street and joined the group with a report for the boss; these visitors enjoyed a quick glass of vodka and after rendering their updates promptly left.

Markov and the others ordered meals including several courses and discussed business between rounds of drinks. Artemi scanned the restaurant every few minutes looking for anyone who looked suspicious. Agent Olsen maintained his focus on his food, his phone, and newspapers to avoid the group's scrutiny. He texted the team at headquarters every ten minutes but today did not present anything noteworthy.

At 12:36 Markov began coughing uncontrollably with his comrades leaning over him to offer assistance. The source of his discomfort, a genuine concern, was determined not to be a piece of food lodged in this throat. Markov mopped his brow with a handkerchief, and his complexion turned pasty and eggshell in color. After several minutes the coughing subsided, and Artemi escorted his boss to the men's room. They returned ten minutes later, and Markov shook hands with all in attendance and left the restaurant.

Olsen feverishly texted Eldrick at headquarters with the alarming news the Russian boss had left early and was probably headed home due to the sudden illness he had suffered.

"Shit. We need to move now!" John Eldrick shouted to his team as they scrambled to the FBI garage hoping to beat Markov to his building and set up the trap. Eldrick knew, however, the Russian had a substantial head start and the team would probably not be in a position to enter the garage before Markov arrived.

Unexpectedly, however, Markov's car stopped in front of a Walgreens drug store with its emergency lights flashing. Artemi dashed in to pick up some medicine for his boss. This unscheduled stop coupled with heavy lunchtime traffic would delay their arrival at Markov's condo building by fifteen to twenty minutes.

The FBI vehicles weaved through traffic from the west side to the lakefront as word from its helicopter indicated Markov's car was now halted at a stoplight on Michigan Avenue, five blocks from his building.

The FBI team arrived and set up quickly inside and outside the garage entrance. Eldrick engaged in an animated conversation with security personnel, finally convincing them this operation was legitimate and obtaining their cooperation. He then hustled inside to take up his position in the garage. He checked by phone with all members of the team to ensure everyone was in place and ready.

Markov's car rounded a corner and headed for the garage. Security opened the door, and the car entered and proceeded toward the curve leading to the second level tenant parking. As the car started to turn, six FBI agents dressed in black stepped out from behind pillars and into the lane to block Markov's car. Two FBI vans blocked the entrance to the rear.

Markov's three henchmen opened windows and fired their Makarov pistols at the lawmen who returned fire, blasting Markov's car, but the rounds failed to penetrate the customized materials added to the vehicle for protection from such surprises. The enclosed garage formed an echo chamber amplifying the ear-piercing blasts from the gunfire. Markov's driver then floored the accelerator and aimed for the agents who had to leap to the sides of the ramp to avoid the speeding car.

Eldrick and two other agents jumped from one of the Suburbans blocking the entrance and raced after the Mercedes while firing at the rear of the car, causing it to careen from side to side as it sped toward another curve. Markov's henchmen returned fire aimed at the agents. One shot hit Eldrick in the thigh and agent Randolph took a round in the outside of the shoulder, which was not covered by the bulletproof vest. Both men fell to the ground as agents in the Suburban jockeyed the large vehicle so that it could pursue the target car.

The Suburban slowed as it crept along the aisle on level two as agents observed each parked vehicle on both sides searching for Markov's car. The quiet presented an ambiguous predicament as agents had to identify the target car but be alert for possible gunfire from Markov's men. At the far end of the row Markov's car was parked at a severe angle and had clipped the right rear of the BMW in the space next to it. Agents could not determine if anyone was still in the car due to the tinted windows, so they pulled to ten feet from the back of the vehicle and cautiously exited the Suburban taking cover behind its open doors.

The Feds shouted commands to possible riders to leave the car with hands up, but the doors did not open. Agent Olsen decided the odds were the car was empty, so he ordered his team to cautiously approach from both sides of the car and check the windshield, which was the only window not clouded by tinting as other agents crouched and opened the doors prepared to shoot. The car was empty.

John Eldrick lay on the floor of the garage while paramedics worked to stop the bleeding from his right thigh. He winced from pain, but maintained constant communication with agents on level two who informed him Markov and his men had left the car. "Damn that little slimeball; he's probably in his unit, or maybe he ducked out of the building through some rear entrance." He summoned security and demanded Markov's condo number and a key; the security chief reluctantly told him the Russian lived in unit 3116 and produced a master key. Eldrick instructed Olsen to come and get the key and then take his team to check Markov's condo and report back.

Olsen's chest heaved from his dash down from the second level. He asked John if the wound was serious, and Eldrick waved him off and told him to hustle up to unit 3116. Olsen raced back up to level two and led his team to the elevators for the ride to the thirty-first floor.

Olsen rang the bell as he and an agent stood to one side of the door and two other agents did the same on the opposite side. Olsen shouted for the occupants to open the door and come out with hands up. After several minutes he used the key to unlock the door and push it open.

The team of agents crept into the living room with their Springfield 1911A1 .45 caliber guns drawn and covered one other as they searched each room, but they found no one. Olsen called Eldrick to report the unit was empty, and John told him to check the stairwells and to find the access door to the roof. "I doubt they went to the roof because they would have no way to make their escape."

"Maybe a helicopter landing up there?"

"I doubt it; they know we have too many drones and choppers of our own, and we would see what they're trying to do immediately. No, Rich, I think they must have gotten out of the building some other way, the bastards."

Paramedics moved Eldrick and Randolph to rolling stretchers and lifted them into ambulances. "We need to do a sweep of the entire building, all floors and units and utility areas to be sure they aren't hiding in here. Take the team and start that process; the Chicago Police will assist you. Let me know how it goes. We're on our way to the hospital," Eldrick instructed.

"Will do, John. Hope everything goes well for you and Bruce."

"Thanks, man; I'm sure we'll be fine. Be careful."

53

Jeremy and his children continued to catch up on their lives, a conversation precipitating periodic bouts of weeping for all three.

At five fifteen Professor Operman appeared behind the sofa and walked around to face the family. He motioned to Jeremy the time had come to take Kelly and Kyle back to their grandparents' home.

Jeremy fought his paternal instinct to resist, but Operman controlled his mind into acquiescence, so a disconsolate father initiated the almost impossible task of convincing the kids they had to return to California. The children clung to their father like barnacles to the hull of a ship for several minutes; Operman determined he would have to intervene. He sent telepathic messages to the weeping kids forcing them to give Jeremy one final kiss then and move away from him.

The professor took the children's' hands and nodded to the despondent father. A soft whoosh and the trio dissolved.

■ ■ ■

Jeremy sank down on the sofa and threw his head back against the cushion, his mind spinning with a crosscurrent of thoughts. Tears continued to drip onto his face and shirt. *I'm glad I got to see them, but the time was so short. Operman said he will try to arrange more visits, but I want to be with them every day and go to their games, concerts, graduations, and weddings someday. I want my old life back; I can't go on being a freak much longer.* Fatigue drained the last drop of adrenaline from the beleaguered dad, and sleep permeated his consciousness and assumed control.

Professor Operman returned at ten thirty having given Jeremy an opportunity to gain some rest and strength. He stood over his sleeping lieutenant and entered his mind to slowly wake him. "I hope you enjoyed your visit with those wonderful children."

"Yes, I sure did. Wish it could have been longer, wish I could go back to my old life."

"I understand. I too, have similar aspirations, but my remaining time on this earth is much shorter than yours. We must remember why we were selected and the contributions we make to achieving peace in this dangerous world."

"I know; I get all that. It's just that I was happy with my life before they took me, and now many people have been hurt, even killed because of me. It's so fucking frustrating."

"Yes it is. But think about all the positive things you've done by assisting on the projects in the other world and the people you've helped since you came back."

"Thanks for the pep talk, but I can't turn the clock back and redo things."

"Quite correct. So, what can you do now?"

"Not sure; I guess keep helping the FBI and hoping someday I can be with my family, to be just a guy with no special powers and all the shit that goes with it. A normal human being."

"Admirable goals; I concur. But for now we need to continue our work. I'll take you back to the Field Museum."

"Okay. Not sure what I can do with no special skills."

"Talk to Mr. Pollard; maybe there's something you can do to help."

"How about you give me my powers back?"

"In due time. Take my hand." Operman extended his hand and Jeremy grasped it for the quick ride back to the boiler room.

■ ■ ■

Jeremy settled into his recliner in his confined quarters, and told Cuthbertson to enter after he knocked to deliver lunch.

The forlorn father munched on his food without seemingly tasting it.

He couldn't kick the depression from his mind after having been with his kids. *Maybe seeing Kelly and Kyle wasn't the best thing right now; after looking into their eyes, I want my old life back more than ever.* His phone buzzed jolting him into the reality of the moment. "Hello, Boss."

"What's happening? Do you have your magic back yet?" Pollard asked.

"No, 'fraid not. The professor brought my kids out last night to visit me and now I want to go back to my old life as soon as possible."

"I understand, but you also know what we're up against and what our mission is, right?"

"Yeah. It's so fucking aggravating, though."

"I can imagine. Here's some news while you were gone. John Eldrick and his team had a great plan to trap and capture Ivan Markov and his band of assholes, but then the little shit Russian boss gets sick and goes home almost before our guys could get to his garage to set up properly. The team was able to beat him to his building by a minute or two but couldn't get everyone into position. They cornered him in the garage and there was a shootout and the little bastard escaped. We swept the building and couldn't find him. John and another agent were wounded, but will be okay. I visited them in the hospital last night, and they're doing well."

"Holy shit, two agents shot? This is getting crazy. Give those guys my best; I hope they recover quick."

"Will do. That's not all. Mark Pawley—I think you remember him helping me from eight years ago out in California—well, he snared Brad Wolfe and the Claypoole brothers after you and Cavallini helped out.

Those three bastards bilked the city of Vista Nueva out of many millions of dollars over the past ten or twelve years. Mark's team is sorting out all the facts to determine how bad the magnitude of the theft is. Stephanie Murphy was the one who uncovered the scheme; if she hadn't kept digging, those assholes might have gotten away with their scam."

"How Is Steph? I'm sure she was scared to death with Brad holding her hostage and pointing a gun at her."

"She's shaken up, but it looks like she'll be fine in time. You and Dominic saved the day on that episode."

"The doc was the one who made it happen since I didn't have my powers."

"You traveled there, even though I wanted you to stay here, and stopped Wolfe before he could hurt Stephanie, so give yourself some credit."

"Well, I'm just glad they got those thieving bastards."

"Right. Let me know if you get your skills back. Talk to you tomorrow."

▪ ▪ ▪

Pollard gave Jeremy some mundane tasks while they both waited for him to become "special" again. He researched FBI intelligence systems on the inner workings of the Russian espionage and counterintelligence operations as well as the Russian mafia. Without his unique skills, however, he could not analyze the data in the manner he would when he had his magic. The data on the screen just stared back at him, posing a dare to divulge their secrets. *Anyone in the bureau could do what I'm doing.* He ploughed ahead, though, hoping a hidden gem of information or a correlation of disparate data sets would reveal their connection but to no avail.

Jeremy's mundane life continued for another week as August gripped the city with hot temperatures and obdurate humidity. The citizens of the Chicago metro area hurried from one air-conditioned home, building, car, and train to another. Cicadas buzzed their shrill songs throughout the days and nights, signaling the waning days of summer.

Jeremy confined his tours of the museum to nighttime after closing hours, following Bob Pollard's original orders and due to the risk posed by his current vulnerability with no special talent. The walls of his accommodations closed on him like a slow-moving vise combined with the extreme boredom of his so-called job with the FBI. However, the pinnacle of his claustrophobia floated up one morning after breakfast. *I can't take it in here anymore; I need to get out and see some humans.*

He ventured up to the main floor and roamed the great hall, weaving between visitors and enjoying the cacophony of voices, especially the children. A two- or three-year-old Asian girl stood in front of Sue, pointing to the great mammal's head, smiling and chattering in her native language. Eventually Jeremy's wandering led to the bench where he had rested in the past.

Conscious that enemies might be covertly mingling with the crowd, he scanned one hundred-eighty degrees every couple of minutes looking for anyone who may be scoping him. A sense of euphoria cascaded over him from being a member of this crowd, although he understood the feeling was ephemeral. From across the room he noted an old man in a sport coat and wearing a black beret moving toward him with stubby, shuffling steps: *Professor Operman?*

"Professor, we have to stop meeting like this."

"I don't think so, Jeremy. I received a vibe you were out of your nest again and without the protection of special skills. I don't want anything bad to happen to you."

"Thanks, but I've been cooped up in my little man cave for a week and was starting to go wacky. I had to get out of there for a while and see some people."

"I understand. I think I will take you to see Megan. I will visit you downstairs tonight. We'll arrive in her room in the middle of the night when you'll have some privacy."

"Are you serious? That's fantastic, I can't wait."

"I'll see you at 2:00 AM, which will be midnight in California."

"What about my powers?"

"Not until we are back from your visit with your wife."

"Well, okay. I'll be ready . . . and thank you in advance."

"You've been a good soldier, and you deserve some family time. Goodbye." He walked into the crowd and disappeared.

. . .

Jeremy watched TV in his subterranean palace and checked the clock on his phone every two minutes beginning at 1:50. *I wonder if the prof will actually show. I hope Megan isn't in a coma or trance like he said; there are so many things I want to tell her, and I want to hear about her life, too.* He glanced at his phone: 1:59. He raised his eyes to see Professor Operman standing near the kitchen.

Jeremy rose and walked toward him. "Wow, you're very punctual, sir."

"Yes, always have been, and don't call me 'sir.' Let's get ready to travel." He extended his right hand and pulled the hopeful husband to his side. Operman closed his eyes and focused his energy inward as both men evaporated.

. . .

The two time travelers emerged quietly in Megan's room at Winston Rehab Facility in Newport Beach. She appeared to be asleep in the darkened, surprisingly spacious accommodations, which included a large sitting area consisting of two cushioned chairs and a two-seat couch next to the windows, and a large bathroom on the other side of the bed.

Operman whispered he would be leaving, but would be close by for the return trip at five thirty before sunrise and that he would program the nurses' and FBI sentry's minds manning the floor administration pod not to disturb the reunited couple. Jeremy thanked him and then turned to the silent figure in the bed. The professor walked toward the window and disappeared.

Eight—almost nine—years had passed since Jeremy last saw his wife. He recalled driving her and the kids to O'Hare Airport to travel and stay with her parents at their home in Orange, California indefinitely. He remembered her fragile state of mind and how frightened she was of who—or what—her husband had become. She had told him her life had been turned upside down and she needed to move the kids to a safe place. He pulled a chair next to the bed and sat with his elbows on the mattress and his hands together supporting his face.

The irony flashed into his mind of his current human condition—no special powers, just a normal human being next to her bed, watching her chest rise and fall in consistent breaths unable to wake and have a conversation with him. He had pictured having the opportunity to be with her, alone as two humans to talk and hug and make love. *This is that moment; we are alone together after all this time and heartache, but once again fate steps between us. I still have to hide, and you have been kidnapped and your mind stolen. What is it they say? Two ships passing in the night. Damn.* He gently grasped her hand. Cold. *Not fair.*

"Megan, open your eyes if you can hear me." No reaction. "I have thought about you every day for as long as I've been gone, and I love you more than ever." He kissed her hand and held it to his face. "I swear to you I'll come back some day, and we'll make up for lost time. We can't get the days and years back, but we can make the most of our life ahead."

He stood, then bent across her torso and kissed her dry lips; they did not return the gesture, and she did not wake. He lay his head on her chest listening to the routine beating of a heart broken—*permanently? I have to find a way to end my life as a freak and come back to living like a husband and father so we can be a family again.* Jeremy sat down and held the cold, lifeless hand and stared at his wife's opaque face as she slept.

At five thirty Operman faded into the room and stood respectfully several feet away from the bed. "Jeremy, it's time."

The young man nodded but did not release his hold on his wife's hand. After several tears slid down his cheeks. He backed up until he stood next to his college professor and took his hand. Operman felt the trembling and squeezed lightly before closing his eyes and concentrating his energy.

The two men vanished in an instant.

ACKNOWLEDGMENTS

Emergence is my third novel and continues the saga of Jeremy Chambers from *Intrusion* and *Phantasm*. Many characters from the first two books transition to the story in this third book. Some new characters are also introduced to amplify the storyline and drama.

Janet Sainsbury contributed story line ideas and invaluable editing regarding female characters. Her ideas and editing enhanced the quality of the story. She also again provided insight on character development identifying nuances of body language, communication, and personality definition.

A sincere thanks to my close friend Dr. Leonard Cerullo, world-renowned neurosurgeon in Chicago. His continuing support and guidance regarding medical issues was critical.

Thanks also to my close friend, John Pankratz, whose extensive business expertise proved invaluable in resolving various accounting rule issues.

Thanks also to my close friend Carl Petruzzelli, who schooled me on various firearms. His expertise again afforded authenticity.

A large dose of gratitude goes to Sabrina Johnson at Mill City Press, whose professional guidance expedited the production process.

Thanks to the designer who skillfully interpreted my ideas for the cover.

Special thanks to the editor who provided professional and insightful editing with respect to both grammar and format.

ABOUT THE AUTHOR

Douglas F. Sainsbury was born and raised in Chicago's west suburbs of Oak Park and River Forest. He attended and graduated from Oak Park-River Forest High School (Ernest Hemingway's alma mater) and then attended the University of Illinois at Urbana-Champaign, graduating with a BA in English. Following college, Doug received a JD from Illinois Institute of Technology's Kent Law School.

World events in the 1960s shaped the next chapter in Doug's life, leading to a tour in the US Army, including fourteen months in Vietnam. His paramount assignments were battalion legal specialist and public information officer (war correspondent-news reporter and photographer).

After military service, Doug spent forty years in the consumer credit and banking industries, the last nine years in the capacity of managing examiner with the Federal Reserve Bank of Chicago.

Doug retired to Southern California in 2012 to be closer to his children and to pursue his lifelong dream of writing fiction. *Intrusion* is his first novel. *Phantasm* and *Emergence* continue the story. Doug can be contacted at doug-sainsbury@gmail.com.